The History of Pendennis by William M

His Fortunes and Misfortunes, His Friends and His

Volume II (of II)

The great author of Vanity Fair and The Luck Of Barry Lyndon was born in India in 1811.

At age 5 his father died and his mother sent him back to England. His education was of the best but he himself seemed unable to apply his talents to a rigorous work ethic.

However, once he harnessed his talents the works flowed in novels, articles, short stories, sketches and lectures.

Sadly, his personal life was rather more difficult. After a few years of marriage his wife began to suffer from depression and over the years became detached from reality. Thackeray himself suffered from ill health later in his life and the one pursuit that kept him moving forward was that of writing. In his life time, he was placed second only to Dickens. High praise indeed.

Index of Contents

CHAPTER I

RELATES TO MR. HARRY FOKER'S AFFAIRS

Since that fatal but delightful night in Grosvenor place, Mr. Harry Foker's heart had been in such a state of agitation as you would hardly have thought so great a philosopher could endure. When we remember what good advice he had given to Pen in former days, how an early wisdom and knowledge of the world had manifested itself in the gifted youth; how a constant course of self-indulgence, such as becomes a gentleman of his means and expectations, ought by right to have increased his cynicism, and made him, with every succeeding day of his life, care less and less for every individual in the world, with the single exception of Mr. Harry Foker, one may wonder that he should fall into the mishap to which most of us are subject once or twice in our lives, and disquiet his great mind about a woman. But Foker, though early wise, was still a man. He could no more escape the common lot than Achilles, or Ajax, or Lord Nelson, or Adam our first father, and now, his time being come, young Harry became a victim to Love, the All-conqueror.

When he went to the Back Kitchen that night after quitting Arthur Pendennis at his staircase-door in Lamb-court, the gin-twist and deviled turkey had no charms for him, the jokes of his companions fell flatly on his ear; and when Mr. Hodgen, the singer of "The Body Snatcher," had a new chant even more dreadful and humorous than that famous composition, Foker, although he appeared his friend, and said "Bravo Hodgen," as common politeness, and his position as one of the chiefs of the Back Kitchen bound him to do, yet never distinctly heard one word of the song, which under its title of "The Cat in the Cupboard," Hodgen has since rendered so famous. Late and very tired, he slipped into his private apartments at home and sought the downy pillow, but his slumbers were disturbed by the fever of his soul, and the very instant that he woke from his agitated sleep, the image of Miss Amory presented itself to him, and said, "Here I am, I am your princess and beauty, you have discovered me, and shall care for nothing else hereafter."

Heavens, how stale and distasteful his former pursuits and friendships appeared to him! He had not been, up to the present time, much accustomed to the society of females of his own rank in life. When he spoke of such, he called them "modest women." That virtue which, let us hope they possessed, had not hitherto compensated to Mr. Foker for the absence of more lively qualities which most of his own relatives did not enjoy, and which he found in Mesdemoiselles, the ladies of the theater. His mother, though good and tender, did not amuse her boy; his cousins, the daughters of his maternal uncle, the respectable Earl of Rosherville, wearied him beyond measure. One was blue, and a geologist; one was a horsewoman, and smoked cigars; one was exceedingly Low Church, and had the most heterodox views on religious matters; at least, so the other said, who was herself of the very Highest Church faction, and made the cupboard in her room into an oratory, and fasted on every Friday in the year. Their paternal house of Drummington, Foker could very seldom be got to visit. He swore he had rather go to the tread-mill than stay there. He was not much beloved by the inhabitants. Lord Erith, Lord Rosherville's heir, considered his cousin a low person, of deplorably vulgar habits and manners; while Foker, and with equal reason, voted Erith a prig and a dullard, the nightcap of the House of Commons, the Speaker's opprobrium, the dreariest of philanthropic spouters. Nor could George Robert, Earl of Gravesend and Rosherville, ever forget that on one evening when he condescended to play at billiards with his nephew, that young gentleman poked his lordship in the side with his cue, and said, "Well, old cock, I've seen many a bad stroke in my life, but I never saw such a bad one as that there." He played the game out with angelic sweetness of temper, for Harry was his guest as well as his nephew; but he was nearly having a fit in the night; and he kept to his own rooms until young Harry quitted Drummington on his return to Oxbridge, where the interesting youth was finishing his education at the time when the occurrence took place. It was an awful blow to the venerable earl; the circumstance was never alluded to in the family: he shunned Foker whenever he came to see them in London or in the country, and could hardly be brought to gasp out a "How d'ye do?" to the young blasphemer. But he would not break his sister Agnes's heart, by banishing Harry from the family altogether; nor, indeed, could he afford to break with Mr. Foker, senior, between whom and his lordship there had been many private transactions, producing an exchange of bank checks from Mr. Foker, and autographs from the earl himself, with the letters I O U written over his illustrious signature.

Besides the four daughters of Lord Gravesend whose various qualities have been enumerated in the former paragraph, his lordship was blessed with a fifth girl, the Lady Ann Milton, who, from her earliest years and nursery, had been destined to a peculiar position in life. It was ordained between her parents and her aunt, that when Mr. Harry Foker attained a proper age, Lady Ann should become his wife. The idea had been familiar to her mind when she yet wore pinafores, and when Harry, the dirtiest of little boys, used to come back with black eyes from school to Drummington, or to his father's house of Logwood, where Lady Ann lived much with her aunt. Both of the young people coincided with the arrangement proposed by the elders, without any protests or difficulty. It no more entered Lady Ann's mind to question the order of her father, than it would have entered Esther's to dispute the commands of Ahasuerus. The heir-apparent of the house of Foker was also obedient, for when the old gentleman said, "Harry, your uncle and I have agreed that when you're of a proper age, you'll marry Lady Ann. She won't have any money, but she's good blood, and a good one to look at, and I shall make you comfortable. If you refuse, you'll have your mother's jointure, and two hundred a year during my life:" Harry, who knew that his sire, though a man of few words, was yet implicitly to be trusted, acquiesced at once in the parental decree, and said, "Well, sir, if Ann's agreeable, I say ditto. She's not a bad-looking girl."

"And she has the best blood in England, sir. Your mother's blood, your own blood, sir," said the brewer. "There's nothing like it, sir."

"Well, sir, as you like it," Harry replied. "When you want me, please ring the bell. Only there's no hurry, and I hope you'll give us a long day. I should like to have my fling out before I marry."

"Fling away, Harry," answered the benevolent father. "Nobody prevents you, do they?" And so very little more was said upon this subject, and Mr. Harry pursued those amusements in life which suited him best; and hung up a little picture of his cousin in his sitting-room, amidst the French prints, the favorite actresses and dancers, the racing and coaching works of art, which suited his taste and formed his gallery. It was an insignificant little picture, representing a simple round face with ringlets; and it made, as it must be confessed, a very poor figure by the side of Mademoiselle Petitot, dancing over a rainbow, or Mademoiselle Redowa, grinning in red boots and a lancer's cap.

Being engaged and disposed of, Lady Ann Milton did not go out so much in the world as her sisters; and often stayed at home in London at the parental house in Gaunt-square, when her mamma with the other ladies went abroad. They talked and they danced with one man after another, and the men came and went, and the stories about them were various. But there was only this one story about Ann: she was engaged to Harry Foker: she never was to think about any body else. It was not a very amusing story.

Well, the instant Foker awoke on the day after Lady Clavering's dinner, there was Blanche's image glaring upon him with its clear gray eyes, and winning smile. There was her tune ringing in his ears, "Yet round about the spot, ofttimes I hover, ofttimes I hover," which poor Foker began piteously to hum, as he sat up in his bed under the crimson silken coverlet. Opposite him was a French print, of a Turkish lady and her Greek lover, surprised by a venerable Ottoman, the lady's husband; on the other wall, was a French print of a gentleman and lady, riding and kissing each other at the full gallop; all round the chaste bed-room were more French prints, either portraits of gauzy nymphs of the Opera or lovely illustrations of the novels; or mayhap, an English chef-d'oeuvre or two, in which Miss Calverley of T. R. E. O. would be represented in tight pantaloons in her favorite page part; or Miss Rougemont as Venus; their value enhanced by the signatures of these ladies, Maria Calverley, or Frederica Rougemont, inscribed underneath the prints in an exquisite fac-simile. Such were the pictures in which honest Harry delighted. He was no worse than many of his neighbors; he was an idle, jovial, kindly fast man about town; and if his rooms were rather profusely decorated with works of French art, so that simple Lady Agnes, his mamma, on entering the apartments where her darling sate enveloped in fragrant clouds of Latakia, was often bewildered by the novelties which she beheld there, why, it must be remembered, that he was richer than most young men, and could better afford to gratify his taste.

A letter from Miss Calverley written in a very dégagé style of spelling and hand-writing, scrawling freely over the filigree paper, and commencing by calling Mr. Harry, her dear Hokey-pokey-fokey, lay on his bed table by his side, amid keys, sovereigns, cigar-cases, and a bit of verbena, which Miss Amory had given him, and reminding him of the arrival of the day when he was "to stand that dinner at the Elefant and Castle, at Richmond, which he had promised;" a card for a private box at Miss Rougemont's approaching benefit, a bundle of tickets for "Ben Budgeon's night, the North Lancashire Pippin, at Martin Faunce's, the Three-corned Hat in St. Martin's Lane; where Conkey Sam, Dick the Nailor, and Deadman (the Worcestershire Nobber), would put on the gloves, and the lovers of the good old British sport were invited to attend"—these and sundry other memoirs of Mr. Foker's pursuits and pleasures lay on the table by his side when he woke.

Ah! how faint all these pleasures seemed now. What did he care for Conkey Sam or the Worcestershire Nobber? What for the French prints ogling him from all sides of the room; those regular stunning slap-up out-and-outers? And Calverley spelling bad, and calling him Hokey-fokey, confound her impudence! The idea of being engaged to a dinner at the Elephant and Castle at Richmond, with that old woman (who was seven and thirty years old, if she was a day), filled his mind with dreary disgust now, instead of that pleasure which he had only yesterday expected to find from the entertainment.

When his fond mamma beheld her boy that morning, she remarked on the pallor of his cheek, and the general gloom of his aspect. "Why do you go on playing billiards at that wicked Spratt's?" Lady Agnes asked. "My dearest child, those billiards will kill you, I'm sure they will."

"It isn't the billiards," Harry said, gloomily. "Then it's the dreadful Back Kitchen," said the Lady Agnes. "I've often thought, d'you know, Harry, of writing to the landlady, and begging that she would have the kindness to put only very little wine in the negus which you take, and see that you have your shawl on before you get into your brougham."

"Do, ma'am. Mrs. Cutts is a most kind, motherly woman," Harry said. "But it isn't the Back Kitchen, neither," he added with a ghastly sigh.

As Lady Agnes never denied her son any thing, and fell into all his ways with the fondest acquiescence, she was rewarded by a perfect confidence on young Harry's part, who never thought to disguise from her a knowledge of the haunts which he frequented; and, on the contrary, brought her home choice anecdotes from the clubs and billiard-rooms, which the simple lady relished, if she did not understand. "My son goes to Spratt's," she would say to her confidential friends. "All the young men go to Spratt's after their balls. It is de rigeur, my dear; and they play billiards as they used to play macao and hazard in Mr. Fox's time. Yes, my dear father often told me that they sate up always until nine o'clock the next morning with Mr. Fox at Brooks's, whom I remember at Drummington, when I was a little girl, in a buff waistcoat and black satin small clothes. My brother Erith never played as a young man, nor sate up late—he had no health for it; but my boy must do as every body does, you know. Yes, and then he often goes to a place called the Back Kitchen, frequented by all the wits and authors, you know, whom one does not see in society, but whom it is a great privilege and pleasure for Harry to meet, and there he hears the questions of the day discussed; and my dear father often said that it was our duty to encourage literature, and he had hoped to see the late Dr. Johnson at Drummington, only Dr. Johnson died. Yes, and Mr. Sheridan came over and drank a great deal of wine—every body drank a great deal of wine in those days—and papa's wine-merchant's bill was ten times as much as Erith's is, who gets it as he wants it from Fortnum and Mason's, and doesn't keep any stock at all."

"That was an uncommon good dinner we had yesterday, ma'am," the artful Harry broke out. "Their clear soup's better than ours. Moufflet will put too much taragon into every thing. The suprème de volaille was very good—uncommon, and the sweets were better than Moufflet's sweets. Did you taste the plombière, ma'am and the maraschino jelly? Stunningly good that maraschino jelly!"

Lady Agnes expressed her agreement in these, as in almost all other sentiments of her son, who continued the artful conversation, saying,

"Very handsome house that of the Claverings. Furniture, I should say, got up regardless of expense. Magnificent display of plate, ma'am." The lady assented to all these propositions.

"Very nice people the Claverings."

"Hem!" said Lady Agnes.

"I know what you mean. Lady C. ain't distangy exactly, but she is very good-natured." "O very," mamma said, who was herself one of the most good-natured of women.

"And Sir Francis, he don't talk much before ladies: but after dinner he comes out uncommon strong, ma'am—a highly agreeable well-informed man. When will you ask them to dinner? Look out for an early day, ma'am;" and looking into Lady Agnes's pocket-book, he chose a day only a fortnight hence (an age that fortnight seemed to the young gentleman), when the Claverings were to be invited to Grosvenor-street.

The obedient Lady Agnes wrote the required invitation. She was accustomed to do so without consulting her husband, who had his own society and habits, and who left his wife to see her own friends alone. Harry looked at the card; but there was an omission in the invitation which did not please him.

"You have not asked Miss Whatdyecallem—Miss Emery, Lady Clavering's daughter."

"O, that little creature!" Lady Agnes cried. "No, I think not, Harry."

"We must ask Miss Amory," Foker said. "I—I want to ask Pendennis; and he's very sweet upon her. Don't you think she sings very well, ma'am?"

"I thought her rather forward, and didn't listen to her singing. She only sang at you and Mr. Pendennis, it seemed to me. But I will ask her if you wish, Harry," and so Miss Amory's name was written on the card with her mother's.

This piece of diplomacy being triumphantly executed, Harry embraced his fond parent with the utmost affection, and retired to his own apartments, where he stretched himself on his ottoman, and lay brooding silently, sighing for the day which was to bring the fair Miss Amory under his paternal roof, and devising a hundred wild schemes for meeting her.

On his return from making the grand tour, Mr. Foker, junior, had brought with him a polyglot valet, who took the place of Stoopid, and condescended to wait at dinner, attired in shirt fronts of worked muslin, with many gold studs and chains, upon his master and the elders of the family. This man, who was of no particular country, and spoke all languages indifferently ill, made himself useful to Mr. Harry in a variety of ways—read all the artless youth's correspondence, knew his favorite haunts and the addresses of his acquaintance, and officiated at the private dinners which the young gentleman gave. As Harry lay upon his sofa after his interview with his mamma, robed in a wonderful dressing-gown, and puffing his pipe in gloomy silence, Anatole, too, must have remarked that something affected his master's spirits; though he did not betray any ill-bred sympathy with Harry's agitation of mind. When Harry began to dress himself in his out-of-door morning costume: he was very hard indeed to please, and particularly severe and snappish about his toilet: he tried, and cursed, pantaloons of many different stripes, checks, and colors: all the boots were villainously varnished, the shirts too "loud" in pattern. He scented his linen and person with peculiar richness this day; and what must have been the valet's astonishment, when, after some blushing and hesitation on Harry's part, the young gentleman asked, "I say, Anatole, when I engaged you, didn't you—hem—didn't you say that you could dress—hem—dress hair?"

The valet said, "Yes, he could."

"Cherchy alors une paire de tongs—et—curly moi un pew" Mr. Foker said, in an easy manner; and the valet wondering whether his master was in love or was going masquerading, went in search of the articles—first from the old butler who waited upon Mr. Foker, senior, on whose bald pate the tongs would have scarcely found a hundred hairs to seize, and finally of the lady who had the charge of the meek auburn fronts of the Lady Agnes. And the tongs being got, Monsieur Anatole twisted his young master's locks until he had made Harry's head as curly as a negro's; after which the youth dressed himself with the utmost care and splendor and proceeded to sally out.

"At what time sall I order de drag, sir, to be to Miss Calverley's door, sir?" the attendant whispered as his master was going forth.

"Confound her! Put the dinner off—I can't go!" said Foker. "No, hang it—I must go. Poyntz and Rougemont, and ever so many more are coming. The drag at Pelham Corner at six o'clock, Anatole."

The drag was not one of Mr. Foker's own equipages, but was hired from a livery stable for festive purposes; Foker, however, put his own carriage into requisition that morning, and for what purpose does the kind reader suppose? Why to drive down to Lamb-court, Temple, taking Grosvenor-place by the way (which lies in the exact direction of the Temple from Grosvenor-street, as every body knows), where he just had the pleasure of peeping upward at Miss Amory's pink window curtains, having achieved which satisfactory feat, he drove off to Pen's chambers. Why did he want to see his dear friend Pen so much? Why did he yearn and long after him; and did it seem necessary to Foker's very existence that he should see Pen that morning, having parted with him in perfect health on the night previous? Pen had lived two years in London, and Foker had not paid half a dozen visits to his chambers. What sent him thither now in such a hurry?

What?—if any young ladies read this page, I have only to inform them that when the same mishap befalls them, which now had for more than twelve hours befallen Harry Foker, people will grow interesting to them for whom they did not care sixpence on the day before; as on the other hand persons of whom they fancied themselves fond will be found to have become insipid and disagreeable. Then your dearest Eliza or Maria of the other day, to whom you wrote letters and sent locks of hair yards long, will on a sudden be as indifferent to you as your stupidest relation: while, on the contrary, about his relations you will begin to feel such a warm interest! such a loving desire to ingratiate yourself with his mamma; such a liking for that dear kind old man his father! If He is in the habit of visiting at any house, what advances you will make in order to visit there too. If He has a married sister you will like to spend long mornings with her. You will fatigue your servant by sending notes to her, for which there will be the most pressing occasion, twice or thrice in a day. You will cry if your mamma objects to your going too often to see His family. The only one of them you will dislike, is perhaps his younger brother, who is at home for the holidays, and who will persist in staying in the room when you come to see your dear new-found friend, his darling second sister. Something like this will happen to you, young ladies, or, at any rate, let us hope it may. Yes, you must go through the hot fits and the cold fits of that pretty fever. Your mothers, if they would acknowledge it, have passed through it before you were born, your dear papa being the object of the passion of course—who could it be but he? And as you suffer it so will your brothers in their way—and after their kind. More selfish than you: more eager and headstrong than you: they will rush on their destiny when the doomed charmer makes her appearance. Or if they don't, and you don't, Heaven help you! As the gambler said of his dice, to love and win is the best thing, to love and lose is the next best. You don't die of the complaint: or very few do. The generous wounded heart suffers and survives it. And he is not a man, or she a woman, who is not conquered by it, or who does not conquer it in his time...... Now, then, if you ask why Henry Foker, Esquire, was in such a hurry to see

Arthur Pendennis, and felt such a sudden value and esteem for him, there is no difficulty in saying it was because Pen had become really valuable in Mr. Foker's eyes; because if Pen was not the rose, he yet had been near that fragrant flower of love. Was not he in the habit of going to her house in London? Did he not live near her in the country?—know all about the enchantress? What, I wonder, would Lady Ann Milton, Mr. Foker's cousin and prétendue, have said, if her ladyship had known all that was going on in the bosom of that funny little gentleman?

Alas! when Foker reached Lamb-court, leaving his carriage for the admiration of the little clerks who were lounging in the arch-way that leads thence into Flag-court which leads into Upper Temple-lane, Warrington was in the chambers, but Pen was absent. Pen was gone to the printing-office to see his proofs. "Would Foker have a pipe, and should the laundress go to the Cock and get him some beer?" — Warrington asked, remarking with a pleased surprise the splendid toilet of this scented and shiny-booted young aristocrat; but Foker had not the slightest wish for beer or tobacco: he had very important business: he rushed away to the "Pall-Mall Gazette" office, still bent upon finding Pen. Pen had quitted that place. Foker wanted him that they might go together to call upon Lady Clavering. Foker went away disconsolate, and whiled away an hour or two vaguely at clubs: and when it was time to pay a visit, he thought it would be but decent and polite to drive to Grosvenor-place and leave a card upon Lady Clavering. He had not the courage to ask to see her when the door was opened, he only delivered two cards, with Mr. Henry Foker engraved upon them, to Jeames, in a speechless agony. Jeames received the tickets bowing his powdered head. The varnished doors closed upon him. The beloved object was as far as ever from him, though so near. He thought he heard the tones of a piano and of a siren singing, coming from the drawing-room and sweeping over the balcony-shrubbery of geraniums. He would have liked to stop and listen, but it might not be. "Drive to Tattersall's," he said to the groom, in a voice smothered with emotion—"And bring my pony round," he added, as the man drove rapidly away.

As good luck would have it, that splendid barouche of Lady Clavering's, which has been inadequately described in a former chapter, drove up to her ladyship's door just as Foker mounted the pony which was in waiting for him. He bestrode the fiery animal, and dodged about the arch of the Green Park, keeping the carriage well in view, until he saw Lady Clavering enter, and with her—whose could be that angel form, but the enchantress's, clad in a sort of gossamer, with a pink bonnet and a light-blue parasol—but Miss Amory?

The carriage took its fair owners to Madame Rigodon's cap and lace shop, to Mrs. Wolsey's Berlin worsted shop—who knows to what other resorts of female commerce? Then it went and took ices at Hunter's, for Lady Clavering was somewhat florid in her tastes and amusements, and not only liked to go abroad in the most showy carriage in London, but that the public should see her in it too. And so, in a white bonnet with a yellow feather, she ate a large pink ice in the sunshine before Hunter's door, till Foker on his pony, and the red jacket who accompanied him, were almost tired of dodging.

Then at last she made her way into the Park, and the rapid Foker made his dash forward. What to do? Just to get a nod of recognition from Miss Amory and her mother; to cross them a half-dozen times in the drive; to watch and ogle them from the other side of the ditch, where the horsemen assemble when the band plays in Kensington Gardens. What is the use of looking at a woman in a pink bonnet across a ditch? What is the earthly good to be got out of a nod of the head? Strange that men will be contented with such pleasures, or if not contented, at least that they will be so eager in seeking them. Not one word did Harry, he so fluent of conversation ordinarily, change with his charmer on that day. Mutely he beheld her return to her carriage, and drive away among rather ironical salutes from the young men in the Park. One said that the Indian widow was making the paternal rupees spin rapidly; another said that she ought to have burned herself alive, and left the money to her daughter. This one asked who Clavering was?—and old Tom Eales, who knew every body, and never missed a day in the Park on his gray cob, kindly said that Clavering had come into an estate over head and heels in mortgage: that there were dev'lish ugly stories about him when he was a young man, and that it was reported of him that he had a share in a gambling house, and had certainly shown the white feather in his regiment. "He plays still; he is in a hell every night almost," Mr. Eales added. "I should think so, since his marriage," said a wag.

"He gives devilish good dinners," said Foker, striking up for the honor of his host of yesterday.

"I daresay, and I daresay he doesn't ask Eales," the wag said. "I say, Eales, do you dine at Clavering's—at the Begum's?"

"I dine there?" said Mr. Eales, who would have dined with Beelzebub, if sure of a good cook, and when he came away, would have painted his host blacker than fate had made him.

"You might, you know, although you do abuse him so," continued the wag. "They say it's very pleasant. Clavering goes to sleep after dinner; the Begum gets tipsy with cherry-brandy, and the young lady sings songs to the young gentlemen. She sings well, don't she, Fo?"

"Slap up," said Fo. "I tell you what, Poyntz, she sings like a— whatdyecallum—you know what I mean— like a mermaid, you know, but that's not their name."

"I never heard a mermaid sing," Mr. Poyntz, the wag replied. "Who ever heard a mermaid? Eales, you are an old fellow, did you?"

"Don't make a lark of me, hang it, Poyntz," said Foker, turning red, and with tears almost in his eyes, "you know what I mean: it's those what's-his-names—in Homer, you know. I never said I was a good scholar."

"And nobody ever said it of you, my boy," Mr. Poyntz remarked, and Foker striking spurs into his pony, cantered away down Rotten Row, his mind agitated with various emotions, ambitions, mortifications. He was sorry that he had not been good at his books in early life—that he might have cut out all those chaps who were about her, and who talked the languages, and wrote poetry, and painted pictures in her album, and—and that. "What am I," thought little Foker, "compared to her? She's all soul, she is, and can write poetry or compose music, as easy as I could drink a glass of beer. Beer?—damme, that's all I'm fit for, is beer. I am a poor, ignorant little beggar, good for nothing but Foker's Entire. I misspent my youth, and used to get the chaps to do my exercises. And what's the consequences now? O, Harry Foker, what a confounded little fool you have been!"

As he made this dreary soliloquy, he had cantered out of Rotten Row into the Park, and there was on the point of riding down a large, old, roomy family carriage, of which he took no heed, when a cheery voice cried out, "Harry, Harry!" and looking up, he beheld his aunt, the Lady Rosherville, and two of her daughters, of whom the one who spoke was Harry's betrothed, the Lady Ann.

He started back with a pale, scared look, as a truth about which he had not thought during the whole day, came across him. There was his fate, there, in the back seat of that carriage.

"What is the matter Harry? why are you so pale? You have been raking and smoking too much, you wicked boy," said Lady Ann.

Foker said, "How do, aunt?" "How do, Ann?" in a perturbed manner—muttered something about a pressing engagement—indeed he saw by the Park clock that he must have been keeping his party in the drag waiting for nearly an hour—and waved a good-by. The little man and the little pony were out of sight in an instant—the great carriage rolled away. Nobody inside was very much interested about his coming or going; the countess being occupied with her spaniel, the Lady Lucy's thoughts and eyes being turned upon a volume of sermons, and those of Lady Ann upon a new novel, which the sisters had just procured from the library.

CHAPTER II

CARRIES THE READER BOTH TO RICHMOND AND GREENWICH

Poor Foker found the dinner at Richmond to be the most dreary entertainment upon which ever mortal man wasted his guineas. "I wonder how the deuce I could ever have liked these people," he thought in his own mind. "Why, I can see the crow's-feet under Rougemont's eyes, and the paint on her cheeks is laid on as thick as clown's in a pantomime! The way in which that Calverley talks slang, is quite disgusting. I hate chaff in a woman. And old Colchicum! that old Col, coming down here in his brougham, with his coronet on it, and sitting bodkin between Mademoiselle Coralie and her mother! It's too bad. An English peer, and a horse-rider of Franconi's! It won't do; by Jove, it won't do. I ain't proud; but it will not do!"

"Twopence-halfpenny for your thoughts, Fokey!" cried out Miss Rougemont, taking her cigar from her truly vermilion lips, as she beheld the young fellow lost in thought, seated at the head of his table, amidst melting ices, and cut pine-apples, and bottles full and empty, and cigar-ashes scattered on fruit, and the ruins of a dessert which had no pleasure for him.

"Does Foker ever think?" drawled out Mr. Poyntz. "Foker, here is a considerable sum of money offered by a fair capitalist at this end of the table for the present emanations of your valuable and acute intellect, old boy!"

"What the deuce is that Poyntz a talking about?" Mrs. Calverley asked of her neighbor. "I hate him. He's a drawlin', sneerin' beast."

"What a droll of a little man is that little Fokare, my lor," Mademoiselle Coralie said, in her own language, and with the rich twang of that sunny Gascony in which her swarthy cheeks and bright black eyes had got their fire. "What a droll of a man! He does not look to have twenty years."

"I wish I were of his age," said the venerable Colchicum, with a sigh, as he inclined his purple face toward a large goblet of claret.

"C'te Jeunesse. Peuh! je m'en fiche," said Madame Brack, Coralie's mamma, taking a great pinch out of Lord Colchicum's delicate gold snuff-box. "Je n'aime que les hommes faits, moi. Comme milor Coralie! n'est ce pas que tu n'aimes que les hommes faits, ma bichette?"

My lord said, with a grin, "You flatter me, Madame Brack."

"Taisez vous, Maman, vous n'êtes qu'une bête," Coralie cried, with a shrug of her robust shoulders; upon which, my lord said that she did not flatter at any rate; and pocketed his snuff-box, not desirous that Madame Brack's dubious fingers should plunge too frequently into his Mackabaw.

There is no need to give a prolonged detail of the animated conversation which ensued during the rest of the banquet; a conversation which would not much edify the reader. And it is scarcely necessary to say, that all ladies of the corps de danse are not like Miss Calverley, any more than that all peers resemble that illustrious member of their order, the late lamented Viscount Colchicum. But there have been such in our memories who have loved the society of riotous youth better than the company of men of their own age and rank, and have given the young ones the precious benefit of their experience and example; and there have been very respectable men too who have not objected so much to the kind of entertainment as to the publicity of it. I am sure, for instance, that our friend Major Pendennis would have made no sort of objection to join a party of pleasure, provided that it were en petit comité, and that such men as my Lord Steyne and my Lord Colchicum were of the society. "Give the young men their pleasures," this worthy guardian said to Pen more than once. "I'm not one of your straight-laced moralists, but an old man of the world, begad; and I know that as long as it lasts, young men will be young men." And there were some young men to whom this estimable philosopher accorded about seventy years as the proper period for sowing their wild oats: but they were men of fashion.

Mr. Foker drove his lovely guests home to Brompton in the drag that night; but he was quite thoughtful and gloomy during the whole of the little journey from Richmond; neither listening to the jokes of the friends behind him and on the box by his side, nor enlivening them, as was his wont, by his own facetious sallies. And when the ladies whom he had conveyed alighted at the door of their house, and asked then accomplished coachman whether he would not step in and take some thing to drink, he declined with so melancholy an air, that they supposed that the governor and he had had a difference, or that some calamity had befallen him: and he did not tell these people what the cause of his grief was, but left Mesdames Rougemont and Calverley, unheeding the cries of the latter, who hung over her balcony like Jezebel, and called out to him to ask him to give another party soon.

He sent the drag home under the guidance of one of the grooms, and went on foot himself; his hands in his pockets, plunged in thought. The stars and moon shining tranquilly over head, looked down upon Mr. Foker that night, as he, in his turn, sentimentally regarded them. And he went and gazed upward at the house in Grosvenor-place, and at the windows which he supposed to be those of the beloved object; and he moaned and he sighed in a way piteous and surprising to witness, which Policeman X. did, who informed Sir Francis Clavering's people, as they took the refreshment of beer on the coach-box at the neighboring public-house, after bringing home their lady from the French play, that there had been another chap hanging about the premises that evening—a little chap, dressed like a swell.

And now with that perspicuity and ingenuity and enterprise which only belongs to a certain passion, Mr. Foker began to dodge Miss Amory through London, and to appear wherever he could meet her. If Lady Clavering went to the French play, where her ladyship had a box, Mr. Foker, whose knowledge of the language, as we have heard, was not conspicuous, appeared in a stall. He found out where her engagements were (it is possible that Anatole, his man, was acquainted with Sir Francis Clavering's gentleman, and so got a sight of her ladyship's engagement-book), and at many of these evening parties Mr. Foker made his appearance, to the surprise of the world, and of his mother especially, whom he ordered to apply for cards to these parties, for which until now he had shown a supreme contempt. He told the pleased and unsuspicious lady that he went to parties because it was right for him to see the world: he told her that he went to the French play because he wanted to perfect himself in the language, and there was no such good lesson as a comedy or vaudeville—and when one night the astonished Lady Agnes saw him stand up and dance, and complimented him upon his elegance and activity, the mendacious little rogue asserted that he had learned to dance in Paris, whereas Anatole knew that his young master used to go off privily to an academy in Brewer-street, and study there for some hours in the morning. The casino of our modern days was not invented, or was in its infancy as yet; and gentlemen of Mr. Foker's time had not the facilities of acquiring the science of dancing which are enjoyed by our present youth.

Old Pendennis seldom missed going to church. He considered it to be his duty as a gentleman to patronize the institution of public worship, and that it was quite a correct thing to be seen in church of a Sunday. One day it chanced that he and Arthur went thither together: the latter, who was now in high favor, had been to breakfast with his uncle, from whose lodging they walked across the Park to a church not far from Belgrave-square. There was a charity sermon at Saint James's, as the major knew by the bills posted on the pillars of his parish church, which probably caused him, for he was a thrifty man, to forsake it for that day: besides he had other views for himself and Pen. "We will go to church, sir, across the Park; and then, begad, we will go to the Claverings' house, and ask them for lunch in a friendly way. Lady Clavering likes to be asked for lunch, and is uncommonly kind, and monstrous hospitable."

"I met them at dinner last week, at Lady Agnes Foker's, sir," Pen said, "and the Begum was very kind indeed. So she was in the country: so she is every where. But I share your opinion about Miss Amory; one of your opinions, that is, uncle, for you were changing, the last time we spoke about her."

"And what do you think of her now?" the elder said.

"I think her the most confounded little flirt in London," Pen answered, laughing. "She made a tremendous assault upon Harry Foker, who sat next to her; and to whom she gave all the talk, though I took her down."

"Bah! Henry Foker is engaged to his cousin, all the world knows it: not a bad coup of Lady Rosherville's, that. I should say, that the young man at his father's death, and old Mr. Foker's life's devilish bad: you know he had a fit, at Arthur's, last year: I should say, that young Foker won't have less than fourteen thousand a year from the brewery, besides Logwood and the Norfolk property. I've no pride about me, Pen. I like a man of birth certainly, but dammy, I like a brewery which brings in a man fourteen thousand a year; hey, Pen? Ha, ha, that's the sort of man for me. And I recommend you now that you are lancéd in the world, to stick to fellows of that sort; to fellows who have a stake in the country, begad."

"Foker sticks to me, sir," Arthur answered. "He has been at our chambers several times lately. He has asked me to dinner. We are almost as great friends, as we used to be in our youth: and his talk is about Blanche Amory from morning till night. I'm sure he's sweet upon her."

"I'm sure he is engaged to his cousin, and that they will keep the young man to his bargain," said the major. "The marriages in these families are affairs of state. Lady Agnes was made to marry old Foker by the late Lord, although she was notoriously partial to her cousin who was killed at Albuera afterward, and who saved her life out of the lake at Drummington. I remember Lady Agnes, sir, an exceedingly fine woman. But what did she do? of course she married her father's man. Why, Mr. Foker sate for

Drummington till the Reform Bill, and paid dev'lish well for his seat, too. And you may depend upon this, sir, that Foker senior, who is a parvenu, and loves a great man, as all parvenus do, has ambitious views for his son as well as himself, and that your friend Harry must do as his father bids him Lord bless you! I've known a hundred cases of love in young men and women: hey, Master Arthur, do you take me? They kick, sir, they resist, they make a deuce of a riot and that sort of thing, but they end by listening to reason, begad."

"Blanche is a dangerous girl, sir," Pen said. "I was smitten with her myself once, and very far gone, too," he added; "but that is years ago."

"Were you? How far did it go? Did she return it?" asked the major, looking hard at Pen.

Pen, with a laugh, said "that at one time he did think he was pretty well in Miss Amory's good graces. But my mother did not like her, and the affair went off." Pen did not think it fit to tell his uncle all the particulars of that courtship which had passed between himself and the young lady.

"A man might go farther and fare worse, Arthur," the major said, still looking queerly at his nephew.

"Her birth, sir; her father was the mate of a ship, they say; and she has not money enough," objected Pen, in a dandyfied manner. "What's ten thousand pound and a girl bred up like her?"

"You use my own words, and it is all very well. But, I tell you in confidence, Pen—in strict honor, mind— that it's my belief she has a devilish deal more than ten thousand pound: and from what I saw of her the other day, and—and have heard of her—I should say she was a devilish accomplished, clever girl: and would make a good wife with a sensible husband."

"How do you know about her money?" Pen asked, smiling. "You seem to have information about every body, and to know about all the town."

"I do know a few things, sir, and I don't tell all I know. Mark that," the uncle replied. "And as for that charming Miss Amory—for charming, begad! she is—if I saw her Mrs. Arthur Pendennis, I should neither be sorry nor surprised, begad! and if you object to ten thousand pound, what would you say, sir, to thirty, or forty, or fifty?" and the major looked still more knowingly, and still harder at Pen.

"Well, sir," he said, to his godfather and namesake, "make her Mrs. Arthur Pendennis. You can do it as well as I."

"Psha! you are laughing at me, sir," the other replied, rather peevishly, and you ought not to laugh so near a church gate. "Here we are at St. Benedict's. They say Mr. Oriel is a beautiful preacher."

Indeed, the bells were tolling, the people were trooping into the handsome church, the carriages of the inhabitants of the lordly quarter poured forth their pretty loads of devotees, in whose company Pen and his uncle, ending their edifying conversation, entered the fane. I do not know whether other people carry their worldly affairs to the church door. Arthur, who, from habitual reverence and feeling, was always more than respectful in a place of worship, thought of the incongruity of their talk, perhaps; while the old gentleman at his side was utterly unconscious of any such contrast. His hat was brushed: his wig was trim: his neckcloth was perfectly tied. He looked at every soul in the congregation, it is true: the bald heads and the bonnets, the flowers and the feathers: but so demurely that he hardly lifted up his eyes from his book—from his book which he could not read without glasses. As for Pen's gravity, it was sorely put to the test when, upon looking by chance toward the seats where the servants were collected, he spied out, by the side of a demure gentleman in plush, Henry Foker, Esquire, who had discovered this place of devotion. Following the direction of Harry's eye, which strayed a good deal from his book, Pen found that it alighted upon a yellow bonnet and a pink one: and that these bonnets were on the heads of Lady Clavering and Blanche Amory. If Pen's uncle is not the only man who has talked about his worldly affairs up to the church door, is poor Harry Foker the only one who has brought his worldly love into the aisle?

When the congregation issued forth at the conclusion of the service, Foker was out among the first, but Pen came up with him presently, as he was hankering about the entrance which he was unwilling to leave, until my lady's barouche, with the bewigged coachman, had borne away its mistress and her daughter from their devotions.

When the two ladies came out, they found together the Pendennises, uncle and nephew, and Harry Foker, Esquire, sucking the crook of his stick, standing there in the sunshine. To see and to ask to eat were simultaneous with the good-natured Begum, and she invited the three gentlemen to luncheon straightway.

Blanche was, too, particularly gracious. "O! do come," she said to Arthur, "if you are not too great a man. I want so to talk to you about—but we mustn't say what, here, you know. What would Mr. Oriel say?" And the young devotee jumped into the carriage after her mamma. "I've read every word of it. It's adorable," she added, still addressing herself to Pen.

"I know who is," said Mr. Arthur, making rather a pert bow.

"What's the row about?" asked Mr. Foker, rather puzzled.

"I suppose Miss Amory means 'Walter Lorraine,'" said the major, looking knowing, and nodding at Pen.

"I suppose so, sir. There was a famous review in the Pall Mall this morning. It was Warrington's doing, though, and I must not be too proud."

"A review in Pall Mall?—Walter Lorraine? What the doose do you mean?" Foker asked. "Walter Lorraine died of the measles, poor little beggar, when we were at Gray Friars. I remember his mother coming up."

"You are not a literary man, Foker," Pen said, laughing, and hooking his arm into his friend's. "You must know I have been writing a novel, and some of the papers have spoken very well of it. Perhaps you don't read the Sunday papers?"

"I read Bell's Life regular, old boy," Mr. Foker answered: at which Pen laughed again, and the three gentlemen proceeded in great good-humor to Lady Clavering's house.

The subject of the novel was resumed after luncheon by Miss Amory, who indeed loved poets and men of letters if she loved any thing, and was sincerely an artist in feeling. "Some of the passages in the book made me cry, positively they did," she said.

Pen said, with some fatuity, "I am happy to think I have a part of vos larmes, Miss Blanche"—And the major (who had not read more than six pages of Pen's book) put on his sanctified look, saying, "Yes, there are some passages quite affecting, mons'ous affecting: and,"—"O, if it makes you cry,"—Lady Amory declared she would not read it, "that she wouldn't."

"Don't, mamma," Blanche said, with a French shrug of her shoulders; and then she fell into a rhapsody about the book, about the snatches of poetry interspersed in it, about the two heroines, Leonora and Neaera; about the two heroes, Walter Lorraine and his rival the young duke—"and what good company you introduce us to," said the young lady, archly, "quel ton! How much of your life have you passed at court, and are you a prime minister's son, Mr. Arthur?"

Pen began to laugh—"It is as cheap for a novelist to create a duke as to make a baronet," he said. "Shall I tell you a secret, Miss Amory? I promoted all my characters at the request of the publisher. The young duke was only a young baron when the novel was first written; his false friend the viscount, was a simple commoner, and so on with all the characters of the story."

"What a wicked, satirical, pert young man you have become! Comme vous voilà formé!" said the young lady, "How different from Arthur Pendennis of the country! Ah! I think I like Arthur Pendennis of the country best, though!" and she gave him the full benefit of her eyes—both of the fond, appealing glance into his own, and of the modest look downward toward the carpet, which showed off her dark eyelids and long fringed lashes.

Pen of course protested that he had not changed in the least, to which the young lady replied by a tender sigh; and thinking that she had done quite enough to make Arthur happy or miserable (as the case might be), she proceeded to cajole his companion, Mr. Harry Foker, who during the literary conversation had sate silently imbibing the head of his cane, and wishing that he was a clever chap, like that Pen.

If the major thought that by telling Miss Amory of Mr. Foker's engagement to his cousin, Lady Ann Milton (which information the old gentleman neatly conveyed to the girl as he sate by her side at luncheon below stairs)—if, we say, the major thought that the knowledge of this fact would prevent Blanche from paying any further attention to the young heir of Foker's Entire, he was entirely mistaken. She became only the more gracious to Foker: she praised him, and every thing belonging to him; she praised his mamma; she praised the pony which he rode in the Park; she praised the lovely breloques or gimcracks which the young gentleman wore at his watch-chain, and that dear little darling of a cane, and those dear little delicious monkeys' heads with ruby eyes, which ornamented Harry's shirt, and formed the buttons of his waistcoat. And then, having praised and coaxed the weak youth until he blushed and tingled with pleasure, and until Pen thought she really had gone quite far enough, she took another theme.

"I am afraid Mr. Foker is a very sad young man," she said, turning round to Pen.

"He does not look so," Pen answered with a sneer.

"I mean we have heard sad stories about him. Haven't we, mamma? What was Mr. Poyntz saying here, the other day, about that party at Richmond? O you naughty creature!" But here, seeing that Harry's countenance assumed a great expression of alarm, while Pen's wore a look of amusement, she turned to the latter and said, "I believe you are just as bad: I believe you would have liked to have been there—wouldn't you? I know you would: yes—and so should I."

"Lor, Blanche!" mamma cried.

"Well, I would. I never saw an actress in my life. I would give any thing to know one; for I adore talent. And I adore Richmond, that I do; and I adore Greenwich, and I say I should like to go there."

"Why should not we three bachelors," the major here broke out, gallantly, and to his nephew's special surprise, "beg these ladies to honor us with their company at Greenwich? Is Lady Clavering to go on forever being hospitable to us, and may we make no return? Speak for yourselves young men—eh, begad! Here is my nephew, with his pockets full of money—his pockets full, begad! and Mr. Henry Foker, who as I have heard say is pretty well to do in the world, how is your lovely cousin, Lady Ann, Mr. Foker?—here are these two young ones—and they allow an old fellow like me to speak. Lady Clavering will you do me the favor to be my guest? and Miss Blanche shall be Arthur's, if she will be so good."

"O delightful," cried Blanche.

"I like a bit of fun, too," said Lady Clavering; "and we will take some day when Sir Francis—"

"When Sir Francis dines out—yes mamma," the daughter said, "it will be charming."

And a charming day it was. The dinner was ordered at Greenwich, and Foker, though he did not invite Miss Amory, had some delicious opportunities of conversation with her during the repast, and afterward on the balcony of their room at the hotel, and again during the drive home in her ladyship's barouche. Pen came down with his uncle, in Sir Hugh Trumpington's brougham, which the major borrowed for the occasion.

"I am an old soldier, begad," he said, "and I learned in early life to make myself comfortable."

And, being an old soldier, he allowed the two young men to pay for the dinner between them, and all the way home in the brougham he rallied Pen about Miss Amory's evident partiality for him: praised her good looks, spirits, and wit: and again told Pen in the strictest confidence, that she would be a devilish deal richer than people thought.

CHAPTER III

CONTAINS A NOVEL INCIDENT

Some account has been given in a former part of this story, how Mr. Pen, during his residence at home, after his defeat at Oxbridge, had occupied himself with various literary compositions, and among other works, had written the greater part of a novel. This book, written under the influence of his youthful embarrassments, amatory and pecuniary, was of a very fierce, gloomy and passionate sort—the Byronic despair, the Wertherian despondency, the mocking bitterness of Mephistopheles of Faust, were all reproduced and developed in the character of the hero; for our youth had just been learning the German language, and imitated, as almost all clever lads do, his favorite poets and writers. Passages in the volumes once so loved, and now read so seldom, still bear the mark of the pencil with which he noted them in those days. Tears fell upon the leaf of the book, perhaps, or blistered the pages of his manuscript as the passionate young man dashed his thoughts down. If he took up the books afterward, he had no ability or wish to sprinkle the leaves with that early dew of former times: his pencil was no longer eager to score its marks of approval: but as he looked over the pages of his manuscript, he remembered what had been the overflowing feelings which had caused him to blot it, and the pain which had inspired the line. If the secret history of books could be written, and the author's private thoughts and meanings noted down alongside of his story, how many insipid volumes would become interesting, and dull tales excite the reader! Many a bitter smile passed over Pen's face as he read his novel, and recalled the time and feelings which gave it birth. How pompous some of the grand passages appeared; and how weak others were in which he thought he had expressed his full heart! This page was imitated from a then favorite author, as he could now clearly see and confess, though he had believed himself to be writing originally then. As he mused over certain lines he recollected the place and hour where he wrote them: the ghost of the dead feeling came back as he mused, and he blushed to review the faint image. And what meant those blots on the page? As you come in the desert to a ground where camels' hoofs are marked in the clay, and traces of withered herbage are yet visible, you know that water was there once; so the place in Pen's mind was no longer green, and the fons lacrymarum was dried up.

He used this simile one morning to Warrington, as the latter sate over his pipe and book, and Pen, with much gesticulation, according to his wont when excited, and with a bitter laugh, thumped his manuscript down on the table, making the tea-things rattle, and the blue milk dance in the jug. On the previous night he had taken the manuscript out of a long neglected chest, containing old shooting jackets, old Oxbridge scribbling books, his old surplice, and battered cap and gown, and other memorials of youth, school, and home. He read in the volume in bed until he fell asleep, for the commencement of the tale was somewhat dull, and he had come home tired from a London evening party.

"By Jove!" said Pen, thumping down his papers, "when I think that these were written but very few years ago, I am ashamed of my memory. I wrote this when I believed myself to be eternally in love with that little coquette, Miss Amory. I used to carry down verses to her, and put them into the hollow of a tree, and dedicate them 'Amori.'"

"That was a sweet little play upon words," Warrington remarked, with a puff "Amory—Amori. It showed profound scholarship. Let us hear a bit of the rubbish." And he stretched over from his easy chair, and caught hold of Pen's manuscript with the fire-tongs, which he was just using in order to put a coal into his pipe. Thus, in possession of the volume, he began to read out from the "Leaves from the Life-book of Walter Lorraine."

"'False as thou art beautiful! heartless as thou art fair! mockery of Passion!' Walter cried, addressing Leonora; 'what evil spirit hath sent thee to torture me so? O Leonora * * * '"

"Cut that part," cried out Pen, making a dash at the book, which, however, his comrade would not release. "Well! don't read it out, at any rate. That's about my other flame, my first—Lady Mirabel that is now. I saw her last night at Lady Whiston's. She asked me to a party at her house, and said, that, as old friends, we ought to meet oftener. She has been seeing me any time these two years in town, and never thought of inviting me before; but seeing Wenham talking to me, and Monsieur Dubois, the French literary man, who had a dozen orders on, and might have passed for a Marshal of France, she condescended to invite me. The Claverings are to be there on the same evening. Won't it be exciting to meet one's two flames at the same table?" "Two flames!—two heaps of burnt-out cinders," Warrington said. "Are both the beauties in this book?"

"Both or something like them," Pen said. "Leonora, who marries the duke, is the Fotheringay. I drew the duke from Magnus Charters, with whom I was at Oxbridge; it's a little like him; and Miss Amory is Neaera. By gad, Warrington, I did love that first woman! I thought of her as I walked home from Lady Whiston's in the moonlight; and the whole early scenes came back to me as if they had been yesterday. And when I got home I pulled out the story which I wrote about her and the other three years ago: do you know, outrageous as it is, it has some good stuff in it, and if Bungay won't publish it, I think Bacon will."

"That's the way of poets," said Warrington. "They fall in love, jilt, or are jilted; they suffer, and they cry out that they suffer more than any other mortals: and when they have experienced feelings enough, they note them down in a book, and take the book to market. All poets are humbugs, all literary men are humbugs; directly a man begins to sell his feelings for money he's a humbug. If a poet gets a pain in his side from too good a dinner, he bellows Ai, Ai, louder than Prometheus."

"I suppose a poet has greater sensibility than another man," said Pen, with some spirit. "That is what makes him a poet. I suppose that he sees and feels more keenly: it is that which makes him speak of what he feels and sees. You speak eagerly enough in your leading articles when you espy a false argument in an opponent, or detect a quack in the House. Paley, who does not care for any thing else in the world, will talk for an hour about a question of law. Give another the privilege which you take yourself, and the free use of his faculty, and let him be what nature has made him. Why should not a man sell his sentimental thoughts as well as you your political ideas, or Paley his legal knowledge? Each alike is a matter of experience and practice. It is not money which causes you to perceive a fallacy, or Paley to argue a point; but a natural or acquired aptitude for that kind of truth: and a poet sets down his thoughts and experiences upon paper as a painter does a landscape or a face upon canvas, to the best of his ability, and according to his particular gift. If ever I think I have the stuff in me to write an epic, by Jove, I will try. If I only feel that I am good enough to crack a joke or tell a story, I will do that."

"Not a bad speech, young one," Warrington said, "but that does not prevent all poets from being humbugs."

"What—Homer, Aeschylus, Shakspeare, and all?"

"Their names are not to be breathed in the same sentence with you pigmies," Mr. Warrington said; "there are men and men, sir."

"Well, Shakspeare was a man who wrote for money, just as you and I do," Pen answered, at which Warrington confounded his impudence, and resumed his pipe and his manuscript.

There was not the slightest doubt then that this document contained a great deal of Pen's personal experiences, and that "Leaves from the Life-book of Walter Lorraine" would never have been written but for Arthur Pendennis's own private griefs, passions, and follies. As we have become acquainted with these in the first volume of his biography, it will not be necessary to make large extracts from the novel of "Walter Lorraine," in which the young gentleman had depicted such of them as he thought were likely to interest the reader, or were suitable for the purposes of his story.

Now, though he had kept it in his box for nearly half of the period during which, according to the Horatian maxim, a work of art ought to lie ripening (a maxim, the truth of which may, by the way, be questioned altogether), Mr. Pen had not buried his novel for this time, in order that the work might improve, but because he did not know where else to bestow it, or had no particular desire to see it. A man who thinks of putting away a composition for ten years before he shall give it to the world, or exercise his own maturer judgment upon it, had best be very sure of the original strength and durability of the work; otherwise, on withdrawing it from its crypt, he may find that, like small wine, it has lost what flavor it once had, and is only tasteless when opened. There are works of all tastes and smacks, the small and the strong, those that improve by age, and those that won't bear keeping at all, but are pleasant at the first draught, when they refresh and sparkle.

Now Pen had never any notion, even in the time of his youthful inexperience and fervor of imagination, that the story he was writing was a masterpiece of composition, or that he was the equal of the great authors whom he admired; and when he now reviewed his little performance, he was keenly enough alive to its faults, and pretty modest regarding its merits. It was not very good, he thought; but it was as good as most books of the kind that had the run of circulating libraries and the career of the season. He had critically examined more than one fashionable novel by the authors of the day then popular, and he thought that his intellect was as good as theirs, and that he could write the English language as well as those ladies or gentlemen; and as he now ran over his early performance, he was pleased to find here and there passages exhibiting both fancy and vigor, and traits, if not of genius, of genuine passion and feeling. This, too, was Warrington's verdict, when that severe critic, after half-an-hour's perusal of the manuscript, and the consumption of a couple of pipes of tobacco, laid Pen's book down, yawning portentously. "I can't read any more of that balderdash now," he said; "but it seems to me there is some good stuff in it, Pen, my boy. There's a certain greenness and freshness in it which I like, somehow. The bloom disappears off the face of poetry after you begin to shave. You can't get up that naturalness and artless rosy tint in after days. Your cheeks are pale, and have got faded by exposure to evening parties, and you are obliged to take curling-irons, and macassar, and the deuce knows what to your whiskers; they curl ambrosially, and you are very grand and genteel, and so forth; but, ah! Pen, the spring time was the best."

"What the deuce have my whiskers to do with the subject in hand?" Pen said (who, perhaps, may have been nettled by Warrington's allusion to those ornaments, which, to say the truth, the young man coaxed, and curled, and oiled, and purfumed, and petted, in rather an absurd manner).

"Do you think we can do any thing with 'Walter Lorraine?' Shall we take him to the publishers, or make an auto-da-fe of him?"

"I don't see what is the good of incremation," Warrington said, "though I have a great mind to put him into the fire, to punish your atrocious humbug and hypocrisy. Shall I burn him indeed? You have much too great a value for him to hurt a hair of his head."

"Have I? Here goes," said Pen, and "Walter Lorraine" went off the table, and was flung on to the coals. But the fire having done its duty of boiling the young man's breakfast-kettle, had given up work for the day, and had gone out, as Pen knew very well; and Warrington, with a scornful smile, once more took up the manuscript with the tongs from out of the harmless cinders.

"O, Pen, what a humbug you are!" Warrington said; "and, what is worst of all, sir, a clumsy humbug. I saw you look to see that the fire was out before you sent 'Walter Lorraine' behind the bars. No, we won't burn him: we will carry him to the Egyptians, and sell him. We will exchange him away for money, yea, for silver and gold, and for beef and for liquors, and for tobacco and for raiment. This youth will fetch some price in the market; for he is a comely lad, though not over strong; but we will fatten him up, and give him the bath, and curl his hair, and we will sell him for a hundred piastres to Bacon or to Bungay. The rubbish is salable enough, sir; and my advice to you is this: the next time you go home for a holiday, take 'Walter Lorraine' in your carpet-bag—give him a more modern air, prune away, though sparingly, some of the green passages, and add a little comedy, and cheerfulness, and satire, and that sort of thing, and then we'll take him to market, and sell him. The book is not a wonder of wonders, but it will do very well."

"Do you think so, Warrington?" said Pen, delighted; for this was great praise from his cynical friend.

"You silly young fool! I think it's uncommonly clever," Warrington said in a kind voice. "So do you, sir." And with the manuscript which he held in his hand he playfully struck Pen on the cheek. That part of Pen's countenance turned as red as it had ever done in the earliest days of his blushes: he grasped the other's hand and said, "Thank you, Warrington," with all his might; and then he retired to his own room with his book, and passed the greater part of the day upon his bed re-reading it: and he did as Warrington had advised, and altered not a little, and added a great deal, until at length he had fashioned "Walter Lorraine" pretty much into the shape in which, as the respected novel-reader knows, it subsequently appeared.

While he was at work upon this performance, the good-natured Warrington artfully inspired the two gentlemen who "read" for Messrs. Bacon and Bungay with the greatest curiosity regarding, "Walter Lorraine," and pointed out the peculiar merits of its distinguished author. It was at the period when the novel, called "The Fashionable," was in vogue among us; and Warrington did not fail to point out, as before, how Pen was a man of the very first fashion himself, and received at the houses of some of the greatest personages in the land. The simple and kind-hearted Percy Popjoy was brought to bear upon Mrs. Bungay, whom he informed that his friend Pendennis was occupied upon a work of the most exciting nature; a work that the whole town would run after, full of wit, genius, satire, pathos, and every conceivable good quality. We have said before, that Bungay knew no more about novels than he did about Hebrew or Algebra, and neither read nor understood any of the books which he published and paid for; but he took his opinions from his professional advisers and from Mrs. B., and, evidently with a view to a commercial transaction, asked Pendennis and Warrington to dinner again. Bacon, when he found that Bungay was about to treat, of course, began to be anxious and curious, and desired to out-bid his rival. Was any thing settled between Mr. Pendennis and the odious house "over the way" about the new book? Mr. Hack, the confidential reader, was told to make inquiries, and see if any thing was to be done, and the result of the inquiries of that diplomatist, was, that one morning, Bacon himself toiled up the staircase of Lamb-court, and to the door on which the names of Mr. Warrington, and Mr. Pendennis were painted.

For a gentleman of fashion as poor Pen was represented to be, it must be confessed, that the apartments he and his friend occupied, were not very suitable. The ragged carpet had grown only more ragged during the two years of joint occupancy: a constant odor of tobacco perfumed the sitting-room: Bacon tumbled over the laundress's buckets in the passage through which he had to pass; Warrington's shooting jacket was as shattered at the elbows as usual; and the chair which Bacon was requested to take on entering, broke down with the publisher. Warrington burst out laughing, said that Bacon had got the game chair, and bawled out to Pen to fetch a sound one from his bedroom. And seeing the publisher looking round the dingy room with an air of profound pity and wonder, asked him whether he didn't think the apartments were elegant, and if he would like, for Mrs. Bacon's drawing-room, any of the articles of furniture? Mr. Warrington's character as a humorist, was known to Mr. Bacon: "I never can make that chap out," the publisher was heard to say, "or tell whether he is in earnest or only chaffing."

It is very possible that Mr. Bacon would have set the two gentlemen down as impostors altogether, but that there chanced to be on the breakfast-table certain cards of invitation which the post of the morning had brought in for Pen, and which happened to come from some very exalted personages of the beau-monde, into which our young man had his introduction. Looking down upon these, Bacon saw that the Marchioness of Steyne would be at home to Mr. Arthur Pendennis upon a given day, and that another lady of distinction proposed to have dancing at her house upon a certain future evening. Warrington saw the admiring publisher eying these documents. "Ah," said he, with an air of simplicity, "Pendennis is one of the most affable young men I ever knew, Mr. Bacon. Here is a young fellow that dines with all the great men in London, and yet he'll take his mutton-chop with you and me quite contentedly. There's nothing like the affability of the old English gentleman."

"O, no, nothing," said Mr. Bacon.

"And you wonder why he should go on living up three pair of stairs with me, don't you, now? Well, it is a queer taste. But we are fond of each other; and as I can't afford to live in a grand house, he comes and stays in these rickety old chambers with me. He's a man that can afford to live any where."

"I fancy it don't cost him much here," thought Mr. Bacon; and the object of these praises presently entered the room from his adjacent sleeping apartment.

Then Mr. Bacon began to speak upon the subject of his visit; said he heard that Mr. Pendennis had a manuscript novel; professed himself anxious to have a sight of that work, and had no doubt that they could come to terms respecting it. What would be his price for it? would he give Bacon the refusal of it? he would find our house a liberal house, and so forth. The delighted Pen assumed an air of indifference, and said that he was already in treaty with Bungay, and could give no definite answer. This piqued the other into such liberal, though vague offers, that Pen began to fancy Eldorado was opening to him, and that his fortune was made from that day.

I shall not mention what was the sum of money which Mr. Arthur Pendennis finally received for the first edition of his novel of "Walter Lorraine," lest other young literary aspirants should expect to be as lucky as he was, and unprofessional persons forsake their own callings, whatever they may be, for the sake of supplying the world with novels, whereof there is already a sufficiency. Let no young people be misled and rush fatally into romance-writing: for one book which succeeds let them remember the many that fail, I do not say deservedly or otherwise, and wholesomely abstain: or if they venture, at least let then do so at their own peril. As for those who have already written novels, this warning is not addressed, of course, to them. Let them take their wares to market; let them apply to Bacon and Bungay, and all the publishers in the Row, or the metropolis, and may they be happy in their ventures. This world is so wide, and the tastes of mankind happily so various, that there is always a chance for every man, and he may win the prize by his genius or by his good fortune. But what is the chance of success or failure; of obtaining popularity, or of holding it, when achieved? One man goes over the ice, which bears him, and a score who follow flounder in. In fine, Mr. Pendennis's was an exceptional case, and applies to himself only: and I assert solemnly, and will to the last maintain, that it is one thing to write a novel, and another to get money for it.

By merit, then, or good fortune, or the skillful playing off of Bungay against Bacon which Warrington performed (and which an amateur novelist is quite welcome to try upon any two publishers in the trade), Pen's novel was actually sold for a certain sum of money to one of the two eminent patrons of letters whom we have introduced to our readers. The sum was so considerable that Pen thought of opening an account at a banker's, or of keeping a cab and horse, or of descending into the first floor of Lamb-court into newly furnished apartments, or of migrating to the fashionable end of the town.

Major Pendennis advised the latter move strongly; he opened his eyes with wonder when he heard of the good luck that had befallen Pen; and which the latter, as soon as it occurred, hastened eagerly to communicate to his uncle. The major was almost angry that Pen should have earned so much money. "Who the doose reads this kind of thing?" he thought to himself, when he heard of the bargain which Pen had made. "I never read your novels and rubbish. Except Paul de Kock, who certainly makes me laugh, I don't think I've looked into a book of the sort these thirty years. 'Gad! Pen's a lucky fellow. I should think he might write one of these in a month now—say a month—that's twelve in a year. Dammy, he may go on spinning this nonsense for the next four or five years, and make a fortune. In the mean time, I should wish him to live properly, take respectable apartments, and keep a brougham." And on this simple calculation it was that the major counseled Pen.

Arthur, laughing, told Warrington what his uncle's advice had been; but he luckily had a much more reasonable counselor than the old gentleman, in the person of his friend, and in his own conscience, which said to him, "Be grateful for this piece of good fortune; don't plunge into any extravagancies. Pay back Laura!" And he wrote a letter to her, in which he told her his thanks and his regard; and inclosed to her such an installment of his debt as nearly wiped it off. The widow and Laura herself might well be affected by the letter. It was written with genuine tenderness and modesty; and old Dr. Portman, when he read a passage in the letter, in which Pen, with an honest heart full of gratitude, humbly thanked Heaven for his present prosperity, and for sending him such dear and kind friends to support him in his ill-fortune,—when Doctor Portman read this portion of the letter, his voice faltered, and his eyes twinkled behind his spectacles. And when he had quite finished reading the same, and had taken his glasses off his nose, and had folded up the paper and given it back to the widow, I am constrained to say, that after holding Mrs. Pendennis's hand for a minute, the doctor drew that lady toward him and fairly kissed her: at which salute, of course, Helen burst out crying on the doctor's shoulder, for her heart was too full to give any other reply: and the doctor, blushing a great deal after his feat, led the lady, with a bow, to the sofa, on which he seated himself by her; and he mumbled out, in a low voice, some words of a Great Poet whom he loved very much, and who describes how in the days of his prosperity he had made "the widow's heart to sing for joy."

"The letter does the boy very great honor, very great honor, my dear," he said, patting it as it lay on Helen's knee—"and I think we have all reason to be thankful for it—very thankful. I need not tell you in what quarter, my dear, for you are a sainted woman: yes, Laura, my love, your mother is a sainted woman. And Mrs. Pendennis, ma'am, I shall order a copy of the book for myself, and another at the Book club."

We may be sure that the widow and Laura walked out to meet the mail which brought them their copy of Pen's precious novel, as soon as that work was printed and ready for delivery to the public; and that they read it to each other: and that they also read it privately and separately, for when the widow came out of her room in her dressing-gown at one o'clock in the morning with volume two, which she had finished, she found Laura devouring volume three in bed. Laura did not say much about the book, but

Helen pronounced that it was a happy mixture of Shakspeare, and Byron, and Walter Scott, and was quite certain that her son was the greatest genius, as he was the best son, in the world.

Did Laura not think about the book and the author, although she said so little? At least she thought about Arthur Pendennis. Kind as his tone was, it vexed her. She did not like his eagerness to repay that money. She would rather that her brother had taken her gift as she intended it; and was pained that there should be money calculations between them. His letters from London, written with the good-natured wish to amuse his mother, were full of descriptions of the famous people and the entertainments, and magnificence of the great city. Every body was flattering him and spoiling him, she was sure. Was he not looking to some great marriage, with that cunning uncle for a Mentor (between whom and Laura there was always an antipathy), that inveterate worldling, whose whole thoughts were bent upon pleasure, and rank, and fortune? He never alluded to—to old times, when he spoke of her. He had forgotten them and her, perhaps: had he not forgotten other things and people?

These thoughts may have passed in Miss Laura's mind, though she did not, she could not, confide them to Helen. She had one more secret, too, from that lady, which she could not divulge, perhaps, because she knew how the widow would have rejoiced to know it. This regarded an event which had occurred during that visit to Lady Rockminster, which Laura had paid in the last Christmas holidays: when Pen was at home with his mother, and when Mr. Pynsent, supposed to be so cold and so ambitious, had formally offered his hand to Miss Bell. No one except herself and her admirer knew of this proposal: or that Pynsent had been rejected by her, and probably the reasons she gave to the mortified young man himself, were not those which actuated her refusal, or those which she chose to acknowledge to herself. "I never," she told Pynsent, "can accept such an offer as that which you make me, which you own is unknown to your family, as I am sure it would be unwelcome to them. The difference of rank between us is too great. You are very kind to me here—too good and kind, dear Mr. Pynsent—but I am little better than a dependent."

"A dependent! who ever so thought of you? You are the equal of all the world," Pynsent broke out.

"I am a dependent at home, too," Laura said, sweetly, "and indeed I would not be otherwise. Left early a poor orphan, I have found the kindest and tenderest of mothers, and I have vowed never to leave her—never. Pray do not speak of this again—here, under your relative's roof, or elsewhere. It is impossible."

"If Lady Rockminster asks you herself, will you listen to her?" Pynsent cried, eagerly.

"No," Laura said. "I beg you never to speak of this any more. I must go away if you do;" and with this she left him.

Pynsent never asked for Lady Rockminster's intercession; he knew how vain it was to look for that: and he never spoke again on that subject to Laura or to any person.

When at length the famous novel appeared, it not only met with applause from more impartial critics than Mrs. Pendennis, but, luckily for Pen, it suited the taste of the public, and obtained a quick and considerable popularity. Before two months were over, Pen had the satisfaction and surprise of seeing the second edition of "Walter Lorraine," advertised in the newspapers; and enjoyed the pleasure of reading and sending home the critiques of various literary journals and reviewers upon his book. Their censure did not much affect him; for the good-natured young man was disposed to accept with considerable humility the dispraise of others. Nor did their praise elate him overmuch; for, like most honest persons, he had his own opinion about his own performance, and when a critic praised him in the wrong place, he was hurt rather than pleased by the compliment. But if a review of his work was very laudatory, it was a great pleasure to him to send it home to his mother at Fairoaks, and to think of the joy which it would give there. There are some natures, and perhaps, as we have said, Pendennis's was one, which are improved and softened by prosperity and kindness, as there are men of other dispositions, who become arrogant and graceless under good fortune. Happy he who can endure one or the other with modesty and good-humor! Lucky he who has been educated to bear his fate, whatsoever it may be, by an early example of uprightness, and a childish training in honor!

CHAPTER IV

ALSATIA

Bred up, like a bailiff or a shabby attorney, about the purlieus of the Inns of Court, Shepherd's Inn is always to be found in the close neighborhood of Lincoln's-Inn-Fields, and the Temple. Somewhere behind the black gables and smutty chimney-stacks of Wych-street, Holywell-street, Chancery-lane, the quadrangle lies, hidden from the outer world; and it is approached by curious passages, and ambiguous smoky alleys, on which the sun has forgotten to shine. Slop-sellers, brandy-ball and hard-bake venders, purveyors of theatrical prints for youth, dealers in dingy furniture, and bedding suggestive of any thing but sleep, line the narrow walls and dark casements with their wares. The doors are many-belled, and crowds of dirty children form endless groups about the steps, or around the shell-fish dealers' trays in these courts, whereof the damp pavements resound with pattens, and are drabbled with a never-failing mud. Ballad-singers come and chant here, in deadly, guttural tones, satirical songs against the Whig administration, against the bishops and dignified clergy, against the German relatives of an august royal family; Punch sets up his theater, sure of an audience, and occasionally of a halfpenny from the swarming occupants of the houses; women scream after their children for loitering in the gutter, or, worse still, against the husband who comes reeling from the gin-shop. There is a ceaseless din and life in these courts, out of which you pass into the tranquil, old-fashioned quadrangle of Shepherd's Inn. In a mangy little grass-plat in the center rises up the statue of Shepherd, defended by iron railings from the assaults of boys. The hall of the Inn, on which the founder's arms are painted, occupies one side of the square, the tall and ancient chambers are carried round other two sides, and over the central archway, which leads into Oldcastle-street, and so into the great London thoroughfare.

The Inn may have been occupied by lawyers once: but the laity have long since been admitted into its precincts, and I do not know that any of the principal legal firms have their chambers here. The offices of the Polwheedle and Tredyddlum Copper Mines occupy one set of the ground-floor chambers; the Registry of Patent Inventions and Union of Genius and Capital Company, another—the only gentleman whose name figures here and in the "Law List," is Mr. Campion, who wears mustaches, and who comes in his cab twice or thrice in a week; and whose West End offices are in Curzon-street, Mayfair, where Mrs. Campion entertains the nobility and gentry to whom her husband lends money. There, and on his glazed cards, he is Mr. Somerset Campion; here he is Campion and Co.; and the same tuft which ornaments his chin, sprouts from the under lip of the rest of the firm. It is splendid to see his cab-horse harness blazing with heraldic bearings, as the vehicle stops at the door leading to his chambers. The horse flings froth off his nostrils as he chafes and tosses under the shining bit. The reins and the breeches of the groom are glittering white—the luster of that equipage makes a sunshine in that shady place.

Our old friend, Captain Costigan, has examined Campion's cab and horse many an afternoon, as he trailed about the court in his carpet slippers and dressing-gown, with his old hat cocked over his eye. He suns himself there after his breakfast when the day is suitable; and goes and pays a visit to the porter's lodge, where he pats the heads of the children, and talks to Mrs. Bolton about the thayatres and me daughter Leedy Mirabel. Mrs. Bolton was herself in the profession once, and danced at the Wells in early days as the thirteenth of Mr. Serle's forty pupils.

Costigan lives in the third floor at No. 4, in the rooms which were Mr. Podmore's, and whose name is still on the door (somebody else's name, by the way, is on almost all the doors in Shepherd's Inn). When Charley Podmore (the pleasing tenor singer, T.R.D.L., and at the Back-Kitchen Concert Rooms), married, and went to live at Lambeth, he ceded his chambers to Mr. Bows and Captain Costigan, who occupy them in common now, and you may often hear the tones of Mr. Bows's piano of fine days when the windows are open, and when he is practicing for amusement, or for the instruction of a theatrical pupil, of whom he has one or two. Fanny Bolton is one, the porteress's daughter, who has heard tell of her mother's theatrical glories, which she longs to emulate. She has a good voice and a pretty face and figure for the stage; and she prepares the rooms and makes the beds and breakfasts for Messrs. Costigan and Bows, in return for which the latter instructs her in music and singing. But for his unfortunate propensity to liquor (and in that excess she supposes that all men of fashion indulge), she thinks the captain the finest gentleman in the world, and believes in all the versions of all his stories; and she is very fond of Mr. Bows, too, and very grateful to him; and this shy, queer old gentleman has a fatherly fondness for her, too, for in truth his heart is full of kindness, and he is never easy unless he loves somebody.

Costigan has had the carriages of visitors of distinction before his humble door in Shepherd's Inn: and to hear him talk of a morning (for his evening song is of a much more melancholy nature) you would fancy that Sir Charles and Lady Mirabel were in the constant habit of calling at his chambers, and bringing with them the select nobility to visit the "old man, the honest old half-pay captain, poor old Jack Costigan," as Cos calls himself.

The truth is, that Lady Mirabel has left her husband's card (which has been stuck in the little looking-glass over the mantle-piece of the sitting-room at No. 4, for these many months past), and has come in person to see her father, but not of late days. A kind person, disposed to discharge her duties gravely, upon her marriage with Sir Charles, she settled a little pension upon her father, who occasionally was admitted to the table of his daughter and son-in-law. At first poor Cos's behavior "in the hoight of poloit societee," as he denominated Lady Mirabel's drawing-room table, was harmless, if it was absurd. As he clothed his person in his best attire, so he selected the longest and richest words in his vocabulary to deck his conversation, and adopted a solemnity of demeanor which struck with astonishment all those persons in whose company he happened to be. "Was your Leedyship in the Pork to-dee?" he would demand of his daughter. "I looked for your equipage in veen:—the poor old man was not gratified by the soight of his daughter's choriot. Sir Chorlus, I saw your neem at the Levée; many's the Levee at the Castle at Dublin that poor old Jack Costigan has attended in his time. Did the Juke look pretty well? Bedad, I'll call at Apsley House and lave me cyard upon 'um. I thank ye, James, a little dthrop more champeane." Indeed, he was magnificent in his courtesy to all, and addressed his observations not only to the master and the guests, but to the domestics who waited at the table, and who had some difficulty in maintaining their professional gravity while they waited on Captain Costigan.

On the first two or three visits to his son-in-law, Costigan maintained a strict sobriety, content to make up for his lost time when he got to the Back-Kitchen, where he bragged about his son-in-law's clart and burgundee, until his own utterance began to fail him, over his sixth tumbler of whiskey-punch. But with familiarity his caution vanished, and poor Cos lamentably disgraced himself at Sir Charles Mirabel's table, by premature inebriation. A carriage was called for him: the hospitable door was shut upon him. Often and sadly did he speak to his friends at the Kitchen of his resemblance to King Lear in the plee—of his having a thankless choild, bedad—of his being a pore worn-out, lonely old man, dthriven to dthrinking by ingratitude, and seeking to dthrown his sorrows in punch.

It is painful to be obliged to record the weaknesses of fathers, but it must be furthermore told of Costigan, that when his credit was exhausted and his money gone, he would not unfrequently beg money from his daughter, and make statements to her not altogether consistent with strict truth. On one day a bailiff was about to lead him to prison, he wrote, "unless the—to you insignificant—sum of three pound five can be forthcoming to liberate a poor man's gray hairs from jail." And the good-natured Lady Mirabel dispatched the money necessary for her father's liberation, with a caution to him to be more economical for the future. On a second occasion the captain met with a frightful accident, and broke a plate-glass window in the Strand, for which the proprietor of the shop held him liable. The money was forthcoming on this time too, to repair her papa's disaster, and was carried down by Lady Mirabel's servant to the slip-shod messenger and aid-de-camp of the captain, who brought the letter announcing his mishap. If the servant had followed the captain's aid-de-camp who carried the remittance, he would have seen that gentleman, a person of Costigan's country too (for have we not said, that however poor an Irish gentleman is, he always has a poorer Irish gentleman to run on his errands and transact his pecuniary affairs?) call a cab from the nearest stand, and rattle down to the Roscius's Head, Harlequin-yard, Drury-lane, where the captain was indeed in pawn, and for several glasses containing rum and water, or other spirituous refreshment, of which he and his staff had partaken. On a third melancholy occasion he wrote that he was attacked by illness, and wanted money to pay the physician whom he was compelled to call in; and this time Lady Mirabel, alarmed about her father's safety, and perhaps reproaching herself that she had of late lost sight of her father, called for her carriage and drove to Shepherd's Inn, at the gate of which she alighted, whence she found the way to her father's chambers, "No. 4, third floor, name of Podmore over the door," the porteress said, with many courtesies, pointing toward the door of the house into which the affectionate daughter entered, and mounted the dingy stair. Alas! the door, surmounted by the name of Podmore, was opened to her by poor Cos in his shirt-sleeves, and prepared with the gridiron to receive the mutton-chops, which Mrs. Bolton had gone to purchase.

Also, it was not pleasant for Sir Charles Mirabel to have letters constantly addressed to him at Brookes's, with the information that Captain Costigan was in the hall waiting for an answer; or when he went to play his rubber at the Travelers', to be obliged to shoot out of his brougham and run up the steps rapidly, lest his father-in-law should seize upon him; and to think that while he read his paper or played his whist, the captain was walking on the opposite side of Pall Mall, with that dreadful cocked hat, and the eye beneath it fixed steadily upon the windows of the club. Sir Charles was a weak man; he was old, and had many infirmities: he cried about his father-in-law to his wife, whom he adored with senile infatuation: he said he must go abroad—he must go and live in the country—he should die, or have another fit if he saw that man again—he knew he should. And it was only by paying a second visit to Captain Costigan, and representing to him, that if he plagued Sir Charles by letters, or addressed him in the street, or made any further applications for loans, his allowance would be withdrawn altogether; that Lady Mirabel was enabled to keep her papa in order, and to restore tranquillity to her husband. And on occasion of this visit, she sternly rebuked Bows for not keeping a better watch over the captain;

desired that he should not be allowed to drink in that shameful way; and that the people at the horrid taverns which he frequented should be told, upon no account to give him credit. "Papa's conduct is bringing me to the grave," she said (though she looked perfectly healthy), "and you, as an old man, Mr. Bows, and one that pretended to have a regard for us, ought to be ashamed of abetting him in it." These were the thanks which honest Bows got for his friendship and his life's devotion. And I do not suppose that the old philosopher was much worse off than many other men, or had greater reason to grumble. On the second floor of the next house to Bows's, in Shepherd's Inn, at No. 3, live two other acquaintances of ours. Colonel Altamont, agent to the Nawaab of Lucknow, and Captain the Chevalier Edward Strong. No name at all is over their door. The captain does not choose to let all the world know where he lives, and his cards bear the address of a Jermyn-street hotel; and as for the Embassador Plenipotentiary of the Indian potentate, he is not an envoy accredited to the Courts of St. James's or Leadenhall-street, but is here on a confidential mission, quite independent of the East India Company or the Board of Control.

"In fact," as Strong says, "Colonel Altamont's object being financial, and to effectuate a sale of some of the principal diamonds and rubies of the Lucknow crown, his wish is not to report himself at the India House or in Cannon-row, but rather to negotiate with private capitalists—with whom he has had important transactions both in this country and on the Continent."

We have said that these anonymous chambers of Strong's had been very comfortably furnished since the arrival of Sir Francis Clavering in London, and the chevalier might boast with reason to the friends who visited him, that few retired captains were more snugly quartered than he, in his crib in Shepherd's Inn. There were three rooms below: the office where Strong transacted his business—whatever that might be—and where still remained the desk and railings of the departed officials who had preceded him, and the chevalier's own bedroom and sitting room; and a private stair led out of the office to two upper apartments, the one occupied by Colonel Altamont, and the other serving as the kitchen of the establishment, and the bedroom of Mr. Grady, the attendant. These rooms were on a level with the apartments of our friends Bows and Costigan next door at No. 4; and by reaching over the communicating leads, Grady could command the mignonnette-box which bloomed in Bows's window.

From Grady's kitchen casement often came odors still more fragrant. The three old soldiers who formed the garrison of No. 4, were all skilled in the culinary art. Grady was great at an Irish stew; the colonel was famous for pillaus and curries; and as for Strong, he could cook any thing. He made French dishes and Spanish dishes, stews, fricassees, and omelettes, to perfection; nor was there any man in England more hospitable than he when his purse was full, or his credit was good. At those happy periods, he could give a friend, as he said, a good dinner, a good glass of wine, and a good song afterward; and poor Cos often heard with envy the roar of Strong's choruses, and the musical clinking of the glasses as he sate in his own room, so far removed and yet so near to those festivities. It was not expedient to invite Mr. Costigan always; his practice of inebriation was lamentable; and he bored Strong's guests with his stories when sober, and with his maudlin tears when drunk.

A strange and motley set they were, these friends of the chevalier; and though Major Pendennis would not much have relished their company, Arthur and Warrington liked it not a little, and Pen thought it as amusing as the society of the finest gentlemen in the finest houses which he had the honor to frequent. There was a history about every man of the set: they seemed all to have had their tides of luck and bad fortune. Most of them had wonderful schemes and speculations in their pockets, and plenty for making rapid and extraordinary fortunes. Jack Holt had been in Don Carlos's army, when Ned Strong had fought on the other side; and was now organizing a little scheme for smuggling tobacco into London, which must bring thirty thousand a year to any man who would advance fifteen hundred, just to bribe the last officer of the Excise who held out, and had wind of the scheme. Tom Diver, who had been in the Mexican navy, knew of a specie-ship which had been sunk in the first year of the war, with three hundred and eighty thousand dollars on board, and a hundred and eighty thousand pounds in bars and doubloons. "Give me eighteen hundred pounds," Tom said, "and I'm off tomorrow. I take out four men, and a diving-bell with me; and I return in ten months to take my seat in parliament, by Jove! and to buy back my family estate." Keightley, the manager of the Tredyddlum and Polwheedle Copper Mines (which were as yet under water), besides singing as good a second as any professional man, and besides the Tredyddlum Office, had a Smyrna Sponge Company, and a little quicksilver operation in view, which would set him straight with the world yet. Filby had been every thing: a corporal of dragoons, a field-preacher, and missionary-agent for converting the Irish; an actor at a Greenwich fair-booth, in front of which his father's attorney found him when the old gentleman died and left him that famous property, from which he got no rents now, and of which nobody exactly knew the situation. Added to these was Sir Francis Clavering, Bart., who liked their society, though he did not much add to its amusements by his convivial powers. But he was made much of by the company now, on account of his wealth and position in the world. He told his little story and sang his little song or two with great affability; and he had had his own history, too, before his accession to good fortune; and had seen the inside of more prisons than one, and written his name on many a stamped paper.

When Altamont first returned from Paris, and after he had communicated with Sir Francis Clavering from the hotel at which he had taken up his quarters (and which he had reached in a very denuded state, considering the wealth of diamonds and rubies with which this honest man was intrusted), Strong was sent to him by his patron the baronet; paid his little bill at the inn, and invited him to come and sleep for a night or two at the chambers, where he subsequently took up his residence. To negotiate with this man was very well, but to have such a person settled in his rooms, and to be constantly burdened with such society, did not suit the chevalier's taste much: and he grumbled not a little to his principal.

"I wish you would put this bear into somebody else's cage," he said to Clavering. "The fellow's no gentleman. I don't like walking with him. He dresses himself like a nigger on a holiday. I took him to the play the other night: and, by Jove, sir, he abused the actor who was doing the part of villain in the play, and swore at him so, that the people in the boxes wanted to turn him out. The after-piece was the 'Brigand,' where Wallack comes in wounded, you know, and dies. When he died, Altamont began to cry like a child, and said it was a d—d shame, and cried and swore so, that there was another row, and every body laughing. Then I had to take him away, because he wanted to take his coat off to one fellow who laughed at him; and bellowed to him to stand up like a man. Who is he? Where the deuce does he come from? You had best tell me the whole story. Frank, you must one day. You and he have robbed a church together, that's my belief. You had better get it off your mind at once, Clavering, and tell me what this Altamont is, and what hold he has over you."

"Hang him! I wish he was dead!" was the baronet's only reply; and his countenance became so gloomy, that Strong did not think fit to question his patron any further at that time; but resolved, if need were, to try and discover for himself what was the secret tie between Altamont and Clavering.

CHAPTER V

IN WHICH THE COLONEL NARRATES SOME OF HIS ADVENTURES

Early in the forenoon of the day after the dinner in Grosvenor-place, at which Colonel Altamont had chosen to appear, the colonel emerged from his chamber in the upper story at Shepherd's Inn, and entered into Strong's sitting-room, where the chevalier sat in his easy-chair with the newspaper and his cigar. He was a man who made his tent comfortable wherever he pitched it, and long before Altamont's arrival, had done justice to a copious breakfast of fried eggs and broiled rashers, which Mr. Grady had prepared secundum artem. Good-humored and talkative, he preferred any company rather than none; and though he had not the least liking for his fellow-lodger, and would not have grieved to hear that the accident had befallen him which Sir Francis Clavering desired so fervently, yet kept on fair terms with him. He had seen Altamont to bed with great friendliness on the night previous, and taken away his candle for fear of accidents; and finding a spirit-bottle empty, upon which he had counted for his nocturnal refreshment, had drunk a glass of water with perfect contentment over his pipe, before he turned into his own crib and to sleep. That enjoyment never failed him: he had always an easy temper, a faultless digestion, and a rosy cheek; and whether he was going into action the next morning or to prison (and both had been his lot), in the camp or the Fleet, the worthy captain snored healthfully through the night, and woke with a good heart and appetite, for the struggles or difficulties or pleasures of the day.

The first act of Colonel Altamont was to bellow to Grady for a pint of pale ale, the which he first poured into a pewter flagon, whence he transferred it to his own lips. He put down the tankard empty, drew a great breath, wiped his mouth in his dressing-gown (the difference of the color of his heard from his dyed whiskers had long struck Captain Strong, who had seen too that his hair was fair under his black wig, but made no remarks upon these circumstances)—the colonel drew a great breath, and professed himself immensely refreshed by his draught. "Nothing like that beer," he remarked, "when the coppers are hot. Many a day I've drunk a dozen of Bass at Calcutta, and—and—"

"And at Lucknow, I suppose," Strong said with a laugh. "I got the beer for you on purpose: knew you'd want it after last night." And the colonel began to talk about his adventures of the preceding evening.

"I can not help myself," the colonel said, beating his head with his big hand. "I'm a madman when I get the liquor on board me; and ain't fit to be trusted with a spirit-bottle. When I once begin I can't stop till I've emptied it; and when I've swallowed it, Lord knows what I say or what I don't say. I dined at home here quite quiet. Grady gave me just my two tumblers, and I intended to pass the evening at the Black and Red as sober as a parson. Why did you leave that confounded sample-bottle of Hollands out of the cupboard, Strong? Grady must go out, too, and leave me the kettle a-boiling for tea. It was of no use, I couldn't keep away from it. Washed it all down, sir, by Jingo. And it's my belief I had some more, too, afterward at that infernal little thieves' den."

"What, were you there, too?" Strong asked, "and before you came to Grosvenor-place? That was beginning betimes."

"Early hours to be drunk and cleared out before nine o'clock, eh? But so it was. Yes, like a great big fool, I must go there; and found the fellows dining, Blackland and young Moss, and two or three more of the thieves. If we'd gone to Rouge et Noir, I must have won. But we didn't try the black and red. No, hang 'em, they know'd I'd have beat 'em at that—I must have beat 'em—I can't help beating 'em, I tell you. But they was too cunning for me. That rascal Blackland got the bones out, and we played hazard on the dining-table. And I dropped all the money I had from you in the morning, be hanged to my luck. It was that that set me wild, and I suppose I must have been very hot about the head, for I went off thinking to get some more money from Clavering, I recollect; and then—and then I don't much remember what happened till I woke this morning, and heard old Bows, at No. 3, playing on his pianner."

Strong mused for a while as he lighted his cigar with a coal. "I should like to know how you always draw money from Clavering, colonel," he said.

The colonel burst out with a laugh, "Ha, ha! he owes it me," he said.

"I don't know that that's a reason with Frank for paying," Strong answered. "He owes plenty besides you."

"Well, he gives it me because he is so fond of me," the other said, with the same grinning sneer. "He loves me like a brother; you know he does, captain. No?—He don't?—Well, perhaps he don't; and if you ask me no questions, perhaps I'll tell you no lies, Captain Strong—put that in your pipe and smoke it, my boy."

"But I'll give up that confounded brandy-bottle," the colonel continued, after a pause. "I must give it up, or it'll be the ruin of me." "It makes you say queer things," said the captain, looking Altamont hard in the face. "Remember what you said last night at Clavering's table."

"Say? What did I say?" asked the other hastily. "Did I split any thing? Dammy, Strong, did I split any thing?"

"Ask me no questions, and I will tell you no lies," the chevalier replied on his part. Strong thought of the words Mr. Altamont had used, and his abrupt departure from the baronet's dining-table and house as soon as he recognized Major Pendennis, or Captain Beak, as he called the major. But Strong resolved to seek an explanation of these words otherwise than from Colonel Altamont, and did not choose to recall them to the other's memory. "No," he said then, "you didn't split as you call it, colonel; it was only a trap of mine to see if I could make you speak; but you didn't say a word that any body could comprehend— you were too far gone for that."

So much the better, Altamont thought; and heaved a great sigh, as if relieved. Strong remarked the emotion, but took no notice, and the other being in a communicative mood, went on speaking.

"Yes, I own to my faults," continued the colonel. "There is some things I can't, do what I will, resist: a bottle of brandy, a box of dice, and a beautiful woman. No man of pluck and spirit, no man as was worth his salt ever could, as I know of. There's hardly p'raps a country in the world in which them three ain't got me into trouble."

"Indeed?" said Strong.

"Yes, from the age of fifteen, when I ran away from home, and went cabin-boy on board an Indiaman, till now, when I'm fifty year old, pretty nigh, them women have always been my ruin. Why, it was one of 'em, and with such black eyes and jewels on her neck, and sattens and ermine like a duchess, I tell you— it was one of 'em at Paris that swept off the best part of the thousand pound as I went off. Didn't I ever tell you of it? Well, I don't mind. At first I was very cautious, and having such a lot of money kep it close and lived like a gentleman—Colonel Altamont, Meurice's hotel, and that sort of thing— never played, except at the public tables, and won more than I lost. Well, sir, there was a chap that I saw at the hotel and the Palace Royal too, a regular swell fellow, with white kid gloves and a tuft to his chin, Bloundell-Bloundell his name was, as I made acquaintance with somehow, and he asked me to dinner, and took me to Madame the Countess de Foljambe's soirées—such a woman, Strong!—such an eye! such a hand at the pianner. Lor bless you, she'd sit down and sing to you, and gaze at you, until she warbled your soul out of your body a'most. She asked me to go to her evening parties every Toosday; and didn't I take opera-boxes and give her dinners at the restaurateurs, that's all? But I had a run of luck at the tables, and it was not in the dinners and opera-boxes that poor Clavering's money went. No, be hanged to it, it was swep off in another way. One night, at the countess's, there was several of us at supper—Mr. Bloundell-Bloundell, the Honorable Deuceace, the Marky de la Tour de Force—all tip-top nobs, sir, and the height of fashion, when we had supper, and champagne, you may be sure, in plenty, and then some of that confounded brandy. I would have it—I would go on at it—the countess mixed the tumblers of punch for me, and we had cards as well as grog after supper, and I played and drank until I don't know what I did. I was like I was last night. I was taken away and put to bed somehow, and never woke until the next day, to a roaring headache, and to see my servant, who said the Honorable Deuceace wanted to see me, and was waiting in the sitting-room. 'How are you, colonel?' says he, a-coming into my bedroom. 'How long did you stay last night after I went away? The play was getting too high for me, and I'd lost enough to you for one night.'

"'To me', says I, 'how's that, my dear feller? (for though he was an earl's son, we was as familiar as you and me). How's that, my dear feller,' says I, and he tells me, that he had borrowed thirty louis of me at vingt-et-un, that he gave me an I.O.U. for it the night before, which I put into my pocket-book before he left the room. I takes out my card-case—it was the countess as worked it for me—and there was the I.O.U. sure enough, and he paid me thirty louis in gold down upon the table at my bed-side. So I said he was a gentleman, and asked him if he would like to take any thing, when my servant should get it for him; but the Honorable Deuceace don't drink of a morning, and he went away to some business which he said he had.

"Presently there's another ring at my outer door: and this time it's Bloundell-Bloundell and the marky that comes in. 'Bong jour, marky,' says I. 'Good morning—no headache,' says he. So I said I had one, and how I must have been uncommon queer the night afore; but they both declared I didn't show no signs of having had too much, but took my liquor as grave as a judge.

"'So,' says the marky, 'Deuceace has been with you; we met him in the Palais Royal as we were coming from breakfast. Has he settled with you? Get it while you can: he's a slippery card; and as he won three ponies of Bloundell, I recommend you to get your money while he has some.'

"'He has paid me,' says I; but I knew no more than the dead that he owed me any thing, and don't remember a bit about lending him thirty louis."

The marky and Bloundell looks and smiles at each other at this; and Bloundell says, 'Colonel, you are a queer feller. No man could have supposed, from your manners, that you had tasted any thing stronger than tea all night, and yet you forget things in the morning. Come, come—tell that to the marines, my friend—we won't have it any price.' 'En effet' says the marky, twiddling his little black mustaches in the chimney-glass, and making a lunge or two as he used to do at the fencing-school. (He was a wonder at the fencing-school, and I've seen him knock down the image fourteen times running, at Lepage's). 'Let us speak of affairs. Colonel, you understand that affairs of honor are best settled at once: perhaps it won't be inconvenient to you to arrange our little matters of last night.'

"'What little matters?' says I. 'Do you owe me any money, marky?'

"'Bah!' says he; 'do not let us have any more jesting. I have your note of hand for three hundred and forty louis. La voici.' says he, taking out a paper from his pocket-book.

"'And mine for two hundred and ten,' says Bloundell-Bloundell, and he pulls out his bit of paper.

"I was in such a rage of wonder at this, that I sprang out of bed, and wrapped my dressing-gown round me. 'Are you come here to make a fool of me?' says I. 'I don't owe you two hundred, or two thousand, or two louis; and I won't pay you a farthing. Do you suppose you can catch me with your notes of hand? I laugh at 'em and at you; and I believe you to be a couple—'

"'A couple of what?' says Mr. Bloundell. 'You, of course, are aware that we are a couple of men of honor, Colonel Altamont, and not come here to trifle or to listen to abuse from you. You will either pay us or we will expose you as a cheat, and chastise you as a cheat, too,' says Bloundell.

"'Oui, parbleu,' says the marky, but I didn't mind him, for I could have thrown the little fellow out of the window; but it was different with Bloundell, he was a large man, that weighs three stone more than me, and stands six inches higher, and I think he could have done for me.

"'Monsieur will pay, or monsieur will give me the reason why. I believe you're little better than a polisson, Colonel Altamont,'—that was the phrase he used"—Altamont said with a grin—and I got plenty more of this language from the two fellows, and was in the thick of the row with them, when another of our party came in. This was a friend of mine—a gent I had met at Boulogne, and had taken to the countess's myself. And as he hadn't played at all on the previous night, and had actually warned me against Bloundell and the others, I told the story to him, and so did the other two.

"'I am very sorry,' says he. 'You would go on playing: the countess entreated you to discontinue. These gentlemen offered repeatedly to stop. It was you that insisted on the large stakes, not they.' In fact he charged dead against me: and when the two others went away, he told me how the marky would shoot me as sure as my name was—was what it is. 'I left the countess crying, too,' said he. 'She hates these two men; she has warned you repeatedly against them,' (which she actually had done, and often told me never to play with them) 'and now, colonel, I have left her in hysterics almost, lest there should be any quarrel between you, and that confounded marky should put a bullet through your head. It's my belief,' says my friend, 'that that woman is distractedly in love with you.'

"'Do you think so?' says I; upon which my friend told me how she had actually gone down on her knees to him and said, 'Save Colonel Altamont!'

"As soon as I was dressed, I went and called upon that lovely woman. She gave a shriek and pretty near fainted when she saw me. She called me Ferdinand—I'm blest if she didn't."

"I thought your name was Jack," said Strong, with a laugh; at which the colonel blushed very much behind his dyed whiskers.

"A man may have more names than one, mayn't he, Strong?" Altamont asked. "When I'm with a lady, I like to take a good one. She called me by my Christian name. She cried fit to break your heart. I can't stand seeing a woman cry—never could—not while I'm fond of her. She said she could not bear to think of my losing so much money in her house. Wouldn't I take her diamonds and necklaces, and pay part?

"I swore I wouldn't touch a farthing's worth of her jewelry, which perhaps I did not think was worth a great deal, but what can a woman do more than give you her all? That's the sort I like, and I know there's plenty of 'em. And I told her to be easy about the money, for I would not pay one single farthing.

"'Then they'll shoot you,' says she; 'they'll kill my Ferdinand.'"

"They'll kill my Jack wouldn't have sounded well in French," Strong said, laughing.

"Never mind about names," said the other, sulkily: "a man of honor may take any name he chooses, I suppose."

"Well, go on with your story," said Strong. "She said they would kill you."

"'No,' says I, 'they won't: for I will not let that scamp of a marquis send me out of the world; and if he lays a hand on me, I'll brain him, marquis as he is.'

"At this the countess shrank back from me as if I had said something very shocking. 'Do I understand Colonel Altamont aright?' says she: 'and that a British officer refuses to meet any person who provokes him to the field of honor?'

"'Field of honor be hanged, countess,' says I, 'You would not have me be a target for that little scoundrel's pistol practice.'

"'Colonel Altamont,' says the countess, 'I thought you were a man of honor—I thought, I—but no matter. Good-by, sir.' And she was sweeping out of the room her voice regular choking in her pocket-handkerchief.

"'Countess,' says I, rushing after her, and seizing her hand.

"'Leave me, Monsieur le Colonel,' says she, shaking me off, 'my father was a general of the Grand Army. A soldier should know how to pay all his debts of honor.'

"What could I do? Every body was against me. Caroline said I had lost the money: though I didn't remember a syllable about the business. I had taken Deuceace's money, too; but then it was because he offered it to me you know, and that's a different thing. Every one of these chaps was a man of fashion and honor; and the marky and the countess of the first families in France. And by Jove, sir, rather than offend her, I paid the money up: five hundred and sixty gold Napoleons, by Jove: besides three hundred which I lost when I had my revenge.

"And I can't tell you at this minute whether I was done or not concluded the colonel, musing. Sometimes I think I was: but then Caroline was so fond of me. That woman would never have seen me done: never, I'm sure she wouldn't: at least, if she would, I'm deceived in woman."

Any further revelations of his past life which Altamont might have been disposed to confide to his honest comrade the chevalier, were interrupted by a knocking at the outer door of their chambers;

which, when opened by Grady the servant, admitted no less a person than Sir Francis Clavering into the presence of the two worthies.

"The governor, by Jove," cried Strong, regarding the arrival of his patron with surprise. "What's brought you here?" growled Altamont, looking sternly from under his heavy eyebrows at the baronet. "It's no good, I warrant." And indeed, good very seldom brought Sir Francis Clavering into that or any other place.

Whenever he came into Shepherd's Inn, it was money that brought the unlucky baronet into those precincts: and there was commonly a gentleman of the money-dealing world in waiting for him at Strong's chambers, or at Campion's below; and a question of bills to negotiate or to renew. Clavering was a man who had never looked his debts fairly in the face, familiar as he had been with them all his life; as long as he could renew a bill, his mind was easy regarding it; and he would sign almost any thing for to-morrow, provided to-day could be left unmolested. He was a man whom scarcely any amount of fortune could have benefited permanently, and who was made to be ruined, to cheat small tradesmen, to be the victim of astuter sharpers: to be niggardly and reckless, and as destitute of honesty as the people who cheated him, and a dupe, chiefly because he was too mean to be a successful knave. He had told more lies in his time, and undergone more baseness of stratagem in order to stave off a small debt, or to swindle a poor creditor, than would have suffered to make a fortune for a braver rogue. He was abject and a shuffler in the very height of his prosperity. Had he been a crown prince, he could not have been more weak, useless, dissolute or ungrateful. He could not move through life except leaning on the arm of somebody: and yet he never had an agent but he mistrusted him; and marred any plans which might be arranged for his benefit, by secretly acting against the people whom he employed. Strong knew Clavering, and judged him quite correctly. It was not as friends that this pair met: but the chevalier worked for his principal, as he would when in the army have pursued a harassing march, or undergone his part in the danger and privations of a siege; because it was his duty, and because he had agreed to it. "What is it he wants," thought the two officers of the Shepherd's Inn garrison, when the baronet came among them.

His pale face expressed extreme anger and irritation. "So, sir," he said, addressing Altamont, "you've been at your old tricks."

"Which of 'um?" asked Altamont, with a sneer.

"You have been at the Rouge et Noir: you were there last night," cried the baronet.

"How do you know—were you there?" the other said. "I was at the Club: but it wasn't on the colors I played—ask the captain—I've been telling him of it. It was with the bones. It was at hazard, Sir Francis, upon my word and honor it was;" and he looked at the baronet with a knowing, humorous mock humility, which only seemed to make the other more angry.

"What the deuce do I care, sir, how a man like you loses his money, and whether it is at hazard or roulette?" screamed the baronet, with a multiplicity of oaths, and at the top of his voice. "What I will not have, sir, is that you should use my name, or couple it with yours. Damn him, Strong, why don't you keep him in better order? I tell you he has gone and used my name again, sir; drawn a bill upon me, and lost the money on the table—I can't stand it—I won't stand it. Flesh and blood won't bear it. Do you know how much I have paid for you, sir?"

"This was only a very little 'un, Sir Francis—only fifteen pound, Captain Strong, they wouldn't stand another: and it oughtn't to anger you, governor. Why it's so trifling, I did not even mention it to Strong,—did I now, captain? I protest it had quite slipped my memory, and all on account of that confounded liquor I took."

"Liquor or no liquor, sir, it is no business of mine. I don't care what you drink, or where you drink it—only it shan't be in my house. And I will not have you breaking into my house of a night, and a fellow like you intruding himself on my company: how dared you show yourself in Grosvenor-place last night, sir—and—and what do you suppose my friends must think of me when they see a man of your sort walking into my dining-room uninvited, and drunk, and calling for liquor as if you were the master of the house."

"They'll think you know some very queer sort of people, I dare say," Altamont said with impenetrable good-humor. "Look here, baronet, I apologize; on my honor, I do, and ain't an apology enough between two gentlemen? It was a strong measure I own, walking into your cuddy, and calling for drink, as if I was the captain: but I had had too much before, you see, that's why I wanted some more; nothing can be more simple—and it was because they wouldn't give me no more money upon your name at the Black and Red, that I thought I would come down and speak to you about it. To refuse me was nothing: but to refuse a bill drawn on you that have been such a friend to the shop, and are a baronet, and a member of parliament, and a gentleman, and no mistake—Damme, it's ungrateful." "By heavens, if ever you do it again. If ever you dare to show yourself in my house; or give my name at a gambling-house or at any other house, by Jove—at any other house—or give any reference at all to me, or speak to me in the street, by Gad, or any where else until I speak to you—I disclaim you altogether—I won't give you another shilling."

"Governor, don't be provoking," Altamont said, surlily. "Don't talk to me about daring to do this thing or t'other, or when my dander is up it's the very thing to urge me on. I oughtn't to have come last night, I know I oughtn't: but I told you I was drunk, and that ought to be sufficient between gentleman and gentleman."

"You a gentleman! dammy, sir," said the baronet, "how dares a fellow like you to call himself a gentleman?"

"I ain't a baronet, I know;" growled the other; "and I've forgotten how to be a gentleman almost now, but—but I was one once, and my father was one, and I'll not have this sort of talk from you, Sir F. Clavering, that's flat. I want to go abroad again. Why don't you come down with the money, and let me go? Why the devil are you to be rolling in riches, and me to have none? Why should you have a house and a table covered with plate, and me be in a garret here in this beggarly Shepherd's Inn? We're partners, ain't we? I've as good a right to be rich as you have, haven't I? Tell the story to Strong here, if you like; and ask him to be umpire between us. I don't mind letting my secret out to a man that won't split. Look here, Strong—perhaps you guess the story already—the fact is, me and the Governor—"

"D—, hold your tongue," shrieked out the baronet in a fury. "You shall have the money as soon as I can get it. I ain't made of money. I'm so pressed and badgered, I don't know where to turn. I shall go mad; by Jove, I shall. I wish I was dead, for I'm the most miserable brute alive. I say, Mr. Altamont, don't mind me. When I'm out of health—and I'm devilish bilious this morning—hang me, I abuse every body, and don't know what I say. Excuse me if I've offended you. I—I'll try and get that little business done. Strong shall try. Upon my word he shall. And I say, Strong, my boy, I want to speak to you. Come into the office for a minute."

Almost all Clavering's assaults ended in this ignominious way, and in a shameful retreat. Altamont sneered after the baronet as he left the room, and entered into the office, to talk privately with his factotum.

"What is the matter now?" the latter asked of him. "It's the old story, I suppose."

"D—it, yes," the baronet said. "I dropped two hundred in ready money at the Little Coventry last night, and gave a check for three hundred more. On her ladyship's bankers, too, for to-morrow; and I must meet it, for there'll be the deuce to pay else. The last time she paid my play-debts, I swore I would not touch a dice-box again, and she'll keep her word, Strong, and dissolve partnership, if I go on. I wish I had three hundred a year, and was away. At a German watering-place you can do devilish well with three hundred a year. But my habits are so d——reckless: I wish I was in the Serpentine. I wish I was dead, by Gad, I wish I was. I wish I had never touched those confounded bones. I had such a run of luck last night, with five for the main, and seven to five all night, until those ruffians wanted to pay me with Altamont's bill upon me. The luck turned from that minute. Never held the box again for three mains, and came away cleaned out, leaving that infernal check behind me. How shall I pay it? Blackland won't hold it over. Hulker and Bullock will write about it directly to her ladyship. By Jove, Ned, I'm the most miserable brute in all England."

It was necessary for Ned to devise some plan to console the baronet under this pressure of grief; and no doubt he found the means of procuring a loan for his patron, for he was closeted at Mr. Campion's offices that day for some time. Altamont had once more a guinea or two in his pocket, with a promise of a farther settlement; and the baronet had no need to wish himself dead for the next two or three months at least. And Strong, putting together what he had learned from the colonel and Sir Francis, began to form in his own mind a pretty accurate opinion as to the nature of the tie which bound the two men together.

CHAPTER VI

A CHAPTER OF CONVERSATIONS

Every day, after the entertainments at Grosvenor-place and Greenwich, of which we have seen Major Pendennis partake, the worthy gentleman's friendship and cordiality for the Clavering family seemed to increase. His calls were frequent; his attentions to the lady of the house unremitting. An old man about town, he had the good fortune to be received in many houses, at which a lady of Lady Clavering's distinction ought also to be seen. Would her ladyship not like to be present at the grand entertainment at Gaunt House? There was to be a very pretty breakfast ball at Viscount Marrowfat's, at Fulham. Every body was to be there (including august personages of the highest rank), and there was to be a Watteau quadrille, in which Miss Amory would surely look charming. To these and other amusements the obsequious old gentleman kindly offered to conduct Lady Clavering, and was also ready to make himself useful to the baronet in any way agreeable to the latter.

In spite of his present station and fortune, the world persisted in looking rather coldly upon Clavering, and strange suspicious rumors followed him about. He was blackballed at two clubs in succession. In the house of commons, he only conversed with a few of the most disreputable members of that famous body, having a happy knack of choosing bad society, and adapting himself naturally to it, as other people do to the company of their betters. To name all the senators with whom Clavering consorted, would be invidious. We may mention only a few. There was Captain Raff, the honorable member for Epsom, who retired after the last Goodwood races, having accepted, as Mr. Hotspur, the whip of the party, said, a mission to the Levant; there was Hustingson, the patriotic member for Islington, whose voice is never heard now denunciating corruption, since his appointment to the Governorship of Coventry Island; there was Bob Freeny, of the Booterstown Freenys, who is a dead shot, and of whom we therefore wish to speak with every respect; and of all these gentlemen, with whom in the course of his professional duty Mr. Hotspur had to confer, there was none for whom he had a more thorough contempt and dislike than for Sir Francis Clavering, the representative of an ancient race, who had sat for their own borough of Clavering time out of mind in the house. "If that man is wanted for a division," Hotspur said, "ten to one he is to be found in a hell. He was educated in the Fleet, and he has not heard the end of Newgate yet, take my word for it. He'll muddle away the Begum's fortune at thimble-rig, be caught picking pockets, and finish on board the hulks." And if the high-born Hotspur, with such an opinion of Clavering, could yet from professional reasons be civil to him, why should not Major Pendennis also have reasons of his own for being attentive to this unlucky gentleman?

"He has a very good cellar and a very good cook," the major said; "as long as he is silent he is not offensive, and he very seldom speaks. If he chooses to frequent gambling-tables, and lose his money to blacklegs, what matters to me? Don't look too curiously into any man's affairs, Pen, my boy; every fellow has some cupboard in his house, begad, which he would not like you and me to peep into. Why should we try, when the rest of the house is open to us? And a devilish good house, too, as you and I know. And if the man of the family is not all one could wish, the women are excellent. The Begum is not over-refined, but as kind a woman as ever lived, and devilish clever too; and as for the little Blanche, you know my opinion about her, you rogue; you know my belief is that she is sweet on you, and would have you for the asking. But you are growing such a great man, that I suppose you won't be content under a duke's daughter—Hey, sir? I recommend you to ask one of them, and try."

Perhaps Pen was somewhat intoxicated by his success in the world; and it may also have entered into the young man's mind (his uncle's perpetual hints serving not a little to encourage the notion) that Miss Amory was tolerably well disposed to renew the little flirtation which had been carried on in the early days of both of them, by the banks of the rural Brawl. But he was little disposed to marriage, he said, at that moment, and, adopting some of his uncle's worldly tone, spoke rather contemptuously of the institution, and in favor of a bachelor life.

"You are very happy, sir," said he, "and you get on very well alone, and so do I. With a wife at my side, I should lose my place in society; and I don't, for my part, much fancy retiring into the country with a Mrs. Pendennis; or taking my wife into lodgings to be waited upon by the servant-of-all-work. The period of my little illusions is over. You cured me of my first love, who certainly was a fool, and would have had a fool for her husband, and a very sulky, discontented husband, too, if she had taken me. We young fellows live fast, sir; and I feel as old at five-and-twenty as many of the old fo—, the old bachelors—whom I see in the bay-window at Bays's. Don't look offended, I only mean that I am blasé about love matters, and that I could no more fan myself into a flame for Miss Amory now, than I could adore Lady Mirabel over again. I wish I could; I rather like old Mirabel for his infatuation about her, and think his passion is the most respectable part of his life."

"Sir Charles Mirabel was always a theatrical man, sir," the major said, annoyed that his nephew should speak flippantly of any person of Sir Charles's rank and station. "He has been occupied with theatricals since his early days. He acted at Carlton House when he was page to the prince; he has been mixed up with that sort of thing; he could afford to marry whom he chooses; and Lady Mirabel is a most respectable woman, received every where—every where, mind. The Duchess of Connaught receives her, Lady Rockminster receives her—it doesn't become young fellows to speak lightly of people in that station. There's not a more respectable woman in England than Lady Mirabel: and the old fogies, as you call them at Bays's, are some of the first gentlemen in England, of whom you youngsters had best learn a little manners, and a little breeding, and a little modesty." And the major began to think that Pen was growing exceedingly pert and conceited, and that the world made a great deal too much of him.

The major's anger amused Pen. He studied his uncle's peculiarities with a constant relish, and was always in a good humor with his worldly old Mentor. "I am a youngster of fifteen years standing, sir," he said, adroitly, "and if you think that we are disrespectful, you should see those of the present generation. A protégé of yours came to breakfast with me the other day. You told me to ask him, and I did it to please you. We had a day's sights together, and dined at the club, and went to the play. He said the wine at the Polyanthus was not so good as Ellis's wine at Richmond, smoked Warrington's cavendish after breakfast, and when I gave him a sovereign as a farewell token, said he had plenty of them, but would take it to show he wasn't proud."

"Did he?—did you ask young Clavering?" cried the major, appeased at once, "fine boy, rather wild, but a fine boy—parents like that sort of attention, and you can't do better than pay it to our worthy friends of Grosvenor-place. And so you took him to the play and tipped him? That was right, sir, that was right;" with which Mentor quitted Telemachus, thinking that the young men were not so very bad, and that he should make something of that fellow yet.

As Master Clavering grew into years and stature, he became too strong for the authority of his fond parents and governess; and rather governed them than permitted himself to be led by their orders. With his papa he was silent and sulky, seldom making his appearance, however, in the neighborhood of that gentleman; with his mamma he roared and fought when any contest between them arose as to the gratification of his appetite, or other wish of his heart; and in his disputes with his governess over his book, he kicked that quiet creature's shins so fiercely, that she was entirely overmastered and subdued by him. And he would have so treated his sister Blanche, too, and did on one or two occasions attempt to prevail over her; but she showed an immense resolution and spirit on her part, and boxed his ears so soundly, that he forebore from molesting Miss Amory, as he did the governess and his mamma, and his mamma's maid.

At length, when the family came to London, Sir Francis gave forth his opinion that "the little beggar had best be sent to school." Accordingly, the young son and heir of the house of Clavering was dispatched to the Rev. Otto Rose's establishment at Twickenham, where young noblemen and gentlemen were received preparatory to their introduction to the great English public schools.

It is not our intention to follow Master Clavering in his scholastic career; the paths to the Temple of learning were made more easy to him than they were to some of us of earlier generations. He advanced toward that fane in a carriage-and-four, so to speak, and might halt and take refreshments almost whenever he pleased. He wore varnished boots from the earliest period of youth, and had cambric handkerchiefs and lemon-colored kid gloves of the smallest size ever manufactured by Privat. They dressed regularly at Mr. Rose's to come down to dinner; the young gentlemen had shawl dressing-gowns, fires in their bedrooms; horse and carriage exercise occasionally, and oil for their hair. Corporal punishment was altogether dispensed with by the principal, who thought that moral discipline was entirely sufficient to lead youth; and the boys were so rapidly advanced in many branches of learning, that they acquired the art of drinking spirits and smoking cigars, even before they were old enough to enter a public school. Young Frank Clavering stole his father's Havannas, and conveyed them to school, or smoked them in the stables, at a surprisingly early period of life, and at ten years old drank his Champagne almost as stoutly as any whiskered cornet of dragoons could do.

When this interesting youth came home for his vacations, Major Pendennis was as laboriously civil and gracious to him as he was to the rest of the family; although the boy had rather a contempt for old Wigsby, as the major was denominated, mimicked him behind his back, as the polite major bowed and smirked with Lady Clavering or Miss Amory; and drew rude caricatures, such as are designed by ingenious youths, in which the major's wig, his nose, his tie, &c., were represented with artless exaggeration. Untiring in his efforts to be agreeable, the major wished that Pen, too, should take particular notice of this child; incited Arthur to invite him to his chambers, to give him a dinner at the club, to take him to Madame Tussaud's, the Tower, the play, and so forth, and to tip him, as the phrase is, at the end of the day's pleasures. Arthur, who was good-natured and fond of children, went through all these ceremonies one day; had the boy to breakfast at the Temple, where he made the most contemptuous remarks regarding the furniture, the crockery, and the tattered state of Warrington's dressing-gown; and smoked a short pipe, and recounted the history of a fight between Tuffy and Long Biggings, at Rose's, greatly to the edification of the two gentlemen his hosts.

As the major rightly predicted, Lady Clavering was very grateful for Arthur's attention to the boy; more grateful than the lad himself, who took attentions as a matter of course, and very likely had more sovereigns in his pocket than poor Pen, who generously gave him one of his own slender stock of those coins.

The major, with the sharp eyes with which nature endowed him, and with the glasses of age and experience, watched this boy, and surveyed his position in the family without seeming to be rudely curious about their affairs. But, as a country neighbor, one who had many family obligations to the Claverings, an old man of the world, he took occasion to find out what Lady Clavering's means were, how her capital was disposed, and what the boy was to inherit. And setting himself to work, for what purposes will appear, no doubt, ulteriorly, he soon had got a pretty accurate knowledge of Lady Clavering's affairs and fortune, and of the prospects of her daughter and son. The daughter was to have but a slender provision; the bulk of the property was, as before has been said, to go to the son, his father did not care for him or any body else, his mother was dotingly fond of him as the child of her latter days, his sister disliked him. Such may be stated, in round numbers, to be the result of the information which Major Pendennis got. "Ah! my dear madam," he would say, patting the head of the boy, "this boy may wear a baron's coronet on his head on some future coronation, if matters are but managed rightly, and if Sir Francis Clavering would but play his cards well."

At this the widow Amory heaved a deep sigh. "He plays only too much of his cards, major, I'm afraid," she said. The major owned that he knew as much; did not disguise that he had heard of Sir Francis Clavering's unfortunate propensity to play; pitied Lady Clavering sincerely; but spoke with such genuine sentiment and sense, that her ladyship, glad to find a person of experience to whom she could confide her grief and her condition, talked about them pretty unreservedly to Major Pendennis, and was eager to have his advice and consolation. Major Pendennis became the Begum's confidante and house-friend, and as a mother, a wife, and a capitalist, she consulted him.

He gave her to understand (showing at the same time a great deal of respectful sympathy) that he was acquainted with some of the circumstances of her first unfortunate marriage, and with even the person of her late husband, whom he remembered in Calcutta—when she was living in seclusion with her father. The poor lady, with tears of shame more than of grief in her eyes, told her version of her story. Going back a child to India after two years at a European school, she had met Amory, and foolishly married him. "O, you don't know how miserable that man made me," she said, "or what a life I passed between him and my father. Before I saw him I had never seen a man except my father's clerks and native servants. You know we didn't go into society in India on account of—" ("I know," said Major Pendennis, with a bow). "I was a wild romantic child, my head was full of novels which I'd read at school—I listened to his wild stories and adventures, for he was a daring fellow, and I thought he talked beautifully of those calm nights on the passage out, when he used to... Well, I married him, and was wretched from that day—wretched with my father, whose character you know, Major Pendennis, and I won't speak of: but he wasn't a good man, sir—neither to my poor mother, nor to me, except that he left me his money—nor to no one else that I ever heard of: and he didn't do many kind actions in his lifetime, I'm afraid. And as for Amory he was almost worse; he was a spendthrift, when my father was close: he drank dreadfully, and was furious when in that way. He wasn't in any way a good or a faithful husband to me, Major Pendennis; and if he'd died in the jail before his trial, instead of afterward, he would have saved me a deal of shame and unhappiness since, sir." Lady Clavering added: "For perhaps I should not have married at all if I had not been so anxious to change his horrid name, and I have not been happy in my second husband, as I suppose you know, sir. Ah, Major Pendennis, I've got money to be sure, and I'm a lady, and people fancy I'm very happy, but I ain't. We all have our cares, and griefs, and troubles: and many's the day that I sit down to one of my grand dinners with an aching heart, and many a night do I lay awake on my fine bed, a great deal more unhappy than the maid that makes it. For I'm not a happy woman, major, for all the world says; and envies the Begum her diamonds, and carriages, and the great company that comes to my house. I'm not happy in my husband; I'm not happy in my daughter. She ain't a good girl like that dear Laura Bell at Fairoaks. She's cost me many a tear though you don't see 'em; and she sneers at her mother because I haven't had learning and that. How should I? I was brought up among natives till I was twelve, and went back to India when I was fourteen. Ah, major I should have been a good woman if I had had a good husband. And now I must go up-stairs and wipe my eyes, for they're red with cryin'. And Lady Rockminster's a-comin, and we're goin to 'ave a drive in the Park. And when Lady Rockminster made her appearance, there was not a trace of tears or vexation on Lady Clavering's face, but she was full of spirits, and bounced out with her blunders and talk, and murdered the king's English, with the utmost liveliness and good humor.

"Begad, she is not such a bad woman!" the major thought within himself. "She is not refined, certainly, and calls 'Apollo' 'Apoller;' but she has some heart, and I like that sort of thing, and a devilish deal of money, too. Three stars in India Stock to her name, begad! which that young cub is to have—is he?" And he thought how he should like to see a little of the money transferred to Miss Blanche, and, better still, one of those stars shining in the name of Mr. Arthur Pendennis.

Still bent upon pursuing his schemes, whatsoever they might be, the old negotiator took the privilege of his intimacy and age, to talk in a kindly and fatherly manner to Miss Blanche, when he found occasion to see her alone. He came in so frequently at luncheon-time, and became so familiar with the ladies, that they did not even hesitate to quarrel before him: and Lady Clavering, whose tongue was loud, and temper brusk, had many a battle with the Sylphide in the family friend's presence. Blanche's wit seldom failed to have the mastery in these encounters, and the keen barbs of her arrows drove her adversary discomfited away. "I am an old fellow," the major said; "I have nothing to do in life. I have my eyes open. I keep good counsel. I am the friend of both of you; and if you choose to quarrel before me, why I shan't tell any one. But you are two good people, and I intend to make it up between you. I have between lots of people—husbands and wives, fathers and sons, daughters and mammas, before this. I like it; I've nothing else to do."

One day, then, the old diplomatist entered Lady Clavering's drawing-room, just as the latter quitted it, evidently in a high state of indignation, and ran past him up the stairs to her own apartments. "She couldn't speak to him now," she said; "she was a great deal too angry with that—that—that little, wicked"—anger choked the rest of the words, or prevented their utterance until Lady Clavering had passed out of hearing.

"My dear, good Miss Amory," the major said, entering the drawing-room, "I see what is happening. You and mamma have been disagreeing. Mothers and daughters disagree in the best families. It was but last week that I healed up a quarrel between Lady Clapperton and her daughter Lady Claudia. Lady Lear and her eldest daughter have not spoken for fourteen years. Kinder and more worthy people than these I never knew in the whole course of my life; for every body but each other admirable. But they can't live together: they oughtn't to live together: and I wish, my dear creature, with all my soul, that I could see you with an establishment of your own—for there is no woman in London who could conduct one better—with your own establishment, making your own home happy."

"I am not very happy in this one," said the Sylphide; "and the stupidity of mamma is enough to provoke a saint."

"Precisely so; you are not suited to one another. Your mother committed one fault in early life—or was it Nature, my dear, in your case?—she ought not to have educated you. You ought not to have been bred up to become the refined and intellectual being you are, surrounded, as I own you are, by those who have not your genius or your refinement. Your place would be to lead in the most brilliant circles, not to follow, and take a second place in any society. I have watched you, Miss Amory: you are ambitious; and your proper sphere is command. You ought to shine; and you never can in this house, I know it. I hope I shall see you in another and a happier one, some day, and the mistress of it."

The Sylphide shrugged her lily shoulders with a look of scorn "Where is the prince, and where is the palace, Major Pendennis?" she said. "I am ready. But there is no romance in the world now, no real affection."

"No, indeed," said the major, with the most sentimental and simple air which he could muster.

"Not that I know any thing about it," said Blanche, casting her eyes down, "except what I have read in novels."

"Of course not," Major Pendennis cried; "how should you, my dear young lady? and novels ain't true, as you remark admirably, and there is no romance left in the world. Begad, I wish I was a young fellow, like my nephew." "And what," continued Miss Amory, musing, "what are the men whom we see about at the balls every night—dancing guardsmen, penniless treasury clerks—boobies! If I had my brother's fortune, I might have such an establishment as you promise me—but with my name, and with my little means, what am I to look to? A country parson, or a barrister in a street near Russell-square, or a captain in a dragoon-regiment, who will take lodgings for me, and come home from the mess tipsy and smelling of smoke like Sir Francis Clavering. That is how we girls are destined to end life. O Major Pendennis, I am sick of London, and of balls, and of young dandies with their chin-tips, and of the insolent great ladies who know us one day and cut us the next—and of the world altogether. I should like to leave it and to go into a convent, that I should. I shall never find any body to understand me. And I live here as much alone in my family and in the world, as if I were in a cell locked up for ever. I wish there were Sisters of Charity here, and that I could be one, and catch the plague, and die of it—I wish to quit the world. I am not very old: but I am tired, I have suffered so much—I've been so disillusionated—I'm weary, I'm weary—O that the Angel of Death would come and beckon me away!"

This speech may be interpreted as follows. A few nights since a great lady, Lady Flamingo, had cut Miss Amory and Lady Clavering. She was quite mad because she could not get an invitation to Lady Drum's ball: it was the end of the season and nobody had proposed to her: she had made no sensation at all, she who was so much cleverer than any girl of the year, and of the young ladies forming her special circle. Dora who had but five thousand pounds, Flora who had nothing, and Leonora who had red hair, were going to be married, and nobody had come for Blanche Amory.

"You judge wisely about the world, and about your position, my dear Miss Blanche," the major said. "The prince don't marry nowadays, as you say: unless the princess has a doosid deal of money in the funds, or is a lady of his own rank. The young folks of the great families marry into the great families: if they haven't fortune they have each other's shoulders, to push on in the world, which is pretty nearly as good. A girl with your fortune can scarcely hope for a great match: but a girl with your genius and your admirable tact and fine manners, with a clever husband by her side, may make any place for herself in the world. We are grown doosid republican. Talent ranks with birth and wealth now, begad: and a clever man with a clever wife, may take any place they please."

Miss Amory did not of course in the least understand what Major Pendennis meant. Perhaps she thought over circumstances in her mind, and asked herself, could he be a negotiator for a former suitor of hers, and could he mean Pen? No, it was impossible; he had been civil, but nothing more. So she said, laughing, "Who is the clever man, and when will you bring him to me, Major Pendennis? I am dying to see him." At this moment a servant threw open the door, and announced Mr. Henry Foker: at which name, and at the appearance of our friend both the lady and the gentleman burst out laughing.

"That is not the man," Major Pendennis said. "He is engaged to his cousin, Lord Gravesend's daughter. Good-by, my dear Miss Amory."

Was Pen growing worldly, and should a man not get the experience of the world and lay it to his account? "He felt, for his part," as he said, "that he was growing very old very soon. How this town forms and changes us," he said once to Warrington. Each had come in from his night's amusement; and Pen was smoking his pipe, and recounting, as his habit was, to his friend the observations and adventures of the evening just past. "How I am changed," he said, "from the simpleton boy at Fairoaks, who was fit to break his heart about his first love? Lady Mirabel had a reception to-night, and was as grave and collected as if she had been born a duchess, and had never seen a trap-door in her life. She gave me the honor of a conversation, and patronized me about Walter Lorraine, quite kindly."

"What condescension," broke in Warrington.

"Wasn't it?" Pen said, simply; at which the other burst out laughing according to his wont. "Is it possible," he said, "that any body should think of patronizing the eminent author of Walter Lorraine?"

"You laugh at both of us," Pen said, blushing a little: "I was coming to that myself. She told me that she had not read the book (as indeed I believe she never read a book in her life), but that Lady Rockminster had, and that the Duchess of Connaught pronounced it to be very clever. In that case, I said I should die happy, for that to please those two ladies was in fact the great aim of my existence, and having their approbation, of course I need look for no other. Lady Mirabel looked at me solemnly out of her fine eyes, and said, 'O indeed,' as if she understood me, and then she asked me whether I went to the duchess's Thursdays; and when I said no, hoped she should see me there, and that I must try and get there, every body went there —every body who was in society: and then we talked of the new embassador from Timbuctoo, and how he was better than the old one; and how Lady Mary Billington was going to marry a clergyman quite below her in rank; and how Lord and Lady Ringdove had fallen out three months after their marriage about Tom Pouter of the Blues, Lady Ringdove's cousin, and so forth. From the gravity of that woman you would have fancied she had been born in a palace, and lived all the seasons of her life in Belgrave-square."

"And you, I suppose you took your part in the conversation pretty well, as the descendant of the earl your father, and the heir of Fairoaks Castle?" Warrington said. "Yes, I remember reading of the festivities which occurred when you came of age. The countess gave a brilliant tea soirée to the neighboring nobility; and the tenantry were regaled in the kitchen with a leg of mutton and a quart of ale. The remains of the banquet were distributed among the poor of the village, and the entrance to the park was illuminated until old John put the candle out on retiring to rest at his usual hour."

"My mother is not a countess," said Pen, "though she has very good blood in her veins, too; but commoner as she is, I have never met a peeress who was more than her peer, Mr. George; and if you will come to Fairoaks Castle you shall judge for yourself of her and of my cousin too. They are not so witty as the London women, but they certainly are as well bred. The thoughts of women in the country are turned to other objects than those which occupy your London ladies. In the country a woman has her household and her poor, her long calm days and long calm evenings."

"Devilish long," Warrington said, "and a great deal too calm; I've tried 'em." "The monotony of that existence must be to a certain degree melancholy—like the tune of a long ballad; and its harmony grave and gentle, sad and tender: it would be unendurable else. The loneliness of women in the country makes them of necessity soft and sentimental. Leading a life of calm duty, constant routine, mystic reverie—a sort of nuns at large—too much gayety or laughter would jar upon their almost sacred quiet, and would be as out of place there as in a church."

"Where you go to sleep over the sermon," Warrington said.

"You are a professed misogynist, and hate the sex because, I suspect, you know very little about them," Mr. Pen continued, with an air of considerable self-complacency. "If you dislike the women in the country for being too slow, surely the London women ought to be fast enough for you. The pace of London life is enormous: how do people last at it, I wonder—male and female? Take a woman of the world: follow her course through the season; one asks how she can survive it? or if she tumbles into a sleep at the end of August, and lies torpid until the spring? She goes into the world every night, and sits watching her marriageable daughters dancing till long after dawn. She has a nursery of little ones, very likely, at home, to whom she administers example and affection; having an eye likewise to bread-and-milk, catechism, music and French, and roast leg of mutton at one o'clock; she has to call upon ladies of her own station, either domestically or in her public character, in which she sits upon Charity Committees, or Ball Committees, or Emigration Committees, or Queen's College Committees, and discharges I don't know what more duties of British stateswomanship. She very likely keeps a poor visiting list; has combinations with the clergyman about soup or flannel, or proper religious teaching for the parish; and (if she lives in certain districts) probably attends early church. She has the newspapers to read, and, at least, must know what her husband's party is about, so as to be able to talk to her neighbor at dinner; and it is a fact that she reads every new book that comes out; for she can talk, and very smartly and well, about them all, and you see them all upon her drawing-room table. She has the cares of her household besides: to make both ends meet; to make the girl's milliner's bills appear not too dreadful to the father and paymaster of the family; to snip off, in secret, a little extra article of expenditure here and there, and convey it, in the shape of a bank-note, to the boys at college or at sea; to check the encroachments of tradesmen, and housekeepers' financial fallacies; to keep upper and lower servants from jangling with one another, and the household in order. Add to this, that she has a secret taste for some art or science, models in clay, makes experiments in chemistry, or plays in private on the violoncello,—and I say, without exaggeration, many London ladies are doing this—and you have a character before you such as our ancestors never heard of, and such as belongs entirely to our era and period of civilization. Ye gods! how rapidly we live and grow! In nine months, Mr. Paxton grows you a pine apple as large as a portmanteau, whereas a little one, no bigger than a Dutch cheese, took three years to attain his majority in old times; and as the race of pine-apples so is the race of man. Hoiaper—what's the Greek for a pine-apple, Warrington?"

"Stop, for mercy's sake, stop with the English and before you come to the Greek," Warrington cried out, laughing. "I never heard you make such a long speech, or was aware that you had penetrated so deeply into the female mysteries. Who taught you all this, and into whose boudoirs and nurseries have you been peeping, while I was smoking my pipe, and reading my book, lying on my straw bed?"

"You are on the bank, old boy, content to watch the waves tossing in the winds, and the struggles of others at sea," Pen said. "I am in the stream now, and, by Jove, I like it. How rapidly we go down it, hey? —strong and feeble, old and young—the metal pitchers and the earthen pitchers—the pretty little china boat swims gayly till the big bruised brazen one bumps him and sends him down—eh, vogue la galère!— you see a man sink in the race, and say good-by to him—look, he has only dived under the other fellow's legs, and comes up shaking his pole, and striking out ever so far ahead. Eh, vogue la galère, I say. It's good sport, Warrington—not winning merely, but playing."

"Well, go in and win, young 'un. I'll sit and mark the game," Warrington said, surveying the ardent young fellow with an almost fatherly pleasure. "A generous fellow plays for the play, a sordid one for the stake; an old fogy sits by and smokes the pipe of tranquillity, while Jack and Tom are pommeling each other in the ring."

"Why don't you come in, George, and have a turn with the gloves? You are big enough and strong enough," Pen said. "Dear old boy, you are worth ten of me."

"You are not quite as tall as Goliath, certainly," the other answered, with a laugh that was rough and yet tender. "And as for me, I am disabled. I had a fatal hit in early life. I will tell you about it some day. You may, too, meet with your master. Don't be too eager, or too confident, or too worldly, my boy."

Was Pendennis becoming worldly, or only seeing the world, or both? and is a man very wrong for being after all only a man? Which is the most reasonable, and does his duty best: he who stands aloof from the struggle of life, calmly contemplating it, or he who descends to the ground, and takes his part in the contest? "That philosopher," Pen said, "had held a great place among the leaders of the world, and enjoyed to the full what it had to give of rank and riches, renown and pleasure, who came, weary-hearted, out of it, and said that all was vanity and vexation of spirit. Many a teacher of those whom we reverence, and who steps out of his carriage up to his carved cathedral place, shakes his lawn ruffles over the velvet cushion, and cries out, that the whole struggle is an accursed one, and the works of the world are evil. Many a conscience-striken mystic flies from it altogether, and shuts himself out from it within convent walls (real or spiritual), whence he can only look up to the sky, and contemplate the heaven out of which there is no rest, and no good. But the earth, where our feet are, is the work of the same Power as the immeasurable blue yonder, in which the future lies into which we would peer. Who ordered toil as the condition of life, ordered weariness, ordered sickness, ordered poverty, failure, success—to this man a foremost place, to the other a nameless struggle with the crowd—to that a shameful fall, or paralyzed limb, or sudden accident—to each some work upon the ground he stands on, until he is laid beneath it." While they were talking, the dawn came shining through the windows of the room, and Pen threw them open to receive the fresh morning air. "Look, George," said he; "look and see the sun rise: he sees the laborer on his way a-field, the work-girl plying her poor needle; the lawyer at his desk, perhaps; the beauty smiling asleep upon her pillow of down; or the jaded reveler reeling to bed; or the fevered patient tossing on it; or the doctor watching by it, over the throes of the mother for the child that is to be born into the world; to be born and to take his part in the suffering and struggling, the tears and laughter, the crime, remorse, love, folly, sorrow, rest."

CHAPTER VII

MISS AMORY'S PARTNERS

The noble Henry Foker, of whom we have lost sight for a few pages, has been in the mean while occupied, as we might suppose a man of his constancy would be, in the pursuit and indulgence of his all-absorbing passion of love.

I wish that a few of my youthful readers who are inclined to that amusement would take the trouble to calculate the time which is spent in the pursuit, when they would find it to be one of the most costly occupations in which a man can possibly indulge. What don't you sacrifice to it, indeed, young gentlemen and young ladies of ill-regulated minds? Many hours of your precious sleep, in the first place, in which you lie tossing and thinking about the adored object, whence you come down late to breakfast, when noon is advancing, and all the family is long since away to its daily occupations. Then when you at length get to these occupations you pay no attention to them, and engage in them with no ardor, all your thoughts and powers of mind being fixed elsewhere. Then the day's work being slurred over, you neglect your friends and relatives, your natural companions and usual associates in life, that you may go and have a glance at the dear personage, or a look up at her windows, or a peep at her carriage in the Park. Then at night the artless blandishments of home bore you; mamma's conversation palls upon you; the dishes which that good soul prepares for the dinner of her favorite are sent away untasted, the whole meal of life, indeed, except one particular plat, has no relish. Life, business, family ties, home, all things useful and dear once become intolerable, and you are never easy except when you are in pursuit of your flame.

Such I believe to be not unfrequently the state of mind among ill-regulated young gentlemen, and such, indeed, was Mr. H. Foker's condition, who, having been bred up to indulge in every propensity toward which he was inclined, abandoned himself to this one with his usual selfish enthusiasm. Nor because he had given his friend Arthur Pendennis a great deal of good advice on a former occasion, need men of the world wonder that Mr. Foker became passion's slave in his turn. Who among us has not given a plenty of the very best advice to his friends? Who has not preached, and who has practiced? To be sure, you, madam, are perhaps a perfect being, and never had a wrong thought in the whole course of your frigid and irreproachable existence: or you, sir, are a great deal too strong-minded to allow any foolish passion to interfere with your equanimity in chambers or your attendance on 'Change; you are so strong that you don't want any sympathy. We don't give you any, then; we keep ours for the humble and weak, that struggle and stumble and get up again, and so march with the rest of mortals. What need have you of a hand who never fall? Your serene virtue is never shaded by passion, or ruffled by temptation, or darkened by remorse; compassion would be impertinence for such an angel: but then, with such a one companionship becomes intolerable; you are, from the very elevation of your virtue and high attributes, of necessity lonely; we can't reach up and talk familiarly with such potentates. Good-by, then; our way lies with humble folks, and not with serene highnesses like you; and we give notice that there are no perfect characters in this history, except, perhaps, one little one, and that one is not perfect either, for she never knows to this day that she is perfect, and with a deplorable misapprehension and perverseness of humility, believes herself to be as great a sinner as need be.

This young person does not happen to be in London at the present period of our story, and it is by no means for the like of her that Mr. Henry Foker's mind is agitated. But what matters a few failings? Need we be angels, male or female, in order to be worshiped as such? Let us admire the diversity of the tastes of mankind, and the oldest, the ugliest, the stupidest and most pompous, the silliest and most vapid, the greatest criminal, tyrant, booby, Bluebeard, Catherine Hayes, George Barnwell, among us, we need never despair. I have read of the passion of a transported pickpocket for a female convict (each of them being advanced in age, repulsive in person, ignorant, quarrelsome, and given to drink), that was as magnificent as the loves of Cleopatra and Antony, or Lancelot and Guinever. The passion which Count Borulawski, the Polish dwarf, inspired in the bosom of the most beautiful baroness at the court of Dresden, is a matter with which we are all of us acquainted: the flame which burned in the heart of young Cornet Tozer but the other day, and caused him to run off and espouse Mrs. Battersby, who was old enough to be his mamma; all these instances are told in the page of history or the newspaper column. Are we to be ashamed or pleased to think that our hearts are formed so that the biggest and highest-placed Ajax among us may some day find himself prostrate before the pattens of his kitchen-maid; as that there is no poverty or shame or crime, which will not be supported, hugged, even with delight, and cherished more closely than virtue would be, by the perverse fidelity and admirable constant folly of a woman?

So then Henry Foker, Esquire, longed after his love, and cursed the fate which separated him from her. When Lord Gravesend's family retired to the country (his lordship leaving his proxy with the venerable Lord Bagwig), Harry still remained lingering on in London, certainly not much to the sorrow of Lady Ann, to whom he was affianced, and who did not in the least miss him. Wherever Miss Clavering went, this infatuated young fellow continued to follow her; and being aware that his engagement to his cousin was known in the world, he was forced to make a mystery of his passion, and confine it to his own breast, so that it was so pent in there and pressed down, that it is a wonder he did not explode some day with the stormy secret, and perish collapsed after the outburst.

There had been a grand entertainment at Gaunt House on one beautiful evening in June, and the next day's journals contained almost two columns of the names of the most closely-printed nobility and gentry who had been honored with invitations to the ball. Among the guests were Sir Francis and Lady Clavering and Miss Amory, for whom the indefatigable Major Pendennis had procured an invitation, and our two young friends Arthur and Harry. Each exerted himself, and danced a great deal with Miss Blanche. As for the worthy major, he assumed the charge of Lady Clavering, and took care to introduce her to that department of the mansion where her ladyship specially distinguished herself, namely, the refreshment-room, where, among pictures of Titian and Giorgione, and regal portraits of Vandyke and Reynolds, and enormous salvers of gold and silver, and pyramids of large flowers, and constellations of wax candles—in a manner perfectly regardless of expense, in a word—a supper was going on all night. Of how many creams, jellies, salads, peaches, white soups, grapes, pâtes, galantines, cups of tea, champagne, and so forth, Lady Clavering partook, it does not become us to say. How much the major suffered as he followed the honest woman about, calling to the solemn male attendants, and lovely servant-maids, and administering to Lady Clavering's various wants with admirable patience, nobody knows; he never confessed. He never allowed his agony to appear on his countenance in the least; but with a constant kindness brought plate after plate to the Begum.

Mr. Wagg counted up all the dishes of which Lady Clavering partook as long as he could count (but as he partook very freely himself of Champagne during the evening, his powers of calculation were not to be trusted at the close of the entertainment), and he recommended Mr. Honeyman, Lady Steyne's medical man, to look carefully after the Begum, and to call and get news of her ladyship the next day.

Sir Francis Clavering made his appearance, and skulked for a while about the magnificent rooms; but the company and the splendor which he met there were not to the baronet's taste, and after tossing off a tumbler of wine or two at the buffet, he quitted Gaunt House for the neighborhood of Jermyn-street, where his friends Loder, Punter, little Moss Abrams, and Captain Skewball were assembled at the familiar green table. In the rattle of the box, and of their agreeable conversation, Sir Francis's spirits rose to their accustomed point of feeble hilarity.

Mr. Pynsent, who had asked Miss Amory to dance, came up on one occasion to claim her hand, but scowls of recognition having already passed between him and Mr. Arthur Pendennis in the dancing-room, Arthur suddenly rose up and claimed Miss Amory as his partner for the present dance, on which Mr. Pynsent, biting his lips and scowling yet more savagely, withdrew with a profound bow, saying that he gave up his claim. There are some men who are always falling in one's way in life. Pynsent and Pen had this view of each other, and regarded each other accordingly.

"What a confounded, conceited provincial fool that is!" thought the one. "Because he has written a twopenny novel, his absurd head is turned, and a kicking would take his conceit out of him."

"What an impertinent idiot that man is!" remarked the other to his partner. "His soul is in Downing-street; his neckcloth is foolscap; his hair is sand; his legs are rulers; his vitals are tape and sealing-wax; he was a prig in his cradle; and never laughed since he was born, except three times at the same joke of his chief. I have the same liking for that man, Miss Amory, that I have for cold boiled veal." Upon which Blanche of course remarked, that Mr. Pendennis was wicked, méchant, perfectly abominable, and wondered what he would say when her back was turned.

"Say!—Say that you have the most beautiful figure and the slimmest waist in the world, Blanche—Miss Amory, I mean. I beg your pardon. Another turn; this music would make an alderman dance."

"And you have left off tumbling, when you waltz now?" Blanche asked, archly looking up at her partner's face.

"One falls and one gets up again in life, Blanche; you know I used to call you so in old times, and it is the prettiest name in the world: besides, I have practiced since then."

"And with a great number of partners, I'm afraid," Blanche said, with a little sham sigh, and a shrug of the shoulders. And so in truth Mr. Pen had practiced a good deal in this life; and had undoubtedly arrived at being able to dance better.

If Pendennis was impertinent in his talk, Foker, on the other hand, so bland and communicative on most occasions, was entirely mum and melancholy when he danced with Miss Amory. To clasp her slender waist was a rapture, to whirl round the room with her was a delirium; but to speak to her, what could he say that was worthy of her? What pearl of conversation could he bring that was fit for the acceptance of such a queen of love and wit as Blanche? It was she who made the talk when she was in the company of this love-stricken partner. It was she who asked him how that dear little pony was, and looked at him and thanked him with such a tender kindness and regret, and refused the dear little pony with such a delicate sigh when he offered it. "I have nobody to ride with in London," she said. "Mamma is timid, and her figure is not pretty on horseback. Sir Francis never goes out with me, He loves me like—like a step-daughter. Oh, how delightful it must be to have a father—a father, Mr. Foker!"

"Oh, uncommon," said Mr. Harry, who enjoyed that blessing very calmly, upon which, and forgetting the sentimental air which she had just before assumed, Blanche's gray eyes gazed at Foker with such an arch twinkle, that both of them burst out laughing, and Harry, enraptured and at his ease, began to entertain her with a variety of innocent prattle—good, kind, simple, Foker talk, flavored with many expressions by no means to be discovered in dictionaries, and relating to the personal history of himself or horses, or other things dear and important to him, or to persons in the ball-room then passing before them, and about whose appearance or character Mr. Harry spoke with artless freedom, and a considerable dash of humor.

And it was Blanche who, when the conversation flagged, and the youth's modesty came rushing back and overpowering him, knew how to reanimate her companion: asked him questions about Logwood, and whether it was a pretty place? Whether he was a hunting-man, and whether he liked women to hunt? (in which case she was prepared to say that she adored hunting)—but Mr. Foker expressing his opinion against sporting females, and pointing out Lady Bullfinch, who happened to pass by, as a horse god-mother, whom he had seen at cover with a cigar in her face, Blanche too expressed her detestation of the sports of the field, and said it would make her shudder to think of a dear, sweet little fox being killed, on which Foker danced and waltzed with renewed vigor and grace.

At the end of the waltz—the last waltz they had on that night— Blanche asked him about Drummington, and whether it was a fine house. His cousins, she had heard, were very accomplished; Lord Erith she had met, and which of his cousins was his favorite? Was it not Lady Ann? Yes, she was sure it was she: sure by his looks and his blushes. She was tired of dancing; it was getting very late; she must go to mamma; and, without another word, she sprang away from Harry Foker's arm, and seized upon Pen's, who was swaggering about the dancing-room, and again said, "Mamma, mamma!—take me to mamma, dear Mr. Pendennis!" transfixing Harry with a Parthian shot, as she fled from him.

My Lord Steyne, with garter and ribbon, with a bald head and shining eyes, and a collar of red whiskers round his face, always looked grand upon an occasion of state; and made a great effect upon Lady Clavering, when he introduced himself to her at the request of the obsequious Major Pendennis. With his own white and royal hand, he handed to her ladyship a glass of wine, said he had heard of her charming daughter, and begged to be presented to her; and, at this very juncture, Mr. Arthur Pendennis came up with the young lady on his arm.

The peer made a profound bow, and Blanche the deepest courtesy that ever was seen. His lordship gave Mr. Arthur Pendennis his hand to shake; said he had read his book, which was very wicked and clever; asked Miss Blanche if she had read it, at which Pen blushed and winced. Why, Blanche was one of the heroines of the novel. Blanche, in black ringlets and a little altered, was the Neaera of Walter Lorraine.

Blanche had read it; the language of the eyes expressed her admiration and rapture at the performance. This little play being achieved, the Marquis of Steyne made other two profound bows to Lady Clavering and her daughter, and passed on to some other of his guests at the splendid entertainment.

Mamma and daughter were loud in their expression of admiration of the noble marquis so soon as his broad back was turned upon them. "He said they make a very nice couple," whispered Major Pendennis to Lady Clavering. Did he now, really? Mamma thought they would; Mamma was so flustered with the honor which had just been shown to her, and with other intoxicating events of the evening, that her good humor knew no bounds. She laughed, she winked, and nodded knowingly at Pen; she tapped him on the arm with her fan; she tapped Blanche; she tapped the major; her contentment was boundless; and her method of showing her joy equally expansive.

As the party went down the great staircase of Gaunt House, the morning had risen stark and clear over the black trees of the square, the skies were tinged with pink; and the cheeks of some of the people at the ball—ah, how ghastly they looked! That admirable and devoted major above all—who had been for hours by Lady Clavering's side, ministering to her and feeding her body with every thing that was nice, and her ear with every thing that was sweet and flattering—oh! what an object he was! The rings round his eyes were of the color of bistre; those orbs themselves were like the plovers' eggs whereof Lady Clavering and Blanche had each tasted; the wrinkles in his old face were furrowed in deep gashes; and a silver stubble, like an elderly morning dew, was glittering on his chin, and alongside the dyed whiskers, now limp and out of curl.

There he stood, with admirable patience, enduring uncomplainingly, a silent agony; knowing that people could see the state of his face (for could he not himself perceive the condition of others, males and females, of his own age?)—longing to go to rest for hours past; aware that suppers disagreed with him, and yet having eaten a little so as to keep his friend, Lady Clavering, in good humor; with twinges of rheumatism in the back and knees; with weary feet burning in his varnished boots; so tired, oh, so tired, and longing for bed! If a man, struggling with hardship and bravely overcoming it, is an object of admiration for the gods, that Power in whose chapels the old major was a faithful worshiper must have looked upward approvingly upon the constancy of Pendennis's martyrdom. There are sufferers in that cause as in the other; the negroes in the service of Mumbo Jumbo tattoo and drill themselves with burning skewers with great fortitude; and we read that the priests in the service of Baal gashed themselves and bled freely. You who can smash the idols, do so with a good courage; but do not be too fierce with the idolaters—they worship the best thing they know.

The Pendennises, the elder and the younger, waited with Lady Clavering and her daughter until her ladyship's carriage was announced, when the elder's martyrdom may be said to have come to an end, for the good-natured Begum insisted upon leaving him at his door in Bury-street; so he took the back seat of the carriage, after a feeble bow or two, and speech of thanks, polite to the last, and resolute in doing his duty. The Begum waved her dumpy little hand by way of farewell to Arthur and Foker, and

Blanche smiled languidly out upon the young men, thinking whether she looked very wan and green under her rose-colored hood, and whether it was the mirrors at Gaunt House, or the fatigue and fever of her own eyes, which made her fancy herself so pale.

Arthur, perhaps, saw quite well how yellow Blanche looked, but did not attribute that peculiarity of her complexion to the effect of the looking-glasses, or to any error in his sight or her own. Our young man of the world could use his eyes very keenly, and could see Blanche's face pretty much as nature had made it. But for poor Foker it had a radiance which dazzled and blinded him: he could see no more faults in it than in the sun, which was now flaring over the house-tops.

Among other wicked London habits which Pen had acquired, the moralist will remark that he had got to keep very bad hours; and often was going to bed at the time when sober country people were thinking of leaving it. Men get used to one hour as to another. Editors of newspapers, Covent-Garden market people, night cabmen, and coffee-sellers, chimney-sweeps, and gentlemen and ladies of fashion who frequent balls, are often quite lively at three or four o'clock of a morning, when ordinary mortals are snoring. We have shown in the last chapter how Pen was in a brisk condition of mind at this period, inclined to smoke his cigar at ease, and to speak freely.

Foker and Pen walked away from Gaunt House, then, indulging in both the above amusements; or rather Pen talked, and Foker looked as if he wanted to say something. Pen was sarcastic and dandyfied when he had been in the company of great folks; he could not help imitating some of their airs and tones, and having a most lively imagination, mistook himself for a person of importance very easily. He rattled away, and attacked this person and that; sneered at Lady John Turnbull's bad French, which her ladyship will introduce into all conversations, in spite of the sneers of every body: at Mrs. Slack Roper's extraordinary costume and sham jewels; at the old dandies and the young ones; at whom didn't he sneer and laugh?

"You fire at everybody, Pen—you're grown awful, that you are," Foker said. "Now, you've pulled about Blondel's yellow wig, and Colchicum's black one, why don't you have a shy at a brown one, hay? you know whose I mean. It got into Lady Clavering's carriage."

"Under my uncle's hat? My uncle is a martyr, Foker, my boy. My uncle has been doing excruciating duties all night. He likes to go to bed rather early. He has a dreadful headache if he sits up and touches supper. He always has the gout if he walks or stands much at a ball. He has been sitting up, and standing up, and supping. He has gone home to the gout and the headache, and for my sake. Shall I make fun of the old boy? no, not for Venice!"

"How do you mean that he has been doing it for your sake?" Foker asked, looking rather alarmed.

"Boy! canst thou keep a secret if I impart it to thee?" Pen cried out, in high spirits. "Art thou of good counsel? Wilt thou swear? Wilt thou be mum, or wilt thou peach? Wilt thou be silent and hear, or wilt thou speak and die?" And as he spoke, flinging himself into an absurd theatrical attitude, the men in the cab-stand in Piccadilly wondered and grinned at the antics of the two young swells.

"What the doose are you driving at?" Foker asked, looking very much agitated.

Pen, however, did not remark this agitation much, but continued in the same bantering and excited vein. "Henry, friend of my youth," he said, "and witness of my early follies, though dull at thy books, yet thou art not altogether deprived of sense; nay, blush not, Henrico, thou hast a good portion of that, and of courage and kindness too, at the service of thy friends. Were I in a strait of poverty, I would come to my Foker's purse. Were I in grief, I would discharge my grief upon his sympathizing bosom—"

"Gammon, Pen; go on," Foker said.

"I would, Henrico, upon thy studs, and upon thy cambric, worked by the hands of beauty, to adorn the breast of valor! Know then, friend of my boyhood's days, that Arthur Pendennis, of the Upper Temple, student-at-law, feels that he is growing lonely, and old Care is furrowing his temples, and Baldness is busy with his crown. Shall we stop and have a drop of coffee at this stall, it looks very hot and nice? Look how that cabman is blowing at his saucer. No, you won't? Aristocrat! I resume my tale. I am getting on in life. I have got devilish little money. I want some. I am thinking of getting some, and settling in life. I'm thinking of settling. I'm thinking of marrying, old boy. I'm thinking of becoming a moral man; a steady port and sherry character: with a good reputation in my quartier, and a moderate establishment of two maids and a man; with an occasional brougham to drive out Mrs. Pendennis, and a house near the Parks for the accommodation of the children. Ha! what sayest thou? Answer thy friend, thou worthy child of beer. Speak, I adjure thee, by all thy vats."

"But you ain't got any money, Pen," said the other, still looking alarmed.

"I ain't? No, but she ave. I tell thee there is gold in store for me —not what you call money, nursed in the lap of luxury, and cradled on grains, and drinking in wealth from a thousand mash-tubs. What do you know about money? What is poverty to you, is splendor to the hardy son of the humble apothecary. You can't live without an establishment, and your houses in town and country. A snug little house somewhere off Belgravia, a brougham for my wife, a decent cook, and a fair bottle of wine for my friends at home sometimes; these simple necessaries suffice for me, my Foker." And here Pendennis began to look more serious. Without bantering further, Pen continued, "I've rather serious thoughts of settling and marrying. No man can get on in the world without some money at his back. You must have a certain stake to begin with, before you can go in and play the great game. Who knows that I'm not going to try, old fellow? Worse men than I have won at it. And as I have not got enough capital from my fathers, I must get some by my wife—that's all."

They were walking down Grosvenor-street, as they talked, or rather as Pen talked, in the selfish fullness of his heart; and Mr. Pen must have been too much occupied with his own affairs to remark the concern and agitation of his neighbor, for he continued, "We are no longer children, you know, you and I, Harry. Bah! the time of our romance has passed away. We don't marry for passion, but for prudence and for establishment. What do you take your cousin for? Because she is a nice girl, and an earl's daughter, and the old folks wish it, and that sort of thing."

"And you, Pendennis," asked Foker, "you ain't very fond of the girl—you're going to marry?"

Pen shrugged his shoulders. "Comme ça," said he; "I like her well enough. She's pretty enough; she's clever enough. I think she'll do very well. And she has got money enough—that's the great point. Psha! you know who she is, don't you? I thought you were sweet on her yourself one night when we dined with her mamma. It's little Amory."

"I—I thought so," Foker said; "and has she accepted you?"

"Not quite," Arthur replied, with a confident smile, which seemed to say, I have but to ask, and she comes to me that instant.

"Oh, not quite," said Foker; and he broke out with such a dreadful laugh, that Pen, for the first time, turned his thoughts from himself toward his companion, and was struck by the other's ghastly pale face.

"My dear fellow, Fo! what's the matter? You're ill," Pen said, in a tone of real concern.

"You think it was the Champagne at Gaunt House, don't you? It ain't that. Come in; let me talk to you for a minute. I'll tell you what it is. D—it, let me tell somebody," Foker said.

They were at Mr. Foker's door by this time, and, opening it, Harry walked with his friend into his apartments, which were situated in the back part of the house, and behind the family dining-room, where the elder Foker received his guests, surrounded by pictures of himself, his wife, his infant son on a donkey, and the late Earl of Gravesend in his robes as a peer. Foker and Pen passed by this chamber, now closed with death-like shutters, and entered into the young man's own quarters. Dusky streams of sunbeams were playing into that room, and lighting up poor Harry's gallery of dancing girls and opera nymphs with flickering illuminations.

"Look here! I can't help telling you, Pen," he said. "Ever since the night we dined there, I'm so fond of that girl, that I think I shall die if I don't get her. I feel as if I should go mad sometimes. I can't stand it, Pen. I couldn't bear to hear you talking about her, just now, about marrying her only because she's money. Ah, Pen! that ain't the question in marrying. I'd bet any thing it ain't. Talking about money and such a girl as that, it's—it's—what-d'ye-callem—you know what I mean—I ain't good at talking—sacrilege, then. If she'd have me, I'd take and sweep a crossing, that I would!"

"Poor Fo! I don't think that would tempt her," Pen said, eying his friend with a great deal of real good-nature and pity. "She is not a girl for love and a cottage."

"She ought to be a duchess, I know that very well, and I know she wouldn't take me unless I could make her a great place in the world—for I ain't good for any thing myself much—I ain't clever and that sort of thing," Foker said, sadly. "If I had all the diamonds that all the duchesses and marchionesses had on to-night, wouldn't I put 'em in her lap? But what's the use of talking? I'm booked for another race. It's that kills me, Pen. I can't get out of it; though I die, I can't get out of it. And though my cousin's a nice girl, and I like her very well, and that, yet I hadn't seen this one when our governors settled that matter between us. And when you talked, just now, about her doing very well, and about her having money enough for both of you, I thought to myself, it isn't money or mere liking a girl, that ought to be enough to make a fellow marry. He may marry, and find he likes somebody else better. All the money in the world won't make you happy then. Look at me; I've plenty of money, or shall have, out of the mash-tubs, as you call 'em. My governor thought he'd made it all right for me in settling my marriage with my cousin. I tell you it won't do; and when Lady Ann has got her husband, it won't be happy for either of us, and she'll have the most miserable beggar in town."

"Poor old fellow!" Pen said, with rather a cheap magnanimity, "I wish I could help you. I had no idea of this, and that you were so wild about the girl. Do you think she would have you without your money? No. Do you think your father would agree to break off your engagement with your cousin? You know him very well, and that he would cast you off rather than do so."

The unhappy Foker only groaned a reply, flinging himself prostrate on the sofa, face forward, his head in his hands.

"As for my affair," Pen went on—"my dear fellow, if I had thought matters were so critical with you, at least I would not have pained you by choosing you as my confidant. And my business is not serious, at least, not as yet. I have not spoken a word about it to Miss Amory. Very likely she would not have me if I asked her. Only I have had a great deal of talk about it with my uncle, who says that the match might be an eligible one for me. I'm ambitious and I'm poor. And it appears Lady Clavering will give her a good deal of money, and Sir Francis might be got to—never mind the rest. Nothing is settled, Harry. They are going out of town directly. I promise you I won't ask her before she goes. There's no hurry: there's time for every body. But, suppose you got her, Foker. Remember what you said about marriages just now, and the misery of a man who doesn't care for his wife: and what sort of a wife would you have who didn't care for her husband?"

"But she would care for me," said Foker, from his sofa—"that is, I think she would. Last night only, as we were dancing, she said—"

"What did she say?" Pen cried, starting up in great wrath. But he saw his own meaning more clearly than Foker, and broke off with a laugh—"Well, never mind what she said, Harry. Miss Amory is a clever girl, and says numbers of civil things—to you—to me, perhaps—and who the deuce knows to whom besides? Nothing's settled, old boy. At least, my heart won't break if I don't get her. Win her if you can, and I wish you joy of her. Good-by! Don't think about what I said to you. I was excited, and confoundedly thirsty in those hot rooms, and didn't, I suppose, put enough Seltzer water into the Champagne. Good night! I'll keep your counsel too. 'Mum' is the word between us; and 'let there be a fair fight, and let the best man win,' as Peter Crawley says."

So saying, Mr. Arthur Pendennis, giving a very queer and rather dangerous look at his companion, shook him by the hand, with something of that sort of cordiality which befitted his just repeated simile of the boxing-match, and which Mr. Bendigo displays when he shakes hands with Mr. Gaunt before they fight each other for the champion's belt and two hundred pounds a side. Foker returned his friend's salute with an imploring look, and a piteous squeeze of the hand, sank back on his cushions again, and Pen, putting on his hat, strode forth into the air, and almost over the body of the matutinal housemaid, who was rubbing the steps at the door.

"And so he wants her too? does he?" thought Pen as he marched along—and noted within himself with a fatal keenness of perception and almost an infernal mischief, that the very pains and tortures which that honest heart of Foker's was suffering gave a zest and an impetus to his own pursuit of Blanche: if pursuit that might be called which had been no pursuit as yet, but mere sport and idle dallying. "She said something to him, did she? perhaps she gave him the fellow flower to this;" and he took out of his coat and twiddled in his thumb and finger a poor little shriveled, crumpled bud that had faded and blackened with the heat and flare of the night. "I wonder to how many more she has given her artless tokens of affection—the little flirt"—and he flung his into the gutter, where the water may have refreshed it, and where any amateur of rosebuds may have picked it up. And then bethinking him that the day was quite bright, and that the passers-by might be staring at his beard and white neckcloth, our modest young gentleman took a cab and drove to the Temple. Ah! is this the boy that prayed at his mother's knee but a few years since, and for whom very likely at this hour of morning she is praying? Is this jaded and selfish worldling the lad who, a short while back, was ready to fling away his worldly all, his hope, his ambition, his chance of life, for his love? This is the man you are proud of, old Pendennis. You boast of having formed him: and of having reasoned him out of his absurd romance and folly—and groaning in your bed over your pains and rheumatisms, satisfy yourself still by thinking, that, at last, that lad will do something to better himself in life, and that the Pendennises will take a good place in the world. And is he the only one, who in his progress through this dark life goes willfully or fatally astray, while the natural truth and love which should illumine him grew dim in the poisoned air, and suffice to light him no more?

When Pen was gone away, poor Harry Foker got up from the sofa, and taking out from his waistcoat— the splendidly buttoned, the gorgeously embroidered, the work of his mamma—a little white rosebud, he drew from his dressing-case, also the maternal present, a pair of scissors, with which he nipped carefully the stalk of the flower, and placing it in a glass of water opposite his bed, he sought refuge there from care and bitter remembrances.

It is to be presumed that Miss Blanche Amory had more than one rose in her bouquet, and why should not the kind young creature give out of her superfluity, and make as many partners as possible happy?

CHAPTER VIII

MONSEIGNEUR S'AMUSE

The exertions of that last night at Gaunt House had proved almost too much for Major Pendennis; and as soon as he could move his weary old body with safety, he transported himself groaning to Buxton, and sought relief in the healing waters of that place. Parliament broke up. Sir Francis Clavering and family left town, and the affairs which we have just mentioned to the reader were not advanced, in the brief interval of a few days or weeks which have occurred between this and the last chapter. The town was, however, emptied since then. The season was now come to a conclusion: Pen's neighbors, the lawyers, were gone upon circuit: and his more fashionable friends had taken their passports for the Continent, or had fled for health or excitement to the Scotch moors. Scarce a man was to be seen in the bay-windows of the Clubs, or on the solitary Pall-Mall pavement. The red jackets had disappeared from before the Palace-gate: the tradesmen of St. James's were abroad taking their pleasure: the tailors had grown mustaches, and were gone up the Rhine: the bootmakers were at Ems or Baden, blushing when they met their customers at those places of recreation, or punting beside their creditors at the gambling tables: the clergymen of St. James's only preached to half a congregation, in which there was not a single sinner of distinction: the band in Kensington Gardens had shut up their instruments of brass and trumpets of silver: only two or three old flies and chaises crawled by the banks of the Serpentine, and Clarence Bulbul, who was retained in town by his arduous duties as a Treasury clerk, when he took his afternoon ride in Rotten Row, compared its loneliness to the vastness of the Arabian desert, and himself to a Bedouin wending his way through that dusty solitude. Warrington stowed away a quantity of Cavendish tobacco in his carpet bag, and betook himself, as his custom was, in the vacation to his brother's house in Norfolk. Pen was left alone in chambers for a while, for this man of fashion could not quit the metropolis when he chose always: and was at present detained by the affairs of his newspaper, the Pall Mall Gazette, of which he acted as the editor and chargé d'affaires during the temporary absence of the chief, Captain Shandon, who was with his family at the salutary watering-place of Boulogne sur Mer.

Although, as we have seen, Mr. Pen had pronounced himself for years past to be a man perfectly blasé and wearied of life, yet the truth is that he was an exceedingly healthy young fellow; still with a fine appetite, which he satisfied with the greatest relish and satisfaction at least once a day; and a constant desire for society, which showed him to be any thing but misanthropical. If he could not get a good dinner he sat down to a bad one with perfect contentment; if he could not procure the company of witty, or great, or beautiful persons, he put up with any society that came to hand; and was perfectly satisfied in a tavern-parlor or on board a Greenwich steam-boat, or in a jaunt to Hampstead with Mr. Finucane, his colleague at the Pall Mall Gazette; or in a visit to the summer theaters across the river; or to the Royal Gardens of Vauxhall, where he was on terms of friendship with the great Simpson, and where he shook the principal comic singer or the lovely equestrian of the arena by the hand. And while he could watch the grimaces or the graces of these with a satiric humor that was not deprived of sympathy, he could look on with an eye of kindness at the lookers on too; at the roystering youth bent upon enjoyment, and here taking it: at the honest parents, with their delighted children laughing and clapping their hands at the show: at the poor outcasts, whose laughter was less innocent, though perhaps louder, and who brought their shame and their youth here, to dance and be merry till the dawn at least; and to get bread and drown care. Of this sympathy with all conditions of men Arthur often boasted: he was pleased to possess it: and said that he hoped thus to the last he should retain it. As another man has an ardor for art or music, or natural science, Mr. Pen said that anthropology was his favorite pursuit; and had his eyes always eagerly open to its infinite varieties and beauties: contemplating with an unfailing delight all specimens of it in all places to which he resorted, whether it was the coqueting of a wrinkled dowager in a ball-room, or a high-bred young beauty blushing in her prime there; whether it was a hulking guardsman coaxing a servant-girl in the Park, or innocent little Tommy that was feeding the ducks while the nurse listened. And indeed a man whose heart is pretty clean, can indulge in this pursuit with an enjoyment that never ceases, and is only perhaps the more keen because it is secret, and has a touch of sadness in it: because he is of his mood and humor lonely, and apart although not alone.

Yes, Pen used to brag and talk in his impetuous way to Warrington. "I was in love so fiercely in my youth, that I have burned out that flame forever, I think, and if ever I marry, it will be a marriage of reason that I will make, with a well-bred, good-tempered, good-looking person who has a little money, and so forth, that will cushion our carriage in its course through life. As for romance, it is all done; I have spent that out, and am old before my time—I'm proud of it."

"Stuff!" growled the other, "you fancied you were getting bald the other day, and bragged about it, as you do about every thing. But you began to use the bear's-grease pot directly the hair-dresser told you; and are scented like a barber ever since."

"You are Diogenes," the other answered, "and you want every man to live in a tub like yourself. Violets smell better than stale tobacco, you grizzly old cynic." But Mr. Pen was blushing while he made this reply to his unromantical friend, and indeed cared a great deal more about himself still than such a philosopher perhaps should have done. Indeed, considering that he was careless about the world, Mr. Pen ornamented his person with no small pains in order to make himself agreeable to it, and for a weary pilgrim as he was, wore very tight boots and bright varnish.

It was in this dull season of the year then, of a shining Friday night in autumn, that Mr. Pendennis, having completed at his newspaper office a brilliant leading article—such as Captain Shandon himself might have written, had the captain been in good humor, and inclined to work, which he never would do except under compulsion—that Mr. Arthur Pendennis having written his article, and reviewed it approvingly as it lay before him in its wet proof-sheet at the office of the paper, bethought him that he would cross the water, and regale himself with the fire-works and other amusements of Vauxhall. So he affably put in his pocket the order which admitted "Editor of Pall Mall Gazette and friend" to that place of recreation, and paid with the coin of the realm a sufficient sum to enable him to cross Waterloo Bridge. The walk thence to the Gardens was pleasant, the stars were shining in the skies above, looking down upon the royal property, whence the rockets and Roman candles had not yet ascended to outshine the stars.

Before you enter the enchanted ground, where twenty thousand additional lamps are burned every night as usual, most of us have passed through the black and dreary passage and wickets which hide the splendors of Vauxhall from uninitiated men. In the walls of this passage are two holes strongly illuminated, in the midst of which you see two gentlemen at desks, where they will take either your money as a private individual, or your order of admission if you are provided with that passport to the Gardens. Pen went to exhibit his ticket at the last-named orifice, where, however, a gentleman and two ladies were already in parley before him.

The gentleman, whose hat was very much on one side, and who wore a short and shabby cloak in an excessively smart manner, was crying out in a voice which Pen at once recognized, "Bedad, sir, if ye doubt me honor, will ye obleege me by stipping out of that box, and—"

"Lor, Capting!" cried the elder lady.

"Don't bother me," said the man in the box.

"And ask Mr. Hodgen himself, who's in the gyardens, to let these leedies pass. Don't be froightened, me dear madam, I'm not going to quarl with this gintleman, at any reet before leedies. Will ye go, sir, and desoire Mr. Hodgen (whose orther I keem in with, and he's me most intemate friend, and I know he's goan to sing the 'Body Snatcher' here to-night), with Captain Costigan's compliments, to stip out and let in the leedies; for meself, sir, oi've seen Vauxhall, and I scawrun any interfayrance on moi account: but for these leedies, one of them has never been there, and oi should think ye'd harly take advantage of me misfartune in losing the tickut, to deproive her of her pleasure."

"It ain't no use, captain. I can't go about your business," the checktaker said; on which the captain swore an oath, and the elder lady said, "Lor, ow provokin!"

As for the young one, she looked up at the captain, and said, "Never mind, Captain Costigan, I'm sure I don't want to go at all. Come away, mamma." And with this, although she did not want to go at all, her feelings overcame her, and she began to cry.

"Me poor child!" the captain said. "Can ye see that, sir, and will ye not let this innocent creature in?"

"It ain't my business," cried the door-keeper, peevishly, out of the illuminated box. And at this minute Arthur came up, and recognizing Costigan, said, "Don't you know me, captain? Pendennis!" And he took off his hat and made a bow to the two ladies. "Me dear boy! Me dear friend!" cried the captain, extending toward Pendennis the grasp of friendship; and he rapidly explained to the other what he called "a most unluckee conthratong." He had an order for Vauxhall, admitting two, from Mr. Hodgen, then within the Gardens, and singing (as he did at the Back Kitchen and the nobility's concerts the "Body Snatcher," the "Death of General Wolfe," the "Banner of Blood," and other favorite melodies); and, having this order for the admission of two persons, he thought that it would admit three, and had come accordingly to the Gardens with his friends. But, on his way, Captain Costigan had lost the paper of admission—it was not forthcoming at all; and the leedies must go back again, to the great disappointment of one of them, as Pendennis saw.

Arthur had a great deal of good nature for everybody, and sympathized with the misfortunes of all sorts of people: how could he refuse his sympathy in such a case as this? He had seen the innocent face as it looked up to the captain, the appealing look of the girl, the piteous quiver of the mouth, and the final outburst of tears. If it had been his last guinea in the world, he must have paid it to have given the poor little thing pleasure. She turned the sad imploring eyes away directly they lighted upon a stranger, and began to wipe them with her handkerchief. Arthur looked very handsome and kind as he stood before the women, with his hat off, blushing, bowing, generous, a gentleman. "Who are they?" he asked of himself. He thought he had seen the elder lady before.

"If I can be of any service to you, Captain Costigan," the young man said, "I hope you will command me; is there any difficulty about taking these ladies into the garden? Will you kindly make use of my purse? And—I have a ticket myself which will admit two—I hope, ma'am, you will permit me?"

The first impulse of the Prince of Fairoaks was to pay for the whole party, and to make away with his newspaper order as poor Costigan had done with his own ticket. But his instinct, and the appearance of the two women told him that they would be better pleased if he did not give himself the airs of a grand seigneur, and he handed his purse to Costigan, and laughingly pulled out his ticket with one hand, as he offered the other to the elder of the ladies—ladies was not the word—they had bonnets and shawls, and collars and ribbons, and the youngest showed a pretty little foot and boot under her modest gray gown, but his Highness of Fairoaks was courteous to every person who wore a petticoat, whatever its texture was, and the humbler the wearer, only the more stately and polite in his demeanor.

"Fanny, take the gentleman's arm," the elder said; "since you will be so very kind; I've seen you often come in at our gate, sir, and go in to Captain Strong's, at No. 4."

Fanny made a little courtesy, and put her hand under Arthur's arm. It had on a shabby little glove, but it was pretty and small. She was not a child, but she was scarcely a woman as yet; her tears had dried up, and her cheek mantled with youthful blushes, and her eyes glistened with pleasure and gratitude, as she looked up into Arthur's kind face.

Arthur, in a protecting way, put his other hand upon the little one resting on his arm. "Fanny's a very pretty little name," he said, "and so you know me, do you?"

"We keep the lodge, sir, at Shepherd's Inn," Fanny said, with a courtesy; "and I've never been at Vauxhall, sir, and Pa didn't like me to go—and—and—O—O—law, how beautiful!" She shrank back as she spoke, starting with wonder and delight as she saw the Royal Gardens blaze before her with a hundred million of lamps, with a splendor such as the finest fairy tale, the finest pantomime she had ever witnessed at the theater, had never realized. Pen was pleased with her pleasure, and pressed to his side the little hand which clung so kindly to him. "What would I not give for a little of this pleasure?" said the blasé young man.

"Your purse, Pendennis, me dear boy," said the captain's voice behind him. "Will ye count it? it's all roight—no—ye thrust in old Jack Costigan (he thrusts me, ye see, madam). Ye've been me preserver,

Pen (I've known um since choildhood, Mrs. Bolton; he's the proproietor of Fairoaks Castle, and many's the cooper of clart I've dthrunk there with the first nobilitee of his native countee)—Mr. Pendennis, ye've been me preserver, and oi thank ye; me daughtther will thank ye: Mr. Simpson, your humble servant, sir."

If Pen was magnificent in his courtesy to the ladies, what was his splendor in comparison to Captain Costigan's bowing here and there, and crying bravo to the singers?

A man, descended like Costigan, from a long line of Hibernian kings, chieftains, and other magnates and sheriffs of the county, had of course too much dignity and self-respect to walk arrum-in-arrum (as the captain phrased it) with a lady who occasionally swept his room out, and cooked his mutton chops. In the course of their journey from Shepherd's Inn to Vauxhall Gardens, Captain Costigan had walked by the side of the two ladies, in a patronizing and affable manner pointing out to them the edifices worthy of note, and discoursing, according to his wont, about other cities and countries which he had visited, and the people of rank and fashion with whom he had the honor of an acquaintance. Nor could it be expected, nor, indeed, did Mrs. Bolton expect, that, arrived in the royal property, and strongly illuminated by the flare of the twenty thousand additional lamps, the captain would relax from his dignity, and give an arm to a lady who was, in fact, little better than a housekeeper or charwoman.

But Pen, on his part, had no such scruples. Miss Fanny Bolton did not make his bed nor sweep his chambers; and he did not choose to let go his pretty little partner. As for Fanny, her color heightened, and her bright eyes shone the brighter with pleasure, as she leaned for protection on the arm of such a fine gentleman as Mr. Pen. And she looked at numbers of other ladies in the place, and at scores of other gentlemen under whose protection they were walking here and there; and she thought that her gentleman was handsomer and grander looking than any other gent in the place. Of course there were votaries of pleasure of all ranks there—rakish young surgeons, fast young clerks and commercialists, occasional dandies of the guard regiments, and the rest. Old Lord Colchicum was there in attendance upon Mademoiselle Caracoline, who had been riding in the ring; and who talked her native French very loud, and used idiomatic expressions of exceeding strength as she walked about, leaning on the arm of his lordship.

Colchicum was in attendance upon Mademoiselle Caracoline, little Tom Tufthunt was in attendance upon Lord Colchicum; and rather pleased, too, with his position. When Don Juan scales the wall, there's never a want of a Leporello to hold the ladder. Tom Tufthunt was quite happy to act as friend to the elderly viscount, and to carve the fowl, and to make the salad at supper. When Pen and his young lady met the viscount's party, that noble peer only gave Arthur a passing leer of recognition as his lordship's eyes passed from Pen's face under the bonnet of Pen's companion. But Tom Tufthunt wagged his head very good-naturedly at Mr. Arthur, and said, "How are you, old boy?" and looked extremely knowing at the god-father of this history.

"That is the great rider at Astley's; I have seen her there," Miss Bolton said, looking after Mademoiselle Caracoline; "and who is that old man? is it not the gentleman in the ring?"

"That is Lord Viscount Colchicum, Miss Fanny," said Pen, with an air of protection. He meant no harm; he was pleased to patronize the young girl, and he was not displeased that she should be so pretty, and that she should be hanging upon his arm, and that yonder elderly Don Juan should have seen her there.

Fanny was very pretty; her eyes were dark and brilliant; her teeth were like little pearls; her mouth was almost as red as Mademoiselle Caracoline's when the latter had put on her vermilion. And what a difference there was between the one's voice and the other's, between the girl's laugh and the woman's! It was only very lately, indeed, that Fanny, when looking in the little glass over the Bows-Costigan mantle-piece as she was dusting it, had begun to suspect that she was a beauty. But a year ago, she was a clumsy, gawky girl, at whom her father sneered, and of whom the girls at the day-school (Miss Minifer's, Newcastle-street, Strand; Miss M., the younger sister, took the leading business at the Norwich circuit in 182-; and she herself had played for two seasons with some credit T.R.E.O., T.R.S.W., until she fell down a trap-door and broke her leg); the girls at Fanny's school, we say, took no account of her, and thought her a dowdy little creature as long as she remained under Miss Minifer's instruction. And it was unremarked and almost unseen in the dark porter's lodge of Shepherd's Inn, that this little flower bloomed into beauty.

So this young person hung upon Mr. Pen's arm, and they paced the gardens together. Empty as London was, there were still some two millions of people left lingering about it, and among them, one or two of the acquaintances of Mr. Arthur Pendennis.

Among them, silent and alone, pale, with his hands in his pockets, and a rueful nod of the head to Arthur as they met, passed Henry Foker, Esq. Young Henry was trying to ease his mind by moving from place to place, and from excitement to excitement. But he thought about Blanche as he sauntered in the dark walks; he thought about Blanche as he looked at the devices of the lamps. He consulted the fortune-teller about her, and was disappointed when that gipsy told him that he was in love with a dark lady who would make him happy; and at the concert, though Mr. Momus sang his most stunning comic songs, and asked his most astonishing riddles, never did a kind smile come to visit Foker's lips. In fact he never heard Mr. Momus at all.

Pen and Miss Bolton were hard by listening to the same concert, and the latter remarked, and Pen laughed at, Mr. Foker's woe-begone face.

Fanny asked what it was that made that odd-looking little man so dismal? "I think he is crossed in love!" Pen said. "Isn't that enough to make any man dismal, Fanny?" And he looked down at her, splendidly protecting her, like Egmont at Clara in Goethe's play, or Leicester at Amy in Scott's novel.

"Crossed in love is he? poor gentleman," said Fanny with a sigh, and her eyes turned round toward him with no little kindness and pity—but Harry did not see the beautiful dark eyes.

"How-dy-do, Mr. Pendennis!"—a voice broke in here—it was that of a young man in a large white coat with a red neckcloth, over which a dingy short collar was turned, so as to exhibit a dubious neck—with a large pin of bullion or other metal, and an imaginative waistcoat with exceedingly fanciful glass buttons, and trowsers that cried with a loud voice, "Come look at me and see how cheap and tawdry I am; my master, what a dirty buck!" and a little stick in one pocket of his coat, and a lady in pink satin on the other arm—"How-dy-do—Forget me, I dare say? Huxter—Clavering."

"How do you do, Mr. Huxter," the Prince of Fairoaks said, in his most princely manner, "I hope you are very well." "Pretty bobbish, thanky." And Mr. Huxter wagged his head. "I say, Pendennis, you've been coming it uncommon strong since we had the row at Wapshot's, don't you remember. Great author, hay? Go about with the swells. Saw your name in the Morning Post. I suppose you're too much of a swell to come and have a bit of supper with an old friend?—Charterhouse-lane to-morrow night—some devilish good fellows from Bartholomew's, and some stunning gin punch. Here's my card." And with this Mr. Huxter released his hand from the pocket where his cane was, and pulling off the top of his card case with his teeth produced thence a visiting ticket, which he handed to Pen.

"You are exceedingly kind, I am sure," said Pen: "but I regret that I have an engagement which will take me out of town to-morrow night." And the Marquis of Fairoaks wondering that such a creature as this could have the audacity to give him a card, put Mr. Huxter's card into his waistcoat pocket with a lofty courtesy. Possibly Mr. Samuel Huxter was not aware that there was any great social difference between Mr. Arthur Pendennis and himself. Mr. Huxter's father was a surgeon and apothecary at Clavering, just as Mr. Pendennis's papa had been a surgeon and apothecary at Bath. But the impudence of some men is beyond all calculation.

"Well, old fellow, never mind," said Mr. Huxter, who, always frank and familiar, was from vinous excitement even more affable than usual. "If ever you are passing, look up at our place—I'm mostly at home Saturdays; and there's generally a cheese in the cupboard. Ta, Ta. There's the bell for the fire-works ringing. Come along, Mary." And he set off running with the rest of the crowd in the direction of the fireworks.

So did Pen presently, when this agreeable youth was out of sight, begin to run with his little companion; Mrs. Bolton following after them, with Captain Costigan at her side. But the captain was too majestic and dignified in his movements to run for friend or enemy, and he pursued his course with the usual jaunty swagger which distinguished his steps, so that he and his companion were speedily distanced by Pen and Miss Fanny.

Perhaps Arthur forgot, or perhaps he did not choose to remember, that the elder couple had no money in their pockets, as had been proved by their adventure at the entrance of the gardens; howbeit, Pen paid a couple of shillings for himself and his partner, and with her hanging close on his arm, scaled the staircase which leads to the fire-work gallery. The captain and mamma might have followed them if they liked, but Arthur and Fanny were too busy to look back. People were pushing and squeezing there beside and behind them. One eager individual rushed by Fanny, and elbowed her so, that she fell back with a little cry, upon which, of course, Arthur caught her adroitly in his arms, and, just for protection, kept her so defended until they mounted the stair, and took their places.

Poor Foker sate alone on one of the highest benches, his face illuminated by the fire-works, or in their absence by the moon. Arthur saw him, and laughed, but did not occupy himself about his friend much. He was engaged with Fanny. How she wondered! how happy she was! how she cried O, O, O, as the rockets soared into the air, and showered down in azure, and emerald, and vermilion. As these wonders blazed and disappeared before her, the little girl thrilled and trembled with delight at Arthur's side—her hand was under his arm still, he felt it pressing him as she looked up delighted.

"How beautiful they are, sir!" she cried.

"Don't call me sir, Fanny," Arthur said.

A quick blush rushed up into the girl's face. "What shall I call you?" she said, in a low voice, sweet and tremulous. "What would you wish me to say, sir?"

"Again, Fanny? Well, I forgot; it is best so, my dear," Pendennis said, very kindly and gently. "I may call you Fanny?"

"O yes!" she said, and the little hand pressed his arm once more very eagerly, and the girl clung to him so that he could feel her heart beating on his shoulder.

"I may call you Fanny, because you are a young girl, and a good girl, Fanny, and I am an old gentleman. But you mustn't call me any thing but sir, or Mr. Pendennis, if you like; for we live in very different stations, Fanny; and don't think I speak unkindly; and—and why do you take your hand away, Fanny? Are you afraid of me? Do you think I would hurt you? Not for all the world, my dear little girl. And—and look how beautiful the moon and stars are, and how calmly they shine when the rockets have gone out, and the noisy wheels have done hissing and blazing. When I came here to-night, I did not think I should have had such a pretty little companion to sit by my side, and see these fine fire-works. You must know I live by myself, and work very hard. I write in books and newspapers, Fanny; and I was quite tired out, and expected to sit alone all night; and—don't cry, my dear, dear, little girl." Here Pen broke out, rapidly putting an end to the calm oration which he had begun to deliver; for the sight of a woman's tears always put his nerves in a quiver, and he began forthwith to coax her and soothe her, and to utter a hundred-and-twenty little ejaculations of pity and sympathy, which need not be repeated here, because they would be absurd in print. So would a mother's talk to a child be absurd in print; so would a lover's to his bride. That sweet, artless poetry bears no translation; and is too subtle for grammarian's clumsy definitions. You have but the same four letters to describe the salute which you perform on your grandmother's forehead, and that which you bestow on the sacred cheek of your mistress; but the same four letters, and not one of them a labial. Do we mean to hint that Mr. Arthur Pendennis made any use of the monosyllable in question? Not so. In the first place it was dark: the fire-works were over, and nobody could see him; secondly, he was not a man to have this kind of secret, and tell it; thirdly and lastly, let the honest fellow who has kissed a pretty girl, say what would have been his own conduct in such a delicate juncture?

Well, the truth is, that however you may suspect him, and whatever you would have done under the circumstances, or Mr. Pen would have liked to do, he behaved honestly, and like a man. "I will not play with this little girl's heart," he said within himself, "and forget my own or her honor. She seems to have a great deal of dangerous and rather contagious sensibility, and I am very glad the fire-works are over; and that I can take her back to her mother. Come along, Fanny; mind the steps, and lean on me. Don't stumble, you heedless little thing; this is the way, and there is your mamma at the door."

And there, indeed, Mrs. Bolton was, unquiet in spirit, and grasping her umbrella. She seized Fanny with maternal fierceness and eagerness, and uttered some rapid abuse to the girl in an under tone. The expression in Captain Costigan's eye—standing behind the matron and winking at Pendennis from under his hat—was, I am bound to say, indefinably humorous.

It was so much so, that Pen could not refrain from bursting into a laugh. "You should have taken my arm, Mrs. Bolton," he said, offering it. "I am very glad to bring Miss Fanny back quite safe to you. We thought you would have followed us up into the gallery. We enjoyed the fire-works, didn't we?"

"Oh, yes!" said Miss Fanny, with rather a demure look.

"And the bouquet was magnificent," said Pen. "And it is ten hours since I had any thing to eat, ladies, and I wish you would permit me to invite you to supper."

"Dad," said Costigan, "I'd loike a snack, tu; only I forgawt me purse, or I should have invoited these leedies to a colleetion."

Mrs. Bolton, with considerable asperity, said, she ad an eadache, and would much rather go home.

"A lobster salad is the best thing in the world for a headache," Pen said, gallantly, "and a glass of wine I'm sure will do you good. Come, Mrs. Bolton, be kind to me, and oblige me. I shan't have the heart to sup without you, and upon my word, I have had no dinner. Give me your arm: give me the umbrella. Costigan, I'm sure you'll take care of Miss Fanny; and I shall think Mrs. Bolton angry with me, unless she will favor me with her society. And we will all sup quietly, and go back in a cab together."

The cab, the lobster salad, the frank and good-humored look of Pendennis, as he smilingly invited the worthy matron, subdued her suspicions and her anger. Since he would be so obliging, she thought she could take a little bit of lobster, and so they all marched away to a box; and Costigan called for a waither with such a loud and belligerent voice, as caused one of those officials instantly to run to him.

The carte was examined on the wall, and Fanny was asked to choose her favorite dish; upon which the young creature said she was fond of lobster, too, but also owned to a partiality for raspberry-tart. This delicacy was provided by Pen, and a bottle of the most frisky Champagne was moreover ordered for the delight of the ladies. Little Fanny drank this: what other sweet intoxication had she not drunk in the course of the night?

When the supper, which was very brisk and gay, was over, and Captain Costigan and Mrs. Bolton had partaken of some of the rack punch that is so fragrant at Vauxhall, the bill was called and discharged by Pen with great generosity, "like a foin young English gentleman of th' olden toime, be Jove," Costigan enthusiastically remarked. And as, when they went out of the box, he stepped forward and gave Mrs. Bolton his arm, Fanny fell to Pen's lot, and the young people walked away in high good-humor together, in the wake of their seniors.

The Champagne and the rack punch, though taken in moderation by all persons, except perhaps poor Cos, who lurched ever so little in his gait, had set them in high spirits and good humor, so that Fanny began to skip and move her brisk little feet in time to the band, which was playing waltzes and galops for the dancers. As they came up to the dancing, the music and Fanny's feet seemed to go quicker together; she seemed to spring, as if naturally, from the ground, and as if she required repression to keep her there.

"Shouldn't you like a turn?" said the Prince of Fairoaks. "What fun it would be! Mrs. Bolton, ma'am, do let me take her once round." Upon which Mr. Costigan said, "Off wid you!" and Mrs. Bolton not refusing (indeed, she was an old war-horse, and would have liked, at the trumpet's sound, to have entered the arena herself), Fanny's shawl was off her back in a minute, and she and Arthur were whirling round in a waltz in the midst of a great deal of queer, but exceedingly joyful company.

Pen had no mishap this time with little Fanny, as he had with Miss Blanche in old days; at least, there was no mishap of his making. The pair danced away with great agility and contentment; first a waltz, then a galop, then a waltz again, until, in the second waltz, they were bumped by another couple who had joined the Terpsichorean choir. This was Mr. Huxter and his pink satin young friend, of whom we have already had a glimpse.

Mr. Huxter very probably had been also partaking of supper, for he was even more excited now than at the time when he had previously claimed Pen's acquaintance; and having run against Arthur and his partner, and nearly knocked them down, this amiable gentleman of course began to abuse the people whom he had injured, and broke out into a volley of slang against the unoffending couple. "Now, then, stoopid! Don't keep the ground if you can't dance, old Slow Coach!" the young surgeon roared out (using, at the same time, other expressions far more emphatic), and was joined in his abuse by the shrill language and laughter of his partner, to the interruption of the ball, the terror of poor little Fanny, and the immense indignation of Pen.

Arthur was furious; and not so angry at the quarrel as at the shame attending it. A battle with a fellow like that! A row in a public garden, and with a porter's daughter on his arm! What a position for Arthur Pendennis! He drew poor little Fanny hastily away from the dancers to her mother, and wished that lady, and Costigan, and poor Fanny underground, rather than there, in his companionship, and under his protection.

When Huxter commenced his attack, that free spoken young gentleman had not seen who was his opponent, and directly he was aware that it was Arthur whom he had insulted, he began to make apologies. "Hold your stoopid tongue, Mary," he said to his partner. "It's an old friend and crony at home. I beg pardon, Pendennis; wasn't aware it was you, old boy" Mr. Huxter had been one of the boys of the Clavering School, who had been present at a combat which has been mentioned in the early part of this story, when young Pen knocked down the biggest champion of the academy, and Huxter knew that it was dangerous to quarrel with Arthur.

His apologies were as odious to the other as his abuse had been. Pen stopped his tipsy remonstrances by telling him to hold his tongue, and desiring him not to use his (Pendennis's) name in that place or any other; and he walked out of the gardens with a titter behind him from the crowd, every one of whom he would have liked to massacre for having been witness to the degrading broil. He walked out of the gardens, quite forgetting poor little Fanny, who came trembling behind him with her mother and the stately Costigan.

He was brought back to himself by a word from the captain, who touched him on the shoulder just as they were passing the inner gate.

"There's no ray-admittance except ye pay again," the captain said. "Hadn't I better go back and take the fellow your message?"

Pen burst out laughing, "Take him a message! Do you think I would fight with such a fellow as that?" he asked.

"No, no! Don't, don't!" cried out little Fanny. "How can you be so wicked, Captain Costigan?" The captain muttered something about honor, and winked knowingly at Pen, but Arthur said gallantly, "No, Fanny, don't be frightened. It was my fault to have danced in such a place. I beg your pardon, to have asked you to dance there." And he gave her his arm once more, and called a cab, and put his three friends into it.

He was about to pay the driver, and to take another carriage for himself, when little Fanny, still alarmed, put her little hand out, and caught him by the coat, and implored him and besought him to come in.

"Will nothing satisfy you," said Pen, in great good-humor, "that I am not going back to fight him? Well, I will come home with you. Drive to Shepherd's Inn, Cab." The cab drove to its destination. Arthur was immensely pleased by the girl's solicitude about him: her tender terrors quite made him forget his previous annoyance.

Pen put the ladies into their lodge, having shaken hands kindly with both of them; and the captain again whispered to him that he would see um in the morning if he was inclined, and take his message to that "scounthrel." But the captain was in his usual condition when he made the proposal; and Pen was perfectly sure that neither he nor Mr. Huxter, when they awoke, would remember any thing about the dispute.

CHAPTER IX

A VISIT OF POLITENESS

Costigan never roused Pen from his slumbers; there was no hostile message from Mr. Huxter to disturb him; and when Pen woke, it was with a brisker and more lively feeling than ordinarily attends that moment in the day of the tired and blasé London man. A city man wakes up to care and consols, and the thoughts of 'Change and the counting-house take possession of him as soon as sleep flies from under his nightcap; a lawyer rouses himself with the early morning to think of the case that will take him all his day to work upon, and the inevitable attorney to whom he has promised his papers ere night. Which of us has not his anxiety instantly present when his eyes are opened, to it and to the world, after his night's sleep? Kind strengthener that enables us to face the day's task with renewed heart! Beautiful ordinance of Providence that creates rest as it awards labor.

Mr. Pendennis's labor, or rather his disposition, was of that sort that his daily occupations did not much interest him, for the excitement of literary composition pretty soon subsides with the hired laborer, and the delight of seeing one's self in print only extends to the first two or three appearances in the magazine or newspaper page. Pegasus put into harness, and obliged to run a stage every day, is as prosaic as any other hack, and won't work without his whip or his feed of corn. So, indeed Mr. Arthur performed his work at the Pall Mall Gazette (and since his success as a novelist with an increased salary), but without the least enthusiasm, doing his best or pretty nearly, and sometimes writing ill and sometimes well. He was a literary hack, naturally fast in pace, and brilliant in action. Neither did society, or that portion which he saw, excite or amuse him overmuch. In spite of his brag and boast to the contrary, he was too young as yet for women's society, which probably can only be had in perfection when a man has ceased to think about his own person, and has given up all designs of being a conqueror of ladies; he was too young to be admitted as an equal among men who had made their mark in the world, and of whose conversation he could scarcely as yet expect to be more than a listener. And he was too old for the men of pleasure of his own age; too much a man of pleasure for the men of business; destined, in a word, to be a good deal alone. Fate awards this lot of solitude to many a man; and many like it from taste, as many without difficulty bear it. Pendennis, in reality, suffered it very equanimously; but in words, and according to his wont, grumbled over it not a little.

"What a nice little artless creature that was," Mr. Pen thought at the very instant of waking after the Vauxhall affair; "what a pretty natural manner she has; how much pleasanter than the minanderies of the young ladies in the ball-rooms" (and here he recalled to himself some instances of what he could not help seeing was the artful simplicity of Miss Blanche, and some of the stupid graces of other young ladies in the polite world); "who could have thought that such a pretty rose could grow in a porter's lodge, or bloom in that dismal old flower-pot of a Shepherd's Inn? So she learns to sing from old Bows? If her singing voice is as sweet as her speaking voice, it must be pretty. I like those low voilées voices. 'What would you like me to call you?' indeed. Poor little Fanny! It went to my heart to adopt the grand air with her, and tell her to call me 'sir.' But we'll have no nonsense of that sort—no Faust and Margaret business for me. That old Bows! So he teaches her to sing, does he? He's a dear old fellow, old Bows: a gentleman in those old clothes: a philosopher, and with a kind heart, too. How good he was to me in the Fotheringay business. He, too, has had his griefs and his sorrows. I must cultivate old Bows. A man ought to see people of all sorts. I am getting tired of genteel society. Besides, there's nobody in town. Yes, I'll go and see Bows, and Costigan, too; what a rich character! begad, I'll study him, and put him into a book." In this way our young anthropologist talked with himself: and as Saturday was the holiday of the week, the "Pall Mall Gazette" making its appearance upon that day, and the contributors to that journal having no further calls upon their brains or ink-bottles, Mr. Pendennis determined he would take advantage of his leisure, and pay a visit to Shepherd's Inn—of course to see old Bows.

The truth is, that if Arthur had been the most determined roué and artful Lovelace who ever set about deceiving a young girl, he could hardly have adopted better means for fascinating and overcoming poor little Fanny Bolton than those which he had employed on the previous night. His dandyfied protecting air, his conceit, generosity, and good humor, the very sense of good and honesty which had enabled him to check the tremulous advances of the young creature, and not to take advantage of that little fluttering sensibility—his faults and his virtues at once contributed to make her admire him; and if we could peep into Fanny's bed (which she shared in a cupboard, along with those two little sisters to whom we have seen Mr. Costigan administering ginger-bread and apples), we should find the poor little maid tossing upon her mattress, to the great disturbance of its other two occupants, and thinking over all the delights and events of that delightful, eventful night, and all the words, looks, and actions of Arthur, its splendid hero. Many novels had Fanny read, in secret and at home, in three volumes and in numbers. Periodical literature had not reached the height which it has attained subsequently, and the girls of Fanny's generation were not enabled to purchase sixteen pages of excitement for a penny, rich with histories of crime, murder, oppressed virtue, and the heartless seductions of the aristocracy; but she had had the benefit of the circulating library which, in conjunction with her school and a small brandy-ball and millinery business, Miss Minifer kept—and Arthur appeared to her at once as the type and realization of all the heroes of all those darling, greasy volumes which the young girl had devoured. Mr. Pen, we have seen, was rather a dandy about shirts and haberdashery in general. Fanny had looked with delight at the fineness of his linen, at the brilliancy of his shirt studs, at his elegant cambric pocket-handkerchief and white gloves, and at the jetty brightness of his charming boots. The prince had appeared and subjugated the poor little handmaid. His image traversed constantly her restless slumbers; the tone of his voice, the blue light of his eyes, the generous look, half love half pity—the manly protecting smile, the frank, winning laughter—all these were repeated in the girl's fond memory. She felt still his arm encircling her, and saw him smiling so grand as he filled up that delicious glass of Champagne. And then she thought of the girls, her friends, who used to sneer at her—of Emma Baker, who was so proud, forsooth, because she was engaged to a cheesemonger, in a white apron, near Clare Market; and of Betsy Rodgers, who made such a to-do about her young man—an attorney's clerk, indeed, that went about with a bag!

So that, at about two o'clock in the afternoon—the Bolton family having concluded, their dinner (and Mr. B., who besides his place of porter of the Inn, was in the employ of Messrs. Tressler, the eminent undertakers of the Strand, being absent in the country with the Countess of Estrich's hearse), when a gentleman in a white hat and white trowsers made his appearance under the Inn archway, and stopped at the porter's wicket, Fanny was not in the least surprised, only delighted, only happy, and blushing beyond all measure. She knew it could be no other than He. She knew He'd come. There he was: there was His Royal Highness beaming upon her from the gate. She called to her mother, who was busy in the upper apartment, "Mamma, mamma," and ran to the wicket at once, and opened it, pushing aside the other children. How she blushed as she gave her hand to him! How affably he took off his white hat as he came in; the children staring up at him! He asked Mrs. Bolton if she had slept well, after the fatigues of the night, and hoped she had no headache: and he said that as he was going that way, he could not pass the door without asking news of his little partner.

Mrs. Bolton was, perhaps, rather shy and suspicious about these advances; but Mr. Pen's good humor was inexhaustible, he could not see that he was unwelcome. He looked about the premises for a seat, and none being disengaged, for a dish-cover was on one, a work-box on the other, and so forth, he took one of the children's chairs, and perched himself upon that uncomfortable eminence. At this, the children began laughing, the child Fanny louder than all; at least, she was more amused than any of them, and amazed at his Royal Highness's condescension. He to sit down in that chair—that little child's chair! Many and many a time after she regarded it: haven't we almost all, such furniture in our rooms, that our fancy peoples with dear figures, that our memory fills with sweet, smiling faces, which may never look on us more?

So Pen sate down, and talked away with great volubility to Mrs. Bolton. He asked about the undertaking business, and how many mutes went down with Lady Estrich's remains; and about the Inn, and who lived there. He seemed very much interested about Mr. Campion's cab and horse, and had met that gentleman in society. He thought he should like shares in the Polwheedle and Pontydiddlum; did Mrs. Bolton do for those chambers? Were there any chambers to let in the Inn? It was better than the Temple: he should like to come to live in Shepherd's Inn. As for Captain Strong and—Colonel Altamont was his name? he was deeply interested in them, too. The captain was an old friend at home. He had dined with him at chambers here, before the colonel came to live with him. What sort of man was the colonel? Wasn't he a stout man, with a large quantity of jewelry, and a wig, and large black whiskers, very black (here Pen was immensely waggish, and caused hysteric giggles of delight from the ladies), very black, indeed; in fact, blue-black; that is to say, a rich greenish purple? That was the man; he had met him, too, at Sir F—in society.

"O, we know!" said the ladies; "Sir F—is Sir F. Clavering; he's often here: two or three times a week with the captain. My little boy has been out for bill stamps for him. Oh, Lor! I beg pardon, I shouldn't have mentioned no secrets," Mrs. Bolton blurted out, being talked perfectly into good-nature by this time. "But we know you to be a gentleman, Mr. Pendennis, for I'm sure you have shown that you can beayve as such. Hasn't Mr. Pendennis, Fanny?"

Fanny loved her mother for that speech. She cast up her dark eyes to the low ceiling, and said, "O, that he has, I'm sure, ma," with a voice full of feeling.

Pen was rather curious about the bill stamps, and concerning the transactions in Strong's chambers. And he asked, when Altamont came and joined the chevalier, whether he, too, sent out for bill stamps, who he was, whether he saw many people, and so forth. These questions, put with considerable adroitness by Pen, who was interested about Sir Francis Clavering's doings from private motives of his own, were artlessly answered by Mrs. Bolton. and to the utmost of her knowledge and ability, which, in truth, were not very great.

These questions answered, and Pen being at a loss for more, luckily recollected his privilege as a member of the press, and asked the ladies whether they would like any orders for the play? The play was their delight, as it is almost always the delight of every theatrical person. When Bolton was away professionally (it appeared that of late the porter of Shepherd's Inn had taken a serious turn, drank a good deal, and otherwise made himself unpleasant to the ladies of his family), they would like of all things to slip out and go to the theater, little Barney their son, keeping the lodge; and Mr. Pendennis's most generous and most genteel compliment of orders was received with boundless gratitude by both mother and daughter.

Fanny clapped her hands with pleasure: her face beamed with it. She looked, and nodded, and laughed at her mamma, who nodded and laughed in her turn. Mrs. Bolton was not superannuated for pleasure yet, or by any means too old for admiration, she thought. And very likely Mr. Pendennis, in his conversation with her, had insinuated some compliments, or shaped his talk so as to please her. At first against Pen, and suspicious of him, she was his partisan now, and almost as enthusiastic about him as her daughter. When two women get together to like a man, they help each other on; each pushes the other forward, and the second, out of sheer sympathy, becomes as eager as the principal: at least, so it is said by philosophers who have examined this science.

So the offer of the play tickets, and other pleasantries, put all parties into perfect good-humor, except for one brief moment, when one of the younger children, hearing the name of "Astley's" pronounced, came forward and stated that she should like very much to go, too; on which Fanny said, "Don't bother!" rather sharply; and mamma said, "Git-long, Betsy Jane, do now, and play in the court:" so that the two little ones, namely, Betsy Jane and Ameliar Ann, went away in their little innocent pinafores, and disported in the court-yard on the smooth gravel, round about the statue of Shepherd the Great.

And here, as they were playing, they very possibly communicated with an old friend of theirs and dweller in the Inn; for while Pen was making himself agreeable to the ladies at the lodge, who were laughing, delighted at his sallies, an old gentleman passed under the archway from the Inn-square, and came and looked in at the door of the lodge.

He made a very blank and rueful face when he saw Mr. Arthur seated upon a table, like Macheath in the play, in easy discourse with Mrs. Bolton and her daughter.

"What! Mr. Bows? How d'you do, Bows!" cried out Pen, in a cheery, loud voice. "I was coming to see you, and was asking your address of these ladies."

"You were coming to see me, were you, sir?" Bows said, and came in with a sad face, and shook hands with Arthur. "Plague on that old man!" somebody thought in the room: and so, perhaps, some one else besides her.

CHAPTER X

IN SHEPHERD'S INN

Our friend Pen said "How d'ye do, Mr. Bows," in a loud, cheery voice, on perceiving that gentleman, and saluted him in a dashing, off-hand manner; yet you could have seen a blush upon Arthur's face (answered by Fanny, whose cheek straightway threw out a similar fluttering red signal), and after Bows and Arthur had shaken hands, and the former had ironically accepted the other's assertion that he was about to pay Mr. Costigan's chambers a visit, there was a gloomy and rather guilty silence in the company, which Pen presently tried to dispel by making a great rattling and noise. The silence of course departed at Mr. Arthur's noise, but the gloom remained and deepened, as the darkness does in a vault if you light up a single taper in it. Pendennis tried to describe, in a jocular manner, the transactions of the night previous, and attempted to give an imitation of Costigan vainly expostulating with the check-taker at Vauxhall. It was not a good imitation. What stranger can imitate that perfection? Nobody laughed. Mrs. Bolton did not in the least understand what part Mr. Pendennis was performing, and whether it was the check-taker or the captain he was taking off. Fanny wore an alarmed face, and tried a timid giggle; old Mr. Bows looked as glum as when he fiddled in the orchestra, or played a difficult piece upon the old piano at the Back-Kitchen. Pen felt that his story was a failure; his voice sank and dwindled away dismally at the end of it—flickered, and went out; and it was all dark again. You could hear the ticket-porter, who lolls about Shepherd's Inn, as he passed on the flags under the archway: the clink of his boot-heels was noted by every body.

"You were coming to see me, sir," Mr. Bows said. "Won't you have the kindness to walk up to my chambers with me? You do them a great honor, I am sure. They are rather high up; but—"

"O! I live in a garret myself, and Shepherd's Inn is twice as cheerful as Lamb Court," Mr. Pendennis broke in.

"I knew that you had third floor apartments," Mr. Bows said; "and was going to say—you will please not take my remark as discourteous—that the air up three pair of stairs is wholesomer for gentlemen, than the air of a porter's lodge."

"Sir!" said Pen, whose candle flamed up again in his wrath, and who was disposed to be as quarrelsome as men are when they are in the wrong. "Will you permit me to choose my society without—"

"You were so polite as to say that you were about to honor my umble domicile with a visit," Mr. Bows said, with a sad voice. "Shall I show you the way? Mr. Pendennis and I are old friends, Mrs. Bolton—very old acquaintances; and at the earliest dawn of his life we crossed each other."

The old man pointed toward the door with a trembling finger, and a hat in the other hand, and in an attitude slightly theatrical; so were his words, when he spoke, somewhat artificial, and chosen from the vocabulary which he had heard all his life from the painted lips of the orators before the stage-lamps. But he was not acting or masquerading, as Pen knew very well, though he was disposed to pooh-pooh the old fellow's melodramatic airs. "Come along, sir," he said, "as you are so very pressing. Mrs. Bolton, I wish you a good day. Good-by, Miss Fanny; I shall always think of our night at Vauxhall with pleasure; and be sure I will remember the theatre-tickets." And he took her hand, pressed it, was pressed by it, and was gone.

"What a nice young man, to be sure!" cried Mrs. Bolton.

"D'you think so, ma?" said Fanny.

"I was a-thinkin who he was like. When I was at the Wells with Mrs. Serle," Mrs. Bolton continued, looking through the window curtain after Pen, as he went up the court with Bows; "there was a young gentleman from the city, that used to come in a tilbry, in a white at, the very image of him, ony his whiskers was black, and Mr. P's. is red.

"Law, ma! they are a most beautiful hawburn," Fanny said.

"He used to come for Emly Budd, who danced Columbine in 'Arleykin Ornpipe, or the Battle of Navarino,' when Miss De la Bosky was took ill—a pretty dancer, and a fine stage figure of a woman—and he was a great sugar-baker in the city, with a country ouse at Omerton; and he used to drive her in the tilbry down Goswell-street-road; and one day they drove and was married at St. Bartholomew's Church Smithfield, where they had their bands read quite private; and she now keeps her carriage; and I sor her name in the paper as patroness of the Manshing-House Ball for the Washywomen's Asylum. And look at Lady Mirabel—Capting Costigan's daughter—she was profeshnl, as all very well know." Thus, and more to this purpose, Mrs. Bolton spoke, now peeping through the window-curtain, now cleaning the mugs and plates, and consigning them to their place in the corner cupboard; and finishing her speech as she and Fanny shook out and folded up the dinner-cloth between them, and restored it to its drawer in the table.

Although Costigan had once before been made pretty accurately to understand what Pen's pecuniary means and expectations were, I suppose Cos had forgotten the information acquired at Chatteris years ago, or had been induced by his natural enthusiasm to exaggerate his friend's income. He had described Fairoaks Park in the most glowing terms to Mrs. Bolton, on the preceding evening, as he was walking about with her during Pen's little escapade with Fanny, had dilated upon the enormous wealth of Pen's famous uncle, the major, and shown an intimate acquaintance with Arthur's funded and landed property. Very likely Mrs. Bolton, in her wisdom, had speculated upon these matters during the night; and had had visions of Fanny driving in her carriage, like Mrs. Bolton's old comrade, the dancer of Sadler's Wells.

In the last operation of table-cloth folding, these two foolish women, of necessity, came close together; and as Fanny took the cloth and gave it the last fold, her mother put her finger under the young girl's chin, and kissed her. Again the red signal flew out, and fluttered on Fanny's cheek. What did it mean? It was not alarm this time. It was pleasure which caused the poor little Fanny to blush so. Poor little Fanny! What? is love sin; that it is so pleasant at the beginning, and so bitter at the end?

After the embrace, Mrs. Bolton thought proper to say that she was a-goin out upon business, and that Fanny must keep the lodge; which Fanny, after a very faint objection indeed, consented to do. So Mrs. Bolton took her bonnet and market-basket, and departed; and the instant she was gone, Fanny went and sate by the window which commanded Bows's door, and never once took her eyes away from that quarter of Shepherd's Inn.

Betsy-Jane and Ameliar-Ann were buzzing in one corner of the place, and making believe to read out of a picture-book, which one of them held topsy-turvy. It was a grave and dreadful tract, of Mr. Bolton's collection. Fanny did not hear her sisters prattling over it. She noticed nothing but Bows's door.

At last she gave a little shake, and her eyes lighted up. He had come out. He would pass the door again. But her poor little countenance fell in an instant more. Pendennis, indeed, came out; but Bows followed after him. They passed under the archway together. He only took off his hat, and bowed as he looked in. He did not stop to speak.

In three or four minutes—Fanny did not know how long, but she looked furiously at him when he came into the lodge—Bows returned alone, and entered into the porter's room.

"Where's your ma, dear?" he said to Fanny.

"I don't know," Fanny said, with an angry toss. "I don't follow ma's steps wherever she goes, I suppose, Mr. Bows."

"Am I my mother's keeper?" Bows said, with his usual melancholy bitterness. "Come here, Betsy-Jane and Amelia-Ann; I've brought a cake for the one who can read her letters best, and a cake for the other who can read them the next best."

When the young ladies had undergone the examination through which Bows put them, they were rewarded with their gingerbread medals, and went off to discuss them in the court. Meanwhile Fanny took out some work, and pretended to busy herself with it, her mind being in great excitement and anger, as she plied her needle, Bows sate so that he could command the entrance from the lodge to the street. But the person whom, perhaps, he expected to see, never made his appearance again. And Mrs. Bolton came in from market, and found Mr. Bows in place of the person whom she had expected to see. The reader perhaps can guess what was his name?

The interview between Bows and his guest, when those two mounted to the apartment occupied by the former in common with the descendant of the Milesian kings, was not particularly satisfactory to either party. Pen was sulky. If Bows had any thing on his mind, he did not care to deliver himself of his thoughts in the presence of Captain Costigan, who remained in the apartment during the whole of Pen's visit; having quitted his bed-chamber, indeed, but a very few minutes before the arrival of that gentleman. We have witnessed the deshabillé of Major Pendennis: will any man wish to be valet-de-chambre to our other hero, Costigan? It would seem that the captain, before issuing from his bedroom, scented himself with otto of whisky. A rich odor of that delicious perfume breathed from out him, as he held out the grasp of cordiality to his visitor. The hand which performed that grasp shook woefully: it was a wonder how it could hold the razor with which the poor gentleman daily operated on his chin.

Bows's room was as neat, on the other hand, as his comrade's was disorderly. His humble wardrobe hung behind a curtain. His books and manuscript music were trimly arranged upon shelves. A lithographed portrait of Miss Fotheringay, as Mrs. Haller, with the actress's sprawling signature at the corner, hung faithfully over the old gentleman's bed. Lady Mirabel wrote much better than Miss Fotheringay had been able to do. Her ladyship had labored assiduously to acquire the art of penmanship since her marriage; and, in a common note of invitation or acceptance, acquitted herself very genteelly. Bows loved the old handwriting best, though; the fair artist's earlier manner. He had but one specimen of the new style, a note in reply to a song composed and dedicated to Lady Mirabel, by her most humble servant Robert Bows; and which document was treasured in his desk among his other state papers. He was teaching Fanny Bolton now to sing and to write, as he had taught Emily in former days. It was the nature of the man to attach himself to something. When Emily was torn from him he took a substitute: as a man looks out for a crutch when he loses a leg, or lashes himself to a raft when he has suffered shipwreck. Latude had given his heart to a woman, no doubt, before he grew to be so fond of a mouse in the Bastille. There are people who in their youth have felt and inspired an heroic passion, and end by being happy in the caresses, or agitated by the illness of a poodle. But it was hard upon Bows, and grating to his feelings as a man and a sentimentalist, that he should find Pen again upon his track, and in pursuit of this little Fanny.

Meanwhile, Costigan had not the least idea but that his company was perfectly welcome to Messrs. Pendennis and Bows, and that the visit of the former was intended for himself. He expressed himself greatly pleased with that mark of poloightness, and promised, in his own mind, that he would repay that obligation at least—which was not the only debt which the captain owed in life—by several visits to his young friend. He entertained him affably with news of the day, or rather of ten days previous; for Pen, in his quality of journalist, remembered to have seen some of the captain's opinions in the Sporting and Theatrical Newspaper, which was Costigan's oracle. He stated that Sir Charles and Lady Mirabel were gone to Baden-Baden, and were most pressing in their invitations that he should join them there. Pen replied with great gravity, that he had heard that Baden was very pleasant, and the Grand Duke exceedingly hospitable to English. Costigan answered, that the laws of hospitalitee bekeam a Grand Juke; that he sariously would think about visiting him; and made some remarks upon the splendid festivities at Dublin Castle, when his Excellency the Earl of Portansherry held the Viceraygal Coort there, and of which he Costigan had been an humble but pleased spectator. And Pen—as he heard these oft-told, well-remembered legends—recollected the time when he had given a sort of credence to them, and had a certain respect for the captain. Emily and first love, and the little room at Chatteris; and the kind talk with Bows on the bridge came back to him. He felt quite kindly disposed toward his two old friends; and cordially shook the hands of both of them when he rose to go away.

He had quite forgotten about little Fanny Bolton while the captain was talking, and Pen himself was absorbed in other selfish meditations, He only remembered her again as Bows came hobbling down the stairs after him, bent evidently upon following him out of Shepherd's Inn.

Mr. Bows's precaution was not a lucky one. The wrath of Mr. Arthur Pendennis rose at the poor old fellow's feeble persecution. Confound him, what does he mean by dogging me? thought Pen. And he burst out laughing when he was in the Strand and by himself, as he thought of the elder's stratagem. It was not an honest laugh, Arthur Pendennis. Perhaps the thought struck Arthur himself, and he blushed at his own sense of humor. He went off to endeavor to banish the thoughts which occupied him, whatever those thoughts might be, and tried various places of amusement with but indifferent success. He struggled up the highest stairs of the Panorama; but when he had arrived, panting, at the height of the eminence, Care had come up with him, and was bearing him company. He went to the Club, and wrote a long letter home, exceedingly witty and sarcastic, and in which, if he did not say a single word about Vauxhall and Fanny Bolton, it was because he thought that subject, however interesting to himself, would not be very interesting to his mother and Laura. Nor could the novels on the library table fix his attention, nor the grave and respectable Jawkins (the only man in town), who wished to engage him in conversation; nor any of the amusements which he tried, after flying from Jawkins. He passed a Comic Theater on his way home, and saw "Stunning Farce," "Roars of Laughter," "Good Old English Fun and Frolic," placarded in vermilion letters on the gate. He went into the pit, and saw the lovely Mrs. Leary, as usual, in a man's attire; and that eminent buffo actor, Tom Horseman, dressed as a woman. Horseman's travestie seemed to him a horrid and hideous degradation; Mrs. Leary's glances and ankles had not the least effect. He laughed again, and bitterly, to himself, as he thought of the effect which she had produced upon him, on the first night of his arrival in London, a short time—what a long, long time ago.

CHAPTER XI

IN OR NEAR THE TEMPLE GARDEN

Fashion has long deserted the green and pretty Temple Garden, in which Shakspeare makes York and Lancaster to pluck the innocent white and red roses which became the badges of their bloody wars; and the learned and pleasant writer of the Handbook of London tells us that "the commonest and hardiest kind of rose has long ceased to put forth a bud" in that smoky air. Not many of the present occupiers of the buildings round about the quarter know, or care, very likely, whether or not roses grow there, or pass the old gate, except on their way to chambers. The attorneys' clerks don't carry flowers in their bags, or posies under their arms, as they run to the counsel's chambers; the few lawyers who take constitutional walks think very little about York and Lancaster, especially since the railroad business is over. Only antiquarians and literary amateurs care to look at the gardens with much interest, and fancy good Sir Roger de Coverley and Mr. Spectator with his short face pacing up and down the road; or dear Oliver Goldsmith in the summer-house, perhaps meditating about the next "Citizen of the World," or the new suit that Mr. Filby, the tailor, is fashioning for him, or the dunning letter that Mr. Newberry has sent. Treading heavily on the gravel, and rolling majestically along in a snuff-colored suit, and a wig that sadly wants the barber's powder and irons, one sees the Great Doctor step up to him, (his Scotch lackey following at the lexicographer's heels, a little the worse for Port wine that they have been taking at the Miter), and Mr. Johnson asks Mr. Goldsmith to come home and take a dish of tea with Miss Williams. Kind faith of Fancy! Sir Hoger and Mr. Spectator are as real to us now as the two doctors and the boozy and faithful Scotchman. The poetical figures live in our memory just as much as the real personages— and as Mr. Arthur Pendennis was of a romantic and literary turn, by no means addicted to the legal pursuits common in the neighborhood of the place, we may presume that he was cherishing some such poetical reflections as these, when, upon the evening after the events recorded in the last chapter the young gentleman chose the Temple Gardens as a place for exercise and meditation.

On the Sunday evening the Temple is commonly calm. The chambers are for the most part vacant; the great lawyers are giving grand dinner parties at their houses in the Belgravian or Tyburnian districts: the agreeable young barristers are absent, attending those parties, and paying their respects to Mr. Kewsy's excellent claret, or Mr. Justice Ermine's accomplished daughters; the uninvited are partaking of the economic joint, and the modest half-pint of wine at the Club, entertaining themselves and the rest of the company in the Club-room, with Circuit jokes and points of wit and law. Nobody is in chambers at all, except poor Mr. Cockle, who is ill, and whose laundress is making him gruel; or Mr. Toodle, who is an amateur of the flute, and whom you may hear piping solitary from his chambers in the second floor: or young Tiger, the student, from whose open windows come a great gush of cigar smoke, and at whose door are a quantity of dishes and covers, bearing the insignia of Dicks' or the Cock. But stop! Whither does Fancy lead us? It is vacation time; and with the exception of Pendennis, nobody is in chambers at all.

Perhaps it was solitude, then, which drove Pen into the Garden; for although he had never before passed the gate, and had looked rather carelessly at the pretty flower-beds, and the groups of pleased citizens sauntering over the trim lawn and the broad gravel-walks by the river, on this evening it happened, as we have said, that the young gentleman, who had dined alone at a tavern in the neighborhood of the Temple, took a fancy, as he was returning home to his chambers, to take a little walk in the gardens, and enjoy the fresh evening air, and the sight of the shining Thames. After walking for a brief space, and looking at the many peaceful and happy groups round about him, he grew tired of the exercise, and betook himself to one of the summer-houses which flank either end of the main walk, and there modestly seated himself. What were his cogitations? The evening was delightfully bright and calm; the sky was cloudless; the chimneys on the opposite bank were not smoking; the wharves and warehouses looked rosy in the sunshine, and as clear as if they too, had washed for the holiday. The steamers rushed rapidly up and down the stream, laden with holiday passengers. The bells of the multitudinous city churches were ringing to evening prayers—such peaceful Sabbath evenings as this Pen may have remembered in his early days, as he paced, with his arm round his mother's waist, on the terrace before the lawn at home. The sun was lighting up the little Brawl, too, as well as the broad Thames, and sinking downward majestically behind the Clavering elms, and the tower of the familiar village church. Was it thoughts of these, or the sunset merely, that caused the blush in the young man's face? He beat time on the bench, to the chorus of the bells without; flicked the dust off his shining boots with his pocket-handkerchief, and starting up, stamped with his foot and said, "No, by Jove, I'll go home." And with this resolution, which indicated that some struggle as to the propriety of remaining where he was, or of quitting the garden, had been going on in his mind, he stepped out of the summer-house.

He nearly knocked down two little children, who did not indeed reach much higher than his knee, and were trotting along the gravel-walk, with their long blue shadows slanting toward the east.

One cried out, "Oh!" the other began to laugh; and with a knowing little infantine chuckle, said, "Missa Pendennis!" And Arthur looking down, saw his two little friends of the day before, Mesdemoiselles Ameliar-Ann and Betsy-Jane. He blushed more than ever at seeing them, and seizing the one whom he had nearly upset, jumped her up into the air, and kissed her; at which sudden assault Ameliar-Ann began to cry in great alarm.

This cry brought up instantly two ladies in clean collars and new ribbons, and grand shawls, namely, Mrs. Bolton in a rich scarlet Caledonian Cashmere, and a black silk dress, and Miss F. Bolton with a yellow scarf and a sweet sprigged muslin, and a parasol—quite the lady. Fanny did not say one single word: though her eyes flashed a welcome, and shone as bright—as bright as the most blazing windows in Paper Buildings. But Mrs. Bolton, after admonishing Betsy-Jane, said, "Lor, sir, how very odd that we should meet you year? I ope you ave your ealth well, sir. Ain't it odd, Fanny, that we should meet Mr. Pendennis?" What do you mean by sniggering, mesdames? When young Croesus has been staying at a country-house, have you never, by any singular coincidence, been walking with your Fanny in the shrubberies? Have you and your Fanny never happened to be listening to the band of the Heavies at Brighton, when young De Boots and Captain Padmore came clinking down the Pier? Have you and your darling Frances never chanced to be visiting old widow Wheezy at the cottage on the common, when the young curate has stepped in with a tract adapted to the rheumatism? Do you suppose that, if singular coincidences occur at the Hall, they don't also happen at the Lodge?

It was a coincidence, no doubt: that was all. In the course of the conversation on the day previous, Mr. Pendennis had merely said, in the simplest way imaginable, and in reply to a question of Miss Bolton, that although some of the courts were gloomy, parts of the Temple were very cheerful and agreeable, especially the chambers looking on the river and around the gardens, and that the gardens were a very pleasant walk on Sunday evenings, and frequented by a great number of people—and here, by the merest chance, all our acquaintances met together, just like so many people in genteel life. What could be more artless, good-natured, or natural?

Pen looked very grave, pompous, and dandified. He was unusually smart and brilliant in his costume. His white duck trowsers and white hat, his neckcloth of many colors, his light waistcoat, gold chains, and shirt studs, gave him the air of a prince of the blood at least. How his splendor became his figure! Was any body ever like him? some one thought. He blushed—how his blushes became him! the same individual, said to herself. The children, on seeing him the day before, had been so struck with him, that after he had gone away they had been playing at him. And Ameliar-Ann, sticking her little chubby fingers into the arm-holes of her pinafore, as Pen was won't to do with his waistcoat, had said, "Now, Bessy-Jane, I'll be Missa Pendennis." Fanny had laughed till she cried, and smothered her sister with kisses for that feat. How happy, too, she was to see Arthur embracing the child!

If Arthur was red, Fanny, on the contrary, was very worn and pale. Arthur remarked it, and asked kindly why she looked so fatigued.

"I was awake all night," said Fanny, and began to blush a little.

"I put out her candle, and hordered her to go to sleep and leave off readin," interposed the fond mother.

"You were reading! And what was it that interested you so?" asked Pen, amused.

"Oh, it's so beautiful!" said Fanny.

"What?"

"Walter Lorraine," Fanny sighed out. "How I do hate that Neara —Neara—I don't know the pronunciation. And how I love Leonora, and Walter, oh, how dear he is!"

How had Fanny discovered the novel of Walter Lorraine, and that Pen was the author? This little person remembered every single word which Mr. Pendennis had spoken on the night previous, and how he wrote in books and newspapers. What books? She was so eager to know, that she had almost a mind to be civil to old Bows, who was suffering under her displeasure since yesterday, but she determined first to make application to Costigan. She began by coaxing the captain and smiling upon him in her most winning way, as she helped to arrange his dinner and set his humble apartment in order. She was sure his linen wanted mending (and indeed the captain's linen-closet contained some curious specimens of manufactured flax and cotton). She would mend his shirts—all his shirts. What horrid holes—what funny holes! She put her little face through one of them, and laughed at the old warrior in the most winning manner. She would have made a funny little picture looking through the holes. Then she daintily removed Costigan's dinner things, tripping about the room as she had seen the dancers do at the play; and she danced to the captain's cupboard, and produced his whisky bottle, and mixed him a tumbler, and must taste a drop of it—a little drop; and the captain must sing her one of his songs, his dear songs, and teach it to her. And when he had sung an Irish melody in his rich quavering voice, fancying it was he who was fascinating the little siren, she put her little question about Arthur Pendennis and his novel, and having got an answer, cared for nothing more, but left the captain at the piano about to sing her another song, and the dinner tray on the passage, and the shirts on the chair, and ran down stairs quickening her pace as she sped.

Captain Costigan, as he said, was not a litherary cyarkter, nor had he as yet found time to peruse his young friend's ellygant perfaurumance, though he intended to teak an early opporchunitee of purchasing a cawpee of his work. But he knew the name of Pen's novel from the fact that Messrs. Finucane, Bludyer, and other frequenters of the Back-Kitchen, spoke of Mr. Pendennis (and not all of them with great friendship; for Bludyer called him a confounded coxcomb, and Hoolan wondered that Doolan did not kick him, &c.) by the sobriquet of Walter Lorraine—and was hence enabled to give Fanny the information which she required.

"And she went and ast for it at the libery," Mrs. Bolton said— "several liberies—and some ad it and it was hout, and some adn't it. And one of the liberies as ad it wouldn't let er ave it without a sovering: and she adn't one, and she came back a-cryin to me—didn't you, Fanny?—and I gave her a sovering."

"And, oh, I was in such a fright lest any one should have come to the libery and took it while I was away," Fanny said, her cheeks and eyes glowing. "And, oh, I do like it so!"

Arthur was touched by this artless sympathy, immensely flattered and moved by it. "Do you like it?" he said. "If you will come up to my chambers I will—No, I will bring you one—no, I will send you one. Good night. Thank you, Fanny. God bless you. I mustn't stay with you. Good-by, good-by." And, pressing her hand once, and nodding to her mother and the other children, he strode out of the gardens.

He quickened his pace as he went from them, and ran out of the gate talking to himself. "Dear, dear little thing," he said, "darling little Fanny! You are worth them all. I wish to heaven Shandon was back, I'd go home to my mother. I mustn't see her. I won't. I won't so help me—"

As he was talking thus, and running, the passers by turning to look at him, he ran against a little old man, and perceived it was Mr. Bows.

"Your very umble servant, sir," said Mr. Bows, making a sarcastic bow, and lifting his old hat from his forehead.

"I wish you a good day," Arthur answered sulkily. "Don't let me detain you, or give you the trouble to follow me again. I am in a hurry, sir. Good evening."

Bows thought Pen had some reason for hurrying to his rooms. "Where are they?" exclaimed the old gentleman. "You know whom I mean. They're not in your rooms, sir, are they? They told Bolton they were going to church at the Temple: they weren't there. They are in your chambers: they mustn't stay in your chambers, Mr. Pendennis."

"Damn it, sir!" cried out Pendennis, fiercely. "Come and see if they are in my chambers: here's the court and the door—come in and see." And Bows, taking off his hat and bowing first, followed the young man.

They were not in Pen's chambers, as we know. But when the gardens were closed, the two women, who had had but a melancholy evening's amusement, walked away sadly with the children, and they entered into Lamb-court, and stood under the lamp-post which cheerfully ornaments the center of that quadrangle, and looked up to the third floor of the house where Pendennis's chambers were, and where they saw a light presently kindled. Then this couple of fools went away, the children dragging wearily after them, and returned to Mr. Bolton, who was immersed in rum-and-water at his lodge in Shepherd's Inn.

Mr. Bows looked round the blank room which the young man occupied, and which had received but very few ornaments or additions since the last time we saw them. Warrington's old book-case and battered library, Pen's writing-table with its litter of papers presented an aspect cheerless enough. "Will you like to look in the bedrooms, Mr. Bows, and see if my victims are there?" he said bitterly; "or whether I have made away with the little girls, and hid them in the coal-hole?"

"Your word is sufficient, Mr. Pendennis," the other said, in his sad tone. "You say they are not here, and I know they are not. And I hope they never have been here, and never will come."

"Upon my word, sir, you are very good, to choose my acquaintances for me," Arthur said, in a haughty tone; "and to suppose that any body would be the worse for my society. I remember you, and owe you kindness from old times, Mr. Bows; or I should speak more angrily than I do, about a very intolerable sort of persecution to which you seem inclined to subject me. You followed me out of your inn yesterday, as if you wanted to watch that I shouldn't steal something." Here Pen stammered and turned red, directly he had said the words; he felt he had given the other an opening, which Bows instantly took.

"I do think you came to steal something, as you say the words, sir," Bows said. "Do you mean to say that you came to pay a visit to poor old Bows, the fiddler; or to Mrs. Bolton at the porter's lodge? O fie! Such a fine gentleman as Arthur Pendennis, Esquire, doesn't condescend to walk up to my garret, or to sit in a laundress's kitchen, but for reasons of his own. And my belief is that you came to steal a pretty girl's heart away, and to ruin it, and to spurn it afterward, Mr. Arthur Pendennis. That's what the world makes of you young dandies, you gentlemen of fashion, you high and mighty aristocrats that trample upon the people. It's sport to you, but what is it, to the poor, think you the toys of your pleasures, whom you play with and whom you fling into the streets when you are tired? I know your order, sir. I know your selfishness, and your arrogance, and your pride. What does it matter to my lord, that the poor man's daughter is made miserable, and her family brought to shame? You must have your pleasures, and the people of course must pay for them. What are we made for, but for that? It's the way with you all—the way with you all, sir."

Bows was speaking beside the question, and Pen had his advantage here, which he was not sorry to take—not sorry to put off the debate from the point upon which his adversary had first engaged it. Arthur broke out with a sort of laugh, for which he asked Bows's pardon. "Yes, I am an aristocrat," he said, "in a palace up three pair of stairs, with a carpet nearly as handsome as yours, Mr. Bows. My life is passed in grinding the people, is it?—in ruining virgins and robbing the poor? My good sir, this is very well in a comedy, where Job Thornberry slaps his breast, and asks my lord how dare he trample on an honest man and poke out an Englishman's fire-side; but in real life, Mr. Bows, to a man who has to work for his bread as much as you do—how can you talk about aristocrats tyrannizing over the people? Have I ever done you a wrong? or assumed airs of superiority over you? Did you not have an early regard for me—in days when we were both of us romantic young fellows, Mr. Bows? Come, don't be angry with me now, and let us be as good friends as we were before."

"Those days were very different," Mr. Bows answered; "and Mr. Arthur Pendennis was an honest, impetuous young fellow then; rather selfish and conceited, perhaps, but honest. And I liked you then, because you were ready to ruin yourself for a woman."

"And now, sir?" Arthur asked.

"And now times are changed, and you want a woman to ruin herself for you," Bows answered. "I know this child, sir. I've always said this lot was hanging over her. She has heated her little brain with novels until her whole thoughts are about love and lovers, and she scarcely sees that she treads on a kitchen floor. I have taught the little thing. She is full of many talents and winning ways, I grant you. I am fond of the girl, sir. I'm a lonely old man; I lead a life that I don't like, among boon companions, who make me melancholy. I have but this child that I care for. Have pity upon me, and don't take her away from me, Mr. Pendennis—don't take her away."

The old man's voice broke as he spoke, its accents touched Pen, much more than the menacing or sarcastic tone which Bows had commenced by adopting.

"Indeed," said he, kindly; "you do me a wrong if you fancy I intend one to poor little Fanny. I never saw her till Friday night. It was the merest chance that our friend Costigan threw her into my way. I have no intentions regarding her—that is—"

"That is, you know very well that she is a foolish girl, and her mother a foolish woman—that is, you meet her in the Temple Gardens, and of course, without previous concert, that is, that when I found her yesterday, reading the book you've wrote, she scorned me," Bows said. "What am I good for but to be laughed at? a deformed old fellow like me; an old fiddler, that wears a thread-bare coat, and gets his bread by playing tunes at an alehouse? You are a fine gentleman, you are. You wear scent in your handkerchief, and a ring on your finger. You go to dine with great people. Who ever gives a crust to old Bows? And yet I might have been as good a man as the best of you. I might have been a man of genius, if I had had the chance; ay, and have lived with the master-spirits of the land. But every thing has failed with me. I'd ambition once, and wrote plays, poems, music—nobody would give me a hearing. I never loved a woman, but she laughed at me; and here I am in my old age alone—alone! Don't take this girl from me, Mr. Pendennis, I say again. Leave her with me a little longer. She was like a child to me till yesterday. Why did you step in and make her mock my deformity and old age?"

CHAPTER XII

THE HAPPY VILLAGE AGAIN

Early in this history, we have had occasion to speak of the little town of Clavering, near which Pen's paternal home of Fairoaks stood, and of some of the people who inhabited the place, and as the society there was by no means amusing or pleasant, our reports concerning it were not carried to any very great length. Mr. Samuel Huxter, the gentleman whose acquaintance we lately made at Vauxhall, was one of the choice spirits of the little town, when he visited it during his vacations, and enlivened the tables of his friends there, by the wit of Bartholomew's and the gossip of the fashionable London circles which he frequented.

Mr. Hobnell, the young gentleman whom Pen had thrashed, in consequence of the quarrel in the Fotheringay affair, was, while a pupil at the Grammar-school at Clavering, made very welcome at the tea-table of Mrs. Huxter, Samuel's mother, and was free of the surgery, where he knew the way to the tamarind-pots, and could scent his pocket-handkerchief with rose-water. And it was at this period of his life that he formed an attachment for Miss Sophy Huxter, whom, on his father's demise, he married, and took home to his house of the Warren, at a few miles from Clavering.

The family had possessed and cultivated an estate there for many years as yeomen and farmers. Mr. Hobnell's father pulled down the old farm-house; built a flaring new white-washed mansion, with capacious stables; and a piano in the drawing-room; kept a pack of harriers; and assumed the title of Squire Hobnell. When he died, and his son reigned in his stead, the family might be fairly considered to be established as county gentry. And Sam Huxter, at London, did no great wrong in boasting about his brother-in-law's place, his hounds, horses, and hospitality, to his admiring comrades at Bartholomew's. Every year, at a time commonly when Mrs. Hobnell could not leave the increasing duties of her nursery, Hobnell came up to London for a lark, had rooms at the Tavistock, and indulged in the pleasures of the town together. Ascott, the theaters, Vauxhall, and the convivial taverns in the joyous neighborhood of Covent Garden, were visited by the vivacious squire, in company with his learned brother. When he was in London, as he said, he liked to do as London does, and to "go it a bit," and when he returned to the west, he took a new bonnet and shawl to Mrs. Hobnell, and relinquished for country sports and occupations, during the next eleven months, the elegant amusements of London life.

Sam Huxter kept up a correspondence with his relative, and supplied him with choice news of the metropolis, in return for the baskets of hares, partridges, and clouted cream which the squire and his good-natured wife forwarded to Sam. A youth more brilliant and distinguished they did not know. He was the life and soul of their house, when he made his appearance in his native place. His songs, jokes, and fun kept the Warren in a roar. He had saved their eldest darling's life, by taking a fish-bone out of her throat; in fine, he was the delight of their circle.

As ill-luck would have it, Pen again fell in with Mr. Huxter, only three days after the rencounter at Vauxhall. Faithful to his vow, he had not been to see little Fanny. He was trying to drive her from his mind by occupation, or other mental excitement. He labored, though not to much profit, incessantly in his rooms; and, in his capacity of critic for the "Pall Mall Gazette," made woeful and savage onslaught on a poem and a romance which came before him for judgment. These authors slain, he went to dine alone at the lonely club of the Polyanthus, where the vast solitudes frightened him, and made him only the more moody. He had been to more theaters for relaxation. The whole house was roaring with laughter and applause, and he saw only an ignoble farce that made him sad. It would have damped the spirits of the buffoon on the stage to have seen Pen's dismal face. He hardly knew what was happening; the scene, and the drama passed before him like a dream or a fever. Then he thought he would go to the Back-Kitchen, his old haunt with Warrington—he was not a bit sleepy yet. The day before he had walked twenty miles in search after rest, over Hampstead Common and Hendon lanes, and had got no sleep at night. He would go to the Back-Kitchen. It was a sort of comfort to him to think he should see Bows. Bows was there, very calm, presiding at the old piano. Some tremendous comic songs were sung, which made the room crack with laughter. How strange they seemed to Pen! He could only see Bows. In an extinct volcano, such as he boasted that his breast was, it was wonderful how he should feel such a flame! Two days' indulgence had kindled it; two days' abstinence had set it burning in fury. So, musing upon this, and drinking down one glass after another, as ill-luck would have it, Arthur's eyes lighted upon Mr. Huxter, who had been to the theater, like himself, and, with two or three comrades, now entered the room, Huxter whispered to his companions, greatly to Pen's annoyance. Arthur felt that the other was talking about him. Huxter then worked through the room, followed by his friends, and came and took a place opposite to Pen, nodding familiarly to him, and holding him out a dirty hand to shake.

Pen shook hands with his fellow townsman. He thought he had been needlessly savage to him on the last night when they had met. As for Huxter, perfectly at good humor with himself and the world, it never entered his mind that he could be disagreeable to any body; and the little dispute, or "chaff," as he styled it, of Vauxhall, was a trifle which he did not in the least regard.

The disciple of Galen having called for "four stouts," with which he and his party refreshed themselves, began to think what would be the most amusing topic of conversation with Pen, and hit upon that precise one which was most painful to our young gentleman.

"Jolly night at Vauxhall—wasn't it?" he said, and winked in a very knowing way.

"I'm glad you liked it," poor Pen said, groaning in spirit.

"I was dev'lish cut—uncommon—been dining with some chaps at Greenwich. That was a pretty bit of muslin hanging on your arm—who was she?" asked the fascinating student.

The question was too much for Arthur. "Have I asked you any questions about yourself, Mr. Huxter?" he said.

"I didn't mean any offense—beg pardon—hang it, you cut up quite savage," said Pen's astonished interlocutor.

"Do you remember what took place between us the other night?" Pen asked, with gathering wrath. "You forget? Very probably. You were tipsy, as you observed just now, and very rude."

"Hang it, sir, I asked your pardon," Huxter said, looking red.

"You did certainly, and it was granted with all my heart, I am sure. But if you recollect I begged that you would have the goodness to omit me from the list of your acquaintance for the future; and when we met in public, that you would not take the trouble to recognize me. Will you please to remember this hereafter; and as the song is beginning, permit me to leave you to the unrestrained enjoyment of the music."

He took his hat, and making a bow to the amazed Mr. Huxter, left the table, as Huxter's comrades, after a pause of wonder, set up such a roar of laughter at Huxter, as called for the intervention of the president of the room; who bawled out, "Silence, gentlemen; do have silence for the Body Snatcher!" which popular song began as Pen left the Back-Kitchen. He flattered himself that he had commanded his temper perfectly. He rather wished that Huxter had been pugnacious. He would have liked to fight him or somebody. He went home. The day's work, the dinner, the play, the whisky-and-water, the quarrel—nothing soothed him. He slept no better than on the previous night.

A few days afterward, Mr. Sam Huxter wrote home a letter to Mr. Hobnell in the country, of which Mr. Arthur Pendennis formed the principal subject. Sam described Arthur's pursuits in London, and his confounded insolence of behavior to his old friends from home. He said he was an abandoned criminal, a regular Don Juan, a fellow who, when he did come into the country, ought to be kept out of honest people's houses. He had seen him at Vauxhall, dancing with an innocent girl in the lower ranks of life, of whom he was making a victim. He had found out from an Irish gentleman (formerly in the army), who frequented a club of which he, Huxter, was member, who the girl was, on whom this conceited humbug was practicing his infernal arts; and he thought he should warn her father, &c., &c.,—the letter then touched on general news, conveyed the writer's thanks for the last parcel and the rabbits, and hinted his extreme readiness for further favors.

About once a year, as we have stated, there was occasion for a christening at the Warren, and it happened that this ceremony took place a day after Hobnell had received the letter of his brother-in-law in town. The infant (a darling little girl) was christened Myra-Lucretia, after its two godmothers, Miss Portman and Mrs. Pybus of Clavering, and as of course Hobnell had communicated Sam's letter to his wife, Mrs. Hobnell imparted its horrid contents to her two gossips. A pretty story it was, and prettily it was told throughout Clavering in the course of that day.

Myra did not—she was too much shocked to do so—speak on the matter to her mamma, but Mrs. Pybus had no such feelings of reserve. She talked over the matter not only with Mrs. Portman, but with Mr. and the Honorable Mrs. Simcoe, with Mrs. Glanders, her daughters being to that end ordered out of the room, with Madame Fribsby, and, in a word, with the whole of the Clavering society. Madam Fribsby looking furtively up at her picture of the dragoon, and inwards into her own wounded memory, said that men would be men, and as long as they were men would be deceivers; and she pensively quoted some lines from Marmion, requesting to know where deceiving lovers should rest? Mrs. Pybus had no words of hatred, horror, contempt, strong enough for a villain who could be capable of conduct so base. This was what came of early indulgence, and insolence, and extravagance, and aristocratic airs (it is certain that Pen had refused to drink tea with Mrs. Pybus), and attending the corrupt and horrid parties in the dreadful modern Babylon! Mrs. Portman was afraid that she must acknowledge that the mother's fatal partiality had spoiled this boy, that his literary successes had turned his head, and his horrid passions had made him forget the principles which Dr. Portman had instilled into him in early life. Glanders, the atrocious Captain of Dragoons, when informed of the occurrence by Mrs. Glanders, whistled and made jocular allusions to it at dinner time; on which Mrs. Glanders called him a brute, and ordered the girls again out of the room, as the horrid captain burst out laughing. Mr. Simcoe was calm under the intelligence; but rather pleased than otherwise; it only served to confirm the opinion which he had always had of that wretched young man: not that he knew any thing about him—not that he had read one line of his dangerous and poisonous works; Heaven forbid that he should: but what could be expected from such a youth, and such frightful, such lamentable, such deplorable want of seriousness? Pen formed the subject for a second sermon at the Clavering chapel of ease: where the dangers of London, and the crime of reading and writing novels, were pointed out on a Sunday evening to a large and warm congregation. They did not wait to hear whether he was guilty or not. They took his wickedness for granted: and with these admirable moralists, it was who should fling the stone at poor Pen.

The next day Mrs. Pendennis, alone and almost fainting with emotion and fatigue, walked or rather ran to Dr. Portman's house, to consult the good doctor. She had had an anonymous letter; some Christian had thought it his or her duty to stab the good soul who had never done mortal a wrong—an anonymous letter with references to Scripture, pointing out the doom of such sinners, and a detailed account of Pen's crime. She was in a state of terror and excitement pitiable to witness. Two or three hours of this pain had aged her already. In her first moment of agitation she had dropped the letter, and Laura had read it. Laura blushed when she read it; her whole frame trembled, but it was with anger. "The cowards," she said. "It isn't true. No, mother, it isn't true."

"It is true, and you've done it, Laura," cried out Helen fiercely. "Why did you refuse him when he asked you? Why did you break my heart and refuse him? It is you who led him into crime. It is you who flung him into the arms of this—this woman. Don't speak to me. Don't answer me. I will never forgive you, never. Martha, bring me my bonnet and shawl. I'll go out. I won't have you come with me. Go away. Leave me, cruel girl; why have you brought this shame on me?" And bidding her daughter and her servants keep away from her, she ran down the road to Clavering.

Doctor Portman, glancing over the letter, thought he knew the hand writing, and, of course, was already acquainted with the charge made against poor Pen. Against his own conscience, perhaps (for the worthy doctor, like most of us, had a considerable natural aptitude for receiving any report unfavorable to his neighbors), he strove to console Helen; he pointed out that the slander came from an anonymous quarter, and therefore must be the work of a rascal; that the charge might not be true—was not true, most likely—at least, that Pen must be heard before he was condemned; that the son of such a mother was not likely to commit such a crime, &c., &c.

Helen at once saw through his feint of objection and denial. "You think he has done it," she said, "you know you think he has done it, Oh, why did I ever leave him, Doctor Portman, or suffer him away from me? But he can't be dishonest—pray God, not dishonest—you don't think that, do you? Remember his conduct about that other—person —how madly he was attached to her. He was an honest boy then— he is now. And I thank God—yes, I fall down on my knees and thank God he paid Laura. You said he was good—you did yourself. And now—if this woman loves him—and you know they must—if he has taken her from her home, or she tempted him, which is most likely-why still, she must be his wife and my daughter. And he must leave the dreadful world and come back to me—to his mother, Doctor Portman. Let us go away and bring him back—yes—bring him back—and there shall be joy for the—the sinner that repenteth. Let us go now, directly, dear friend—this very—"

Helen could say no more. She fell back and fainted. She was carried to a bed in the house of the pitying doctor, and the surgeon was called to attend her. She lay all night in an alarming state. Laura came to her, or to the rectory rather; for she would not see Laura. And Doctor Portman, still beseeching her to be tranquil, and growing bolder and more confident of Arthur's innocence as he witnessed the terrible grief of the poor mother, wrote a letter to Pen warning him of the rumors that were against him, and earnestly praying that he would break off and repent of a connection so fatal to his best interests and his soul's welfare.

And Laura?—was her heart not wrung by the thought of Arthur's crime and Helen's estrangement? Was it not a bitter blow for the innocent girl to think that at one stroke she should lose all the love which she cared for in the world?

CHAPTER XIII

WHICH HAD VERY NEARLY BEEN THE LAST OF THE STORY

Doctor Portman's letter was sent off to its destination in London, and the worthy clergyman endeavored to sooth down Mrs. Pendennis into some state of composure until an answer should arrive, which the doctor tried to think, or, at any rate, persisted in saying, would be satisfactory as regarded the morality of Mr. Pen. At least Helen's wish of moving upon London and appearing in person to warn her son of his wickedness, was impracticable for a day or two. The apothecary forbade her moving even so far as Fairoaks for the first day, and it was not until the subsequent morning that she found herself again back on her sofa at home, with the faithful, though silent Laura, nursing at her side.

Unluckily for himself and all parties, Pen never read that homily which Doctor Portman addressed to him, until many weeks after the epistle had been composed; and day after day, the widow waited for her son's reply to the charges against him; her own illness increasing with every day's delay. It was a hard task for Laura to bear the anxiety; to witness her dearest friend's suffering: worst of all, to support Helen's estrangement, and the pain caused to her by that averted affection. But it was the custom of this young lady to the utmost of her power, and by means of that gracious assistance which Heaven awarded to her pure and constant prayers, to do her duty. And, as that duty was performed quite noiselessly—while, the supplications, which endowed her with the requisite strength for fulfilling it, also took place in her own chamber, away from all mortal sight,—we, too, must be perforce silent about these virtues of hers, which no more bear public talking about, than a flower will bear to bloom in a ball-room. This only we will say-that a good woman is the loveliest flower that blooms under Heaven; and that we look with love and wonder upon its silent grace, its pure fragrance, its delicate bloom of beauty. Sweet and beautiful!—the fairest and the most spotless!—is it not pity to see them bowed down or devoured by Grief or Death inexorable—wasting in disease-pining with long pain-or cut off by sudden fate in their prime? We may deserve grief—but why should these be unhappy?—except that we know that Heaven chastens those whom it loves best; being pleased, by repeated trials, to make these pure spirits more pure.

So Pen never got the letter, although it was duly posted and faithfully discharged by the postman into his letter-box in Lamb Court, and thence carried by the laundress to his writing-table with the rest of his lordship's correspondence; into which room, have we not seen a picture of him, entering from his little bedroom adjoining, as Mrs. Flanagan, his laundress, was in the act of drinking his gin?

Those kind readers who have watched Mr. Arthur's career hitherto, and have made, as they naturally would do, observations upon the moral character and peculiarities of their acquaintance, have probably discovered by this time what was the prevailing fault in Mr. Pen's disposition, and who was that greatest enemy, artfully indicated in the title-page, with whom he had to contend. Not a few of us, my beloved public, have the very same rascal to contend with: a scoundrel who takes every opportunity of bringing us into mischief, of plunging us into quarrels, of leading us into idleness and unprofitable company, and what not. In a word, Pen's greatest enemy was himself: and as he had been pampering, and coaxing, and indulging that individual all his life, the rogue grew insolent, as all spoiled servants will be; and at the slightest attempt to coerce him, or make him do that which was unpleasant to him, became frantically rude and unruly. A person who is used to making sacrifices—Laura, for instance, who had got such a habit of giving up her own pleasure for others-can do the business quite easily; but Pen, unaccustomed as he was to any sort of self-denial, suffered woundily when called on to pay his share, and savagely grumbled at being obliged to forego any thing he liked.

He had resolved in his mighty mind then that he would not see Fanny; and he wouldn't. He tried to drive the thoughts of that fascinating little person out of his head, by constant occupation, by exercise, by dissipation, and society. He worked, then, too much; he walked and rode too much; he ate, drank, and smoked too much; nor could all the cigars and the punch of which he partook drive little Fanny's image out of his inflamed brain, and at the end of a week of this discipline and self-denial our young gentleman was in bed with a fever. Let the reader who has never had a fever in chambers pity the wretch who is bound to undergo that calamity.

A committee of marriageable ladies, or of any Christian persons interested in the propagation of the domestic virtues, should employ a Cruikshank, or a Leech, or some other kindly expositor of the follies of the day, to make a series of designs representing the horrors of a bachelor's life in chambers, and leading the beholder to think of better things, and a more wholesome condition. What can be more uncomfortable than the bachelor's lonely breakfast?—with the black kettle in the dreary fire in

Midsummer; or, worse still, with the fire gone out at Christmas, half an hour after the laundress has quitted the sitting-room? Into this solitude the owner enters shivering, and has to commence his day by hunting for coals and wood: and before he begins the work of a student, has to discharge the duties of a housemaid, vice Mrs. Flanagan, who is absent without leave. Or, again, what can form a finer subject for the classical designer than the bachelor's shirt—that garment which he wants to assume just at dinner-time, and which he finds without any buttons to fasten it? Then there is the bachelor's return to chambers after a merry Christmas holiday, spent in a cozy country-house, full of pretty faces, and kind welcomes and regrets. He leaves his portmanteau at the barber's in the court: he lights his dismal old candle at the sputtering little lamp on the stair: he enters the blank familiar room, where the only tokens to greet him, that show any interest in his personal welfare, are the Christmas bills, which are lying in wait for him, amicably spread out on his reading-table. Add to these scenes an appalling picture of bachelor's illness, and the rents in the Temple will begin to fall from the day of the publication of the dismal diorama. To be well in chambers is melancholy, and lonely and selfish enough; but to be ill in chambers—to pass nights of pain and watchfulness—to long for the morning and the laundress—to serve yourself your own medicine by your own watch—to have no other companion for long hours but your own sickening fancies and fevered thoughts: no kind hand to give you drink if you are thirsty, or to smooth the hot pillow that crumples under you—this indeed, is a fate so dismal and tragic, that we shall not enlarge upon its horrors; and shall only heartily pity those bachelors in the Temple who brave it every day.

This lot befell Arthur Pendennis after the various excesses which we have mentioned, and to which he had subjected his unfortunate brains. One night he went to bed ill, and next the day awoke worse. His only visitor that day, besides the laundress, was the Printer's Devil, from the "Pall Mall Gazette Office," whom the writer endeavored, as best he could, to satisfy. His exertions to complete his work rendered his fever the greater: he could only furnish a part of the quantity of "copy" usually supplied by him; and Shandon being absent, and Warrington not in London to give a help, the political and editorial columns of the "Gazette" looked very blank indeed; nor did the sub-editor know how to fill them. Mr. Finucane rushed up to Pen's Chambers, and found that gentleman so exceedingly unwell, that the good-natured Irishman set to work to supply his place, if possible, and produced a series of political and critical compositions, such as no doubt greatly edified the readers of the periodical in which he and Pen were concerned. Allusions to the greatness of Ireland, and the genius and virtue of the inhabitants of that injured country, flowed magnificently from Finucane's pen; and Shandon, the Chief of the paper, who was enjoying himself placidly at Boulogne-sur-mer, looking over the columns of the journal, which was forwarded to him, instantly recognized the hand of the great sub-editor, and said, laughing, as he flung over the paper to his wife, "Look here, Mary, my dear, here is Jack at work again." Indeed, Jack was a warm friend, and a gallant partisan, and when he had the pen in hand, seldom let slip an opportunity of letting the world know that Rafferty was the greatest painter in Europe, and wondering at the petty jealousy of the Academy, which refused to make him an R. A.: of stating that it was generally reported at the West End, that Mr. Rooney, M. P. was appointed Governor of Barataria; or of introducing into the subject in hand, whatever it might be, a compliment to the Round Towers, or the Giant's Causeway. And besides doing Pen's work for him, to the best of his ability, his kind-hearted comrade offered to forego his Saturday's and Sunday's holiday, and pass those days of holiday and rest as nurse-tender to Arthur, who, however, insisted, that the other should not forego his pleasure, and thankfully assured him that he could bear best his malady alone.

Taking his supper at the Back-Kitchen on the Friday night, after having achieved the work of the paper, Finucane informed Captain Costigan of the illness of their young friend in the Temple; and remembering the fact two days afterward, the captain went to Lamb Court and paid a visit to the invalid on Sunday afternoon. He found Mrs. Flanagan, the laundress, in tears in the sitting-room, and got a bad report of the poor dear young gentleman within. Pen's condition had so much alarmed her, that she was obliged to have recourse to the stimulus of brandy to enable her to support the grief which his illness occasioned. As she hung about his bed, and endeavored to minister to him, her attentions became intolerable to the invalid, and he begged her peevishly not to come near him. Hence the laundress's tears and redoubled grief, and renewed application to the bottle, which she was accustomed to use as an anodyne. The captain rated the woman soundly for her intemperance, and pointed out to her the fatal consequences which must ensue if she persisted in her imprudent courses. Pen, who was by this time in a very fevered state, was yet greatly pleased to receive Costigan's visit. He heard the well-known voice in his sitting-room, as he lay in the bedroom within, and called the captain eagerly to him, and thanked him for coming, and begged him to take a chair and talk to him. The captain felt the young man's pulse with great gravity—(his own tremulous and clammy hand growing steady for the instant while his finger pressed Arthur's throbbing vein)—the pulse was beating very fiercely—Pen's face was haggard and hot—his eyes were bloodshot and gloomy; his "bird," as the captain pronounced the word, afterward giving a description of his condition, had not been shaved for nearly a week. Pen made his visitor sit down, and, tossing and turning in his comfortless bed, began to try and talk to the captain in a lively manner, about the Back-Kitchen, about Vauxhall and when they should go again, and about Fanny—how was little Fanny?

Indeed how was she? We know how she went home very sadly on the previous Sunday evening, after she had seen Arthur light his lamp in his chambers, while he was having his interview with Bows. Bows came back to his own rooms presently, passing by the Lodge door, and looking into Mrs. Bolton's, according to his wont, as he passed, but with a very melancholy face. She had another weary night that night. Her restlessness wakened her little bedfellows more than once. She daren't read more of Walter Lorraine: Father was at home, and would suffer no light. She kept the book under her pillow, and felt for it in the night. She had only just got to sleep, when the children began to stir with the morning, almost as early as the birds. Though she was very angry with Bows, she went to his room at her accustomed hour in the day, and there the good-hearted musician began to talk to her.

"I saw Mr. Pendennis last night, Fanny," he said.

"Did you? I thought you did," Fanny answered, looking fiercely at the melancholy old gentleman.

"I've been fond of you ever since we came to live in this place," he continued. "You were a child when I came; and you used to like me, Fanny, until three or four days ago: until you saw this gentleman."

"And now, I suppose, you are going to say ill of him," said Fanny. "Do, Mr. Bows—that will make me like you better."

"Indeed I shall do no such thing," Bows answered; "I think he is a very good and honest young man."

"Indeed, you know that if you said a word against him, I would never speak a word to you again—never!" cried Miss Fanny; and clenched her little hand, and paced up and down the room. Bows noted, watched, and followed the ardent little creature with admiration and gloomy sympathy. Her cheeks flushed, her frame trembled; her eyes beamed love, anger, defiance. "You would like to speak ill of him," she said; "but you daren't—you know you daren't!"

"I knew him many years since," Bows continued, "when he was almost as young as you are, and he had a romantic attachment for our friend the captain's daughter—Lady Mirabel that is now."

Fanny laughed. "I suppose there was other people, too, that had a romantic attachment for Miss Costigan," she said: "I don't want to hear about 'em."

"He wanted to marry her; but their ages were quite disproportionate: and their rank in life. She would not have him because he had no money. She acted very wisely in refusing him; for the two would have been very unhappy, and she wasn't a fit person to go and live with his family, or to make his home comfortable. Mr. Pendennis has his way to make in the world, and must marry a lady of his own rank. A woman who loves a man will not ruin his prospects, cause him to quarrel with his family, and lead him into poverty and misery for her gratification. An honest girl won't do that, for her own sake, or for the man's."

Fanny's emotion, which but now had been that of defiance and anger, here turned to dismay and supplication. "What do I know about marrying, Bows?" she said; "When was there any talk of it? What has there been between this young gentleman and me that's to make people speak so cruel? It was not my doing; nor Arthur's—Mr. Pendennis's—that I met him at Vauxhall. It was the captain took me and ma there. We never thought of nothing wrong, I'm sure. He came and rescued us, and was so very kind. Then he came to call and ask after us: and very, very good it was of such a grand gentleman to be so polite to humble folks like us! And yesterday ma and me just went to walk in the Temple Gardens, and—and"—here she broke out with that usual, unanswerable female argument of tears—and cried, "Oh! I wish I was dead! I wish I was laid in my grave; and had never, never seen him!"

"He said as much himself, Fanny," Bows said; and Fanny asked through her sobs, Why, why should he wish he had never seen her? Had she ever done him any harm? Oh, she would perish rather than do him any harm. Whereupon the musician informed her of the conversation of the day previous, showed her that Pen could not and must not think of her as a wife fitting for him, and that she, as she valued her honest reputation, must strive too to forget him. And Fanny, leaving the musician, convinced but still of the same mind, and promising that she would avoid the danger which menaced her, went back to the Porter's Lodge, and told her mother all. She talked of her love for Arthur, and bewailed, in her artless manner, the inequality of their condition, that set barriers between them. "There's the Lady of Lyons," Fanny said; "Oh, ma! how I did love Mr. Macready when I saw him do it; and Pauline, for being faithful to poor Claude, and always thinking of him; and he coming back to her, an officer, through all his dangers! And if every body admires Pauline—and I'm sure every body does, for being so true to a poor man—why should a gentleman be ashamed of loving a poor girl? Not that Mr. Arthur loves me—Oh, no, no! I ain't worthy of him; only a princess is worthy of such a gentleman as him. Such a poet!—writing so beautifully, and looking so grand! I'm sure he's a nobleman, and of ancient family, and kep out of his estate. Perhaps his uncle has it. Ah, if I might, oh, how I'd serve him, and work for him, and slave for him, that I would. I wouldn't ask for more than that, ma—just to be allowed to see him of a morning; and sometimes he'd say 'How d'you do, Fanny?' or, 'God bless you Fanny!' as he said on Sunday. And I'd work, and work; and I'd, sit up all night, and read, and learn, and make myself worthy of him. The captain says his mother lives in the country, and is a grand lady there. Oh, how I wish I might go and be her servant, ma! I can do plenty of things, and work very neat; and—and sometimes he'd come home, and I should see him!"

The girl's head fell on her mother's shoulder as she spoke, and she gave way to a plentiful outpouring of girlish tears, to which the matron, of course, joined her own. "You mustn't think no more of him, Fanny," she said. "If he don't come to you, he's a horrid, wicked man."

"Don't call him so, mother," Fanny replied. "He's the best of men, the best and the kindest. Bows says he thinks he is unhappy at leaving poor little Fanny. It wasn't his fault, was it, that we met?—and it ain't his that I mustn't see him again. He says I mustn't—and I mustn't, mother. He'll forget me, but I shall never forget him. No! I'll pray for him, and love him always—until I die—and I shall die, I know I shall—and then my spirit will always go and be with him."

"You forget your poor mother, Fanny, and you'll break my heart by goin' on so," Mrs. Bolton said. "Perhaps you will see him. I'm sure you'll see him. I'm sure he'll come to-day. If ever I saw a man in love, that man is him. When Emily Budd's young man first came about her, he was sent away by old Budd, a most respectable man, and violoncello in the orchestra at the Wells; and his own family wouldn't hear of it neither. But he came back. We all knew he would. Emily always said so; and he married her; and this one will come back too; and you mark a mother's words, and see if he don't, dear."

At this point of the conversation Mr. Bolton entered the Lodge for his evening meal. At the father's appearance, the talk between mother and daughter ceased instantly. Mrs. Bolton caressed and cajoled the surly undertaker's aid-de-camp, and said, "Lor, Mr. B., who'd have thought to see you away from the Club of a Saturday night. Fanny, dear, get your pa some supper. What will you have, B.? The poor gurl's got a gathering in her eye, or somethink in it—I was looking at it just now as you came in." And she squeezed her daughter's hand as a signal of prudence and secrecy; and Fanny's tears were dried up likewise; and by that wondrous hypocrisy and power of disguise which women practice, and with which weapons of defense nature endows them, the traces of her emotion disappeared; and she went and took her work, and sat in the corner so demure and quiet, that the careless male parent never suspected that any thing ailed her.

Thus, as if fate seemed determined to inflame and increase the poor child's malady and passion, all circumstances and all parties round about her urged it on. Her mother encouraged and applauded it; and the very words which Bows used in endeavoring to repress her flame only augmented this unlucky fever. Pen was not wicked and a seducer: Pen was high-minded in wishing to avoid her. Pen loved her: the good and the great, the magnificent youth, with the chains of gold and the scented auburn hair! And so he did; or so he would have loved her five years back, perhaps, before the world had hardened the ardent and reckless boy—before he was ashamed of a foolish and imprudent passion, and strangled it as poor women do their illicit children, not on account of the crime, but of the shame, and from dread that the finger of the world should point to them.

What respectable person in the world will not say he was quite right to avoid a marriage with an ill-educated person of low degree, whose relations a gentleman could not well acknowledge, and whose manners would not become her new station?—and what philosopher would not tell him that the best thing to do with these little passions if they spring up, is to get rid of them, and let them pass over and cure them: that no man dies about a woman, or vice versâ: and that one or the other having found the impossibility of gratifying his or her desire in the particular instance, must make the best of matters, forget each other, look out elsewhere, and choose again? And yet, perhaps, there may be something said on the other side. Perhaps Bows was right in admiring that passion of Pen's, blind and unreasoning as it was, that made him ready to stake his all for his love; perhaps, if self-sacrifice is a laudable virtue, mere worldly self-sacrifice is not very much to be praised;—in fine, let this be a reserved point to be settled by the individual moralist who chooses to debate it.

So much is certain, that with the experience of the world which Mr. Pen now had, he would have laughed at and scouted the idea of marrying a penniless girl out of a kitchen. And this point being fixed in his mind, he was but doing his duty as an honest man, in crushing any unlucky fondness which he might feel toward poor little Fanny.

So she waited and waited in hopes that Arthur would come. She waited for a whole week, and it was at the end of that time that the poor little creature heard from Costigan of the illness under which Arthur was suffering.

It chanced on that very evening after Costigan had visited Pen, that Arthur's uncle, the excellent major, arrived in town from Buxton, where his health had been mended, and sent his valet Morgan to make inquiries for Arthur, and to request that gentleman to breakfast with the major the next morning. The major was merely passing through London on his way to the Marquis of Steyne's house of Stillbrook, where he was engaged to shoot partridges.

Morgan came back to his master with a very long face. He had seen Mr. Arthur; Mr. Arthur was very bad indeed; Mr. Arthur was in bed with a fever. A doctor ought to be sent to him; and Morgan thought his case most alarming.

Gracious goodness! this was sad news indeed. He had hoped that Arthur could come down to Stillbrook: he had arranged that he should go, and procured an invitation for his nephew from Lord Steyne. He must go himself; he couldn't throw Lord Steyne over; the fever might be catching: it might be measles: he had never himself had the measles; they were dangerous when contracted at his age. Was any body with Mr. Arthur?

Morgan said there was somebody a nussing of Mr. Arthur.

The major then asked, had his nephew taken any advice? Morgan said he had asked that question, and had been told that Mr. Pendennis had had no doctor.

Morgan's master was sincerely vexed at hearing of Arthur's calamity. He would have gone to him, but what good could it do Arthur that he, the major, should catch a fever? His own ailments rendered it absolutely impossible that he should attend to any body but himself. But the young man must have advice—the best advice; and Morgan was straightway dispatched with a note from Major Pendennis to his friend Doctor Goodenough, who by good luck happened to be in London and at home, and who quitted his dinner instantly, and whose carriage was in half an hour in Upper Temple Lane, near Pen's chambers. The major had asked the kind-hearted physician to bring him news of his nephew at the Club where he himself was dining, and in the course of the night the doctor made his appearance. The affair was very serious: the patient was in a high fever: he had had Pen bled instantly: and would see him the first thing in the morning. The major went disconsolate to bed with this unfortunate news. When Goodenough came to see him according to his promise the next day, the doctor had to listen for a quarter of an hour to an account of the major's own maladies, before the latter had leisure to hear about Arthur.

He had had a very bad night—his—his nurse said; at one hour he had been delirious. It might end badly: his mother had better be sent for immediately. The major wrote the letter to Mrs. Pendennis with the greatest alacrity, and at the same time with the most polite precautions. As for going himself to the lad, in his state it was impossible. "Could I be of any use to him, my dear doctor?" he asked.

The doctor, with a peculiar laugh, said, No: he didn't think the major could be of any use; that his own precious health required the most delicate treatment, and that he had best go into the country and stay: that he himself would take care to see the patient twice a day, and do all in his power for him.

The major declared upon his honor, that if he could be of any use he would rush to Pen's chambers. As it was, Morgan should go and see that every thing was right. The doctor must write to him by every post to Stillbrook; it was but forty miles distant from London, and if any thing happened he would come up at any sacrifice.

Major Pendennis transacted his benevolence by deputy and by post. "What else could he do," as he said? "Gad, you know, in these cases, it's best not disturbing a fellow. If a poor fellow goes to the bad, why, Gad, you know, he's disposed of. But in order to get well (and in this, my dear doctor, I'm sure that you will agree with me), the best way is to keep him quiet—perfectly quiet."

Thus it was the old gentleman tried to satisfy his conscience; and he went his way that day to Stillbrook by railway (for railways have sprung up in the course of this narrative, though they have not quite penetrated into Pen's country yet), and made his appearance in his usual trim order and curly wig, at the dinner-table of the Marquis of Steyne. But we must do the major the justice to say, that he was very unhappy and gloomy in demeanor. Wagg and Wenham rallied him about his low spirits; asked whether he was crossed in love? and otherwise diverted themselves at his expense. He lost his money at whist after dinner, and actually trumped his partner's highest spade. And the thoughts of the suffering boy, of whom he was proud, and whom he loved after his manner, kept the old fellow awake half through the night, and made him feverish and uneasy.

On the morrow he received a note in a handwriting which he did not know: it was that of Mr. Bows, indeed, saying, that Mr. Arthur Pendennis had had a tolerable night; and that as Dr. Goodenough had stated that the major desired to be informed of his nephew's health, he, R. B., had sent him the news per rail.

The next day he was going out shooting, about noon, with some of the gentlemen staying at Lord Steyne's house; and the company, waiting for the carriages, were assembled on the terrace in front of the house, when a fly drove up from the neighboring station, and a gray-headed, rather shabby old gentleman, jumped out, and asked for Major Pendennis? It was Mr. Bows. He took the major aside and spoke to him; most of the gentlemen round about saw that something serious had happened, from the alarmed look of the major's face.

Wagg said, "It's a bailiff come down to nab the major;" but nobody laughed at the pleasantry.

"Hullo! What's the matter, Pendennis?" cried Lord Steyne, with his strident voice; "any thing wrong?"

"It's—it's my boy that's dead," said the major, and burst into a sob—the old man was quite overcome.

"Not dead, my lord; but very ill when I left London," Mr. Bows said, in a low voice.

A britzka came up at this moment as the three men were speaking. The peer looked at his watch. "You've twenty minutes to catch the mail-train. Jump in, Pendennis; and drive like h—, sir, do you hear?"

The carriage drove off swiftly with Pendennis and his companions, and let us trust that the oath will be pardoned to the Marquis of Steyne.

The major drove rapidly from the station to the Temple, and found a traveling carriage already before him, and blocking up the narrow Temple Lane. Two ladies got out of it, and were asking their way of the porters; the major looked by chance at the panel of the carriage, and saw the worn-out crest of the eagle looking at the sun, and the motto, "nec tenui pennâ," painted beneath. It was his brother's old carriage, built many, many years ago. It was Helen and Laura that were asking their way to poor Pen's room.

He ran up to them; hastily clasped his sister's arm and kissed her hand; and the three entered into Lamb-court, and mounted the long, gloomy stair.

They knocked very gently at the door, on which Arthur's name was written, and it was opened by Fanny Bolton.

CHAPTER XIV

A CRITICAL CHAPTER

As Fanny saw the two ladies and the anxious countenance of the elder, who regarded her with a look of inscrutable alarm and terror, the poor girl at once knew that Pen's mother was before her; there was a resemblance between the widow's haggard eyes and Arthur's as he tossed in his bed in fever. Fanny looked wistfully at Mrs. Pendennis, and at Laura afterward; there was no more expression in the latter's face than if it had been a mass of stone. Hard-heartedness and gloom dwelt on the figures of both the new comers; neither showed any the faintest gleam of mercy or sympathy for Fanny. She looked desperately from them to the major behind them. Old Pendennis dropped his eyelids, looking up ever so stealthily from under them at Arthur's poor little nurse.

"I—I wrote to you yesterday, if you please, ma'am," Fanny said, trembling in every limb as she spoke; and as pale as Laura, whose sad menacing face looked over Mrs. Pendennis's shoulder.

"Did you, madam?" Mrs. Pendennis said, "I suppose I may now relieve you from nursing my son. I am his mother, you understand."

"Yes, ma'am. I—this is the way to his—O, wait a minute," cried out Fanny. "I must prepare you for his—"

The widow, whose face had been hopelessly cruel and ruthless, here started back with a gasp and a little cry, which she speedily stifled. "He's been so since yesterday," Fanny said, trembling very much, and with chattering teeth.

A horrid shriek of laughter came out of Pen's room, whereof the door was open; and, after several shouts, the poor wretch began to sing a college drinking song, and then to hurra and to shout as if he was in the midst of a wine party, and to thump with his fist against the wainscot. He was quite delirious.

"He does not know me, ma'am," Fanny said.

"Indeed. Perhaps he will know his mother; let me pass, if you please, and go into him." And the widow hastily pushed by little Fanny, and through the dark passage which led into Pen's sitting-room.

Laura sailed by Fanny, too, without a word; and Major Pendennis followed them. Fanny sat down on a bench in the passage, and cried, and prayed as well as she could. She would have died for him; and they hated her. They had not a word of thanks or kindness for her, the fine ladies. She sate there in the passage, she did not know how long. They never came out to speak to her. She sate there until doctor Goodenough came to pay his second visit that day; he found the poor little thing at the door.

"What, nurse? How's your patient?" asked the good-natured doctor. "Has he had any rest?"

"Go and ask them. They're inside," Fanny answered.

"Who? his mother?"

Fanny nodded her head and didn't speak.

"You must go to bed yourself, my poor little maid," said the doctor. "You will be ill too, if you don't."

"O, mayn't I come and see him: mayn't I come and see him! I—I—love him so," the little girl said; and as she spoke she fell down on her knees and clasped hold of the doctor's hand in such an agony that to see her melted the kind physician's heart, and caused a mist to come over his spectacles.

"Pooh, pooh! Nonsense! Nurse, has he taken his draught? Has he had any rest? Of course you must come and see him. So must I."

"They'll let me sit here, won't they, sir? I'll never make no noise. I only ask to stop here," Fanny said. On which the doctor called her a stupid little thing; put her down upon the bench where Pen's printer's devil used to sit so many hours; tapped her pale cheek with his finger, and bustled into the further room.

Mrs. Pendennis was ensconced, pale and solemn, in a great chair by Pen's bed-side. Her watch was on the bed-table by Pen's medicines. Her bonnet and cloaks were laid in the window. She had her Bible in her lap, without which she never traveled. Her first movement, after seeing her son, had been to take Fanny's shawl and bonnet which were on his drawers, and bring them out and drop them down upon his study-table. She had closed the door upon Major Pendennis, and Laura too; and taken possession of her son.

She had had a great doubt and terror lest Arthur should not know her; but that pang was spared to her, in part at least. Pen knew his mother quite well, and familiarly smiled and nodded at her. When she came in, he instantly fancied that they were at home at Fairoaks; and began to talk and chatter and laugh in a rambling wild way. Laura could hear him outside. His laughter shot shafts of poison into her heart. It was true then. He had been guilty—and with that creature!—an intrigue with a servant maid; and she had loved him—and he was dying most likely—raving and unrepentant. The major now and then hummed out a word of remark or consolation, which Laura scarce heard. A dismal sitting it was for all parties; and when Goodenough appeared, he came like an angel into the room.

It is not only for the sick man, it is for the sick man's friends that the doctor comes. His presence is often as good for them as for the patient, and they long for him yet more eagerly. How we have all watched after him! what an emotion the thrill of his carriage-wheels in the street, and at length at the door, has made us feel! how we hang upon his words, and what a comfort we get from a smile or two, if he can vouchsafe that sunshine to lighten our darkness! Who hasn't seen the mother praying into his face, to know if there is hope for the sick infant that can not speak, and that lies yonder, its little frame battling with fever? Ah, how she looks into his eyes! What thanks if there is light there; what grief and pain if he casts them down, and dares not say "hope!" Or it is the house-father who is stricken. The terrified wife looks on, while the physician feels his patient's wrist, smothering her agonies, as the children have been called upon to stay their plays and their talk. Over the patient in the fever, the wife expectant, the children unconscious, the doctor stands as if he were Fate, the dispenser of life and death: he must let the patient off this time; the woman prays so for his respite! One can fancy how awful the responsibility must be to a conscientious man: how cruel the feeling that he has given the wrong remedy, or that it might have been possible to do better: how harassing the sympathy with survivors, if the case is unfortunate—how immense the delight of victory!

Having passed through a hasty ceremony of introduction to the new comers, of whose arrival he had been made aware by the heart-broken little nurse in waiting without, the doctor proceeded to examine the patient, about whose condition of high fever there could be no mistake, and on whom he thought it necessary to exercise the strongest antiphlogistic remedies in his power. He consoled the unfortunate mother as best he might; and giving her the most comfortable assurances on which he could venture, that there was no reason to despair yet, that every thing might still be hoped from his youth, the strength of his constitution, and so forth, and having done his utmost to allay the horrors of the alarmed matron, he took the elder Pendennis aside into the vacant room (Warrington's bed-room), for the purpose of holding a little consultation.

The case was very critical. The fever, if not stopped, might and would carry off the young fellow: he must be bled forthwith: the mother must be informed of this necessity. Why was that other young lady brought with her? She was out of place in a sick room.

"And there was another woman still, be hanged to it!" the major said, "the—the little person who opened the door." His sister-in-law had brought the poor little devil's bonnet and shawl out, and flung them upon the study-table. Did Goodenough know any thing about the—the little person? "I just caught a glimpse of her as we passed in," the major said, "and begad she was uncommonly nice-looking." The doctor looked queer: the doctor smiled—in the very gravest moments, with life and death pending, such strange contrasts and occasions of humor will arise, and such smiles will pass, to satirize the gloom, as it were, and to make it more gloomy!

"I have it," at last he said, re-entering the study; and he wrote a couple of notes hastily at the table there, and sealed one of them. Then, taking up poor Fanny's shawl and bonnet, and the notes, he went out in the passage to that poor little messenger, and said, "Quick, nurse; you must carry this to the surgeon, and bid him come instantly: and then go to my house, and ask for my servant, Harbottle, and tell him to get this prescription prepared; and wait until I—until it is ready. It may take a little time in preparation."

So poor Fanny trudged away with her two notes, and found the apothecary, who lived in the Strand hard by, and who came straightway, his lancet in his pocket, to operate on his patient; and then Fanny made for the doctor's house, in Hanover-square.

The doctor was at home again before the prescription was made up, which took Harbottle, his servant, such a long time in compounding: and, during the remainder of Arthur's illness, poor Fanny never made her appearance in the quality of nurse at his chambers any more. But for that day and the next, a little figure might be seen lurking about Pen's staircase—a sad, sad little face looked at and interrogated the apothecary and the apothecary's boy, and the laundress, and the kind physician himself, as they passed out of the chambers of the sick man. And on the third day, the kind doctor's chariot stopped at Shepherd's Inn, and the good, and honest, and benevolent man went into the Porter's Lodge, and tended a little patient he had there, for whom the best remedy he found was on the day when he was enabled to tell Fanny Bolton that the crisis was over, and that there was at length every hope for Arthur Pendennis.

J. Costigan, Esquire, late of her Majesty's service, saw the doctor's carriage, and criticised its horses and appointments. "Green liveries, bedad!" the general said, "and as foin a pair of high-stepping bee horses as ever a gentleman need sit behoind, let alone a docthor. There's no ind to the proide and ar'gance of them docthors nowadays—not but that is a good one, and a scoientific cyarkter, and a roight good fellow, bedad; and he's brought the poor little girl well troo her faver, Bows, me boy;" and so pleased was Mr. Costigan with the doctor's behavior and skill, that, whenever he met Dr. Goodenough's carriage in future, he made a point of saluting it and the physician inside, in as courteous and magnificent a manner, as if Dr. Goodenough had been the Lord Liftenant himself, and Captain Costigan had been in his glory in Phaynix Park.

The widow's gratitude to the physician knew no bounds—or scarcely any bounds, at least. The kind gentleman laughed at the idea of taking a fee from a literary man, or the widow of a brother practitioner; and she determined when she got back to Fairoaks that she would send Goodenough the silver-gilt vase, the jewel of the house, and the glory of the late John Pendennis, preserved in green baize, and presented to him at Bath, by the Lady Elizabeth Firebrace, on the recovery of her son, the late Sir Anthony Firebrace, from the scarlet fever. Hippocrates, Hygeia, King Bladud, and a wreath of serpents surmount the cup to this day; which was executed in their finest manner, by Messrs. Abednego, of Milsom-street; and the inscription was by Mr. Birch tutor to the young baronet.

This priceless gem of art the widow determined to devote to Goodenough, the preserver of her son; and there was scarcely any other favor which her gratitude would not have conferred upon him, except one, which he desired most, and which was that she should think a little charitably and kindly of poor Fanny, of whose artless, sad story, he had got something during his interviews with her, and of whom he was induced to think very kindly—not being disposed, indeed, to give much credit to Pen for his conduct in the affair, or not knowing what that conduct had been. He knew, enough, however, to be aware that the poor infatuated little girl was without stain as yet; that while she had been in Pen's room it was to see the last of him, as she thought, and that Arthur was scarcely aware of her presence; and that she suffered under the deepest and most pitiful grief, at the idea of losing him, dead or living.

But on the one or two occasions when Goodenough alluded to Fanny, the widow's countenance, always soft and gentle, assumed an expression so cruel and inexorable, that the doctor saw it was in vain to ask her for justice or pity, and he broke off all entreaties, and ceased making any further allusions regarding his little client. There is a complaint which neither poppy, nor mandragora, nor all the drowsy syrups of the East could allay, in the men in his time, as we are informed by a popular poet of the days of Elizabeth; and which, when exhibited in women, no medical discoveries or practice subsequent — neither homoeopathy, nor hydropathy, nor mesmerism, nor Dr. Simpson, nor Dr. Locock can cure, and that is—we won't call it jealousy, but rather gently denominate rivalry and emulation, in ladies.

Some of those mischievous and prosaic people who carp and calculate at every detail of the romancer, and want to know, for instance, how when the characters "in the Critic" are at a dead lock with their daggers at each other's throats, they are to be got out of that murderous complication of circumstances, may be induced to ask how it was possible in a set of chambers in the Temple, consisting of three rooms, two cupboards, a passage, and a coal-box, Arthur a sick gentleman, Helen his mother, Laura her adopted daughter, Martha their country attendant, Mrs. Wheezer a nurse from St. Bartholomew's Hospital, Mrs. Flanagan an Irish laundress, Major Pendennis a retired military officer, Morgan his valet, Pidgeon Mr. Arthur Pendennis's boy, and others could be accommodated—the answer is given at once, that almost every body in the Temple was out of town, and that there was scarcely a single occupant of Pen's house in Lamb Court except those who were occupied round the sick bed of the sick gentleman, about whose fever we have not given a lengthy account, neither shall we enlarge very much upon the more cheerful theme of his recovery.

Every body we have said was out of town, and of course such a fashionable man as young Mr. Sibwright, who occupied chambers on the second floor in Pen's staircase, could not be supposed to remain in London. Mrs. Flanagan, Mr. Pendennis's laundress, was acquainted with Mrs. Rouncy who did for Mr. Sibwright, and that gentleman's bedroom was got ready for Miss Bell, or Mrs. Pendennis, when the latter should be inclined to leave her son's sick room, to try and seek for a little rest for herself.

If that young buck and flower of Baker-street, Percy Sibwright could have known who was the occupant of his bedroom, how proud he would have been of that apartment: what poems he would have written about Laura! (several of his things have appeared in the annuals, and in manuscript in the nobility's albums)—he was a Camford man and very nearly got the English Prize Poem, it was said—Sibwright, however, was absent and his bed given up to Miss Bell. It was the prettiest little brass bed in the world, with chintz curtains lined with pink—he had a mignonette box in his bedroom window, and the mere sight of his little exhibition of shiny boots, arranged in trim rows over his wardrobe, was a gratification to the beholder. He had a museum of scent, pomatum, and bears' grease pots, quite curious to examine, too; and a choice selection of portraits of females almost always in sadness and generally in disguise or dishabille, glittered round the neat walls of his elegant little bower of repose. Medora with disheveled hair was consoling herself over her banjo for the absence of her Conrad—the Princesse Fleur de Marie (of Rudolstein and the Mystères de Paris) was sadly ogling out of the bars of her convent cage, in which, poor prisoned bird, she was moulting away—Dorothea of Don Quixote was washing her eternal feet:— in fine, it was such an elegant gallery as became a gallant lover of the sex. And in Sibwright's sitting-room, while there was quite an infantine law library clad in skins of fresh new born calf, there was a tolerably large collection of classical books which he could not read, and of English and French works of poetry and fiction which he read a great deal too much. His invitation cards of the past season still decorated his looking glass: and scarce any thing told of the lawyer but the wig-box beside the Venus upon the middle shelf of the bookcase, on which the name of P. Sibwright, Esquire, was gilded.

With Sibwright in chambers was Mr. Bangham. Mr. Bangham was a sporting man married to a rich widow. Mr. Bangham had no practice—did not come to chambers thrice in a term: went a circuit for those mysterious reasons which make men go circuit—and his room served as a great convenience to Sibwright when that young gentleman gave his little dinners. It must be confessed that these two gentlemen have nothing to do with our history, will never appear in it again probably, but we can not help glancing through their doors as they happen to be open to us, and as we pass to Pen's rooms; as in the pursuit of our own business in life through the Strand, at the Club, nay at Church itself, we can not help peeping at the shops on the way, or at our neighbor's dinner, or at the faces under the bonnets in the next pew.

Very many years after the circumstances about which we are at present occupied, Laura with a blush and a laugh showing much humor owned to having read a French novel once much in vogue, and when her husband asked her, wondering where on earth she could have got such a volume, she owned that it was in the Temple, when she lived in Mr. Percy Sibwright's chambers.

"And, also, I never confessed," she said, "on that same occasion, what I must now own to; that I opened the japanned box, and took out that strange-looking wig inside it, and put it on and looked at myself in the glass in it."

Suppose Percy Sibwright had come in at such a moment as that? What would he have said—the enraptured rogue? What would have been all the pictures of disguised beauties in his room compared to that living one? Ah, we are speaking of old times, when Sibwright was a bachelor and before he got a county court—when people were young—when most people were young. Other people are young now; but we no more.

When Miss Laura played this prank with the wig, you can't suppose that Pen could have been very ill upstairs; otherwise, though she had grown to care for him ever so little, common sense of feeling and decorum would have prevented her from performing any tricks or trying any disguises.

But all sorts of events had occurred in the course of the last few days which had contributed to increase or account for her gayety, and a little colony of the reader's old friends and acquaintances was by this time established in Lamb Court, Temple, and round Pen's sick bed there. First, Martha, Mrs. Pendennis's servant, had arrived from Fairoaks, being summoned thence by the major, who justly thought her presence would be comfortable and useful to her mistress and her young master, for neither of whom the constant neighborhood of Mrs. Flanagan (who during Pen's illness required more spirituous consolation than ever to support her) could be pleasant. Martha then made her appearance in due season to wait upon Mrs. Pendennis, nor did that lady go once to bed until the faithful servant had reached her, when, with a heart full of maternal thankfulness, she went and lay down upon Warrington's straw mattress, and among his mathematical books as has been already described.

It is true ere that day a great and delightful alteration in Pen's condition had taken place. The fever, subjugated by Dr. Goodenough's blisters, potions, and lancet, had left the young man, or only returned at intervals of feeble intermittance; his wandering senses had settled in his weakened brain: he had had time to kiss and bless his mother for coming to him, and calling for Laura and his uncle (who were both affected according to their different natures by his wan appearance, his lean shrunken hands, his hollow eyes and voice, his thin bearded face) to press their hands and thank them affectionately; and after this greeting, and after they had been turned out of the room by his affectionate nurse, he had sunk into a fine sleep which had lasted for about sixteen hours, at the end of which period he awoke calling out that he was very hungry. If it is hard to be ill and to loathe food, oh, how pleasant to be getting well and to be feeling hungry—how hungry! Alas, the joys of convalescence become feebler with increasing years, as other joys do—and then—and then comes that illness when one does not convalesce at all.

On the day of this happy event, too, came another arrival in Lambcourt. This was introduced into the Pen-Warrington sitting-room by large puffs of tobacco smoke—the puffs of smoke were followed by an individual with a cigar in his mouth, and a carpet bag under his arm— this was Warrington, who had run back from Norfolk, when Mr. Bows thoughtfully wrote to inform him of his friend's calamity. But he had been from home when Bows's letter had reached his brother's house— the Eastern Counties did not then boast of a railway (for we beg the reader to understand that we only commit anachronisms when we choose, and when by a daring violation of those natural laws some great ethical truth is to be advanced)—in fine, Warrington only appeared with the rest of the good luck upon the lucky day after Pen's convalescence may have been said to have begun.

His surprise was, after all, not very great when he found the chambers of his sick friend occupied, and his old acquaintance the major seated demurely in an easy chair, (Warrington had let himself into the rooms with his own pass-key), listening, or pretending to listen, to a young lady who was reading to him a play of Shakspeare in a low sweet voice. The lady stopped and started, and laid down her book, at the apparition of the tall traveler with the cigar and the carpet-bag. He blushed, he flung the cigar into the passage: he took off his hat, and dropped that too, and going up to the major, seized that old gentleman's hand, and asked questions about Arthur.

The major answered in a tremulous, though cheery voice—it was curious how emotion seemed to olden him—and returning Warrington's pressure with a shaking hand, told him the news—of Arthur's happy crisis, of his mother's arrival—with her young charge—with Miss—

"You need not tell me her name," Mr. Warrington said with great animation, for he was affected and elated with the thought of his friend's recovery—"you need not tell me your name. I knew at once it was Laura." And he held out his hand and took hers. Immense kindness and tenderness gleamed from under his rough eyebrows, and shook his voice as he gazed at her and spoke to her. "And this is Laura !" his looks seemed to say. "And this is Warrington," the generous girl's heart beat back. "Arthur's hero—the brave and the kind—he has come hundreds of miles to succor him, when he heard of his friend's misfortune!"

"Thank you, Mr. Warrington," was all that Laura said, however; and as she returned the pressure of his kind hand, she blushed so, that she was glad the lamp was behind her to conceal her flushing face.

As these two were standing in this attitude, the door of Pen's bed-chamber was opened stealthily as his mother was wont to open it, and Warrington saw another lady, who first looked at him, and then turning round toward the bed, said, "Hsh!" and put up her hand. It was to Pen Helen was turning, and giving caution. He called out with a feeble, tremulous, but cheery voice, "Come in, Stunner—come in, Warrington. I knew it was you—by the—by the smoke, old boy," he said, as holding his worn hand out, and with tears at once of weakness and pleasure in his eyes, he greeted his friend.

"I—I beg pardon, ma'am, for smoking," Warrington said, who now almost for the first time blushed for his wicked propensity.

Helen only said, "God bless you, Mr. Warrington." She was so happy, she would have liked to kiss George. Then, and after the friends had had a brief, very brief interview, the delighted and inexorable mother, giving her hand to Warrington, sent him out of the room too, back to Laura and the major, who had not resumed their play of Cymbeline where they had left it off at the arrival of the rightful owner of Pen's chambers.

CHAPTER XV

CONVALESCENCE

Our duty now is to record a fact concerning Pendennis, which, however shameful and disgraceful, when told regarding the chief personage and Godfather of a novel, must, nevertheless, be made known to the public who reads his veritable memoirs. Having gone to bed ill with fever, and suffering to a certain degree under the passion of love, after he had gone through his physical malady, and had been bled and had been blistered, and had had his head shaved, and had been treated and medicamented as the doctor ordained: it is a fact, that, when he rallied up from his bodily ailment, his mental malady had likewise quitted him, and he was no more in love with Fanny Bolton than you or I, who are much too wise, or too moral, to allow our hearts to go gadding after porters' daughters.

He laughed at himself as he lay on his pillow, thinking of this second cure which had been effected upon him. He did not care the least about Fanny now; he wondered how he ever should have cared: and according to his custom made an autopsy of that dead passion, and anatomized his own defunct sensation for his poor little nurse. What could have made him so hot and eager about her but a few weeks back: Not her wit, not her breeding, not her beauty—there were hundreds of women better looking than she. It was out of himself that the passion had gone: it did not reside in her. She was the same; but the eyes which saw her were changed; and, alas, that it should be so! were not particularly eager to see her any more. He felt very well disposed toward the little thing, and so forth, but as for violent personal regard, such as he had but a few weeks ago, it had fled under the influence of the pill and lancet, which had destroyed the fever in his frame. And an immense source of comfort and gratitude it was to Pendennis (though there was something selfish in that feeling, as in most others of our young man), that he had been enabled to resist temptation at the time when the danger was greatest, and had no particular cause of self-reproach as he remembered his conduct toward the young girl. As from a precipice down which he might have fallen, so from the fever from which he had recovered, he reviewed the Fanny Bolton snare, now that he had escaped out of it, but I'm not sure that he was not ashamed of the very satisfaction which he experienced. It is pleasant, perhaps, but it is humiliating to own that you love no more.

Meanwhile the kind smiles and tender watchfulness of the mother at his bed-side, filled the young man with peace and security. To see that health was returning, was all the unwearied nurse demanded: to execute any caprice or order of her patient's, her chiefest joy and reward. He felt himself environed by her love, and thought himself almost as grateful for it as he had been when weak and helpless in childhood.

Some misty notions regarding the first part of his illness, and that Fanny had nursed him, Pen may have had, but they were so dim that he could not realize them with accuracy, or distinguish them from what he knew to be delusions which had occurred and were remembered during the delirium of his fever. So as he had not thought proper on former occasions to make any allusions about Fanny Bolton to his mother, of course he could not now confide to her his sentiments regarding Fanny, or make this worthy lady a confidante. It was on both sides an unlucky precaution and want of confidence; and a word or two in time might have spared the good lady and those connected with her, a deal of pain and anguish.

Seeing Miss Bolton installed as nurse and tender to Pen, I am sorry to say Mrs. Pendennis had put the worst construction on the fact of the intimacy of these two unlucky young persons, and had settled in her own mind that the accusations against Arthur were true. Why not have stopped to inquire?—There are stories to a man's disadvantage that the women who are fondest of him are always the most eager to believe. Isn't a man's wife often the first to be jealous of him? Poor Pen got a good stock of this suspicious kind of love from the nurse who was now watching over him; and the kind and pure creature thought that her boy had gone through a malady much more awful and debasing than the mere physical fever, and was stained by crime as well as weakened by illness. The consciousness of this she had to bear perforce silently, and to try to put a mask of cheerfulness and confidence over her inward doubt and despair and horror.

When Captain Shandon, at Boulogne, read the next number of the "Pall-Mall Gazette," it was to remark to Mrs. Shandon that Jack Finucane's hand was no longer visible in the leading articles, and that Mr. Warrington must be at work there again. "I know the crack of his whip in a hundred, and the cut which the fellow's thong leaves. There's Jack Bludyer, goes to work like a butcher, and mangles a subject. Mr. Warrington finishes a man, and lays his cuts neat and regular, straight down the back, and drawing blood every line;" at which dreadful metaphor, Mrs. Shandon said, "Law, Charles, how can you talk so! I always thought Mr. Warrington very high, but a kind gentleman; and I'm sure he was most kind to the children." Upon which Shandon said, "Yes; he's kind to the children; but he's savage to the men; and to be sure, my dear, you don't understand a word about what I'm saying; and it's best you shouldn't; for it's little good comes out of writing for newspapers; and it's better here, living easy at Boulogne, where the wine's plenty, and the brandy costs but two francs a bottle. Mix us another tumbler, Mary, my dear; we'll go back into harness soon. 'Cras ingens iterabimus aequor'—bad luck to it."

In a word, Warrington went to work with all his might, in place of his prostrate friend, and did Pen's portion of the "Pall-Mall Gazette" "with a vengeance," as the saying is. He wrote occasional articles and literary criticisms; he attended theatres and musical performances, and discoursed about them with his usual savage energy. His hand was too strong for such small subjects, and it pleased him to tell Arthur's mother, and uncle, and Laura, that there was no hand in all the band of penmen more graceful and light, more pleasant and more elegant, than Arthur's. "The people in this country, ma'am, don't understand what style is, or they would see the merits of our young one," he said to Mrs. Pendennis. "I call him ours, ma'am, for I bred him; and I am as proud of him as you are; and, bating a little willfulness, and a little selfishness, and a little dandyfication, I don't know a more honest, or loyal, or gentle creature. His pen is wicked sometimes, but he is as kind as a young lady—as Miss Laura here—and I believe he would not do any living mortal harm."

At this, Helen, though she heaved a deep, deep sigh, and Laura, though she, too, was sadly wounded, nevertheless were most thankful for Warrington's good opinion of Arthur, and loved him for being so attached to their Pen. And Major Pendennis was loud in his praises of Mr. Warrington—more loud and enthusiastic than it was the major's wont to be. "He is a gentleman, my dear creature," he said to Helen, "every inch a gentleman, my good madam—the Suffolk Warringtons —Charles the First's baronets: what could he be but a gentleman, come out of that family?—father—Sir Miles Warrington; ran away with— beg your pardon, Miss Bell. Sir Miles was a very well-known man in London, and a friend of the Prince of

Wales. This gentleman is a man of the greatest talents, the very highest accomplishments —sure to get on, if he had a motive to put his energies to work."

Laura blushed for herself while the major was talking and praising Arthur's hero. As she looked at Warrington's manly face and dark, melancholy eyes, this young person had been speculating about him, and had settled in her mind that he must have been the victim of an unhappy attachment; and as she caught herself so speculating, why, Miss Bell blushed.

Warrington got chambers hard by—Grenier's chambers in Flagcourt; and having executed Pen's task with great energy in the morning, his delight and pleasure of an afternoon was to come and sit with the sick man's company in the sunny autumn evenings; and he had the honor more than once of giving Miss Bell his arm for a walk in the Temple Gardens; to take which pastime, when the frank Laura asked of Helen permission, the major eagerly said, "Yes, yes, begad—of course you go out with him—it's like the country, you know; everybody goes out with every body in the gardens, and there are beadles, you know, and that sort of thing—every body walks in the Temple Gardens." If the great arbiter of morals did not object, why should simple Helen? She was glad that her girl should have such fresh air as the river could give, and to see her return with heightened color and spirits from these harmless excursions.

Laura and Helen had come, you must know, to a little explanation. When the news arrived of Pen's alarming illness, Laura insisted upon accompanying the terrified mother to London, would not hear of the refusal which the still angry Helen gave her, and, when refused a second time yet more sternly, and when it seemed that the poor lost lad's life was despaired of, and when it was known that his conduct was such as to render all thoughts of union hopeless, Laura had, with many tears told her mother a secret with which every observant person who reads this story is acquainted already. Now she never could marry him, was she to be denied the consolation of owning how fondly, how truly, how entirely she had loved him? The mingling tears of the women appeased the agony of their grief somewhat, and the sorrows and terrors of their journey were at least in so far mitigated that they shared them together.

What could Fanny expect when suddenly brought up for sentence before a couple of such judges? Nothing but swift condemnation, awful punishment, merciless dismissal! Women are cruel critics in cases such as that in which poor Fanny was implicated; and we like them to be so: for, besides the guard which a man places round his own harem, and the defenses which a woman has in her heart, her faith, and honor, hasn't she all her own friends of her own sex to keep watch that she does not go astray, and to tear her to pieces if she is found erring? When our Mahmouds or Selims of Baker-street or Belgrave-square visit their Fatimas with condign punishment, their mothers sew up Fatima's sack for her, and her sisters and sisters-in-law see her well under water. And this present writer does not say nay. He protests most solemnly he is a Turk, too. He wears a turban and a beard like another, and is all for the sack practice, Bismillah! But O you spotless, who have the right of capital punishment vested in you, at least be very cautious that you make away with the proper (if so she may be called) person. Be very sure of the fact before you order the barge out: and don't pop your subject into the Bosphorus, until you are quite certain that she deserves it. This is all I would urge in Poor Fatima's behalf—absolutely all—not a word more, by the beard of the Prophet. If she's guilty, down with her—heave over the sack, away with it into the Golden Horn bubble and squeak, and justice being done, give away, men, and let us pull back to supper.

So the major did not in any way object to Warrington's continued promenades with Miss Laura, but, like a benevolent old gentleman, encouraged in every way the intimacy of that couple. Were there any exhibitions in town? he was for Warrington conducting her to them. If Warrington had proposed to take her to Vauxhall itself, this most complaisant of men would have seen no harm—nor would Helen, if Pendennis the elder had so ruled it—nor would there have been any harm between two persons whose honor was entirely spotless—between Warrington, who saw in intimacy a pure, and high-minded, and artless woman for the first time in his life—and Laura, who too for the first time was thrown into the constant society of a gentleman of great natural parts and powers of pleasing; who possessed varied acquirements, enthusiasm, simplicity, humor, and that freshness of mind which his simple life and habits gave him, and which contrasted so much with Pen's dandy indifference of manner and faded sneer. In Warrington's very uncouthness there was a refinement, which the other's finery lacked. In his energy, his respect, his desire to please, his hearty laughter, or simple confiding pathos, what a difference to Sultan Pen's yawning sovereignty and languid acceptance of homage! What had made Pen at home such a dandy and such a despot? The women had spoiled him, as we like them and as they like to do. They had cloyed him with obedience, and surfeited him with sweet respect and submission, until he grew weary of the slaves who waited upon him, and their caresses and cajoleries excited him no more. Abroad, he was brisk and lively, and eager and impassioned enough—most men are so constituted and so nurtured. Does this, like the former sentence, run a chance of being misinterpreted, and does any one dare to suppose that the writer would incite the women to revolt? Never, by the whiskers of the Prophet, again he says. He wears a beard, and he likes his women to be slaves. What man doesn't? What man would be henpecked, I say?—We will cut off all the heads in Christendom or Turkeydom rather than that.

Well, then, Arthur being so languid, and indifferent, and careless about the favors bestowed upon him, how came it that Laura should have such a love and rapturous regard for him, that a mere inadequate expression of it should have kept the girl talking all the way from Fairoaks to London, as she and Helen traveled in the post-chaise? As soon as Helen had finished one story about the dear fellow, and narrated, with a hundred sobs and ejaculations, and looks up to heaven, some thrilling incidents which occurred about the period when the hero was breeched, Laura began another equally interesting, and equally ornamented with tears, and told how heroically he had a tooth out or wouldn't have it out, or how daringly he robbed a bird's nest, or how magnanimously he spared it; or how he gave a shilling to the old woman on the common, or went without his bread and butter for the beggar-boy who came into the yard—and so on. One to another the sobbing women sang laments upon their hero, who, my worthy reader has long since perceived, is no more a hero than either one of us. Being as he was, why should a sensible girl be so fond of him?

This point has been argued before in a previous unfortunate sentence (which lately drew down all the wrath of Ireland upon the writer's head), and which said that the greatest rascal-cutthroats have had somebody to be fond of them, and if those monsters, why not ordinary mortals? And with whom shall a young lady fall in love but with the person she sees? She is not supposed to lose her heart in a dream, like a Princess in the Arabian Nights; or to plight her young affections to the portrait of a gentleman in the Exhibition, or a sketch in the Illustrated London News. You have an instinct within you which inclines you to attach yourself to some one: you meet Somebody: you hear Somebody constantly praised: you walk, or ride, or waltz, or talk, or sit in the same pew at church with Somebody: you meet again, and again, and—"Marriages are made in Heaven," your dear mamma says, pinning your orange flowers wreath on, with her blessed eyes dimmed with tears—and there is a wedding breakfast, and you take off your white satin and retire to your coach and four, and you and he are a happy pair. Or, the affair is broken off and then, poor dear wounded heart! why then you meet Somebody Else and twine your young affections round number two. It is your nature so to do. Do you suppose it is all for the man's sake that you love, and not a bit for your own? Do you suppose you would drink if you were not thirsty, or eat if you were not hungry?

So then Laura liked Pen because she saw scarcely any body else at Fairoaks except Doctor Portman and Captain Glanders, and because his mother constantly praised her Arthur, and because he was gentleman-like, tolerably good-looking and witty, and because, above all, it was of her nature to like somebody. And having once received this image into her heart, she there tenderly nursed it and clasped it—she there, in his long absences and her constant solitudes, silently brooded over it and fondled it— and when after this she came to London, and had an opportunity of becoming rather intimate with Mr. George Warrington, what on earth was to prevent her from thinking him a most odd, original, agreeable, and pleasing person?

A long time afterward, when these days were over, and Fate in its own way had disposed of the various persons now assembled in the dingy building in Lamb-court, perhaps some of them looked back and thought how happy the time was, and how pleasant had been their evening talks and little walks and simple recreations round the sofa of Pen the convalescent. The major had a favorable opinion of September in London from that time forward, and declared at his clubs and in society that the dead season in town was often pleasant, doosid pleasant, begad. He used to go home to his lodgings in Bury-street of a night, wondering that it was already so late, and that the evening had passed away so quietly. He made his appearance at the Temple pretty constantly in the afternoon, and tugged up the long, black staircase with quite a benevolent activity and perseverance. And he made interest with the chef at Bays's (that renowned cook, the superintendence of whose work upon Gastronomy compelled the gifted author to stay in the metropolis), to prepare little jellies, delicate clear soups, aspics, and other trifles good for invalids, which Morgan the valet constantly brought down to the little Lamb-court colony. And the permission to drink a glass or two of pure sherry being accorded to Pen by Doctor Goodenough, the major told with almost tears in his eyes how his noble friend the Marquis of Steyne, passing through London on his way to the Continent, had ordered any quantity of his precious, his priceless Amontillado, that had been a present from King Ferdinand to the noble marquis, to be placed at the disposal of Mr. Arthur Pendennis. The widow and Laura tasted it with respect (though they didn't in the least like the bitter flavor), but the invalid was greatly invigorated by it, and Warrington pronounced it superlatively good, and proposed the major's health in a mock speech after dinner on the first day when the wine was served, and that of Lord Steyne and the aristocracy in general.

Major Pendennis returned thanks with the utmost gravity and in a speech in which he used the words "the present occasion," at least the proper number of times. Pen cheered with his feeble voice from his arm-chair. Warrington taught Miss Laura to cry "Hear! hear!" and tapped the table with his knuckles. Pidgeon the attendant grinned, and honest Doctor Goodenough found the party so merrily engaged, when he came in to pay his faithful, gratuitous visit.

Warrington knew Sibwright, who lived below, and that gallant gentleman, in reply to a letter informing him of the use to which his apartments had been put, wrote back the most polite and flowery letter of acquiescence. He placed his chambers at the service of their fair occupants, his bed at their disposal, his carpets at their feet. Everybody was kindly disposed toward the sick man and his family. His heart (and his mother's too, as we may fancy) melted within him at the thought of so much good feeling and good nature. Let Pen's biographer be pardoned for alluding to a time, not far distant, when a somewhat similar mishap brought him a providential friend, a kind physician, and a thousand proofs of a most touching and surprising kindness and sympathy There was a piano in Mr. Sibwright's chamber (indeed this gentleman, a lover of all the arts, performed himself—and exceedingly ill too—upon the instrument); and had had a song dedicated to him (the words by himself, the air by his devoted friend Leopoldo Twankidillo), and at this music-box, as Mr. Warrington called it, Laura, at first with a great deal of tremor and blushing (which became her very much), played and sang, sometimes of an evening, simple airs, and old songs of home. Her voice was a rich contralto, and Warrington, who scarcely knew one tune from another, and who had but one time or bray in his repertoire—a most discordant imitation of God save the King—sat rapt in delight listening to these songs. He could follow their rhythm if not their harmony; and he could watch, with a constant and daily growing enthusiasm, the pure, and tender, and generous creature who made the music.

I wonder how that poor pale little girl in the black bonnet, who used to stand at the lamp-post in Lamb-court sometimes of an evening looking up to the open windows from which the music came, liked to hear it? When Pen's bed-time came the songs were hushed. Lights appeared in the upper room: his room, whither the widow used to conduct him; and then the major and Mr. Warrington, and sometimes Miss Laura, would have a game at écarté or backgammon; or she would sit by working a pair of slippers in worsted—a pair of gentleman's slippers—they might have been for Arthur, or for George, or for Major Pendennis: one of those three would have given any thing for the slippers.

While such business as this was going on within, a rather shabby old gentleman would come and lead away the pale girl in the black bonnet; who had no right to be abroad in the night air, and the Temple porters, the few laundresses, and other amateurs who had been listening to the concert, would also disappear.

Just before ten o'clock there was another musical performance, namely, that of the chimes of St. Clement's clock in the Strand, which played the clear, cheerful notes of a psalm, before it proceeded to ring its ten fatal strokes. As they were ringing, Laura began to fold up the slippers; Martha from Fairoaks appeared with a bed-candle, and a constant smile on her face; the major said, "God bless my soul, is it so late?" Warrington and he left their unfinished game, and got up and shook hands with Miss Bell. Martha from Fairoaks lighted them out of the passage and down the stair, and, as they descended, they could hear, her bolting and locking "the sporting door" after them, upon her young mistress and herself. If there had been any danger, grinning Martha said she would have got down "that thar hooky soord which hung up in gantleman's room,"—meaning the Damascus scimitar with the names of the Prophet engraved on the blade and the red-velvet scabbard, which Percy Sibwright, Esquire, brought back from his tour in the Levant, along with an Albanian dress, and which he wore with such elegant effect at Lady Mullinger's fancy ball, Gloucester-square, Hyde Park. It entangled itself in Miss Kewsey's train, who appeared in the dress in which she, with her mamma, had been presented to their sovereign (the latter by the L—d Ch-nc-ll-r's lady), and led to events which have nothing to do with this history. Is not Miss Kewsey now Mrs. Sibwright? Has Sibwright not got a county court?—Good night, Laura and Fairoaks Martha. Sleep well and wake happy, pure and gentle lady.

Sometimes after these evenings Warrington would walk a little way with Major Pendennis—just a little way—just as far as the Temple gate—as the Strand—as Charing Cross—as the Club—he was not going into the Club? Well, as far as Bury-street where he would laughingly shake hands on the major's own door-step. They had been talking about Laura all the way. It was wonderful how enthusiastic the major, who, as we know, used to dislike her, had grown to be regarding the young lady. "Dev'lish fine girl, begad. Dev'lish well-mannered girl—my sister-in-law has the manners of a duchess and would bring up any girl well. Miss Bell's a little countryfied. But the smell of the hawthorn is pleasant, demmy. How she blushes! Your London girls would give many a guinea for a bouquet like that—natural flowers, begad! And she's a little money too—nothing to speak of—but a pooty little bit of money." In all which opinions no doubt Mr. Warrington agreed; and though he laughed as he shook hands with the major, his face fell as he left his veteran companion; and he strode back to chambers, and smoked pipe after pipe long into the night, and wrote article upon article, more and more savage, in lieu of friend Pen disabled.

Well, it was a happy time for almost all parties concerned. Pen mended daily. Sleeping and eating were his constant occupations. His appetite was something frightful. He was ashamed of exhibiting it before Laura, and almost before his mother, who laughed and applauded him. As the roast chicken of his dinner went away he eyed the departing friend with sad longing, and began to long for jelly, or tea, or what not. He was like an ogre in devouring. The doctor cried stop, but Pen would not. Nature called out to him more loudly than the doctor, and that kind and friendly physician handed him over with a very good grace to the other healer.

And here let us speak very tenderly and in the strictest confidence of an event which befell him, and to which he never liked an allusion. During his delirium the ruthless Goodenough ordered ice to be put to his head, and all his lovely hair to be cut. It was done in the time of—of the other nurse, who left every single hair of course in a paper for the widow to count and treasure up. She never believed but that the girl had taken away some of it, but then women are so suspicious upon these matters.

When this direful loss was made visible to Major Pendennis, as of course it was the first time the elder saw the poor young man's shorn pate, and when Pen was quite out of danger, and gaining daily vigor, the major, with something like blushes and a queer wink of his eyes, said he knew of a—a person—a coiffeur, in fact—a good man, whom he would send down to the Temple, and who would—a—apply—a—a temporary remedy to that misfortune.

Laura looked at Warrington with the archest sparkle in her eyes— Warrington fairly burst out into a boohoo of laughter: even the widow was obliged to laugh: and the major erubescent confounded the impudence of the young folks, and said when he had his hair cut he would keep a lock of it for Miss Laura.

Warrington voted that Pen should wear a barrister's wig. There was Sibwright's down below, which would become him hugely. Pen said "Stuff," and seemed as confused as his uncle; and the end was that a gentleman from Burlington Arcade waited next day upon Mr. Pendennis, and had a private interview with him in his bedroom; and a week afterward the same individual appeared with a box under his arm, and an ineffable grin of politeness on his face, and announced that he had brought 'ome Mr. Pendennis's 'ead of 'air.

It must have been a grand but melancholy sight to see Pen in the recesses of his apartment, sadly contemplating his ravaged beauty, and the artificial means of hiding its ruin. He appeared at length in the 'ead of 'air; but Warrington laughed so that Pen grew sulky, and went back for his velvet cap, a neat turban which the fondest of mammas had worked for him. Then Mr. Warrington and Miss Bell got some flowers off the ladies' bonnets and made a wreath, with which they decorated the wig and brought it out in procession, and did homage before it. In fact they indulged in a hundred sports, jocularities, waggeries, and petits jeux innocens: so that the second and third floors of number 6, Lambcourt, Temple, rang with more cheerfulness and laughter than had been known in those precincts for many a long day.

At last, after about ten days of this life, one evening when the little spy of the court came out to take her usual post of observation at the lamp, there was no music from the second floor window, there were no lights in the third story chambers, the windows of each were open, and the occupants were gone. Mrs. Flanagan the laundress, told Fanny what had happened. The ladies and all the party had gone to Richmond for change of air. The antique traveling chariot was brought out again and cushioned with many pillows for Pen and his mother; and Miss Laura went in the most affable manner in the omnibus under the guardianship of Mr. George Warrington. He came back and took possession of his old bed that night in the vacant and cheerless chambers, and to his old books and his old pipes, but not perhaps to his old sleep.

The widow had left a jar full of flowers upon his table, prettily arranged, and when he entered they filled the solitary room with odor. They were memorials of the kind, gentle souls who had gone away, and who had decorated for a little while that lonely, cheerless place. He had had the happiest days of his whole life, George felt—he knew it now they were just gone: he went and took up the flowers and put his face to them, smelt them—perhaps kissed them. As he put them down, he rubbed his rough hand across his eyes with a bitter word and laugh. He would have given his whole life and soul to win that prize which Arthur rejected. Did she want fame? he would have won it for her: devotion?—a great heart full of pent-up tenderness and manly love and gentleness was there for her, if she might take it. But it might not be. Fate had ruled otherwise. "Even if I could, she would not have me," George thought. "What has an ugly, rough old fellow like me, to make any woman like him? I'm getting old, and I've made no mark in life. I've neither good looks, nor youth, nor money, nor reputation. A man must be able to do something besides stare at her and offer on his knees his uncouth devotion, to make a woman like him. What can I do? Lots of young fellows have passed me in the race—what they call the prizes of life didn't seem to me worth the trouble of the struggle. But for her. If she had been mine and liked a diamond—ah! shouldn't she have worn it! Psha, what a fool I am to brag of what I would have done! We are the slaves of destiny. Our lots are shaped for us, and mine is ordained long ago. Come, let us have a pipe, and put the smell of these flowers out of court. Poor little silent flowers! you'll be dead to-morrow. What business had you to show your red cheeks in this dingy place?"

By his bed-side George found a new Bible which the widow had placed there, with a note inside saying that she had not seen the book among his collection in a room where she had spent a number of hours, and where God had vouchsafed to her prayers the life of her son, and that she gave to Arthur's friend the best thing she could, and besought him to read in the volume sometimes, and to keep it as a token of a grateful mother's regard and affection. Poor George mournfully kissed the book as he had done the flowers; and the morning found him still reading in its awful pages, in which so many stricken hearts, in which so many tender and faithful souls, have found comfort under calamity and refuge and hope in affliction.

CHAPTER XVI

FANNY'S OCCUPATION'S GONE

Good Helen, ever since her son's illness, had taken, as we have seen, entire possession of the young man, of his drawers and closets and all which they contained: whether shirts that wanted buttons, or stockings that required mending, or, must it be owned? letters that lay among those articles of raiment, and which of course it was necessary that somebody should answer during Arthur's weakened and incapable condition. Perhaps Mrs. Pendennis was laudably desirous to have some explanations about the dreadful Fanny Bolton mystery, regarding which she had never breathed a word to her son, though it was present in her mind always, and occasioned her inexpressible anxiety and disquiet. She had caused the brass knocker to be screwed off the inner door of the chambers, whereupon the postman's startling double rap would, as she justly argued, disturb the rest of her patient, and she did not allow him to see any letter which arrived, whether from boot-makers who importuned him, or hatters who had a heavy account to make up against next Saturday, and would be very much obliged if Mr. Arthur Pendennis would have the kindness to settle, &c. Of these documents, Pen, who was always free-handed and careless, of course had his share, and though no great one, one quite enough to alarm his scrupulous and conscientious mother. She had some savings; Pen's magnificent self-denial, and her own economy amounting from her great simplicity and avoidance of show to parsimony almost, had enabled her to put by a little sum of money, a part of which she delightedly consecrated to the paying off the young gentleman's obligations. At this price, many a worthy youth and respected reader would hand over his correspondence to his parents; and, perhaps, there is no greater test of a man's regularity and easiness of conscience, than his readiness to face the postman. Blessed is he who is made happy by the sound of the rat-tat! The good are eager for it: but the naughty tremble at the sound thereof. So it was very kind of Mrs. Pendennis doubly to spare Pen the trouble of hearing or answering letters during his illness.

There could have been nothing in the young man's chests of drawers and wardrobes which could be considered as inculpating him in any way, nor any satisfactory documents regarding the Fanny Bolton affair found there, for the widow had to ask her brother-in-law if he knew any thing about the odious transaction; and the dreadful intrigue about which her son was engaged. When they were at Richmond one day, and Pen with Warrington had taken a seat on a bench on the terrace, the widow kept Major Pendennis in consultation, and laid her terrors and perplexities before him, such of them at least (for as is the wont of men and women, she did not make quite a clean confession, and I suppose no spendthrift asked for a schedule of his debts, no lady of fashion asked by her husband for her dress-maker's bills ever sent in the whole of them yet)—such, we say, of her perplexities, at least, as she chose to confide to her director for the time being.

When, then, she asked the major what course she ought to pursue, about this dreadful—this horrid affair, and whether he knew any thing regarding it? the old gentleman puckered up his face, so that you could not tell whether he was smiling or not; gave the widow one queer look with his little eyes; cast them down to the carpet again, and said, "My dear, good creature, I don't know any thing about it; and I don't wish to know any thing about it; and, as you ask me my opinion, I think you had best know nothing about it too. Young men will be young men; and, begad, my good ma'am, if you think our boy is a Jo—"

"Pray, spare me this," Helen broke in, looking very stately.

"My dear creature, I did not commence the conversation, permit me to say," the major said, bowing very blandly.

"I can't bear to hear such a sin—such a dreadful sin—spoken of in such a way," the widow said, with tears of annoyance starting from her eyes. "I can't bear to think that my boy should commit such a crime. I wish he had died, almost, before he had done it. I don't know how I survive it myself; for it is breaking my heart, Major Pendennis, to think that his father's son—my child—whom I remember so good—oh, so good, and full of honor!—should be fallen so dreadfully low, as to—as to—"

"As to flirt with a little grisette? my dear creature," said the major. "Egad, if all the mothers in England were to break their hearts because—Nay, nay; upon my word and honor, now, don't agitate yourself—

don't cry. I can't bear to see a woman's tears—I never could—never. But how do we know that any thing serious has happened? Has Arthur said any thing?"

"His silence confirms it," sobbed Mrs. Pendennis, behind her pocket-handkerchief.

"Not at all. There are subjects, my dear, about which a young fellow can not surely talk to his mamma," insinuated the brother-in-law.

"She has written to him" cried the lady, behind the cambric.

"What, before he was ill? Nothing more likely."

"No, since;" the mourner with the batiste mask gasped out; "not before; that is, I don't think so—that is, I—"

"Only since; and you have—yes, I understand. I suppose when he was too ill to read his own correspondence, you took charge of it, did you?"

"I am the most unhappy mother in the world," cried out the unfortunate Helen.

"The most unhappy mother in the world, because your son is a man and not a hermit! Have a care, my dear sister. If you have suppressed any letters to him, you may have done yourself a great injury; and, if I know any thing of Arthur's spirit, may cause a difference between him and you, which you'll rue all your life—a difference that's a dev'lish deal more important, my good madam, than the little—little — trumpery cause which originated it."

"There was only one letter," broke out Helen—"only a very little one—only a few words. Here it is—O— how can you, how can you speak so?"

When the good soul said only "a very little one," the major could not speak at all, so inclined was he to laugh, in spite of the agonies of the poor soul before him, and for whom he had a hearty pity and liking too. But each was looking at the matter with his or her peculiar eyes and view of morals, and the major's morals, as the reader knows, were not those of an ascetic.

"I recommend you," he gravely continued, "if you can, to seal it up —those letters ain't unfrequently sealed with wafers—and to put it among Pen's other letters, and let him have them when he calls for them. Or if we can't seal it, we mistook it for a bill."

"I can't tell my son a lie," said the widow. It had been put silently into the letter-box two days previous to their departure from the Temple, and had been brought to Mrs. Pendennis by Martha. She had never seen Fanny's handwriting of course; but when the letter was put into her hands, she knew the author at once. She had been on the watch for that letter every day since Pen had been ill. She had opened some of his other letters because she wanted to get at that one. She had the horrid paper poisoning her bag at that moment. She took it out and offered it to her brother-in-law.

"Arthur Pendennis, Esq.," he read in a timid little sprawling handwriting, and with a sneer on his face. "No, my dear, I won't read any more. But you, who have read it, may tell me what the letter contains— only prayers for his health in bad spelling, you say—and a desire to see him? Well—there's no harm in that. And as you ask me"—here the major began to look a little queer for his own part, and put on his demure look—"as you ask me, my dear, for information, why, I don't mind telling you that—ah—that—Morgan, my man, has made some inquiries regarding this affair, and that—my friend Doctor Goodenough also looked into it—and it appears that this person was greatly smitten with Arthur; that he paid for her and took her to Vauxhall Gardens, as Morgan heard from an old acquaintance of Pen's and ours, an Irish gentleman, who was very nearly once having the honor of being the—from an Irishman, in fact;—that the girl's father, a violent man of intoxicated habits, has beaten her mother, who persists in declaring her daughter's entire innocence to her husband on the one hand, while on the other she told Goodenough that Arthur had acted like a brute to her child. And so you see the story remains in a mystery. Will you have it cleared up? I have but to ask Pen, and he will tell me at once—he is as honorable a man as ever lived."

"Honorable!" said the widow, with bitter scorn. "O, brother, what is this you call honor? If my boy has been guilty, he must marry her. I would go down on my knees and pray him to do so."

"Good God! are you mad?" screamed out the major; and remembering former passages in Arthur's history and Helen's, the truth came across his mind that, were Helen to make this prayer to her son, he would marry the girl: he was wild enough and obstinate enough to commit any folly when a woman he loved was in the case. "My dear sister, have you lost your senses?" he continued (after an agitated pause, during which the above dreary reflection crossed him), and in a softened tone. "What right have we to suppose that any thing has passed between this girl and him? Let's see the letter. Her heart is breaking; pray, pray, write to me—home unhappy—unkind father—your nurse—poor little Fanny—spelt, as you say, in a manner to outrage all sense of decorum. But, good heavens! my dear, what is there in this? only that the little devil is making love to him still. Why she didn't come into his chambers until he was so delirious that he didn't know her. Whatd'youcallem, Flanagan, the laundress, told Morgan, my man, so. She came in company with an old fellow, an old Mr. Bows, who came most kindly down to Stillbrook and brought me away—by the way, I left him in the cab, and never paid the fare; and dev'lish kind it was of him. No, there's nothing in the story."

"Do you think so? Thank Heaven—thank God!" Helen cried. "I'll take the letter to Arthur and ask him now. Look at him there. He's on the terrace with Mr. Warrington. They are talking to some children. My boy was always fond of children. He's innocent, thank God—thank God! Let me go to him."

Old Pendennis had his own opinion. When he briskly took the not guilty side of the case, but a moment before, very likely the old gentleman had a different view from that which he chose to advocate, and judged of Arthur by what he himself would have done. If she goes to Arthur, and he speaks the truth, as the rascal will, it spoils all, he thought. And he tried one more effort.

"My dear, good soul," he said, taking Helen's hand and kissing it, "as your son has not acquainted you with this affair, think if you have any right to examine it. As you believe him to be a man of honor, what right have you to doubt his honor in this instance? Who is his accuser? An anonymous scoundrel who has brought no specific charge against him. If there were any such, wouldn't the girl's parents have come forward? He is not called upon to rebut, nor you to entertain an anonymous accusation; and as for believing him guilty because a girl of that rank happened to be in his rooms acting as nurse to him, begad you might as well insist upon his marrying that dem'd old Irish gin-drinking laundress, Mrs. Flanagan."

The widow burst out laughing through her tears—the victory was gained by the old general.

"Marry Mrs. Flanagan, by Ged," he continued, tapping her slender hand. "No. The boy has told you nothing about it, and you know nothing about it. The boy is innocent—of course. And what, my good soul, is the course for us to pursoo? Suppose he is attached to this girl—don't look sad again, it's merely a supposition—and begad a young fellow may have an attachment, mayn't he?—Directly he gets well he will be at her again."

"He must come home! We must go directly to Fairoaks," the widow cried out.

"My good creature, he'll bore himself to death at Fairoaks. He'll have nothing to do but to think about his passion there. There's no place in the world for making a little passion into a big one, and where a fellow feeds on his own thoughts, like a dem'd lonely country-house where there's nothing to do. We must occupy him: amuse him: we must take him abroad: he's never been abroad except to Paris for a lark. We must travel a little. He must have a nurse with him, to take great care of him, for Goodenough says he had a dev'lish narrow squeak of it (don't look frightened), and so you must come and watch: and I suppose you'll take Miss Bell, and I should like to ask Warrington to come. Arthur's dev'lish fond of Warrington. He can't do without Warrington. Warrington's family is one of the oldest in England, and he is one of the best young fellows I ever met in my life. I like him exceedingly."

"Does Mr. Warrington know any thing about this—this affair?" asked Helen. "He had been away, I know, for two months before it happened: Pen wrote me so."

"Not a word—I—I've asked him about it. I've pumped him. He never heard of the transaction, never; I pledge you my word," cried out the major, in some alarm. "And, my dear, I think you had much best not talk to him about it—much best not—of course not: the subject is most delicate and painful."

The simple widow took her brother's hand and pressed it. "Thank you, brother," she said. "You have been very, very kind to me. You have given me a great deal of comfort. I'll go to my room, and think of what you have said. This illness and these—these—emotions—have agitated me a great deal; and I'm not very strong, you know. But I'll go and thank God that my boy is innocent. He is innocent. Isn't he, sir?"

"Yes, my dearest creature, yes," said the old fellow, kissing her affectionately, and quite overcome by her tenderness. He looked after her as she retreated, with a fondness which was rendered more piquant, as it were, by the mixture of a certain scorn which accompanied it. "Innocent!" he said; "I'd swear, till I was black in the face, he was innocent, rather than give that good soul pain."

Having achieved this victory, the fatigued and happy warrior laid himself down on the sofa, and put his yellow silk pocket-handkerchief over his face, and indulged in a snug little nap, of which the dreams, no doubt, were very pleasant, as he snored with refreshing regularity. The young men sate, meanwhile, dawdling away the sunshiny hours on the terrace, very happy, and Pen, at least, very talkative. He was narrating to Warrington a plan for a new novel, and a new tragedy. Warrington laughed at the idea of his writing a tragedy? By Jove, he would show that he could; and he began to spout some of the lines of his play.

The little solo on the wind instrument which the major was performing was interrupted by the entrance of Miss Bell. She had been on a visit to her old friend, Lady Rockminster, who had taken a summer villa in the neighborhood; and who, hearing of Arthur's illness, and his mother's arrival at Richmond, had visited the latter; and, for the benefit of the former, whom she didn't like, had been prodigal of grapes, partridges, and other attentions. For Laura the old lady had a great fondness, and longed that she should come and stay with her; but Laura could not leave her mother at this juncture. Worn out by constant watching over Arthur's health, Helen's own had suffered very considerably; and Doctor Goodenough had had reason to prescribe for her as well as for his younger patient.

Old Pendennis started up on the entrance of the young lady. His slumbers were easily broken. He made her a gallant speech—he had been full of gallantry toward her of late. Where had she been gathering those roses which she wore on her cheeks? How happy he was to be disturbed out of his dreams by such a charming reality! Laura had plenty of humor and honesty; and these two caused her to have on her side something very like a contempt for the old gentleman. It delighted her to draw out his worldlinesses, and to make the old habitue of clubs and drawing-rooms tell his twaddling tales about great folks, and expound his views of morals.

Not in this instance, however, was she disposed to be satirical. She had been to drive with Lady Rockminster in the Park, she said; and she had brought home game for Pen, and flowers for mamma. She looked very grave about mamma. She had just been with Mrs. Pendennis. Helen was very much worn, and she feared she was very, very ill. Her large eyes filled with tender marks of the sympathy which she felt in her beloved friend's condition. She was alarmed about her. "Could not that good—that dear Dr. Goodenough cure her?"

"Arthur's illness, and other mental anxiety," the major slowly said, "had, no doubt, shaken Helen." A burning blush upon the girl's face showed that she understood the old man's allusions. But she looked him full in the face and made no reply. "He might have spared me that," she thought. "What is he aiming at in recalling that shame to me?" That he had an aim in view is very possible. The old diplomatist seldom spoke without some such end. Dr. Goodenough had talked to him, he said, about their dear friend's health, and she wanted rest and change of scene—yes, change of scene. Painful circumstances which had occurred must be forgotten and never alluded to; he begged pardon for even hinting at them to Miss Bell—he never should do so again—nor, he was sure, would she. Every thing must be done to soothe and comfort their friend, and his proposal was that they should go abroad for the autumn to a watering-place in the Rhine neighborhood, where Helen might rally her exhausted spirits, and Arthur try and become a new man. Of course, Laura would not forsake her mother?

Of course not. It was about Helen, and Helen only—that is, about Arthur too for her sake that Laura was anxious. She would go abroad or any where with Helen.

And Helen having thought the matter over for an hour in her room, had by that time grown to be as anxious for the tour as any school-boy, who has been reading a book of voyages, is eager to go to sea. Whither should they go? the farther the better—to some place so remote that even recollection could not follow them thither: so delightful that Pen should never want to leave it—any where so that he could be happy. She opened her desk with trembling fingers and took out her banker's book, and counted up her little savings. If more was wanted, she had the diamond cross. She would borrow from Laura again. "Let us go—let us go," she thought; "directly he can bear the journey let us go away. Come, kind Doctor Goodenough—come quick, and give us leave to quit England."

The good doctor drove over to dine with them that very day. "If you agitate yourself so," he said to her, "and if your heart beats so, and if you persist in being so anxious about a young gentleman who is getting well as fast as he can, we shall have you laid up, and Miss Laura to watch you: and then it will be her turn to be ill, and I should like to know how the deuce a doctor is to live who is obliged to come and attend you all for nothing? Mrs. Goodenough is already jealous of you, and says, with perfect justice, that I fall in love with my patients. And you must please to get out of the country as soon as ever you can, that I may have a little peace in my family."

When the plan of going abroad was proposed to Arthur, it was received by that gentleman with the greatest alacrity and enthusiasm. He longed to be off at once. He let his mustaches grow from that very moment, in order, I suppose, that he might get his mouth into training for a perfect French and German pronunciation; and he was seriously disquieted in his mind because the mustaches, when they came, were of a decidedly red color. He had looked forward to an autumn at Fairoaks; and perhaps the idea of passing two or three months there did not amuse the young man. "There is not a soul to speak to in the place," he said to Warrington. "I can't stand old Portman's sermons, and pompous after-dinner conversation. I know all old Glanders's stories about the Peninsular war. The Claverings are the only Christian people in the neighborhood, and they are not to be at home before Christmas, my uncle says: besides, Warrington, I want to get out of the country. While you were away, confound it, I had a temptation, from which I am very thankful to have escaped, and which I count that even my illness came very luckily to put an end to." And here he narrated to his friend the circumstances of the Vauxhall affair, with which the reader is already acquainted.

Warrington looked very grave when he heard this story. Putting the moral delinquency out of the question, he was extremely glad for Arthur's sake that the latter had escaped from a danger which might have made his whole life wretched; "which certainly," said Warrington, "would have occasioned the wretchedness and ruin of the other party. And your mother—and your friends—what a pain it would have been to them!" urged Pen's companion, little knowing what grief and annoyance these good people had already suffered.

"Not a word to my mother!" Pen cried out, in a state of great alarm, "She would never get over it. An esclandre of that sort would kill her, I do believe. And," he added, with a knowing air, and as if, like a young rascal of a Lovelace, he had been engaged in what are called affairs de coeur, all his life; "the best way, when a danger of that sort menaces, is not to face it, but to turn one's back on it and run."

"And were you very much smitten?" Warrington asked.

"Hm!" said Lovelace. "She dropped her h's, but she was a dear little girl."

O Clarissas of this life, O you poor little ignorant vain foolish maidens! if you did but know the way in which the Lovelaces speak of you: if you could but hear Jack talking to Tom across the coffee-room of a Club; or see Ned taking your poor little letters out of his cigar-case and handing them over to Charley, and Billy, and Harry across the mess-room table, you would not be so eager to write, or so ready to listen! There's a sort of crime which is not complete unless the lucky rogue boasts of it afterward; and the man who betrays your honor in the first place, is pretty sure, remember that, to betray your secret too.

"It's hard to fight, and it's easy to fall," Warrington said gloomily. "And as you say, Pendennis, when a danger like this is imminent, the best way is to turn your back on it and run."

After this little discourse upon a subject about which Pen would have talked a great deal more eloquently a month back, the conversation reverted to the plans for going abroad, and Arthur eagerly pressed his
friend to be of the party. Warrington was a part of the family—a part of the cure. Arthur said he should not have half the pleasure without Warrington.

But George said no, he couldn't go. He must stop at home and take Pen's place. The other remarked that that was needless, for Shandon was now come back to London, and Arthur was entitled to a holiday.

"Don't press me," Warrington said, "I can't go. I've particular engagements. I'm best at home. I've not got the money to travel, that's the long and short of it, for traveling costs money, you know."

This little obstacle seemed fatal to Pen. He mentioned it to his mother: Mrs. Pendennis was very sorry; Mr. Warrington had been exceedingly kind; but she supposed he knew best about his affairs. And then, no doubt, she reproached herself, for selfishness in wishing to carry the boy off and have him to herself altogether.

"What is this I hear from Pen, my dear Mr. Warrington?" the major asked one day, when the pair were alone, and after Warrington's objection had been stated to him. "Not go with us? We can't hear of such a thing—Pen won't get well without you. I promise you, I'm not going to be his nurse. He must have somebody with him that's stronger and gayer and better able to amuse him than a rheumatic old fogy like me. I shall go to Carlsbad very likely, when I've seen you people settle down. Traveling costs nothing nowadays—or so little! And—and pray, Warrington, remember that I was your father's very old friend, and if you and your brother are not on such terms as to enable you to—to anticipate you younger brother's allowance, I beg you to make me your banker, for hasn't Pen been getting into your debt these three weeks past, during which you have been doing what he informs me is his work, with such exemplary talent and genius, begad?"

Still, in spite of this kind offer and unheard-of generosity on the part of the major, George Warrington refused, and said he would stay at home. But it was with a faltering voice and an irresolute accent which showed how much he would like to go, though his tongue persisted in saying nay.

But the major's persevering benevolence was not to be balked in this way. At the tea-table that evening, Helen happening to be absent from the room for the moment, looking for Pen who had gone to roost, old Pendennis returned to the charge, and rated Warrington for refusing to join in their excursion. "Isn't it ungallant, Miss Bell?" he said, turning to that young lady. "Isn't it unfriendly? Here we have been the happiest party in the world, and this odious, selfish creature breaks it up!"

Miss Bell's long eye-lashes looked down toward her tea-cup: and Warrington blushed hugely but did not speak. Neither did Miss Bell speak: but when he blushed she blushed too.

"You ask him to come, my dear," said the benevolent old gentleman, "and then perhaps he will listen to you—" "Why should Mr. Warrington listen to me?" asked the young lady, putting her query to her tea-spoon, seemingly, and not to the major.

"Ask him; you have not asked him," said Pen's artless uncle.

"I should be very glad, indeed, if Mr. Warrington would come," remarked Laura to the tea-spoon.

"Would you?" said George.

She looked up and said, "Yes." Their eyes met. "I will go any where you ask me, or do any thing," said George, lowly, and forcing out the words as if they gave him pain.

Old Pendennis was delighted; the affectionate old creature clapped his hands and cried "Bravo! bravo! It's a bargain—a bargain, begad! Shake hands on it, young people!" And Laura, with a look full of tender brightness, put out her hand to Warrington. He took hers: his face indicated a strange agitation. He seemed to be about to speak, when, from Pen's neighboring room Helen entered, looking at them as the candle which she held lighted her pale, frightened face.

Laura blushed more red than ever and withdrew her hand.

"What is it?" Helen asked.

"It's a bargain we have been making, my dear creature," said the major in his most caressing voice. "We have just bound over Mr. Warrington in a promise to come abroad with us."

"Indeed!" Helen said.

CHAPTER XVII

IN WHICH FANNY ENGAGES A NEW MEDICAL MAN

Could Helen have suspected that, with Pen's returning strength, his unhappy partiality for little Fanny would also reawaken? Though she never spoke a word regarding that young person, after her conversation with the major, and though, to all appearance, she utterly ignored Fanny's existence, yet Mrs. Pendennis kept a particularly close watch upon all Master Arthur's actions; on the plea of ill-health, would scarcely let him out of her sight; and was especially anxious that he should be spared the trouble of all correspondence for the present at least. Very likely Arthur looked at his own letters with some tremor; very likely, as he received them at the family table, feeling his mother's watch upon him (though the good soul's eye seemed fixed upon her tea-cup or her book), he expected daily to see a little handwriting, which he would have known, though he had never seen it yet, and his heart beat as he received the letters to his address. Was he more pleased or annoyed, that, day after day, his expectations were not realized; and was his mind relieved, that there came no letter from Fanny? Though, no doubt, in these matters, when Lovelace is tired of Clarissa (or the contrary), it is best for both parties to break at once, and each, after the failure of the attempt at union, to go his own way, and pursue his course through life solitary; yet our self-love, or our pity, or our sense of decency, does not like that sudden bankruptcy. Before we announce to the world that our firm of Lovelace and Co. can't meet its engagements, we try to make compromises: we have mournful meetings of partners: we delay the putting up of the shutters, and the dreary announcement of the failure. It must come: but we pawn our jewels to keep things going a little longer. On the whole, I dare say, Pen was rather annoyed that he had no remonstrances from Fanny. What! could she part from him, and never so much as once look round? could she sink, and never once hold a little hand out, or cry, "Help, Arthur?" Well, well: they don't all go down who venture on that voyage. Some few drown when the vessel founders; but most are only ducked, and scramble to shore. And the reader's experience of A. Pendennis, Esquire, of the Upper Temple, will enable him to state whether that gentleman belonged to the class of persons who were likely to sink or to swim.

Though Pen was as yet too weak to walk half a mile; and might not, on account of his precious health, be trusted to take a drive in a carriage by himself, and without a nurse in attendance; yet Helen could not keep watch over Mr. Warrington too, and had no authority to prevent that gentleman from going to London if business called him thither. Indeed, if he had gone and staid, perhaps the widow, from reasons of her own, would have been glad; but she checked these selfish wishes as soon as she ascertained or owned them; and, remembering Warrington's great regard and services, and constant friendship for her boy, received him as a member of her family almost, with her usual melancholy kindness and submissive acquiescence. Yet somehow, one morning when his affairs called him to town, she divined what Warrington's errand was, and that he was gone to London, to get news about Fanny for Pen.

Indeed, Arthur had had some talk with his friend, and told him more at large what his adventures had been with Fanny (adventures which the reader knows already), and what were his feelings respecting her. He was very thankful that he had escaped the great danger, to which Warrington said Amen heartily: that he had no great fault wherewith to reproach himself in regard of his behavior to her, but that if they parted, as they must, he would be glad to say a God bless her, and to hope that she would remember him kindly. In his discourse with Warrington he spoke upon these matters with so much gravity, and so much emotion, that George, who had pronounced himself most strongly for the separation too, began to fear that his friend was not so well cured as he boasted of being; and that, if the two were to come together again, all the danger and the temptation might have to be fought once more. And with what result? "It is hard to struggle, Arthur, and it is easy to fall," Warrington said: "and the best courage for us poor wretches is to fly from danger. I would not have been what I am now, had I practiced what I preach."

"And what did you practice, George?" Pen asked, eagerly. "I knew there was something. Tell us about it, Warrington."

"There was something that can't be mended, and that shattered my whole fortunes early," Warrington answered, "I said I would tell you about it some day, Pen: and will, but not now. Take the moral without the fable now, Pen, my boy; and if you want to see a man whose whole life has been wrecked, by an unlucky rock against which he struck as a boy—here he is, Arthur: and so I warn you."

We have shown how Mr. Huxter, in writing home to his Clavering friends, mentioned that there was a fashionable club in London of which he was an attendant, and that he was there in the habit of meeting an Irish officer of distinction, who, among other news, had given that intelligence regarding Pendennis, which the young surgeon had transmitted to Clavering. This club was no other than the Back Kitchen, where the disciple of Saint Bartholomew was accustomed to meet the general, the peculiarities of whose brogue, appearance, disposition, and general conversation, greatly diverted many young gentlemen who used the Back Kitchen as a place of nightly entertainment and refreshment. Huxter, who had a fine natural genius for mimicking every thing, whether it was a favorite tragic or comic actor, a cock on a dunghill, a corkscrew going into a bottle and a cork issuing thence, or an Irish officer of genteel connections who offered himself as an object of imitation with only too much readiness, talked his talk, and twanged his poor old long bow whenever drink, a hearer, and an opportunity occurred, studied our friend the general with peculiar gusto, and drew the honest fellow out many a night. A bait, consisting of sixpenny-worth of brandy and water, the worthy old man was sure to swallow: and under the influence of this liquor, who was more happy than he to tell his stories of his daughter's triumphs and his own, in love, war, drink, and polite society? Thus Huxter was enabled to present to his friends many pictures of Costigan: of Costigan fighting a jewel in the Phaynix—of Costigan and his interview with the Juke of York—of Costigan at his sonunlaw's teeble, surrounded by the nobilitee of his countree—of Costigan, when crying drunk, at which time he was in the habit of confidentially lamenting his daughter's ingratichewd, and stating that his gray hairs were hastening to a praymachure greeve, And thus our friend was the means of bringing a number of young fellows to the Back Kitchen, who consumed the landlord's liquors while they relished the general's peculiarities, so that mine host pardoned many of the latter's foibles, in consideration of the good which they brought to his house. Not the highest position in life was this certainly, or one which, if we had a reverence for an old man, we would be anxious that he should occupy: but of this aged buffoon it may be mentioned that he had no particular idea that his condition of life was not a high one, and that in his whiskied blood there was not a black drop, nor in his muddled brains a bitter feeling, against any mortal being. Even his child, his cruel Emily, he would have taken to his heart and forgiven with tears; and what more can one say of the Christian charity of a man than that he is actually ready to forgive those who have done him every kindness, and with whom he is wrong in a dispute?

There was some idea among the young men who frequented, the Back Kitchen, and made themselves merry with the society of Captain Costigan, that the captain made a mystery regarding his lodgings for fear of duns, or from a desire of privacy, and lived in some wonderful place. Nor would the landlord of the premises, when questioned upon this subject, answer any inquiries; his maxim being that he only knew gentlemen who frequented that room, in that room; that when they quitted that room, having paid their scores as gentlemen, and behaved as gentlemen, his communication with them ceased; and that, as a gentleman himself, he thought it was only impertinent curiosity to ask where any other gentleman lived. Costigan, in his most intoxicated and confidential moments, also evaded any replies to questions or hints addressed to him on this subject: there was no particular secret about it, as we have seen, who have had more than once the honor of entering his apartments, but in the vicissitudes of a long life he had been pretty often in the habit of residing in houses where privacy was necessary to his comfort, and where the appearance of some visitors would have brought him any thing but pleasure. Hence all sorts of legends were formed by wags or credulous persons respecting his place of abode. It was stated that he slept habitually in a watch-box in the city; in a cab at a mews, where a cab proprietor gave him a shelter; in the Duke of York's Column, &c., the wildest of these theories being put abroad by the facetious and imaginative Huxter. For Huxey, when not silenced by the company of "swells," and when in the society of his own friends, was a very different fellow to the youth whom we have seen cowed by Pen's impertinent airs; and, adored by his family at home, was the life and soul of the circle whom he met, either round the festive board or the dissecting table.

On one brilliant September morning, as Huxter was regaling himself with a cup of coffee at a stall in Covent Garden, having spent a delicious night dancing at Vauxhall, he spied the general reeling down Henrietta-street, with a crowd of hooting, blackguard boys at his heels, who had left their beds under the arches of the river betimes, and were prowling about already for breakfast, and the strange livelihood of the day. The poor old general was not in that condition when the sneers and jokes of these young beggars had much effect upon him: the cabmen and watermen at the cab-stand knew him, and passed their comments upon him: the policemen gazed after him, and warned the boys off him, with looks of scorn and pity; what did the scorn and pity of men, the jokes of ribald children, matter to the general? He reeled along the street with glazed eyes, having just sense enough to know whither he was bound, and to pursue his accustomed beat homeward. He went to bed not knowing how he had reached it, as often as any man in London. He woke and found himself there, and asked no questions, and he was tacking about on this daily though perilous voyage, when, from his station at the coffee-stall, Huxter spied him. To note his friend, to pay his twopence (indeed, he had but eightpence left, or he would have had a cab from Vauxhall to take him home), was with the eager Huxter the work of an instant—Costigan dived down the alleys by Drury-lane Theater, where gin-shops, oyster-shops, and theatrical wardrobes abound, the proprietors of which were now asleep behind the shutters, as the pink morning lighted up their chimneys; and through these courts Huxter followed the general, until he reached Oldcastle-street, in which is the gate of Shepherd's Inn.

Here, just as he was within sight of home, a luckless slice of orange-peel came between the general's heel and the pavement, and caused the poor fellow to fall backward.

Huxter ran up to him instantly, and after a pause, during which the veteran, giddy with his fall and his previous whisky, gathered as he best might, his dizzy brains together, the young surgeon lifted up the limping general, and very kindly and good-naturedly offered to conduct him to his home. For some time, and in reply to the queries which the student of medicine put to him, the muzzy general refused to say where his lodgings were, and declared that they were hard by, and that he could reach them without difficulty; and he disengaged himself from Huxter's arm, and made a rush, as if to get to his own home unattended: but he reeled and lurched so, that the young surgeon insisted upon accompanying him, and, with many soothing expressions and cheering and consolatory phrases, succeeded in getting the general's dirty old hand under what he called his own fin, and led the old fellow, moaning piteously, across the street. He stopped when he came to the ancient gate, ornamented with the armorial bearings of the venerable Shepherd. "Here 'tis," said he, drawing up at the portal, and he made a successful pull at the gatebell, which presently brought out old Mr. Bolton, the porter, scowling fiercely, and grumbling as he was used to do every morning when it became his turn to let in that early bird.

Costigan tried to hold Bolton for a moment in genteel conversation, but the other surlily would not. "Don't bother me," he said; "go to your hown bed, capting, and don't keep honest men out of theirs." So the captain tacked across the square and reached his own staircase, up which he stumbled with the worthy Huxter at his heels. Costigan had a key of his own, which Huxter inserted into the keyhole for him, so that there was no need to call up little Mr. Bows from the sleep into which the old musician had not long since fallen, and Huxter having aided to disrobe his tipsy patient, and ascertained that no bones were broken, helped him to bed, and applied compresses and water to one of his knees and shins, which, with the pair of trowsers which encased them, Costigan had severely torn in his fall. At the general's age, and with his habit of body, such wounds as he had inflicted on himself are slow to heal: a good deal of inflammation ensued, and the old fellow lay ill for some days suffering both pain and fever.

Mr. Huxter undertook the case of his interesting patient with great confidence and alacrity, and conducted it with becoming skill. He visited his friend day after day, and consoled him with lively rattle and conversation, for the absence of the society which Costigan needed, and of which he was an ornament; and he gave special instructions to the invalid's nurse about the quantity of whisky which the patient was to take—instructions which, as the poor old fellow could not for many days get out of his bed or sofa himself, he could not by any means infringe. Bows, Mrs. Bolton, and our little friend Fanny, when able to do so, officiated at the general's bedside, and the old warrior was made as comfortable as possible under his calamity.

Thus Huxter, whose affable manners and social turn made him quickly intimate with persons in whose society he fell, and whose over-refinement did not lead them to repulse the familiarities of this young gentleman, became pretty soon intimate in Shepherd's Inn, both with our acquaintances in the garrets and those in the Porter's Lodge. He thought he had seen Fanny somewhere: he felt certain that he had: but it is no wonder that he should not accurately remember her, for the poor little thing never chose to tell him where she had met him: he himself had seen her at a period, when his own views both of persons and of right and wrong were clouded by the excitement of drinking and dancing, and also little Fanny was very much changed and worn by the fever and agitation, and passion and despair, which the past three weeks had poured upon the head of that little victim. Borne down was the head now, and very pale and wan the face; and many and many a time the sad eyes had looked into the postman's, as he came to the Inn, and the sickened heart had sunk as he passed away. When Mr. Costigan's accident occurred, Fanny was rather glad to have an opportunity of being useful and doing something kind— something that would make her forget her own little sorrows perhaps: she felt she bore them better while she did her duty, though I dare say many a tear dropped into the old Irishman's gruel. Ah, me! stir the gruel well, and have courage, little Fanny! If every body who has suffered from your complaint were to die of it straightway, what a fine year the undertakers would have!

Whether from compassion for his only patient, or delight in his society, Mr. Huxter found now occasion to visit Costigan two or three times in the day at least, and if any of the members of the Porter's Lodge family were not in attendance on the general, the young doctor was sure to have some particular directions to address to those at their own place of habitation. He was a kind fellow; he made or purchased toys for the children; he brought them apples and brandy balls; he brought a mask and frightened them with it, and caused a smile upon the face of pale Fanny. He called Mrs. Bolton Mrs. B., and was very intimate, familiar, and facetious with that lady, quite different from that "aughty artless beast," as Mrs. Bolton now denominated a certain young gentleman of our acquaintance, and whom she now vowed she never could abear.

It was from this lady, who was very free in her conversation, that Huxter presently learned what was the illness which was evidently preying upon little Fan, and what had been Pen's behavior regarding her. Mrs. Bolton's account of the transaction was not, it may be imagined, entirely an impartial narrative. One would have thought from her story that the young gentleman had employed a course of the most persevering and flagitious artifices to win the girl's heart, had broken the most solemn promises made to her, and was a wretch to be hated and chastised by every champion of woman. Huxter, in his present frame of mind respecting Arthur, and suffering under the latter's contumely, was ready, of course, to take all for granted that was said in the disfavor of this unfortunate convalescent. But why did he not write home to Clavering, as he had done previously, giving an account of Pen's misconduct, and of the particulars regarding it, which had now come to his knowledge? He once, in a letter to his brother-in-law, announced that that nice young man, Mr. Pendennis, had escaped narrowly from a fever, and that no doubt all Clavering, where he was so popular, would be pleased at his recovery; and he mentioned that he had an interesting case of compound fracture, an officer of distinction, which kept him in town; but as for Fanny Bolton, he made no more mention of her in his letters—no more than Pen himself had made mention of her. O you mothers at home, how much do you think you know about your lads? How much do you think you know?

But with Bows, there was no reason why Huxter should not speak his mind, and so, a very short time after his conversation with Mrs. Bolton. Mr. Sam talked to the musician about his early acquaintance with Pendennis; described him as a confounded conceited blackguard, and expressed a determination to punch, his impudent head as soon as ever he should be well enough to stand up like a man.

Then it was that Bows on his part spoke, and told his version of the story, whereof Arthur and little Fan were the hero and heroine; how they had met by no contrivance of the former, but by a blunder of the old Irishman, now in bed with a broken shin—how Pen had acted with manliness and self-control in the business—how Mrs. Bolton was an idiot; and he related the conversation which he, Bows, had had with Pen, and the sentiments uttered by the young man. Perhaps Bows's story caused some twinges of conscience in the breast of Pen's accuser, and that gentleman frankly owned that he had been wrong with regard to Arthur, and withdrew his project for punching Mr. Pendennis's head.

But the cessation of his hostility for Pen did not diminish Huxter's attentions to Fanny, which unlucky Mr. Bows marked with his usual jealousy and bitterness of spirit. "I have but to like any body," the old fellow thought, "and somebody is sure to come and be preferred to me. It has been the same ill-luck with me since I was a lad, until now that I am sixty years old. What can such a man as I am expect better than to be laughed at? It is for the young to succeed, and to be happy, and not for old fools like me. I've played a second fiddle all through life," he said, with a bitter laugh; "how can I suppose the luck is to change after it has gone against me so long?" This was the selfish way in which Bows looked at the state of affairs: though few persons would have thought there was any cause for his jealousy, who looked at the pale and grief-stricken countenance of the hapless little girl, its object. Fanny received Huxter's good-natured efforts at consolation and kind attentions kindly. She laughed now and again at his jokes and games with her little sisters, but relapsed quickly into a dejection which ought to have satisfied Mr. Bows that the new-comer had no place in her heart as yet, had jealous Mr. Bows been enabled to see with clear eyes.

But Bows did not. Fanny attributed Pen's silence somehow to Bows's interference. Fanny hated him. Fanny treated Bows with constant cruelty and injustice. She turned from him when he spoke—she loathed his attempts at consolation. A hard life had Mr. Bows, and a cruel return for his regard.

When Warrington came to Shepherd's Inn as Pen's embassador, it was for Mr. Bows's apartments he inquired (no doubt upon a previous agreement with the principal for whom he acted in this delicate negotiation), and he did not so much as catch a glimpse of Miss Fanny when he stopped at the inn-gate and made his inquiry. Warrington was, of course, directed to the musician's chambers, and found him tending the patient there, from whose chamber he came out to wait upon his guest. We have said that they had been previously known to one another, and the pair shook hands with sufficient cordiality. After a little preliminary talk, Warrington said that he had come from his friend Arthur Pendennis, and from his family, to thank Bows for his attention at the commencement of Pen's illness, and for his kindness in hastening into the country to fetch the major.

Bows replied that it was but his duty: he had never thought to have seen the young gentleman alive again when he went in search of Pen's relatives, and he was very glad of Mr. Pendennis's recovery, and that he had his friends with him. "Lucky are they who have friends, Mr. Warrington," said the musician. "I might be up in this garret and nobody would care for me, or mind whether I was alive or dead."

"What! not the general, Mr. Bows?" Warrington asked.

"The general likes his whisky-bottle more than any thing in life," the other answered; "we live together from habit and convenience; and he cares for me no more than you do. What is it you want to ask me, Mr. Warrington? You ain't come to visit me, I know very well. Nobody comes to visit me. It is about Fanny, the porter's daughter, you are come—I see that very well. Is Mr. Pendennis, now he has got well, anxious to see her again? Does his lordship the Sultan propose to throw his 'andkerchief to her? She has been very ill, sir, ever since the day when Mrs. Pendennis turned her out of doors—kind of a lady, wasn't it? The poor girl and myself found the young gentleman raving in a fever, knowing nobody, with nobody to tend him but his drunken laundress—she watched day and night by him. I set off to fetch his uncle. Mamma comes and turns Fanny to the right about. Uncle comes and leaves me to pay the cab. Carry my compliments to the ladies and gentleman, and say we are both very thankful, very. Why, a countess couldn't have behaved better, and for an apothecary's lady, as I'm given to understand Mrs. Pendennis was—I'm sure her behavior is most uncommon aristocratic and genteel. She ought to have a double gilt pestle and mortar to her coach."

It was from Mr. Huxter that Bows had learned Pen's parentage, no doubt, and if he took Pen's part against the young surgeon, and Fanny's against Mr. Pendennis, it was because the old gentleman was in so savage a mood, that his humor was to contradict every body.

Warrington was curious, and not ill pleased at the musician's taunts and irascibility. "I never heard of these transactions," he said, "or got but a very imperfect account of them from Major Pendennis. What was a lady to do? I think (I have never spoken with her on the subject) she had some notion that the young woman and my friend Pen were on—on terms of—of an intimacy which Mrs. Pendennis could not, of course, recognize—"

"Oh, of course not, sir. Speak out, sir; say what you mean at once, that the young gentleman of the Temple had made a victim of the girl of Shepherd's Inn, eh? And so she was to be turned out of doors—or brayed alive in the double gilt pestle and mortar, by Jove! No, Mr. Warrington, there was no such thing: there was no victimizing, or if there was, Mr. Arthur was the victim, not the girl. He is an honest fellow, he is, though he is conceited, and a puppy sometimes. He can feel like a man, and run away from temptation like a man. I own it, though I suffer by it, I own it. He has a heart, he has: but the girl hasn't sir. That girl will do any thing to win a man, and fling him away without a pang, sir. If she flung away herself, sir, she'll feel it and cry. She had a fever when Mrs. Pendennis turned her out of doors; and she made love to the doctor, Doctor Goodenough, who came to cure her. Now she has taken on with another chap—another sawbones ha, ha! d——it, sir, she likes the pestle and mortar, and hangs round the pill boxes, she's so fond of 'em, and she has got a fellow from Saint Bartholomew's, who grins through a horse collar for her sisters, and charms away her melancholy. Go and see, sir: very likely he's in the lodge now. If you want news about Miss Fanny, you must ask at the doctor's shop, sir, not of an old fiddler like me—Good-by, sir. There's my patient calling."

And a voice was heard from the captain's bedroom, a well-known voice, which said, "I'd loike a dthrop of dthrink, Bows, I'm thirstee." And not sorry, perhaps, to hear that such was the state of things, and that Pen's forsaken was consoling herself, Warrington took his leave of the irascible musician.

As luck would have it, he passed the lodge door just as Mr. Huxter was in the act of frightening the children with the mask whereof we have spoken, and Fanny was smiling languidly at his farces. Warrington laughed bitterly. "Are all women like that?" he thought. "I think there's one that's not," he added, with a sigh.

At Piccadilly, waiting for the Richmond omnibus, George fell in with Major Pendennis, bound in the same direction, and he told the old gentleman of what he had seen and heard respecting Fanny.

Major Pendennis was highly delighted: and as might be expected of such a philosopher, made precisely the same observation as that which had escaped from Warrington. "All women are the same," he said.

"La petite se console. Dayme, when I used to read 'Télémaque' at school, Calypso ne pouvait se consoler—you know the rest, Warrington—I used to say it was absard. Absard, by Gad, and so it is. And so she's got a new soupirant has she, the little porteress? Dayvlish nice little girl. How mad Pen will be— eh, Warrington? But we must break it to him gently, or he'll be in such a rage that he will be going after her again. We must ménager the young fellow."

"I think Mrs. Pendennis ought to know that Pen acted very well in the business. She evidently thinks him guilty, and according to Mr. Bows, Arthur behaved like a good fellow," Warrington said.

"My dear Warrington," said the major, with a look of some alarm. "In Mrs. Pendennis's agitated state of health and that sort of thing, the best way, I think, is not to say a single word about the subject—or, stay, leave it to me: and I'll talk to her—break it to her gently, you know, and that sort of a thing. I give you my word I will. And so Calypso's consoled, is she?" And he sniggered over this gratifying truth, happy in the corner of the omnibus during the rest of the journey.

Pen was very anxious to hear from his envoy what had been the result of the latter's mission; and as soon as the two young men could be alone, the embassador spoke in reply to Arthur's eager queries.

"You remember your poem, Pen, of Ariadne in Naxos," Warrington said; "devilish bad poetry it was, to be sure."

"Apres?" asked Pen, in a great state of excitement.

"When Theseus left Ariadne, do you remember what happened to her, young fellow?"

"It's a lie, it's a lie! You don't mean that!" cried out Pen, starting up, his face turning red.

"Sit down, stoopid," Warrington said, and with two fingers pushed Pen back into his seat again. "It's better for you as it is, young one;" he said sadly, in reply to the savage flush in Arthur's face.

CHAPTER XVIII

FOREIGN GROUND

Worth Major Pendennis fulfilled his promise to Warrington so far as to satisfy his own conscience, and in so far to ease poor Helen with regard to her son, as to make her understand that all connection between Arthur and the odious little gate-keeper was at an end, and that she need have no further anxiety with respect to an imprudent attachment or a degrading marriage on Pen's part. And that young fellow's mind was also relieved (after he had recovered the shock to his vanity) by thinking that Miss Fanny was not going to die of love for him, and that no unpleasant consequences were to be apprehended from the luckless and brief connection.

So the whole party were free to carry into effect their projected Continental trip, and Arthur Pendennis, rentier, voyageant avec Madame Pendennis and Mademoiselle Bell, and George Warrington, particulier, age de 32 ans, taille 6 pieds (Anglais), figure ordinaire, cheveux noirs, barbe idem, &c., procured passports from the consul of H.M. the King of the Belgians at Dover, and passed over from that port to

Ostend, whence the party took their way leisurely, visiting Bruges and Ghent on their way to Brussels and the Rhine. It is not our purpose to describe this oft-traveled tour, or Laura's delight at the tranquil and ancient cities which she saw for the first time, or Helen's wonder and interest at the Beguine convents which they visited, or the almost terror with which she saw the black-veiled nuns with out-stretched arms kneeling before the illuminated altars, and beheld the strange pomps and ceremonials of the Catholic worship. Bare-footed friars in the streets, crowned images of Saints and Virgins in the churches before which people were bowing down and worshiping, in direct defiance, as she held, of the written law; priests in gorgeous robes, or lurking in dark confessionals, theatres opened, and people dancing on Sundays; all these new sights and manners shocked and bewildered the simple country lady; and when the young men after their evening drive or walk returned to the widow and her adopted daughter, they found their books of devotion on the table, and at their entrance Laura would commonly cease reading some of the psalms or the sacred pages which, of all others Helen loved. The late events connected with her son had cruelly shaken her; Laura watched with intense, though hidden anxiety, every movement of her dearest friend; and poor Pen was most constant and affectionate in waiting upon his mother, whose wounded bosom yearned with love toward him, though there was a secret between them, and an anguish or rage almost on the mother's part, to think that she was dispossessed somehow of her son's heart, or that there were recesses in it which she must not or dared not enter. She sickened as she thought of the sacred days of boyhood when it had not been so—when her Arthur's heart had no secrets, and she was his all in all: when he poured his hopes and pleasures, his childish griefs, vanities, triumphs into her willing and tender embrace; when her home was his nest still; and before fate, selfishness, nature, had driven him forth on wayward wings—to range on his own flight—to sing his own song—and to seek his own home and his own mate. Watching this devouring care and racking disappointment in her friend, Laura once said to Helen, "If Pen had loved me as you wished, I should have gained him, but I should have lost you, mamma, I know I should; and I like you to love me best. Men do not know what it is to love as we do, I think,"—and Helen, sighing, agreed to this portion of the young lady's speech, though she protested against the former part. For my part, I suppose Miss Laura was right in both statements, and with regard to the latter assertion especially, that it is an old and received truism—love is an hour with us: it is all night and all day with a woman. Damon has taxes, sermon, parade, tailors' bills, parliamentary duties, and the deuce knows what to think of; Delia has to think about Damon—Damon is the oak (or the post), and stands up, and Delia is the ivy or the honey-suckle whose arms twine about him. Is it not so, Delia? Is it not your nature to creep about his feet and kiss them, to twine round his trunk and hang there; and Damon's to stand like a British man with his hands in his breeches pocket, while the pretty fond parasite clings round him?

Old Pendennis had only accompanied our friends to the water's edge, and left them on board the boat, giving the chief charge of the little expedition to Warrington. He himself was bound on a brief visit to the house of a great man, a friend of his, after which sojourn he proposed to join his sister-in-law at the German watering-place, whither the party was bound. The major himself thought that his long attentions to his sick family had earned for him a little relaxation—and though the best of the partridges were thinned off, the pheasants were still to be shot at Stillbrook, where the noble owner still was; old Pendennis betook himself to that hospitable mansion and disported there with great comfort to himself. A royal duke, some foreigners of note, some illustrious statesmen, and some pleasant people visited it: it did the old fellow's heart good to see his name in the "Morning Post," among the list of the distinguished company which the Marquis of Steyne was entertaining at his country house at Stillbrook. He was a very useful and pleasant personage in a country house. He entertained the young men with queer little anecdotes and grivoises stories on their shooting parties, or in their smoking-room, where they laughed at him and with him. He was obsequious with the ladies of a morning, in the rooms dedicated to them. He walked the new arrivals about the park and gardens, and showed them the carte du pays, and where there was the best view of the mansion, and where the most favorable point to look at the lake: he showed where the timber was to be felled, and where the old road went before the new bridge was built, and the hill cut down; and where the place in the wood was where old Lord Lynx discovered Sir Phelim O'Neal on his knees before her ladyship, &c. &c.; he called the lodge keepers and gardeners by their names; he knew the number of domestics that sat down in the housekeeper's room, and how many dined in the servants' hall; he had a word for every body, and about every body, and a little against every body. He was invaluable in a country house, in a word: and richly merited and enjoyed his vacation after his labors. And perhaps while he was thus deservedly enjoying himself with his country friends, the major was not ill-pleased at transferring to Warrington the command of the family expedition to the Continent, and thus perforce keeping him in the service of the ladies—a servitude which George was only too willing to undergo for his friend's sake, and for that of a society which he found daily more delightful. Warrington was a good German scholar and was willing to give Miss Laura lessons in the language, who was very glad to improve herself, though Pen, for his part, was too weak or lazy now to resume his German studies. Warrington acted as courier and interpreter; Warrington saw the baggage in and out of ships, inns, and carriages, managed the money matters, and put the little troop into marching order. Warrington found out where the English church was, and, if Mrs. Pendennis and Miss Laura were inclined to go thither, walked with great decorum along with them. Warrington walked by Mrs. Pendennis's donkey, when that lady went out on her evening excursions; or took carriages for her; or got "Galignani" for her; or devised comfortable seats under the lime trees for her, when the guests paraded after dinner, and the Kursaal band at the bath, where our tired friends stopped, performed their pleasant music under the trees. Many a fine whiskered Prussian or French dandy, come to the bath for the "Trente et quarante" cast glances of longing toward the pretty, fresh-colored English girl who accompanied the pale widow, and would have longed to take a turn with her at the galop or the waltz. But Laura did not appear in the ball-room, except once or twice, when Pen vouchsafed to walk with her; and as for Warrington that rough diamond had not had the polish of a dancing master, and he did not know how to waltz—though he would have liked to learn, if he could have had such a partner as Laura. Such a partner! psha, what had a stiff bachelor to do with partners and waltzing? what was he about, dancing attendance here? drinking in sweet pleasure at a risk he knows not of what after sadness and regret, and lonely longing? But yet he staid on. You would have said he was the widow's son, to watch his constant care and watchfulness of her; or that he was an adventurer, and wanted to marry her fortune, or at any rate, that he wanted some very great treasure or benefit from her —and very likely he did—for ours, as the reader has possibly already discovered, is a Selfish Story, and almost every person, according to his nature, more or less generous than George, and according to the way of the world as it seems to us, is occupied about Number One. So Warrington selfishly devoted himself to Helen, who selfishly devoted herself to Pen, who selfishly devoted himself to himself at this present period, having no other personage or object to occupy him, except, indeed, his mother's health, which gave him a serious and real disquiet; but though they sate together, they did not talk much, and the cloud was always between them.

Every day Laura looked for Warrington, and received him with more frank and eager welcome. He found himself talking to her as he didn't know himself that he could talk. He found himself performing acts of gallantry which astounded him after the performance: he found himself looking blankly in the glass at the crow's-feet round his eyes, and at some streaks of white in his hair, and some intrusive silver bristles in his grim, blue beard. He found himself looking at the young bucks at the bath—at the blond, tight-waisted Germans—at the capering Frenchmen, with their lackered mustaches and trim varnished boots—at the English dandies, Pen among them, with their calm domineering air, and insolent languor: and envied each one of these some excellence or quality of youth, or good looks which he possessed, and of which Warrington felt the need. And every night, as the night came, he quitted the little circle with greater reluctance; and, retiring to his own lodging in their neighborhood, felt himself the more lonely and unhappy. The widow could not help seeing his attachment. She understood, now, why Major Pendennis (always a tacit enemy of her darling project) had been so eager that Warrington should be of their party. Laura frankly owned her great, her enthusiastic, regard for him: and Arthur would make no movement. Arthur did not choose to see what was going on; or did not care to prevent, or actually encouraged, it. She remembered his often having said that he could not understand how a man proposed to a woman twice. She was in torture—at secret feud with her son, of all objects in the world the dearest to her—in doubt, which she dared not express to herself, about Laura—averse to Warrington, the good and generous. No wonder that the healing waters of Rosenbad did not do her good, or that Doctor von Glauber, the bath physician, when he came to visit her, found that the poor lady made no progress to recovery. Meanwhile Pen got well rapidly; slept with immense perseverance twelve hours out of the twenty-four; ate huge meals; and, at the end of a couple of months, had almost got back the bodily strength and weight which he had possessed before his illness.

After they had passed some fifteen days at their place of rest and refreshment, a letter came from Major Pendennis announcing his speedy arrival at Rosenbad, and, soon after the letter, the major himself made his appearance accompanied by Morgan his faithful valet, without whom the old gentleman could not move. When the major traveled he wore a jaunty and juvenile traveling costume; to see his back still you would have taken him for one of the young fellows whose slim waist and youthful appearance Warrington was beginning to envy. It was not until the worthy man began to move, that the observer remarked that Time had weakened his ancient knees, and had unkindly interfered to impede the action of the natty little varnished boots in which the old traveler still pinched his toes. There were magnates both of our own country and of foreign nations present that autumn at Rosenbad. The elder Pendennis read over the strangers' list with great gratification on the night of his arrival, was pleased to find several of his acquaintances among the great folks, and would have the honor of presenting his nephew to a German Grand Duchess, a Russian Princess, and an English Marquis, before many days were over: nor was Pen by any means averse to making the acquaintance of these great personages, having a liking for polite life, and all the splendors and amenities belonging to it. That very evening the resolute old gentlemen, leaning on his nephew's arm, made his appearance in the halls of the Kursaal, and lost or won a napoleon or two at the table of Trente et quarante. He did not play to lose, he said, or to win, but he did as other folks did, and betted his napoleon and took his luck as it came. He pointed out the Russians and Spaniards gambling for heaps of gold, and denounced their eagerness as something sordid and barbarous; an English gentleman should play where the fashion is play, but should not elate or depress himself at the sport; and he told how he had seen his friend the Marquis of Steyne, when Lord Gaunt, lose eighteen thousand at a sitting, and break the bank three nights running at Paris, without ever showing the least emotion at his defeat or victory—"And that's what I call being an English gentleman, Pen, my dear boy," the old gentleman said, warming as he prattled about his recollections—"what I call the great manner only remains with us and with a few families in France." And as Russian princesses passed him, whose reputation had long ceased to be doubtful, and damaged English ladies, who are constantly seen in company of their faithful attendant for the time being in these gay haunts of dissipation, the old major, with eager garrulity and mischievous relish told his nephew wonderful particulars regarding the lives of these heroines; and diverted the young man with a thousand scandals. Egad, he felt himself quite young again, he remarked to Pen, as, rouged and grinning, her enormous chasseur behind her bearing her shawl, the Princess Obstropski smiled and recognized and accosted him. He remembered her in '14 when she was an actress of the Paris Boulevard, and the Emperor Alexander's aid-de-camp Obstropski (a man of great talents, who knew a good deal about the Emperor Paul's death, and was a devil to play) married her. He most courteously and respectfully asked leave to call upon the princess, and to present to her his nephew,

Mr. Arthur Pendennis; and he pointed out to the latter a half-dozen of other personages whose names were as famous, and whose histories were as edifying. What would poor Helen have thought, could she have heard those tales, or known to what kind of people her brother-in-law was presenting her son? Only once, leaning on Arthur's arm, she had passed through the room where the green tables were prepared for play, and the croaking croupiers were calling out their fatal words of Rouge gagne and Couleur perd. She had shrunk terrified out of the pandemonium, imploring Pen, extorting from him a promise, on his word of honor, that he would never play at those tables; and the scene which so frightened the simple widow, only amused the worldly old veteran, and made him young again! He could breath the air cheerfully which stifled her. Her right was not his right: his food was her poison. Human creatures are constituted thus differently, and with this variety the marvelous world is peopled. To the credit of Mr. Pen, let it be said, that he kept honestly the promise made to his mother, and stoutly told his uncle of his intention to abide by it.

When the major arrived, his presence somehow cast a damp upon at least three persons of our little party—upon Laura, who had any thing but respect for him; upon Warrington, whose manner toward him showed an involuntary haughtiness and contempt; and upon the timid and alarmed widow, who dreaded lest he should interfere with her darling, though almost desperate projects for her boy. And, indeed, the major, unknown to himself, was the bearer of tidings which were to bring about a catastrophe in the affairs of all our friends.

Pen with his two ladies had apartments in the town of Rosenbad; honest Warrington had lodgings hard by; the major, on arrival at Rosenbad, had, as befitted his dignity, taken up his quarters at one of the great hotels, at the Roman Emperor or the Four Seasons, where two or three hundred gamblers, pleasure-seekers, or invalids, sate down and over-ate themselves daily at the enormous table d'hote. To this hotel Pen went on the morning after the major's arrival dutifully to pay his respects to his uncle, and found the latter's sitting-room duly prepared and arranged by Mr. Morgan, with the major's hats brushed, and his coats laid out: his dispatch-boxes and umbrella-cases, his guide-books, passports, maps, and other elaborate necessaries of the English traveler, all as trim and ready as they could be in their master's own room in Jermyn-street. Every thing was ready, from the medicine-bottle fresh filled from the pharmacien's, down to the old fellow's prayer-book, without which he never traveled, for he made a point of appearing at the English church at every place which he honored with a stay. "Every body did it," he said; "every English gentleman did it," and this pious man would as soon have thought of not calling upon the English embassador in a continental town, as of not showing himself at the national place of worship.

The old gentleman had been to take one of the baths for which Rosenbad is famous, and which every body takes, and his after-bath toilet was not yet completed when Pen arrived. The elder called out to Arthur in a cheery voice from the inner apartment, in which he and Morgan were engaged, and the valet presently came in, bearing a little packet to Pen's address—Mr. Arthur's letters and papers, Morgan said, which he had brought from Mr. Arthur's chambers in London, and which consisted chiefly of numbers of the "Pall Mall Gazette," which our friend Mr. Finucane thought his collaborateur would like to see. The papers were tied together: the letters in an envelope, addressed to Pen, in the last-named gentleman's handwriting.

Among the letters there was a little note addressed, as a former letter we have heard of had been, to "Arthur Pendennis, Esquire," which Arthur opened with a start and a blush, and read with a very keen pang of interest, and sorrow, and regard. She had come to Arthur's house, Fanny Bolton said—and found that he was gone—gone away to Germany without ever leaving a word for her—or answer to her last letter, in which she prayed but for one word of kindness—or the books which he had promised her in happier times, before he was ill, and which she would like to keep in remembrance of him. She said she would not reproach those who had found her at his bedside when he was in the fever, and knew nobody, and who had turned the poor girl away without a word. She thought she should have died, she said, of that, but Doctor Goodenough had kindly tended her, and kept her life, when, perhaps, the keeping of it was of no good, and she forgave every body: and as for Arthur, she would pray for him forever. And when he was so ill, and they cut off his hair, she had made so free as to keep one little lock for herself, and that she owned. And might she still keep it, or would his mamma order that that should be gave up too? She was willing to obey him in all things, and couldn't but remember that once he was so kind, oh! so good and kind! to his poor Fanny. When Major Pendennis, fresh and smirking from his toilet, came out of his bedroom to his sitting-room, he found Arthur with this note before him, and an expression of savage anger on his face, which surprised the elder gentleman. "What news from London, my boy?" he rather faintly asked; "are the duns at you that you look so glum?"

"Do you know any thing about this letter, sir?" Arthur asked.

"What letter, my good sir?" said the other drily, at once perceiving what had happened.

"You know what I mean—about, about Miss—about Fanny Bolton—the poor dear little girl," Arthur broke out. "When was she in my room? Was she there when I was delirious—I fancied she was—was she? Who sent her out of my chambers? Who intercepted her letters to me? Who dared to do it? Did you do it, uncle?"

"It's not my practice to tamper with gentlemen's letters, or to answer damned impertinent questions," Major Pendennis cried out, in a great tremor of emotion and indignation. "There was a girl in your rooms when I came up at great personal inconveinence, daymy—and to meet with a return of this kind for my affection to you, is not pleasant, by Gad, sir—not at all pleasant."

"That's not the question, sir," Arthur said hotly—"and—and, I beg your pardon, uncle. You were, you always have been, most kind to me: but I say again, did you say any thing harsh to this poor girl. Did you send her away from me?"

"I never spoke a word to the girl," the uncle said, "and I never sent her away from you, and know no more about her, and wish to know no more about her, than about the man in the moon."

"Then it's my mother that did it," Arthur broke out. "Did my mother send that poor child away?"

"I repeat I know nothing about it, sir," the elder said testily. "Let's change the subject, if you please."

"I'll never forgive the person who did it," said Arthur, bouncing up and seizing his hat.

The major cried out, "Stop, Arthur, for God's sake, stop;" but before he had uttered his sentence Arthur had rushed out of the room, and at the next minute the major saw him striding rapidly down the street that led toward his home.

"Get breakfast!" said the old fellow to Morgan, and he wagged his head and sighed as he looked out of the window. "Poor Helen—poor soul! There'll be a row. I knew there would: and begad all the fat's in the fire."

When Pen reached home he only found Warrington in the ladies' drawing-room, waiting their arrival in order to conduct them to the room where the little English colony at Rosenbad held their Sunday church. Helen and Laura had not appeared as yet; the former was ailing, and her daughter was with her. Pen's wrath was so great that he could not defer expressing it. He flung Fanny's letter across the table to his friend. "Look there, Warrington," he said; "she tended me in my illness, she rescued me out of the jaws of death, and this is the way they have treated the dear little creature. They have kept her letters from me; they have treated me like a child, and her like a dog, poor thing! My mother has done this."

"If she has, you must remember it is your mother," Warrington interposed.

"It only makes the crime the greater, because it is she who has done it," Pen answered. "She ought to have been the poor girl's defender, not her enemy: she ought to go down on her knees and ask pardon of her. I ought! I will! I am shocked at the cruelty which has been shown her. What? She gave me her all, and this is her return! She sacrifices every thing for me, and they spurn her."

"Hush!" said Warrington, "they can hear you from the next room."

"Hear; let them hear!" Pen cried out, only so much the louder. "Those may overhear my talk who intercept my letters. I say this poor girl has been shamefully used, and I will do my best to right her; I will."

The door of the neighboring room opened and Laura came forth with pale and stern face. She looked at Pen with glances from which beamed pride, defiance, aversion. "Arthur, your mother is very ill," she said; "it is a pity that you should speak so loud as to disturb her."

"It is a pity that I should have been obliged to speak at all," Pen answered. "And I have more to say before I have done."

"I should think what you have to say will hardly be fit for me to hear," Laura said, haughtily.

"You are welcome to hear it or not, as you like," said Mr. Pen. "I shall go in now and speak to my mother."

Laura came rapidly forward, so that she should not be overheard by her friend within. "Not now, sir," she said to Pen. "You may kill her if you do. Your conduct has gone far enough to make her wretched."

"What conduct?" cried out Pen, in a fury. "Who dares impugn it? Who dares meddle with me? Is it you who are the instigator of this persecution?"

"I said before it was a subject of which it did not become me to hear or to speak," Laura said. "But as for mamma, if she had acted otherwise than she did with regard to—to the person about whom you seem to take such an interest, it would have been I that must have quitted your house, and not that—that person."

"By heavens! this is too much," Pen cried out, with a violent execration.

"Perhaps that is what you wished," Laura said, tossing her head up. "No more of this, if you please; I am not accustomed to hear such subjects spoken of in such language;" and with a stately courtesy the young lady passed to her friend's room, looking her adversary full in the face as she retreated and closed the door upon him.

Pen was bewildered with wonder, perplexity, fury, at this monstrous and unreasonable persecution. He burst out into a loud and bitter laugh as Laura quitted him, and with sneers and revilings, as a man who jeers under an operation, ridiculed at once his own pain and his persecutor's anger. The laugh, which was one of bitter humor, and no unmanly or unkindly expression of suffering under most cruel and unmerited torture, was heard in the next apartment, as some of his unlucky previous expressions had been, and, like them, entirely misinterpreted by the hearers. It struck like a dagger into the wounded and tender heart of Helen; it pierced Laura, and inflamed the high-spirited girl, with scorn and anger. "And it was to this hardened libertine," she thought—"to this boaster of low intrigues, that I had given my heart away." "He breaks the most sacred laws," thought Helen. "He prefers the creature of his passion to his own mother; and when he is upbraided, he laughs, and glories in his crime. 'She gave me her all,' I heard him say it," argued the poor widow; "and he boasts of it, and laughs, and breaks his mother's heart." The emotion, the shame, the grief, the mortification almost killed her. She felt she should die of his unkindness.

Warrington thought of Laura's speech—"Perhaps that is what you wished." "She loves Pen still," he said. "It was jealousy made her speak."—"Come away, Pen. Come away, and let us go to church and get calm. You must explain this matter to your mother. She does not appear to know the truth: nor do you quite, my good fellow. Come away, and let us talk about it." And again he muttered to himself, "'Perhaps that is what you wished.' Yes, she loves him. Why shouldn't she love him? Whom else would I have her love? What can she be to me but the dearest, and the fairest, and the best of women?"

So, leaving the women similarly engaged within, the two gentlemen walked away, each occupied with his own thoughts, and silent for a considerable space. "I must set this matter right," thought honest George, "as she loves him still—I must set his mind right about the other woman." And with this charitable thought, the good fellow began to tell more at large what Bows had said to him regarding Miss Bolton's behavior and fickleness, and he described how the girl was no better than a little light-minded flirt; and, perhaps, he exaggerated the good humor and contentedness which he had himself, as he thought, witnessed in her behavior in the scene with Mr. Huxter.

Now, all Bows's statements had been colored by an insane jealousy and rage on that old man's part; and instead of allaying Pen's renascent desire to see his little conquest again, Warrington's accounts inflamed and angered Pendennis, and made him more anxious than before to set himself right, as he persisted in phrasing it, with Fanny. They arrived at the church-door presently; but scarce one word of the service, and not a syllable of Mr. Shamble's sermon, did either of them comprehend, probably—so much was each engaged with his own private speculations. The major came up to them after the service, with his well-brushed hat and wig, and his jauntiest, most cheerful air. He complimented them upon being seen at church; again he said that every comme-il-faut person made a point of attending the English service abroad; and he walked back with the young men, prattling to them in garrulous good-humor, and making bows to his acquaintances as they passed; and thinking innocently that Pen and George were both highly delighted by his anecdotes, which they suffered to run on in a scornful and silent acquiescence.

At the time of Mr. Shamble's sermon (an erratic Anglican divine hired for the season at places of English resort, and addicted to debts, drinking, and even to roulette, it was said), Pen, chafing under the persecution which his womankind inflicted upon him, had been meditating a great act of revolt and of justice, as he had worked himself up to believe; and Warrington on his part had been thinking that a crisis in his affairs had likewise come, and that it was necessary for him to break away from a connection which every day made more and more wretched and dear to him. Yes, the time was come. He took those fatal words, "Perhaps that is what you wished," as a text for a gloomy homily, which he preached to himself, in the dark pew of his own heart, while Mr. Shamble was feebly giving utterance to his sermon.

CHAPTER XIX

"FAIROAKS TO LET."

Our poor widow (with the assistance of her faithful Martha of Fairoaks, who laughed and wondered at the German ways, and superintended the affairs of the simple household) had made a little feast in honor of Major Pendennis's arrival, of which, however, only the major and his two younger friends partook, for Helen sent to say that she was too unwell to dine at their table, and Laura bore her company. The major talked for the party, and did not perceive, or choose to perceive, what a gloom and silence pervaded the other two sharers of the modest dinner. It was evening before Helen and Laura came into the sitting-room to join the company there. She came in leaning on Laura, with her back to the waning light, so that Arthur could not see how pallid and woe-stricken her face was, and as she went up to Pen, whom she had not seen during the day, and placed her fond arms on his shoulder and kissed him tenderly, Laura left her, and moved away to another part of the room. Pen remarked that his mother's voice and her whole frame trembled, her hand was clammy cold as she put it up to his forehead, piteously embracing him. The spectacle of her misery only added, somehow, to the wrath and testiness of the young man. He scarcely returned the kiss which the suffering lady gave him: and the countenance with which he met the appeal of her look was hard and cruel. "She persecutes me," he thought within himself, "and she comes to me with the air of a martyr." "You look very ill, my child," she said. "I don't like to see you look in that way." And she tottered to a sofa, still holding one of his passive hands in her thin, cold, clinging fingers.

"I have had much to annoy me, mother," Pen said with a throbbing breast: and as he spoke Helen's heart began to beat so, that she sate almost dead and speechless with terror.

Warrington, Laura, and Major Pendennis, all remained breathless, aware that a storm was about to break.

"I have had letters from London," Arthur continued, "and one that has given me more pain than I ever had in my life. It tells me that former letters of mine have been intercepted and purloined away from me; that—that a young creature who has shown the greatest love and care for me, has been most cruelly used by—by you, mother."

"For God's sake stop," cried out Warrington. "She's ill—don't you see she is ill?"

"Let him go on," said the widow faintly.

"Let him go on and kill her," said Laura, rushing up to her mother's side. "Speak on, sir, and see her die."

"It is you who are cruel," cried Pen, more exasperated and more savage, because his own heart, naturally soft and weak, revolted indignantly at the injustice of the very suffering which was laid at his door. "It is you that are cruel, who attribute all this pain to me: it is you who are cruel with your wicked reproaches, your wicked doubts of me, your wicked persecutions of those who love me—yes, those who love me, and who brave every thing for me, and whom you despise and trample upon because they are of lower degree than you. Shall I tell you what I will do—what I am resolved to do, now that I know what your conduct has been? I will, go back to this poor girl whom you turned out of my doors, and ask her to come back and share my home with me. I'll defy the pride which persecutes her, and the pitiless suspicion which insults her and me."

"Do you mean, Pen, that you—" here the widow, with eager eyes and out-stretched hands, was breaking out, but Laura stopped her; "Silence, hush, dear mother," she cried and the widow hushed. Savagely as Pen spoke, she was only too eager to hear what more he had to say, "Go on, Arthur, go on, Arthur," was all she said, almost swooning away as she spoke.

"By Gad, I say he shan't go on, or I won't hear him, by Gad," the major said, trembling too in his wrath. "If you choose, sir, after all we've done for you, after all I've done for you myself, to insult your mother and disgrace your name, by allying yourself with a low-born kitchen-girl, go and do it, by Gad, but let us, ma'am have no more to do with him. I wash my hands of you, sir—I wash my hands of you. I'm an old fellow—I ain't long for this world. I come of as ancient and honorable a family as any in England, by Gad, and I did hope, before I went off the hooks, by Gad, that the fellow that I'd liked, and brought up, and nursed through life, by Jove, would do something to show me that our name—yes, the name of Pendennis, by Gad, was left undishonored behind us, but if he won't, dammy, I say, amen. By G—, both my father and my brother Jack were the proudest men in England, and I never would have thought that there would come this disgrace to my name—never—and—and I'm ashamed that it's Arthur Pendennis." The old fellow's voice here broke off into a sob: it was a second time that Arthur had brought tears from those wrinkled lids.

The sound of his breaking voice stayed Pen's anger instantly, and he stopped pacing the room, as he had been doing until that moment. Laura was by Helen's sofa; and Warrington had remained hitherto an almost silent, but not uninterested spectator of the family storm. As the parties were talking, it had grown almost dark; and after the lull which succeeded the passionate outbreak of the major, George's deep voice, as it here broke trembling into the twilight room, was heard with no small emotion by all.

"Will you let me tell you something about myself, my kind friends?" he said, "you have been so good to me, ma'am—you have been so kind to me, Laura—I hope I may call you so sometimes—my dear Pen and I have been such friends that—that I have long wanted to tell you my story, such as it is, and would have told it to you earlier but that it is a sad one, and contains another's secret. However, it may do good for Arthur to know it—it is right that every one here should. It will divert you from thinking about a subject, which, out of a fatal misconception, has caused a great deal of pain to all of you. May I please tell you, Mrs. Pendennis?"

"Pray speak," was all Helen said; and indeed she was not much heeding; her mind was full of another idea with which Pen's words had supplied her, and she was in a terror of hope that what he had hinted might be as she wished.

George filled himself a bumper of wine and emptied it, and began to speak. "You all of you know how you see me," he said, "A man without a desire to make an advance in the world; careless about reputation; and living in a garret and from hand to mouth, though I have friends and a name, and I dare say capabilities of my own, that would serve me if I had a mind. But mind I have none. I shall die in that garret most likely, and alone. I nailed myself to that doom in early life. Shall I tell you what it was that interested me about Arthur years ago, and made me inclined toward him when first I saw him? The men from our college at Oxbridge brought up accounts of that early affair with the Chatteris actress, about whom Pen has often talked to me since; and who, but for the major's generalship, might have been your daughter-in-law, ma'am. I can't see Pen in the dark, but he blushes, I'm sure; and I dare say Miss Bell does; and my friend Major Pendennis, I dare say, laughs as he ought to do—for he won. What would have been Arthur's lot now had he been tied at nineteen to an illiterate woman older than himself, with no qualities in common between them to make one a companion for the other, no equality, no confidence, and no love speedily? What could he have been but most miserable? And when he spoke just now and threatened a similar union, be sure it was but a threat occasioned by anger, which you must give me leave to say, ma'am, was very natural on his part, for after a generous and manly conduct—let me say who know the circumstances well—most generous and manly and self-denying (which is rare with him)—he has met from some friends of his with a most unkind suspicion, and has had to complain of the unfair treatment of another innocent person, toward whom he and you all are under much obligation."

The widow was going to get up here, and Warrington, seeing her attempt to rise, said, "Do I tire you, ma'am?"

"O no—go on—go on," said Helen, delighted, and he continued.

"I liked him, you see, because of that early history of his, which had come to my ears in college gossip, and because I like a man, if you will pardon me for saying so, Miss Laura, who shows that he can have a great unreasonable attachment for a woman. That was why we became friends—and are all friends here—for always, aren't we?" he added, in a lower voice, leaning over to her, "and Pen has been a great comfort and companion to a lonely and unfortunate man.

"I am not complaining of my lot, you see; for no man's is what he would have it; and up in my garret, where you left the flowers, and with my old books and my pipe for a wife, I am pretty contented, and only occasionally envy other men, whose careers in life are more brilliant, or who can solace their ill fortune by what Fate and my own fault has deprived me of—the affection of a woman or a child." Here there came a sigh from somewhere near Warrington in the dark, and a hand was held out in his direction, which, however, was instantly withdrawn, for the prudery of our females is such, that before all expression of feeling, or natural kindness and regard, a woman is taught to think of herself and the proprieties, and to be ready to blush at the very slightest notice; and checking, as, of course, it ought, this spontaneous motion, modesty drew up again, kindly friendship shrank back ashamed of itself, and Warrington resumed his history. "My fate is such as I made it, and not lucky for me or for others involved in it.

"I, too, had an adventure before I went to college; and there was no one to save me as Major Pendennis saved Pen. Pardon me, Miss Laura, if I tell this story before you. It is as well that you all of you should hear my confession. Before I went to college, as a boy of eighteen, I was at a private tutor's and there, like Arthur, I became attached, or fancied I was attached, to a woman of a much lower degree and a greater age than my own. You shrink from me—"

"No I don't," Laura said, and here the hand went out resolutely, and laid itself in Warrington's. She had divined his story from some previous hints let fall by him, and his first words at its commencement.

"She was a yeoman's daughter in the neighborhood," Warrington said, with rather a faltering voice, "and I fancied—what all young men fancy. Her parents knew who my father was, and encouraged me, with all sorts of coarse artifices and scoundrel flatteries, which I see now, about their house. To do her justice, I own she never cared for me but was forced into what happened by the threats and compulsion of her family. Would to God that I had not been deceived: but in these matters we are deceived because we wish to be so, and I thought I loved that poor woman.

"What could come of such a marriage? I found, before long, that I was married to a boor. She could not comprehend one subject that interested me. Her dullness palled upon me till I grew to loathe it. And after some time of a wretched, furtive union—I must tell you all —I found letters somewhere (and such letters they were!) which showed me that her heart, such as it was, had never been mine, but had always belonged to a person of her own degree.

"At my father's death, I paid what debts I had contracted at college, and settled every shilling which remained to me in an annuity upon— upon those who bore my name, on condition that they should hide themselves away, and not assume it. They have kept that condition, as they would break it, for more money. If I had earned fame or reputation, that woman would have come to claim it: if I had made a name for myself, those who had no right to it would have borne it; and I entered life at twenty, God help me—hopeless and ruined beyond remission. I was the boyish victim of vulgar cheats, and, perhaps, it is only of late I have found out how hard—ah, how hard—it is to forgive them. I told you the moral before, Pen; and now I have told you the fable. Beware how you marry out of your degree. I was made for a better lot than this, I think: but God has awarded me this one—and so, you see, it is for me to look on, and see others successful and others happy, with a heart that shall be as little bitter as possible."

"By Gad, sir," cried the major, in high good humor, "I intended you to marry Miss Laura here."

"And, by Gad, Master Shallow, I owe you a thousand pound," Warrington said.

"How d'ye mean a thousand? it was only a pony, sir," replied the major simply, at which the other laughed.

As for Helen, she was so delighted, that she started up, and said, "God bless you—God forever bless you, Mr. Warrington;" and kissed both his hands, and ran up to Pen, and fell into his arms.

"Yes, dearest mother," he said as he held her to him, and with a noble tenderness and emotion, embraced and forgave her. "I am innocent, and my dear, dear mother has done me a wrong."

"Oh, yes, my child, I have wronged you, thank God, I have wronged you!" Helen whispered. "Come away, Arthur—not here—I want to ask my child to forgive me—and—and my God, to forgive me; and to bless you, and love you, my son."

He led her, tottering, into her room, and closed the door, as the three touched spectators of the reconciliation looked on in pleased silence. Ever after, ever after, the tender accents of that voice faltering sweetly at his ear—the look of the sacred eyes beaming with an affection unutterable—the quiver of the fond lips smiling mournfully—were remembered by the young man. And at his best moments, and at his hours of trial and grief, and at his times of success or well doing, the mother's face looked down upon him, and blessed him with its gaze of pity and purity, as he saw it in that night when she yet lingered with him; and when she seemed, ere she quite left him, an angel, transfigured and glorified with love—for which love, as for the greatest of the bounties and wonders of God's provision for us, let us kneel and thank Our Father.

The moon had risen by this time; Arthur recollected well afterward how it lighted up his mother's sweet pale face. Their talk, or his rather, for she scarcely could speak, was more tender and confidential than it had been for years before. He was the frank and generous boy of her early days and love. He told her the story, the mistake regarding which had caused her so much pain—his struggles to fly from temptation, and his thankfulness that he had been able to overcome it. He never would do the girl wrong, never; or wound his own honor or his mother's pure heart. The threat that he would return was uttered in a moment of exasperation, of which he repented. He never would see her again. But his mother said yes he should; and it was she who had been proud and culpable—and she would like to give Fanny Bolton something—and she begged her dear boy's pardon for opening the letter —and she would write to the young girl, if—if she had time. Poor thing! was it not natural that she should love her Arthur? And again she kissed him, and she blessed him.

As they were talking the clock struck nine, and Helen reminded him how, when he was a little boy, she used to go up to his bedroom at that hour, and hear him say Our Father. And once more, oh, once more, the young man fell down at his mother's sacred knees, and sobbed out the prayer which the Divine Tenderness uttered for us, and which has been echoed for twenty ages since by millions of sinful and humbled men. And as he spoke the last words of the supplication, the mother's head fell down on her boy's, and her arms closed round him, and together they repeated the words "for ever and ever," and "Amen."

A little time after, it might have been a quarter of an hour, Laura heard Arthur's voice calling from within, "Laura! Laura!" She rushed into the room instantly, and found the young man still on his knees and holding his mother's hand. Helen's head had sunk back and was quite pale in the moon. Pen looked round, scared with a ghastly terror "Help, Laura, help!" he said—"she's fainted—she's—"

Laura screamed, and fell by the side of Helen. The shriek brought Warrington and Major Pendennis and the servants to the room. The sainted woman was dead. The last emotion of her soul here was joy, to be henceforth uncheckered and eternal. The tender heart beat no more— it was to have no more pangs, no more doubts, no more griefs and trials. Its last throb was love; and Helen's last breath was a benediction.

The melancholy party bent their way speedily homewards, and Helen was laid by her husband's side at Clavering, in the old church where she had prayed so often. For a while Laura went to stay with Dr. Portman, who read the service over his dear sister departed, amidst his own sobs and those of the little congregation which assembled round Helen's tomb. There were not many who cared for her, or who spoke of her when gone. Scarcely more than of a nun in a cloister did people know of that pious and gentle lady. A few words among the cottagers whom her bounty was accustomed to relieve, a little talk from house to house, at Clavering, where this lady, told how their neighbor died of a complaint in the heart; while that speculated upon the amount of property which the widow had left; and a third wondered whether Arthur would let Fairoaks or live in it, and expected that he would not be long getting through his property—this was all, and except with one or two who cherished her, the kind soul was forgotten by the next market-day. Would you desire that grief for you should last for a few more weeks? and does after-life seem less solitary, provided that our names, when we "go down into silence," are echoing on this side of the grave yet for a little while, and human voices are still talking about us? She was gone, the pure soul, whom only two or three loved and knew. The great blank she left was in Laura's heart, to whom her love had been every thing, and who had now but to worship her memory. "I am glad that she gave me her blessing before she went away," Warrington said to Pen; and as for Arthur, with a humble acknowledgment and wonder at so much affection, he hardly dared to ask of Heaven to make him worthy of it, though he felt that a saint there was interceding for him.

All the lady's affairs were found in perfect order, and her little property ready for transmission to her son, in trust for whom she held it. Papers in her desk showed that she had long been aware of the complaint, one of the heart, under which she labored, and knew it would suddenly remove her: and a prayer was found in her hand-writing, asking that her end might be, as it was, in the arms of her son.

Laura and Arthur talked over her sayings, all of which the former most fondly remembered, to the young man's shame somewhat, who thought how much greater her love had been for Helen than his own. He referred himself entirely to Laura to know what Helen would have wished should be done; what poor persons she would have liked to relieve; what legacies or remembrances she would have wished to transmit. They packed up the vase which Helen in her gratitude had destined to Dr. Goodenough, and duly sent it to the kind doctor: a silver coffee-pot, which she used, was sent off to Portman: a diamond ring with her hair, was given with affectionate greeting to Warrington.

It must have been a hard day for poor Laura when she went over to Fairoaks first, and to the little room which she had occupied, and which was hers no more, and to the widow's own blank chamber in which those two had passed so many beloved hours. There, of course, were the clothes in the wardrobe, the cushion on which she prayed, the chair at the toilet: the glass that was no more to reflect her dear sad face. After she had been here awhile, Pen knocked and led her down stairs to the parlor again, and made her drink a little wine, and said, "God bless you," as she touched the glass. "Nothing shall ever be changed in your room," he said, "it is always your room—it is always my sister's room. Shall it not be so, Laura?" and Laura said, "Yes!"

Among the widow's papers was found a packet, marked by the widow "Letters from Laura's father," and which Arthur gave to her. They were the letters which had passed between the cousins in the early days before the marriage of, either of them. The ink was faded in which they were written: the tears dried out that both perhaps had shed over them: the grief healed now whose bitterness they chronicled: the friends doubtless united whose parting on earth had caused to both pangs so cruel. And Laura learned fully now for the first time what the tie was which had bound her so tenderly to Helen: how faithfully her more than mother had cherished her father's memory, how truly she had loved him, how meekly resigned him.

One legacy of his mother's Pen remembered, of which Laura could have no cognizance. It was that wish of Helen's to make some present to Fanny Bolton; and Pen wrote to her, putting his letter under an envelope to Mr. Bows, and requesting that gentleman to read it before he delivered it to Fanny. "Dear Fanny," Pen said, "I have to acknowledge two letters from you, one of which was delayed in my illness," (Pen found the first letter in his mother's desk after her decease, and the reading it gave him a strange pang), "and to thank you, my kind nurse and friend, who watched me so tenderly during my fever. And I have to tell you that the last words of my dear mother, who is no more, were words of good-will and gratitude to you for nursing me: and she said she would have written to you had she had time—that she would like to ask your pardon if she had harshly treated you—and that she would beg you to show your forgiveness by accepting some token of friendship and regard from her." Pen concluded by saying that his friend, George Warrington, Esq., of Lamb-court Temple, was trustee of a little sum of money, of which the interest would be paid to her until she became of age, or changed her name, which would always be affectionately remembered by her grateful friend, A. Pendennis. The sum was in truth but small, although enough to make a little heiress of Fanny Bolton, whose parents were appeased, and whose father said Mr. P. had acted quite as the gentleman—though Bows growled out that to plaster a wounded heart with a bank-note was an easy kind of sympathy; and poor Fanny felt only too clearly that Pen's letter was one of farewell.

"Sending hundred-pound notes to porters' daughters is all dev'lish well," old Major Pendennis said to his nephew (whom, as the proprietor of Fairoaks and the head of the family, he now treated with marked deference and civility), "and as there was a little ready money at the bank, and your poor mother wished it, there's perhaps no harm done. But my good lad, I'd have you to remember that you've not above five hundred a year, though, thanks to me, the world gives you credit for being a doosid deal better off; and, on my knees, I beg you, my boy, don't break into your capital. Stick to it, sir; don't speculate with it, sir; keep your land, and don't borrow on it. Tatham tells me that the Chatteris branch of the railway may— will almost certainly pass through Chatteris, and if it can be brought on this side of the Brawl, sir, and through your fields, they'll be worth a dev'lish deal of money, and your five hundred a year will jump up to eight or nine. Whatever it is, keep it, I implore you, keep it. And I say, Pen, I think you should give up living in those dirty chambers in the Temple and get a decent lodging. And I should have a man, sir, to wait upon me; and a horse or two in town in the season. All this will pretty well swallow up your income, and I know you must live close. But remember you have a certain place in society, and you can't afford to cut a poor figure in the world. What are you going to do in the winter? You don't intend to stay down here, or, I suppose, to go on writing for that—what-d'ye-call'em—that newspaper?"

"Warrington and I are going abroad again, sir, for a little, and then we shall see what is to be done," Arthur replied.

"And you'll let Fairoaks, of course? Good school in the neighborhood; cheap country: dev'lish nice place for East India Colonels or families wanting to retire. I'll speak about it at the club; there are lots of fellows at the club want a place of that sort."

"I hope Laura will live in it for the winter, at least, and will make it her home," Arthur replied: at which the major pish'd, and psha'd, and said that there ought to be convents, begad, for English ladies, and wished that Miss Bell had not been there to interfere with the arrangements of the family, and that she would mope herself to death alone in that place.

Indeed, it would have been a very dismal abode for poor Laura, who was not too happy either in Doctor Portman's household, and in the town where too many things reminded her of the dear parent whom she had lost. But old Lady Rockminster, who adored her young friend Laura, as soon as she read in the paper of her loss, and of her presence in the country, rushed over from Baymouth, where the old lady was staying, and insisted that Laura should remain six months, twelve months, all her life with her; and to her ladyship's house, Martha from Fairoaks, as femme de chambre, accompanied her young mistress.

Pen and Warrington saw her depart. It was difficult to say which of the young men seemed to regard her the most tenderly. "Your cousin is pert and rather vulgar, my dear, but he seems to have a good heart," little Lady Rockminster said, who said her say about every body—"but I like Bluebeard best. Tell, me is he touche au coeur?"

"Mr. Warrington has been long—engaged," Laura said dropping her eyes.

"Nonsense, child! And good heavens, my dear! that's a pretty diamond cross. What do you mean by wearing it in the morning?"

"Arthur—my brother gave it to me just now. It was—it was—" She could not finish the sentence. The carriage passed over the bridge, and by the dear, dear gate of Fairoaks—home no more.

CHAPTER XX

OLD FRIENDS

It chanced at that great English festival, at which all London takes a holiday upon Epsom Downs, that a great number of the personages to whom we have been introduced in the course of this history, were assembled to see the Derby. In a comfortable open carriage, which had been brought to the ground by a pair of horses, might be seen Mrs. Bungay, of Paternoster-row, attired like Solomon in all his glory, and having by her side modest Mrs. Shandon, for whom, since the commencement of their acquaintance, the worthy publisher's lady had maintained a steady friendship. Bungay, having recreated himself with a copious luncheon, was madly shying at the sticks hard by, till the perspiration ran off his bald pate. Shandon was shambling about among the drinking tents and gipsies: Finucane constant in attendance on the two ladies, to whom gentlemen of their acquaintance, and connected with the publishing house, came up to pay a visit.

Among others, Mr. Archer came up to make her his bow, and told Mrs. Bungay who was on the course. Yonder was the prime minister: his lordship had just told him to back Borax for the race; but Archer thought Muffineer the better horse. He pointed out countless dukes and grandees to the delighted Mrs. Bungay. "Look yonder in the Grand Stand," he said. "There sits the Chinese embassador with the mandarins of his suite. Fou-choo-foo brought me over letters of introduction from the Governor-general of India, my most intimate friend, and I was for some time very kind to him, and he had his chop-sticks laid for him at my table whenever he chose to come and dine. But he brought his own cook with him, and—would you believe it, Mrs. Bungay?—one day, when I was out, and the embassador was with Mrs. Archer in our garden eating gooseberries, of which the Chinese are passionately fond, the beast of a cook, seeing my wife's dear little Blenheim spaniel (that we had from the Duke of Maryborough himself, whose ancestor's life Mrs. Archer's great-great-grandfather saved at the battle of Malplaquet), seized upon the poor little devil, cut his throat, and skinned him, and served him up stuffed with forced meat in the second course."

"Law!" said Mrs. Bungay.

"You may fancy my wife's agony when she knew what had happened! The cook came screaming up-stairs, and told us that she had found poor Fido's skin in the area, just after we had all of us tasted of the dish! She never would speak to the embassador again—never; and, upon my word, he has never been to dine with us since. The Lord Mayor, who did me the honor to dine, liked the dish very much; and, eaten with green peas, it tastes rather like duck."

"You don't say so, now!" cried the astonished publisher's lady.

"Fact, upon my word. Look at that lady in blue, seated by the embassador: that is Lady Flamingo, and they say she is going to be married to him, and return to Pekin with his Excellency. She is getting her feet squeezed down on purpose. But she'll only cripple herself, and will never be able to do it—never. My wife has the smallest foot in England, and wears shoes for a six-year's old child; but what is that to a Chinese lady's foot, Mrs. Bungay?"

"Who is that carriage as Mr. Pendennis is with, Mr. Archer?" Mrs. Bungay presently asked. "He and Mr. Warrington was here just now. He's 'aughty in his manners, that Mr. Pendennis, and well he may be, for I'm told he keeps tip-top company. As he 'ad a large fortune left him, Mr. Archer? He's in black still, I see."

"Eighteen hundred a year in land, and twenty-two thousand five hundred in the three-and-a-half per cents.; that's about it," said Mr. Archer.

"Law! why you know every thing Mr. A.!" cried the lady of Paternoster Row.

"I happen to know, because I was called in about poor Mrs. Pendennis's will," Mr. Archer replied. "Pendennis's uncle, the major, seldom does any thing without me; and as he is likely to be extravagant we've tied up the property, so that he can't make ducks and drakes with it. How do you do, my Lord?— Do you know that gentleman, ladies? You have read his speeches in the House; it is Lord Rochester."

"Lord Fiddlestick," cried out Finucane, from the box. "Sure it's Tom Staples, of the Morning Advertiser, Archer."

"Is it?" Archer said, simply. "Well I'm very short-sighted, and upon my word I thought it was Rochester. That gentleman with the double opera-glass (another nod) is Lord John; and the tall man with him, don't you know him? is Sir James."

"You know 'em because you see 'em in the house," growled Finucane.

"I know them because they are kind enough to allow me to call them my most intimate friends," Archer continued. "Look at the Duke of Hampshire; what a pattern of a fine old English gentleman! He never misses 'the Derby.' 'Archer,' he said to me only yesterday, 'I have been at sixty-five Derbies! appeared on the field for the first time on a piebald pony when I was seven years old, with my father, the Prince of Wales, and Colonel Hanger; and only missing two races—one when I had the measles at Eton, and one in the Waterloo year, when I was with my friend Wellington in Flanders.'"

"And who is that yellow carriage, with the pink and yellow parasols, that Mr. Pendennis is talking to, and ever so many gentlemen?" asked Mrs. Bungay.

"That is Lady Clavering, of Clavering Park, next estate to my friend Pendennis. That is the young son and heir upon the box; he's awfully tipsy, the little scamp! and the young lady is Miss Amory, Lady

Clavering's daughter by a first marriage, and uncommonly sweet upon my friend Pendennis; but I've reason to think he has his heart fixed elsewhere. You have heard of young Mr. Foker—the great brewer, Foker, you know—he was going to hang himself in consequence of a fatal passion for Miss Amory, who refused him, but was cut down just in time by his valet, and is now abroad, under a keeper."

"How happy that young fellow is!" sighed Mrs. Bungay. "Who'd have thought when he came so quiet and demure to dine with us, three or four years ago, he would turn out such a grand character! Why, I saw his name at court the other day, and presented by the Marquis of Steyne and all; and in every party of the nobility his name's down, as sure as a gun."

"I introduced him a good deal when he first came up to town," Mr. Archer said, "and his uncle, Major Pendennis, did the rest. Halloo! There's Cobden here, of all men in the world! I must go and speak to him. Good-by, Mrs. Bungay. Good morning, Mrs. Shandon."

An hour previous to this time, and at a different part of the course, there might have been seen an old stage-coach, on the battered roof of which a crowd of shabby raffs were stamping and hallooing, as the great event of the day—the Derby race—rushed over the green sward, and by the shouting millions of people assembled to view that magnificent scene. This was Wheeler's (the "Harlequin's Head") drag, which had brought down a company of choice spirits from Bow-street, with a slap-up luncheon in the "boot." As the whirling race flashed by, each of the choice spirits bellowed out the name of the horse or the colors which he thought or he hoped might be foremost. "The Cornet!" "It's Muffineer!" "It's blue sleeves!'" "Yellow cap! yellow cap! yellow cap!" and so forth, yelled the gentlemen sportsmen during that delicious and thrilling minute before the contest was decided; and as the fluttering signal blew out, showing the number of the famous horse Podasokus as winner of the race, one of the gentlemen on the "Harlequin's Head" drag sprang up off the roof, as if he was a pigeon and about to fly away to London or York with the news.

But his elation did not lift him many inches from his standing-place, to which he came down again on the instant, causing the boards of the crazy old coach-roof to crack with the weight of his joy. "Hurrah, hurrah!" he bawled out, "Podasokus is the horse! Supper for ten Wheeler, my boy. Ask you all round of course, and damn the expense."

And the gentlemen on the carriage, the shabby swaggerers, the dubious bucks, said, "Thank you—congratulate you, colonel; sup with you with pleasure:" and whispered to one another, "The colonel stands to win fifteen hundred, and he got the odds from a good man, too."

And each of the shabby bucks and dusky dandies began to eye his neighbor with suspicion, lest that neighbor, taking his advantage, should get the colonel into a lonely place and borrow money of him. And the winner on Podasokus could not be alone during the whole of that afternoon, so closely did his friends watch him and each other.

At another part of the course you might have seen a vehicle, certainly more modest, if not more shabby than that battered coach which had brought down the choice spirits from the Harlequin's Head; this was cab No. 2002, which had conveyed a gentleman and two ladies from the cab-stand in the Strand: whereof one of the ladies, as she sate on the box of the cab enjoying with her mamma and their companion a repast of lobster-salad and bitter ale, looked so fresh and pretty that many of the splendid young dandies who were strolling about the course, and enjoying themselves at the noble diversion of sticks, and talking to the beautifully dressed ladies in the beautiful carriages on the hill, forsook these fascinations to have a glance at the smiling and rosy-cheeked lass on the cab. The blushes of youth and good-humor mantled on the girl's cheeks, and played over that fair countenance like the pretty shining cloudlets on the serene sky over head; the elder lady's cheek was red too; but that was a permanent mottled rose, deepening only as it received fresh draughts of pale ale and brandy-and-water, until her face emulated the rich shell of the lobster which she devoured.

The gentleman who escorted these two ladies was most active in attendance upon them: here on the course, as he had been during the previous journey. During the whole of that animated and delightful drive from London, his jokes had never ceased. He spoke up undauntedly to the most awful drags full of the biggest and most solemn guardsmen; as to the humblest donkey-chaise in which Bob the dustman was driving Molly to the race. He had fired astonishing volleys of what is called "chaff" into endless windows as he passed; into lines of grinning girls' schools; into little regiments of shouting urchins hurrahing behind the railings of their classical and commercial academies; into casements whence smiling maid-servants, and nurses tossing babies, or demure old maiden ladies with dissenting countenances, were looking. And the pretty girl in the straw bonnet with pink ribbon, and her mamma the devourer of lobsters, had both agreed that when he was in "spirits" there was nothing like that Mr. Sam. He had crammed the cab with trophies won from the bankrupt proprietors of the sticks hard by, and with countless pincushions, wooden-apples, backy-boxes, Jack-in-the-boxes, and little soldiers. He had brought up a gipsy with a tawny child in her arms to tell the fortunes of the ladies; and the only cloud which momentarily obscured the sunshine of that happy party, was when the teller of fate informed the young lady that she had had reason to beware of a fair man, who was false to her: that she had had a bad illness, and that she would find that a dark man would prove true.

The girl looked very much abashed at this news: her mother and the young man interchanged signs of wonder and intelligence. Perhaps the conjuror had used the same words to a hundred different carriages on that day.

Making his way solitary among the crowd and the carriages, and noting, according to his wont, the various circumstances and characters which the animated scene presented, a young friend of ours came suddenly upon cab 2002, and the little group of persons assembled on the outside of the vehicle. As he caught sight of the young lady on the box, she started and turned pale: her mother became redder than ever: the heretofore gay and triumphant Mr. Sam. immediately assumed a fierce and suspicious look, and his eyes turned savagely from Fanny Bolton (whom the reader no doubt, has recognized in the young lady of the cab) to Arthur Pendennis, advancing to meet her.

Arthur too, looked dark and suspicious on perceiving Mr. Samuel Huxter in company with his old acquaintances: but his suspicion was that of alarmed morality, and, I dare say, highly creditable to Mr. Arthur: like the suspicion of Mrs. Lynx, when she sees Mr. Brown and Mrs. Jones talking together, or when she remarks Mrs. Lamb twice or thrice in a handsome opera-box. There may be no harm in the conversation of Mr. B. and Mrs. J.: and Mrs. Lamb's opera box (though she notoriously can't afford one) may be honestly come by: but yet a moralist like Mrs. Lynx has a right to the little precautionary fright: and Arthur was no doubt justified in adopting that severe demeanor of his.

Fanny's heart began to patter violently: Huxter's fists, plunged into the pockets of his paletot, clenched themselves involuntarily, and armed themselves, as it were, in ambush: Mrs. Bolton began to talk with all her might, and with a wonderful volubility: and Lor! she was so 'appy to see Mr. Pendennis, and how well he was a lookin', and we'd been talkin' about Mr. P. only jest before; hadn't we, Fanny? and if this was the famous Hepsom races that they talked so much about, she didn't care, for her part, if she never saw them again. And how was Major Pendennis, and that kind Mr. Warrington, who brought Mr. P's great kindness to Fanny; and she never would forget it, never: and Mr. Warrington was so tall, he almost broke his 'ead up against their lodge door. You recollect Mr. Warrington a knockin' of his head—don't you, Fanny?

While Mrs. Bolton was so discoursing, I wonder how many thousands of thoughts passed through Fanny's mind, and what dear times, sad struggles, lonely griefs, and subsequent shame-faced consolations were recalled to her? What pangs had the poor little thing, as she thought how much she had loved him, and that she loved him no more? There he stood, about whom she was going to die ten months since, dandified, supercilious, with a black crape to his white hat, and jet buttons in his shirt front: and a pink in his coat, that some one else had probably given him: with the tightest lavender-colored gloves sewn with black: and the smallest of canes. And Mr. Huxter wore no gloves, and great blucher boots, and smelt very much of tobacco certainly; and looked, oh, it must be owned, he looked as if a bucket of water would do him a great deal of good! All these thoughts, and a myriad of others rushed through Fanny's mind as her mamma was delivering herself of her speech, and as the girl, from under her eyes, surveyed Pendennis—surveyed him entirely from head to foot, the circle on his white forehead that his hat left when he lifted it (his beautiful, beautiful hair had grown again), the trinkets at his watch-chain, the ring on his hand under his glove, the neat shining boot, so, so unlike Sam's high-low!—and after her hand had given a little twittering pressure to the lavender-colored kid grasp which was held out to it, and after her mother had delivered herself of her speech, all Fanny could find to say was, "This is Mr. Samuel Huxter whom you knew formerly, I believe, sir; Mr. Samuel, you know you knew Mr. Pendennis formerly—and—and—will you take a little refreshment?" These little words tremulous and uncolored as they were, yet were understood by Pendennis in such a manner as to take a great load of suspicion from off his mind—of remorse, perhaps from his heart. The frown on the countenance of the prince of Fairoaks disappeared, and a good-natured smile and a knowing twinkle of the eyes illuminated his highness's countenance. "I am very thirsty," he said, "and I will be glad to drink your health, Fanny; and I hope Mr. Huxter will pardon me for having been very rude to him the last time we met, and when I was so ill and out of spirits, that indeed I scarcely knew what I said." And herewith the lavender-colored dexter kid-glove was handed out, in token of amity, to Huxter.

The dirty fist in the young surgeon's pocket was obliged to undouble itself, and come out of its ambush disarmed. The poor fellow himself felt, as he laid it in Pen's hand, how hot his own was, and how black—it left black marks on Pen's gloves; he saw them—he would have liked to have clenched it again and dashed it into the other's good-humored face; and have seen, there upon that ground, with Fanny, with all England looking on, which was the best man—he Sam Huxter of Bartholomew's, or that grinning dandy.

Pen with ineffable good-humor took a glass—he didn't mind what it was—he was content to drink after the ladies; and he filled it with frothing lukewarm beer, which he pronounced to be delicious, and which he drank cordially to the health of the party.

As he was drinking and talking on in an engaging manner, a young lady in a shot dove-colored dress, with a white parasol lined with pink, and the prettiest dove-colored boots that ever stepped, passed by Pen, leaning on the arm of a stalwart gentleman with a military mustache. The young lady clenched her little fist, and gave a mischievous side-look as she passed Pen. He of the mustaches burst out into a jolly laugh. He had taken off his hat to the ladies of cab No. 2002. You should have seen Fanny Bolton's eyes watching after the dove-colored young lady. Immediately Huxter perceived the direction which they took, they ceased looking after the dove-colored nymph, and they turned and looked into Sam Huxter's orbs with the most artless good-humored expression.

"What a beautiful creature!" Fanny said. "What a lovely dress! Did you remark, Mr. Sam, such little, little hands?"

"It was Capting Strong," said Mrs. Bolton: "and who was the young woman, I wonder?"

"A neighbor of mine in the country—Miss Amory," Arthur said—"Lady Clavering's daughter. You've seen Sir Francis often in Shepherd's Inn, Mrs. Bolton."

As he spoke, Fanny built up a perfect romance in three volumes— love—faithlessness—splendid marriage at St. George's, Hanover-square —broken-hearted maid—and Sam Huxter was not the hero of that story—poor Sam, who by this time had got out an exceedingly rank Cuba cigar, and was smoking it under Fanny's little nose.

After that confounded prig Pendennis joined and left the party the sun was less bright to Sam Huxter, the sky less blue—the sticks had no attraction for him—the bitter beer hot and undrinkable—the world was changed. He had a quantity of peas and a tin pea-shooter in the pocket of the cab for amusement on the homeward route. He didn't take them out, and forgot their existence until some other wag, on their return from the races, fired a volley into Sam's sad face; upon which salute, after a few oaths indicative of surprise, he burst into a savage and sardonic laugh.

But Fanny was charming all the way home. She coaxed, and snuggled, and smiled. She laughed pretty laughs; she admired everything; she took out the darling little jack-in-the-boxes, and was so obliged to Sam. And when they got home, and Mr. Huxter, still with darkness on his countenance, was taking a frigid leave of her—she burst into tears, and said he was a naughty, unkind thing.

Upon which, with a burst of emotion, almost as emphatic as hers, the young surgeon held the girl in his arms—swore that she was an angel, and that he was a jealous brute; owned that he was unworthy of her, and that he had no right to hate Pendennis; and asked her, implored her, to say once more that she—

That she what?—The end of the question and Fanny's answer were pronounced by lips that were so near each other, that no bystander could hear the words. Mrs. Bolton only said, "Come, come, Mr. H.— no nonsense, if you please; and I think you've acted like a wicked wretch, and been most uncommon cruel to Fanny, that I do."

When Arthur left No. 2002, he went to pay his respects to the carriage to which, and to the side of her mamma, the dove colored author of Mes Larmes had by this time returned. Indefatigable old Major Pendennis was in waiting upon Lady Clavering, and had occupied the back seat in her carriage; the box being in possession of young Hopeful, under the care of Captain Strong.

A number of dandies, and men of a certain fashion—of military bucks, of young rakes of the public offices, of those who may be styled men's men rather than ladies'—had come about the carriage during its station on the hill—and had exchanged a word or two with Lady Clavering, and a little talk (a little "chaff" some of the most elegant of the men styled their conversation) with Miss Amory. They had offered her sportive bets, and exchanged with her all sorts of free-talk and knowing innuendoes. They pointed out to her who was on the course: and the "who" was not always the person a young lady should know.

When Pen came up to Lady Clavering's carriage, he had to push his way through a crowd of these young bucks who were paying their court to Miss Amory, in order to arrive as near that young lady, who beckoned him by many pretty signals to her side.

"Je l'ai vue," she said; "elle a de bien beaux yeux; vous êtes un monstre!"

"Why monster?" said Pen, with a laugh; "Honi soit qui mal y pense. My young friend, yonder, is as well protected as any young lady in Christendom. She has her mamma on one side, her 'prétendu' on the other. Could any harm happen to a girl between those two?"

"One does not know what may or may not arrive," said Miss Blanche. in French, "when a girl has the mind, and when she is pursued by a wicked monster like you. Figure to yourself, colonel, that I come to find monsieur, your nephew, near to a cab, by two ladies, and a man, oh, such a man! and who ate lobsters, and who laughed, who laughed!"

"It did not strike me that the man laughed," Pen said. "And as for lobsters, I thought he would have liked to eat me after the lobsters. He shook hands with me, and griped me so, that he bruised my glove black and blue. He is a young surgeon. He comes from Clavering. Don't you remember the gilt pestle and mortar in High-street?"

"If he attends you when you are sick," continued Miss Amory, "he will kill you. He will serve you right; for you are a monster."

The perpetual recurrence to the word "monster" jarred upon Pen. "She speaks about these matters a great deal too lightly," he thought. "If I had been a monster, as she calls it, she would have received me just the same. This is not the way in which an English lady should speak or think. Laura would not speak in that way, thank God!" and as he thought so, his own countenance fell.

"Of what are you thinking? Are you going to bouder me at present?" Blanche asked. "Major, scold your méchant nephew. He does not amuse me at all. He is as béte as Captain Crackenbury."

"What are you saying about me, Miss Amory?" said the guardsman, with a grin. "If it's any thing good, say it in English, for I don't understand French when it's spoke so devilish quick."

"It ain't any thing good, Crack," said Crackenbury's fellow, Captain Clinker. "Let's come away, and don't spoil sport. They say Pendennis is sweet upon her."

"I'm told he's a devilish clever fellow," sighed Crackenbury. "Lady Violet Lebas says he's a devilish clever fellow. He wrote a work, or a poem, or something; and he writes those devilish clever things in the—in the papers you know. Dammy, I wish I was a clever fellow, Clinker."

"That's past wishing for, Crack, my boy," the other said. "I can't write a good book, but I think I can make a pretty good one on the Derby. What a flat Clavering is! And the Begum! I like that old Begum. She's worth ten of her daughter. How pleased the old girl was at winning the lottery!"

"Clavering's safe to pay up, ain't he?" asked Captain Crackenbury. "I hope so," said his friend; and they disappeared, to enjoy themselves among the sticks.

Before the end of the day's amusements, many more gentlemen of Lady Clavering's acquaintance came up to her carriage, and chatted with the party which it contained. The worthy lady was in high spirits and good-humor, laughing and talking according to her wont, and offering refreshments to all her friends, until her ample baskets and bottles were emptied, and her servants and postillions were in such a royal state of excitement as servants and postillions commonly are upon the Derby day.

The major remarked that some of the visitors to the carriage appeared to look with rather queer and meaning glances toward its owner. "How easily she takes it!" one man whispered to another. "The Begum's made of money," the friend replied. "How easily she takes what?" thought old Pendennis. "Has any body lost any money?" Lady Clavering said she was happy in the morning because Sir Francis had promised her not to bet.

Mr. Welbore, the country neighbor of the Claverings, was passing the carriage, when he was called back by the Begum, who rallied him for wishing to cut her. "Why didn't he come before? Why didn't he come to lunch?" Her ladyship was in great delight, she told him—she told every body—that she had won five pounds in a lottery. As she conveyed this piece of intelligence to him, Mr. Welbore looked so particularly knowing, and withal melancholy, that a dismal apprehension seized upon Major Pendennis. "He would go and look after the horses and those rascals of postillions, who were so long in coming round." When he came back to the carriage, his usually benign and smirking countenance was obscured by some sorrow. "What is the matter with you now?" the good-natured Begum asked. The major pretended a headache from the fatigue and sunshine of the day. The carriage wheeled off the course and took its way Londonwards, not the least brilliant equipage in that vast and picturesque procession. The tipsy drivers dashed gallantly over the turf, amid the admiration of foot-passengers, the ironical cheers of the little donkey-carriages and spring vans, and the loud objurgations of horse-and-chaise men, with whom the reckless post-boys came in contact. The jolly Begum looked the picture of good humor as she reclined on her splendid cushions; the lovely Sylphide smiled with languid elegance. Many an honest holiday-maker with his family wadded into a tax-cart, many a cheap dandy working his way home on his weary hack, admired that brilliant turn-out, and thought, no doubt, how happy those "swells" must be. Strong sat on the box still, with a lordly voice calling to the post-boys and the crowd. Master Frank had been put inside of the carriage and was asleep there by the side of the major, dozing away the effects of the constant luncheon and champagne of which he had freely partaken.

The major was revolving in his mind meanwhile the news the receipt of which had made him so grave. "If Sir Francis Clavering goes on in this way," Pendennis the elder thought, "this little tipsy rascal will be as bankrupt as his father and grandfather before him. The Begum's fortune can't stand such drains upon it: no fortune can stand them: she has paid his debts half-a-dozen times already. A few years more of the turf, and a few coups like this will ruin her."

"Don't you think we could get up races at Clavering, mamma?" Miss Amory asked. "Yes, we must have them there again. There were races there in the old times, the good old times. It's a national amusement you know: and we could have a Clavering ball: and we might have dances for the tenantry, and rustic sports in the park—Oh, it would he charming."

"Capital fun," said mamma. "Wouldn't it, major?"

"The turf is a very expensive amusement, my dear lady," Major Pendennis answered, with such a rueful face, that the Begum rallied him, and asked laughingly whether he had lost money on the race?

After a slumber of about an hour and a half, the heir of the house began to exhibit symptoms of wakefulness, stretching his youthful arms over the major's face, and kicking his sister's knees as she sate opposite to him. When the amiable youth was quite restored to consciousness, he began a sprightly conversation.

"I say, ma," he said, "I've gone and done it this time, I have." "What have you gone and done, Franky, dear?" asked mamma. "How much is seventeen half-crowns?" "Two pound and half-a-crown, ain't it? I drew Borax in our lottery, but I bought Podasokus and Man-milliner of Leggat minor for two open tarts and a bottle of ginger beer."

"You little wicked gambling creature, how dare you begin so soon?" cried Miss Amory.

"Hold your tongue, if you please. Who ever asked your leave, miss?" the brother said. "And I say, ma—"

"Well, Franky, dear?"

"You'll tip me all the same, you know, when I go back—" and here he broke out into a laugh. "I say, ma, shall I tell you something?"

The Begum expressed her desire to hear this something, and her son and heir continued:

"When me and Strong was down at the grand stand after the race, and I was talking to Leggat minor, who was there with his governor; I saw pa look as savage as a bear. And I say, ma, Leggat minor told me that he heard his governor say that pa had lost seven thousand backing the favorite. I'll never back the favorite when I'm of age. No, no—hang me if I do: leave me alone, Strong, will you?"

"Captain Strong! Captain Strong! is this true?" cried out the unfortunate Begum. "Has Sir Francis been betting again? He promised me he wouldn't. He gave me his word of honor he wouldn't."

Strong, from his place on the box, had overheard the end of young Clavering's communication, and was trying in vain to stop his unlucky tongue.

"I'm afraid it's true, ma'am," he said, turning round. "I deplore the loss as much as you can. He promised me as he promised you; but the play is too strong for him! he can't refrain from it."

Lady Clavering at this sad news burst into a fit of tears. She deplored her wretched fate as the most miserable of woman. She declared she would separate, and pay no more debts for this ungrateful man. She narrated with tearful volubility a score of stories only too
 authentic, which showed how her husband had deceived, and how constantly she had befriended him: and in this melancholy condition, while young Hopeful was thinking about the two guineas which he himself had won; and the major revolving, in his darkened mind, whether certain plans which he had been forming had better not be abandoned; the splendid carriage drove up at length to the Begum's house in Grosvenor-place; the idlers and boys lingering about the place to witness, according to public wont, the close of the Derby day, cheering the carriage as it drew up, and envying the happy folks who descended from it.

"And it's for the son of this man that I am made a beggar!" Blanche said, quivering with anger, as she walked up stairs leaning on the major's arm—"for this cheat—for this black-leg—for this liar—for this robber of women."

"Calm yourself, my dear Miss Blanche," the old gentleman said; "I pray calm yourself. You have been hardly treated, most unjustly. But remember that you have always a friend in me; and trust to an old fellow who will try and serve you."

And the young lady, and the heir of the hopeful house of Clavering, having retired to their beds, the remaining three of the Epsom party remained for some time in deep consultation.

CHAPTER XXI

EXPLANATIONS

Almost a year, as the reader will perceive, has passed since an event described a few pages back. Arthur's black coat is about to be exchanged for a blue one. His person has undergone other more pleasing and remarkable changes. His wig has been laid aside, and his hair, though somewhat thinner, has returned to public view. And he has had the honor of appearing at court in the uniform of a cornet of the Clavering troop of the——shire Yeomanry Cavalry, being presented to the sovereign by the Marquis of Steyne.

This was a measure strongly and pathetically urged by Arthur's uncle. The major would not hear of a year passing before this ceremony of gentlemanhood was gone through. The old gentleman thought that his nephew should belong to some rather more select club than the Megatherium; and has announced every where in the world his disappointment that the young man's property has turned out not by any means as well as he could have hoped, and is under fifteen hundred a year.

That is the amount at which Pendennis's property is set down in the world, where his publishers begin to respect him much more than formerly, and where even mammas are by no means uncivil to him. For if the pretty daughters are, naturally, to marry people of very different expectations, at any rate, he will be eligible for the plain ones; and if the brilliant and fascinating Myra is to hook an earl, poor little Beatrice, who has one shoulder higher than the other, must hang on to some boor through life, and why should not Mr. Pendennis be her support? In the very first winter after the accession to his mother's fortune, Mrs. Hawxby in a country-house caused her Beatrice to learn billiards from Mr. Pendennis, and would be driven by nobody but him in the pony carriage, because he was literary and her Beatrice was literary too, and declared that the young man, under the instigation of his horrid old uncle, had behaved most infamously in trifling with Beatrice's feelings. The truth is, the old gentleman, who knew Mrs. Hawxby's character, and how desperately that lady would practice upon unwary young men, had come to the country-house in question and carried Arthur out of the danger of her immediate claws, though not out of the reach of her tongue. The elder Pendennis would have had his nephew pass a part of the Christmas at Clavering, whither the family had returned; but Arthur had not the heart for that. Clavering was too near poor old Fairoaks; and that was too full of sad recollections for the young man.

We have lost sight of the Claverings, too, until their reappearance upon the Epsom race-ground, and must give a brief account of them in the interval. During the past year, the world has not treated any member of the Clavering family very kindly. Lady Clavering, one of the best-natured women that ever enjoyed a good dinner, or made a slip in grammar, has had her appetite and good-nature sadly tried by constant family grievances, and disputes such as make the efforts of the best French cook unpalatable, and the most delicately-stuffed sofa-cushion hard to lie on. "I'd rather have a turnip, Strong, for dessert, than that pineapple, and all them Muscatel grapes, from Clavering," says poor Lady Clavering, looking at her dinner-table, and confiding her griefs to her faithful friend, "if I could but have a little quiet to eat it with. Oh, how much happier I was when I was a widow, and before all this money fell in to me!"

The Clavering family had indeed made a false start in life, and had got neither comfort, nor position, nor thanks for the hospitalities which they administered, nor a return of kindness from the people whom they entertained. The success of their first London season was doubtful; and their failure afterward notorious. "Human patience was not great enough to put up with Sir Francis Clavering," people said. "He was too hopelessly low, dull, and disreputable. You could not say what, but there was a taint about the house and its entourages. Who was the Begum, with her money, and without her h's, and where did she come from? What an extraordinary little piece of conceit the daughter was, with her Gallicised graces and daring affectations, not fit for well-bred English girls to associate with! What strange people were those they assembled round about them! Sir Francis Clavering was a gambler, living notoriously in the society of blacklegs and profligates. Hely Clinker, who was in his regiment, said that he not only cheated at cards, but showed the white feather. What could Lady Rockminster have meant by taking her up?" After the first season, indeed, Lady Rockminster, who had taken up Lady Clavering, put her down; the great ladies would not take their daughters to her parties; the young men who attended them behaved with the most odious freedom and scornful familiarity; and poor Lady Clavering herself avowed that she was obliged to take what she called "the canal" into her parlor, because the tiptops wouldn't come.

She had not the slightest ill-will toward "the canal," the poor, dear lady, or any pride about herself, or idea that she was better than her neighbor; but she had taken implicitly the orders which, on her entry into the world, her social godmother had given her: she had been willing to know whom they knew, and ask whom they asked. The "canal," in fact, was much pleasanter than what is called "society;" but, as we said before, that to leave a mistress is easy, while, on the contrary, to be left by her is cruel; so you may give up society without any great pang, or any thing but a sensation of relief at the parting; but severe are the mortifications and pains you have if society gives up you.

One young man of fashion we have mentioned, who at least, it might have been expected, would have been found faithful among the faithless, and Harry Foker, Esq., was indeed that young man. But he had not managed matters with prudence, and the unhappy passion at first confided to Pen became notorious and ridiculous to the town, was carried to the ears of his weak and fond mother, and finally brought under the cognizance of the bald-headed and inflexible Foker senior.

When Mr. Foker learned this disagreeable news, there took place between him and his son a violent and painful scene which ended in the poor little gentleman's banishment from England for a year, with a positive order to return at the expiration of that time and complete his marriage with his cousin, or to retire into private life and three hundred a year altogether, and never see parent or brewery more. Mr. Henry Foker went away, then, carrying with him that grief and care which passes free at the strictest custom-houses, and which proverbially accompanies the exile, and with this crape over his eyes, even the Parisian Boulevard looked melancholy to him, and the sky of Italy black.

To Sir Francis Clavering, that year was a most unfortunate one. The events described in the last chapter came to complete the ruin of the year. It was that year of grace in which, as our sporting readers may remember, Lord Harrowhill's horse (he was a classical young nobleman, and named his stud out of the Iliad)—when Podasokus won the "Derby," to the dismay of the knowing ones, who pronounced the winning horse's name in various extraordinary ways, and who backed Borax, who was nowhere in the race. Sir Francis Clavering, who was intimate with some of the most rascally characters of the turf, and, of course, had valuable "information," had laid heavy odds against the winning horse, and backed the favorite freely, and the result of his dealings was, as his son correctly stated to poor Lady Clavering, a loss of seven thousand pounds.

Indeed, it was a cruel blow upon the lady, who had discharged her husband's debts many times over; who had received as many times his oaths and promises of amendment; who had paid his money-lenders and horse-dealers; who had furnished his town and country houses, and who was called upon now instantly to meet this enormous sum, the penalty of her cowardly husband's extravagance. It has been described in former pages how the elder Pendennis had become the adviser of the Clavering family, and, in his quality of intimate friend of the house, had gone over every room of it, and even seen that ugly closet which we all of us have, and in which, according to the proverb, the family skeleton is locked up. About the baronet's pecuniary matters, if the major did not know, it was because Clavering himself did not know them, and hid them from himself and others in such a hopeless entanglement of lies that it was impossible for adviser or attorney or principal to get an accurate knowledge of his affairs. But, concerning Lady Clavering, the major was much better informed; and when the unlucky mishap of the "Derby" arose, he took upon himself to become completely and thoroughly acquainted with all her means, whatsoever they where; and was now accurately informed of the vast and repeated sacrifices which the widow Amory had made in behalf of her present husband.

He did not conceal—and he had won no small favor from Miss Blanche by avowing it—his opinion, that Lady Clavering's daughter had been hardly treated at the expense of her son by her second marriage: and in his conversations with Lady Clavering had fairly hinted that he thought Miss Blanche ought to have a better provision. We have said that he had already given the widow to understand that he knew all the particulars of her early and unfortunate history, having been in India at the time when—when the painful circumstances occurred which had ended in her parting from her first husband. He could tell her where to find the Calcutta newspaper which contained the account of Amory's trial, and he showed, and the Begum was not a little grateful to him for his forbearance, how being aware all along of this mishap which had befallen her, he had kept all knowledge of it to himself, and been constantly the friend of her family.

"Interested motives, my dear Lady Clavering," he said, "of course I may have had. We all have interested motives, and mine I don't conceal from you, was to make a marriage between my nephew and your daughter." To which Lady Clavering, perhaps with some surprise that the major should choose her family for a union with his own, said she was quite willing to consent.

But frankly he said, "My dear lady, my boy has but five hundred a year, and a wife with ten thousand pounds to her fortune would scarcely better him. We could do better for him than that, permit me to say, and he is a shrewd, cautious young fellow who has sown his wild oats now—who has very good parts and plenty of ambition—and whose object in marrying is to better himself. If you and Sir Francis chose—and Sir Francis, take my word for it, will refuse you nothing—you could put Arthur in a way to advance very considerably in the world, and show the stuff which he has in him. Of what use is that seat in Parliament to Clavering, who scarcely ever shows his face in the House, or speaks a word there? I'm

told by gentlemen who heard my boy at Oxbridge, that he was famous as an orator, begad!—and once put his foot into the stirrup and mount him, I've no doubt he won't be the
last of the field ma'am. I've tested the chap, and know him pretty well, I think. He is much too lazy, and careless, and flighty a fellow, to make a jog-trot journey, and arrive, as your lawyers do, at the end of their lives! but give him a start and good friends, and an opportunity, and take my word for it, he'll make himself a name that his sons shall be proud of. I don't see any way for a fellow like him to parvenir, but by making a prudent marriage—not with a beggarly heiress—to sit down for life upon a miserable fifteen hundred a year—but with somebody whom he can help, and who can help him forward in the world, and whom he can give a good name and a station in the country, begad, in return for the advantages which she brings him. It would be better for you to have a distinguished son-in-law, than to keep your husband on in Parliament, who's of no good to himself or to any body else there, and that's, I say, why I've been interested about you, and offer you what I think a good bargain for both."

"You know I look upon Arthur as one of the family almost now," said the good-natured Begum; "he comes and goes when he likes; and the more I think of his dear mother, the more I see there's few people so good—none so good to me. And I'm sure I cried when I heard of her death, and would have gone into mourning for her myself, only black don't become me. And I know who his mother wanted him to marry —Laura, I mean—whom old Lady Rockminster has taken such a fancy to, and no wonder. She's a better girl than my girl. I know both, And my Betsy—Blanche, I mean—ain't been a comfort to me, major. It's Laura Penn ought to marry."

"Marry on five hundred a year! My dear good soul, you are mad!" Major Pendennis said. "Think over what I have said to you. Do nothing in your affairs with that unhappy husband of yours without consulting me; and remember that old Pendennis is always your friend."

For some time previous, Pen's uncle had held similar language to Miss Amory. He had pointed out to her the convenience of the match which he had at heart, and was bound to say, that mutual convenience was of all things the very best in the world to marry upon—the only thing. "Look at your love-marriages, my dear young creature. The love-match people are the most notorious of all for quarreling, afterward; and a girl who runs away with Jack to Gretna Green, constantly runs away with Tom to Switzerland afterward. The great point in marriage is for people to agree to be useful to one another. The lady brings the means, and the gentleman avails himself of them. My boy's wife brings the horse, and begad, Pen goes in and wins the plate. That's what I call a sensible union. A couple like that have something to talk to each other about when they come together. If you had Cupid himself to talk to—if Blanche and Pen were Cupid and Psyche, begad—they'd begin to yawn after a few evenings, if they had nothing but sentiment to speak on."

As for Miss Amory, she was contented enough with Pen as long as there was nobody better. And how many other young ladies are like her?—and how many love marriages carry on well to the last?—and how many sentimental firms do not finish in bankruptcy?—and how many heroic passions don't dwindle down into despicable indifference, or end in shameful defeat?

These views of life and philosophy the major was constantly, according to his custom, inculcating to Pen, whose mind was such that he could see the right on both sides of many questions, and comprehending the sentimental life which was quite out of the reach of the honest major's intelligence, could understand the practical life too, and accommodate himself, or think he could accommodate himself to it. So it came to pass that during the spring succeeding his mother's death he became a good deal under the influence of his uncle's advice, and domesticated in Lady Clavering's house; and in a measure was accepted by Miss Amory without being a suitor, and was received without being engaged. The young people were extremely familiar, without being particularly sentimental, and met and parted with each other in perfect good-humor. "And I," thought Pendennis, "am the fellow who eight years ago had a grand passion, and last year was raging in a fever about Briseis!"

Yes, it was the same Pendennis, and time had brought to him, as to the rest of us, its ordinary consequences, consolations, developments. We alter very little. When we talk of this man or that woman being no longer the same person whom we remember in youth, and remark (of course to deplore) changes in our friends, we don't, perhaps, calculate that circumstance only brings out the latent defect or quality, and does not create it. The selfish languor and indifference of to-day's possession is the consequence of the selfish ardor of yesterday's pursuit: the scorn and weariness which cries vanitas vanitatum is but the lassitude of the sick appetite palled with pleasure: the insolence of the successful parvenu is only the necessary continuance of the career of the needy struggler: our mental changes are like our gray hairs or our wrinkles—but the fulfillment of the plan of mortal growth and decay: that which is snow-white now was glossy black once; that which is sluggish obesity to-day was boisterous rosy health a few years back; that calm weariness, benevolent, resigned, and disappointed, was ambition, fierce and violent, but a few years since, and has only settled into submissive repose after many a battle and defeat. Lucky he who can bear his failure so generously, and give up his broken sword to Fate the Conqueror with a manly and humble heart! Are you not awe-stricken, you, friendly reader, who, taking the page up for a moment's light reading, lay it down, perchance, for a graver reflection—to think how you, who have consummated your success or your disaster, may be holding marked station, or a hopeless and nameless place, in the crowds who have passed through how many struggles of defeat, success, crime, remorse, to yourself only known!—who may have loved and grown cold, wept and laughed again, how often!—to think how you are the same, You, whom in childhood you remember, before the voyage of life began? It has been prosperous, and you are riding into port, the people huzzaing and the guns saluting,—and the lucky captain bows from the ship's side, and there is a care under the star on his breast which no body knows of: or you are wrecked, and lashed, hopeless, to a solitary spar out at sea:—the sinking man and the successful one are thinking each about home, very likely, and remembering the time when they were children; alone on the hopeless spar, drowning out of sight; alone in the midst of the crowd applauding you.

CHAPTER XXII

CONVERSATIONS

Our good-natured Begum was at first so much enraged at this last instance of her husband's duplicity and folly, that she refused to give Sir Francis Clavering any aid in order to meet his debts of honor, and declared that she would separate from him, and leave him to the consequences of his incorrigible weakness and waste. After that fatal day's transactions at the Derby, the unlucky gambler was in such a condition of mind that he was disposed to avoid every body—alike his turf-associates with whom he had made debts which he trembled lest he should not have the means of paying, and his wife, his long-suffering banker, on whom he reasonably doubted whether he should be allowed any longer to draw. When Lady Clavering asked the next morning whether Sir Francis was in the house, she received answer that he had not returned that night, but had sent a messenger to his valet, ordering him to forward clothes and letters by the bearer. Strong knew that he should have a visit or a message from him in the course of that or the subsequent day, and accordingly got a note beseeching him to call upon his distracted friend F. C., at Short's Hotel, Blackfriars, and ask for Mr. Francis there. For the baronet was a gentleman of that peculiarity of mind that he would rather tell a lie than not, and always began a contest with fortune by running away and hiding himself. The boots of Mr. Short's establishment, who carried Clavering's message to Grosvenor-place, and brought back his carpet-bag, was instantly aware who was the owner of the bag, and he imparted his information to the footman who was laying the breakfast-table, who carried down the news to the servant's hall, who took it to Mrs. Bonner, my lady's housekeeper and confidential maid, who carried it to my lady. And thus every single person in the Grosvenor-place establishment knew that Sir Francis was in hiding, under the name of Francis, at an inn in the Blackfriar's-road. And Sir Francis's coachman told the news to other gentlemen's coachmen, who carried it to their masters, and to the neighboring Tattersall's, where very gloomy anticipations were formed that Sir Francis Clavering was about to make a tour in the Levant.

In the course of that day the number of letters addressed to Sir Francis Clavering, Bart., which found their way to his hall table, was quite remarkable. The French cook sent in his account to my lady; the tradesmen who supplied her ladyship's table, and Messrs. Finer and Gimcrack, the mercers and ornamental dealers, and Madame Crinoline, the eminent milliner, also forwarded their little bills to her ladyship in company with Miss Amory's private, and by no means inconsiderable, account at each establishment.

In the afternoon of the day after the Derby, when Strong (after a colloquy with his principal at Short's hotel, whom he found crying and drinking Curaçoa) called to transact business according to his custom at Grosvenor-place, he found all these suspicious documents ranged in the baronet's study; and began to open them and examine them with a rueful countenance.

Mrs. Bonner, my lady's maid and housekeeper, came down upon him while engaged in this occupation. Mrs. Bonner, a part of the family, and as necessary to her mistress as the chevalier was to Sir Francis, was of course on Lady Clavering's side in the dispute between her and her husband, and as by duty bound even more angry than her ladyship herself.

"She won't pay if she takes my advice," Mrs. Bonner said. "You'll please to go back to Sir Francis, Captain—and he lurking about in a low public-house and don't dare to face his wife like a man;—and say that we won't pay his debts no longer. We made a man of him, we took him out of jail (and other folks too perhaps), we've paid his debts over and over again—we set him up in Parliament and gave him a house in town and country, and where he don't dare to show his face, the shabby sneak! We've given him the horse he rides, and the dinner he eats, and the very clothes he has on his back; and we will give him no more. Our fortune, such as is left of it, is left to ourselves, and we wont waste any more of it on this ungrateful man. We'll give him enough to live upon and leave him, that's what we'll do: and that's what you may tell him from Susan Bonner."

Susan Bonner's mistress hearing of Strong's arrival sent for him at this juncture, and the chevalier went up to her ladyship not without hopes that he should find her more tractable than her factotum Mrs. Bonner. Many a time before had he pleaded his client's cause with Lady Clavering and caused her good-nature to relent. He tried again once more. He painted in dismal colors the situation in which he had found Sir Francis: and would not answer for any consequences which might ensue if he could not find means of meeting his engagements. "Kill hisself," laughed Mrs. Bonner, "kill hisself, will he? Dying's the best thing he could do." Strong vowed that he had found him with the razors on the table; but at this, in her turn, Lady Clavering laughed bitterly. "He'll do himself no harm, as long as there's a shilling left of which he can rob a poor woman. His life's quite safe, captain: you may depend upon that. Ah! it was a bad day that ever I set eyes on him."

"He's worse than the first man," cried out my lady's aid-de-camp. "He was a man, he was—a wild devil, but he had the courage of a man—whereas this fellow—what's the use of my lady paying his bills, and selling her diamonds, and forgiving him? He'll be as bad again next year. The very next chance he has he'll be a cheating of her, and robbing of her; and her money will go to keep a pack of rogues and swindlers—I don't mean you, captain—you've been a good friend to us enough, bating we wish we'd never set eyes on you."

The chevalier saw from the words which Mrs. Bonner had let slip regarding the diamonds, that the kind Begum was disposed to relent once more at least, and that there were hopes still for his principal.

"Upon my word, ma'am," he said, with a real feeling of sympathy for Lady Clavering's troubles, and admiration for her untiring good-nature, and with a show of enthusiasm which advanced not a little his graceless patron's cause—"any thing you say against Clavering, or Mrs. Bonner here cries out against me, is no better than we deserve, both of us, and it was an unlucky day for you when you saw either. He has behaved cruelly to you; and if you were not the most generous and forgiving woman in the world, I know there would be no chance for him. But you can't let the father of your son be a disgraced man, and send little Frank into the world with such a stain upon him. Tie him down; bind him by any promises you like: I vouch for him that he will subscribe them."

"And break 'em," said Mrs. Bonner.

"And keep 'em this time," cried out Strong. "He must keep them. If you could have seen how he wept, ma'am! 'Oh, Strong,' he said to me, 'it's not for myself I feel now: it's for my boy—it's for the best woman in England, whom I have treated basely—I know I have.' He didn't intend to bet upon this race, ma'am—indeed he didn't. He was cheated into it: all the ring was taken in. He thought he might make the bet quite safely, without the least risk. And it will be a lesson to him for all his life long. To see a man cry—Oh, it's dreadful."

"He don't think much of making my dear missus cry," said Mrs. Bonner—"poor dear soul!—look if he does, captain."

"If you've the soul of a man, Clavering," Strong said to his principal, when he recounted this scene to him, "you'll keep your promise this time: and, so help me Heaven! if you break word with her, I'll turn against you, and tell all."

"What, all?" cried Mr. Francis, to whom his embassador brought the news back at Short's hotel, where Strong found the baronet crying and drinking Curaçoa.

"Psha! Do you suppose I am a fool?" burst out Strong. "Do you suppose I could have lived so long in the world, Frank Clavering, with out having my eyes about me? You know I have but to speak, and you are a beggar to-morrow. And I am not the only man who knows your secret."

"Who else does?" gasped Clavering.

"Old Pendennis does, or I am very much mistaken. He recognized the man the first night he saw him, when he came drunk into your house."

"He knows it, does he?" shrieked out Clavering. "Damn him—kill him."

"You'd like to kill us all, wouldn't you old boy?" said Strong, with a sneer, puffing his cigar.

The baronet dashed his weak hand against his forehead; perhaps the other had interpreted his wish rightly. "Oh, Strong!" he cried, "if I dared, I'd put an end to myself, for I'm the d—est miserable dog in all England. It's that that makes me so wild and reckless. It's that which makes me take to drink (and he drank, with a trembling hand, a bumper of his fortifier—the Curaçoa), and to live about with these thieves. I know they're thieves, every one of em, d—d thieves. And—and how can I help it?—and I didn't know it, you know—and, by gad, I'm innocent—and until I saw the d—d scoundrel first, I knew no more about it than the dead—and I'll fly, and I'll go abroad out of the reach of the confounded hells, and I'll bury myself in a forest, by gad! and hang myself up to a tree—and, oh—I'm the most miserable beggar in all England!" And so with more tears, shrieks, and curses, the impotent wretch vented his grief and deplored his unhappy fate; and, in the midst of groans and despair and blasphemy, vowed his miserable repentance.

The honored proverb which declares that to be an ill wind which blows good to nobody, was verified in the case of Sir Francis Clavering, and another of the occupants of Mr. Strong's chambers in Shepherd's Inn. The man was "good," by a lucky hap, with whom Colonel Altamont made his bet; and on the settling day of the Derby—as Captain Clinker, who was appointed to settle Sir Francis Clavering's book for him (for Lady Clavering, by the advice of Major Pendennis, would not allow the baronet to liquidate his own money transactions), paid over the notes to the baronet's many creditors—Colonel Altamont had the satisfaction of receiving the odds of thirty to one in fifties, which he had taken against the winning horse of the day.

Numbers of the colonel's friends were present on the occasion to congratulate him on his luck—all Altamont's own set, and the gents who met in the private parlor of the convivial Wheeler, my host of the Harlequin's Head, came to witness their comrade's good fortune, and would have liked, with a generous sympathy for success, to share in it. "Now was the time," Tom Driver had suggested to the colonel, "to have up the specie ship that was sunk in the Gulf of Mexico, with the three hundred and eighty thousand dollars on board, besides bars and doubloons." "The Tredyddlums were very low—to be bought for an old song—never was such an opportunity for buying shares," Mr. Keightley insinuated; and Jack Holt pressed forward his tobacco-smuggling scheme, the audacity of which pleased the colonel more than any other of the speculations proposed to him. Then of the Harlequin's Head boys: there was Jack Hackstraw, who knew of a pair of horses which the colonel must buy; Tom Fleet, whose satirical paper, "The Swell," wanted but two hundred pounds of capital to be worth a thousand a year to any man—"with such a power and influence, colonel, you rogue, and the entrée of all the green-rooms in London," Tom urged; while little Moss Abrams entreated the colonel not to listen to these absurd fellows with their humbugging speculations, but to invest his money in some good bills which Moss could get for him, and which would return him fifty per cent, as safe as the Bank of England.

Each and all of these worthies came round the colonel with their various blandishments; but he had courage enough to resist them, and to button up his notes in the pocket of his coat, and go home to Strong, and "sport" the outer door of the chambers. Honest Strong had given his fellow-lodger good advice about all his acquaintances; and though, when pressed, he did not mind frankly taking twenty pounds himself out of the colonel's winnings, Strong was a great deal too upright to let others cheat him.

He was not a bad fellow when in good fortune, this Altamont. He ordered a smart livery for Grady, and made poor old Costigan shed tears of quickly dried gratitude by giving him a five-pound note after a snug dinner at the Back-Kitchen, and he bought a green shawl for Mrs. Bolton, and a yellow one for Fanny: the most brilliant "sacrifices" of a Regent-street haberdasher's window. And a short time after this, upon her birth-day, which happened in the month of June, Miss Amory received from "a friend" a parcel containing an enormous brass-inlaid writing-desk, in which there was a set of amethysts, the most hideous eyes ever looked upon—a musical snuff-box, and two keepsakes of the year before last, and accompanied with a couple of gown-pieces of the most astounding colors, the receipt of which goods made the Sylphide laugh and wonder immoderately. Now it is a fact that Colonel Altamont had made a purchase of cigars and French silks from some duffers in Fleet-street about this period; and he was found by Strong in the open Auction-room, in Cheapside, having invested some money in two desks, several pairs of richly-plated candlesticks, a dinner épergne and a bagatelle-board. The dinner épergne remained at chambers and figured at the banquets there, which the colonel gave pretty freely. It seemed beautiful in his eyes, until Jack Holt said it looked as if it had been taken in "a bill." And Jack Holt certainly knew.

The dinners were pretty frequent at chambers, and Sir Francis Clavering condescended to partake of them constantly. His own house was shut up; the successor of Mirobolant, who had sent in his bills so prematurely, was dismissed by the indignant Lady Clavering; the luxuriance of the establishment was greatly pruned and reduced. One of the large footmen was cashiered, upon which the other gave warning, not liking to serve without his mate, or in a family where on'y one footman was kep'. General and severe economical reforms were practiced by the Begum in her whole household, in consequence of the extravagance of which her graceless husband had been guilty. The major, as her ladyship's friend; Strong, on the part of poor Clavering; her ladyship's lawyer, and the honest Begum herself, executed these reforms with promptitude and severity. After paying the baronet's debts, the settlement of which occasioned considerable public scandal, and caused the baronet to sink even lower in the world's estimation than he had been before, Lady Clavering quitted London for Tunbridge Wells in high dudgeon, refusing to see her reprobate husband, whom nobody pitied. Clavering remained in London patiently, by no means anxious to meet his wife's just indignation, and sneaked in and out of the House of Commons, whence he and Captain Raff and Mr. Marker would go to have a game at billiards and a cigar: or showed in the sporting public-houses; or might be seen lurking about Lincoln's Inn and his lawyers', where the principals kept him for hours waiting, and the clerks winked at each other, as he sat in their office. No wonder that he relished the dinners at Shepherd's Inn, and was perfectly resigned there: resigned? he was so happy nowhere else; he was wretched among his equals, who scorned him; but here he was the chief guest at the table, where they continually addressed him with "Yes, Sir Francis," and "No, Sir Francis," where he told his wretched jokes, and where he quavered his dreary little French song, after Strong had sung his jovial chorus, and honest Costigan had piped his Irish ditties. Such a jolly menage as Strong's, with Grady's Irish stew, and the chevalier's brew of punch after dinner, would have been welcome to many a better man than Clavering, the solitude of whose great house at home frightened him, where he was attended only by the old woman who kept the house, and his valet who sneered at him.

"Yes, dammit," said he, to his friends in Shepherd's Inn. "That fellow of mine, I must turn him away, only I owe him two years' wages, curse him, and can't ask my lady. He brings me my tea cold of a morning, with a dem'd leaden tea-spoon, and he says my lady's sent all the plate to the banker's because it ain't safe. Now ain't it hard that she won't trust me with a single tea-spoon—ain't it ungentlemanlike, Altamont? You know my lady's of low birth—that is—I beg your pardon—hem—that is, it's most cruel of her not to show more confidence in me. And the very servants begin to laugh—the dam scoundrels! I'll break every bone in their great hulking bodies, curse 'em, I will. They don't answer my bell: and—and, my man was at Vauxhall last night with one of my dress shirts and my velvet waistcoat on, I know it was mine—the confounded impudent blackguard—and he went on dancing before my eyes, confound him; I'm sure he'll live to be hanged—he deserves to be hanged—all those infernal rascals of valets."

He was very kind to Altamont now: he listened to the colonel's loud stories when Altamont described how—when he was working his way home once from New Zealand, where he had been on a whaling expedition—he and his comrades had been obliged to shirk on board at night, to escape from their wives, by Jove—and how the poor devils put out in their canoes when they saw the ship under sail, and paddled madly after her: how he had been lost in the bush once for three months in New South Wales, when he was there once on a trading speculation: how he had seen Boney at Saint Helena, and been presented to him with the rest of the officers of the Indiaman of which he was a mate—to all these tales (and over his cups Altamont told many of them; and, it must be owned, lied and bragged a great deal) Sir Francis now listened with great attention; making a point of drinking wine with Altamont at dinner and of treating him with every distinction.

"Leave him alone, I know what he's a-coming to," Altamont said, laughing to Strong, who remonstrated with him, "and leave me alone; I know what I'm a-telling, very well. I was officer on board an Indiaman, so I was; I traded to New South Wales, so I did, in a ship of my own, and lost her. I became officer to the Nawaub, so I did; only me and my royal master have had a difference, Strong—that's it. Who's the better or the worse for what I tell? or knows any thing about me? The other chap is dead—shot in the bush, and his body reckonized at Sydney. If I thought any body would split, do you think I wouldn't wring his neck? I've done as good before now, Strong—I told you how I did for the overseer before I took leave—but in fair fight, I mean—in fair fight; or, rayther, he had the best of it. He had his gun and bay'net, and I had only an ax. Fifty of 'em saw it—ay, and cheered me when I did it—and I'd do it again,—him, wouldn't I? I ain't afraid of any body; and I'd have the life of the man who split upon me. That's my maxim, and pass me the liquor—You wouldn't turn on a man. I know you. You're an honest feller, and will stand by a feller, and have looked death in the face like a man. But as for that lily-livered sneak—that poor lyin', swindlin', cringin' cur of a Clavering—who stands in my shoes—stands in my shoes, hang him! I'll make him pull my boots off and clean 'em, I will. Ha, ha!" Here he burst out into a wild laugh, at which Strong got up and put away the brandy-bottle. The other still laughed good-humoredly. "You're right, old boy," he said; "you always keep your head cool, you do—and when I begin to talk too much—I say, when I begin to pitch, I authorize you, and order you, and command you, to put away the rum-bottle."

"Take my counsel, Altamont," Strong said, gravely, "and mind how you deal with that man. Don't make it too much his interest to get rid of you; or who knows what he may do?"

The event for which, with cynical enjoyment, Altamont had been on the look-out, came very speedily. One day, Strong being absent upon an errand for his principal, Sir Francis made his appearance in the chambers, and found the envoy of the Nawaub alone. He abused the world in general for being heartless and unkind to him: he abused his wife for being ungenerous to him: he abused Strong for being ungrateful—hundreds of pounds had he given Ned Strong—been his friend for life and kept him out of jail, by Jove—and now Ned was taking her ladyship's side against him and abetting her in her infernal, unkind treatment of him. "They've entered into a conspiracy to keep me penniless, Altamont," the baronet said: "they don't give me as much pocket-money as Frank has at school."

"Why don't you go down to Richmond and borrow of him, Clavering?" Altamont broke out with a savage laugh. "He wouldn't see his poor old beggar of a father without pocket-money, would he?"

"I tell you, I've been obliged to humiliate myself cruelly," Clavering said. "Look here, sir—look here, at these pawn-tickets! Fancy a member of Parliament and an old English baronet, by gad! obliged to put a drawing-room clock and a Buhl inkstand up the spout; and a gold duck's head paper-holder, that I dare say cost my wife five pound, for which they'd only give me fifteen-and-six! Oh, it's a humiliating thing, sir, poverty to a man of my habits; and it's made me shed tears, sir—tears; and that d—d valet of mine—curse him, I wish he was hanged!—has had the confounded impudence to threaten to tell my lady: as if the things in my own house weren't my own, to sell or to keep, or to fling out of window if I chose—by gad! the confounded scoundrel."

"Cry a little; don't mind cryin' before me—it'll relieve you, Clavering" the other said. "Why, I say, old feller, what a happy feller I once thought you, and what a miserable son of a gun you really are!"

"It's a shame that they treat me so, ain't it," Clavering went on—for, though ordinarily silent and apathetic, about his own griefs the baronet could whine for an hour at a time. "And—and, by gad, sir, I haven't got the money to pay the very cab that's waiting for me at the door; and the porteress, that Mrs. Bolton, lent me three shillin's, and I don't like to ask her for any more: and I asked that d—d old Costigan, the confounded old penniless Irish miscreant, and he hadn't got a shillin', the beggar; and Campion's out of town, or else he'd do a little bill for me, I know he would."

"I thought you swore on your honor to your wife that you wouldn't put your name to paper," said Mr. Altamont, puffing at his cigar.

"Why does she leave me without pocket-money then? Damme, I must have money," cried out the baronet. "Oh, Am—, Oh, Altamont, I'm the most miserable beggar alive."

"You'd like a chap to lend you a twenty-pound-note, wouldn't you now?" the other asked.

"If you would, I'd be grateful to you forever—forever, my dearest friend," cried Clavering. "How much would you give? Will you give a fifty-pound bill, at six months, for half down and half in plate," asked Altamont.

"Yes, I would, so help me—, and pay it on the day," screamed Clavering. "I'll make it payable at my banker's: I'll do any thing you like."

"Well, I was only chaffing you. I'll give you twenty pound."

"You said a pony," interposed Clavering; "my dear fellow, you said a pony, and I'll be eternally obliged to you; and I'll not take it as a gift—only as a loan, and pay you back in six months. I take my oath I will."

"Well—well—there's the money, Sir Francis Clavering. I ain't a bad fellow. When I've money in my pocket, dammy, I spend it like a man. Here's five-and-twenty for you. Don't be losing it at the hells now. Don't be making a fool of yourself. Go down to Clavering Park, and it'll keep you ever so long. You needn't 'ave butchers' meat: there's pigs I dare say on the premises: and you can shoot rabbits for dinner, you know, every day till the game comes in. Besides, the neighbors will ask you about to dinner, you know, sometimes: for you are a baronet, though you have outrun the constable. And you've got this comfort, that I'm off your shoulders for a good bit to come—p'raps this two years—if I don't play; and I don't intend to touch the confounded black and red: and by that time my lady, as you call her— Jimmy, I used to say—will have come round again; and you'll be ready for me, you know, and come down handsomely to yours truly."

At this juncture of their conversation Strong returned, nor did the baronet care much about prolonging the talk, having got the money: and he made his way from Shepherd's Inn, and went home and bullied his servant in a manner so unusually brisk and insolent, that the man concluded his master must have pawned some more of the house furniture, or at any rate, have come into possession of some ready money.

"And yet I've looked over the house, Morgan, and I don't think he has took any more of the things," Sir Francis's valet said to Major Pendennis's man, as they met at their club soon after. "My lady locked up a'most all the befews afore she went away, and he couldn't take away the picters and looking-glasses in a cab: and he wouldn't spout the fenders and fire-irons—he ain't so bad as that. But he's got money somehow. He's so dam'd imperent when he have. A few nights ago I sor him at Vauxhall, where I was a polkin with Lady Hemly Babewood's gals—a wery pleasant room that is, and an uncommon good lot in it, hall except the 'ousekeeper, and she's methodisticle—I was a polkin—you're too old a cove to polk, Mr. Morgan—and 'ere's your 'ealth—and I 'appened to 'ave on some of Clavering's abberdashery, and he sor it too; and he didn't dare so much as speak a word."

"How about the house in St. John's Wood?" Mr. Morgan asked.

"Execution in it.—Sold up hevery thing: ponies and pianna, and Brougham, and all. Mrs. Montague Rivers hoff to Boulogne—non est inwentus, Mr. Morgan. It's my belief she put the execution in herself: and was tired of him."

"Play much?" asked Morgan.

"Not since the smash. When your governor, and the lawyers, and my lady and him had that tremenduous scene: he went down on his knees, my lady told Mrs. Bonner, as told me—and swoar as he never more would touch a card or a dice, or put his name to a bit of paper; and my lady was a-goin' to give him the notes down to pay his liabilities after the race: only your governor said (which he wrote it on a piece of paper, and passed it across the table to the lawyer and my lady), that some one else had better book up for him, for he'd have kep' some of the money. He's a sly old cove, your gov'nor." The expression of "old cove," thus flippantly applied by the younger gentleman to himself and his master, displeased Mr. Morgan exceedingly. On the first occasion, when Mr. Lightfoot used the obnoxious expression, his comrade's anger was only indicated by a silent frown; but on the second offense, Morgan, who was smoking his cigar elegantly, and holding it on the tip of his penknife, withdrew the cigar from his lips, and took his young friend to task.

"Don't call Major Pendennis an old cove, if you'll 'ave the goodness, Lightfoot, and don't call me an old cove, nether. Such words ain't used in society; and we have lived in the fust society, both at 'ome and foring. We've been intimate with the fust statesmen of Europe. When we go abroad we dine with Prince Metternitch and Louy Philup reg'lar. We go here to the best houses, the tip-tops, I tell you. We ride with

Lord John and the noble Whycount at the edd of Foring Affairs. We dine with the Earl of Burgrave, and are consulted by the Marquis of Steyne in every think. We ought to know a thing or two, Mr. Lightfoot. You're a young man, I'm an old cove, as you say. We've both seen the world, and we both know that it ain't money, nor bein' a baronet, nor 'avin' a town and country 'ouse, nor a paltry five or six thousand a year."

"It's ten, Mr. Morgan," cried Mr. Lightfoot, with great animation.

"It may have been, sir," Morgan said, with calm severity; "it may have been Mr. Lightfoot, but it ain't six now, nor five, sir. It's been doosedly dipped and cut into, sir, by the confounded extravygance of your master, with his helbow-shakin' and his bill discountin', and his cottage in the Regency Park, and his many wickednesses. He's a bad un, Mr. Lightfoot—a bad lot, sir, and that you know. And it ain't money, sir—not such money as that, at any rate, come from a Calcuttar attorney, and I dessay wrung out of the pore starving blacks—that will give a pusson position in society, as you know very well. We've no money, but we go every where; there's not a housekeeper's room, sir, in this town of any consiquince, where James Morgan ain't welcome. And it was me who got you into this club, Lightfoot, as you very well know, though I am an old cove, and they would have blackballed you without me, as sure as your name is Frederic."

"I know they would, Mr. Morgan," said the other, with much humility.

"Well, then, don't call me an old cove, sir. It ain't gentlemanlike, Frederic Lightfoot, which I knew you when you was a cab-boy, and when your father was in trouble, and got you the place you have now when the Frenchman went away. And if you think, sir, that because you're making up to Mrs. Bonner, who may have saved her two thousand pound—and I dare say she has in five-and-twenty years as she have lived confidential maid to Lady Clavering—yet, sir, you must remember who put you into that service, and who knows what you were before, sir, and it don't become you, Frederic Lightfoot, to call me an old cove."

"I beg your pardon, Mr. Morgan—I can't do more than make an apology—will you have a glass, sir, and let me drink your 'ealth?" "You know I don't take sperrits, Lightfoot," replied Morgan, appeased. "And so you and Mrs. Bonner is going to put up together, are you?"

"She's old, but two thousand pound's a good bit, you see, Mr. Morgan. And we'll get the 'Clavering Arms' for a very little; and that'll be no bad thing when the railroad runs through Clavering. And when we are there, I hope you'll come and see us, Mr. Morgan."

"It's a stoopid place, and no society," said Mr. Morgan. "I know it well. In Mrs. Pendennis's time we used to go down reg'lar, and the hair refreshed me after the London racket."

"The railroad will improve Mr. Arthur's property," remarked Lightfoot. "What's about the figure of it, should you say, sir?"

"Under fifteen hundred, sir," answered Morgan; at which the other, who knew the extent of poor Arthur's acres, thrust his tongue in his cheek, but remained wisely silent.

"Is his man any good, Mr. Morgan?" Lightfoot resumed.

"Pigeon ain't used to society as yet; but he's young and has good talents, and has read a good deal, and I dessay he will do very well," replied Morgan. "He wouldn't quite do for this kind of thing, Lightfoot, for he ain't seen the world yet."

When the pint of sherry for which Mr. Lightfoot called, upon Mr. Morgan's announcement that he declined to drink spirits, had been discussed by the two gentlemen, who held the wine up to the light, and smacked their lips, and winked their eyes at it, and rallied the landlord as to the vintage, in the most approved manner of connoisseurs, Morgan's ruffled equanimity was quite restored, and he was prepared to treat his young friend with perfect good-humor.

"What d'you think about Miss Amory, Lightfoot?—tell us in confidence, now—do you think we should do well—you understand—if we make Miss A. into Mrs. A. P.? Comprendy vous?"

"She and her ma's always quarrelin'," said Mr. Lightfoot. "Bonner is more than a match for the old lady, and treats Sir Francis like that—like this year spill, which I fling into the grate. But she daren't say a word to Miss Amory. No more dare none of us. When a visitor comes in, she smiles and languishes, you'd think that butter wouldn't melt in her mouth: and the minute he is gone, very likely, she flares up like a little demon, and says things fit to send you wild. If Mr. Arthur comes, it's 'Do let's sing that there delightful song!' or, 'Come and write me them pooty verses in this halbum!' and very likely she's been a rilin' her mother, or sticking pins into her maid, a minute before. She do stick pins into her and pinch her. Mary Hann showed me one of her arms quite black and blue; and I recklect Mrs. Bonner, who's as jealous of me as a old cat, boxed her ears for showing me. And then you should see Miss at luncheon, when there's nobody but the family! She makes b'leave she never eats, and my! you should only jest see her. She has Mary Hann to bring her up plum-cakes and creams into her bedroom; and the cook's the only man in the house she's civil to. Bonner says, how, the second season in London, Mr. Soppington was a-goin' to propose for her, and actially came one day, and sor her fling a book into the fire, and scold her mother so, that he went down softly by the back droring-room door, which he came in by; and next thing we heard of him was, he was married to Miss Rider. Oh, she's a devil, that little Blanche, and that's my candig apinium, Mr. Morgan."

"Apinion, not apinium, Lightfoot, my good fellow," Mr. Morgan said, with parental kindness, and then asked of his own bosom with a sigh, why the deuce does my governor want Master Arthur to marry such a girl as this? and the tête-à-tête of the two gentlemen was broken up by the entry of other gentlemen, members of the club—when fashionable town-talk, politics, cribbage, and other amusements ensued, and the conversation became general.

The Gentleman's Club was held in the parlor of the Wheel of Fortune public-house, in a snug little by-lane, leading out of one of the great streets of May Fair, and frequented by some of the most select gentlemen about town. Their masters' affairs, debts, intrigues, adventures; their ladies' good and bad qualities and quarrels with their husbands; all the family secrets were here discussed with perfect freedom and confidence, and here, when about to enter into a new situation, a gentleman was enabled to get every requisite information regarding the family of which he proposed to become a member. Liveries it may be imagined were excluded from this select precinct; and the powdered heads of the largest metropolitan footmen might bow down in vain, entreating admission into the Gentleman's Club. These outcast giants in plush took their beer in an outer apartment of the Wheel of Fortune, and could no more get an entry into the club room than a Pall Mall tradesman or a Lincoln's Inn attorney could get admission into Bay's or Spratt's. And it is because the conversation which we have been permitted to overhear here, in some measure explains the characters and bearings of our story, that we have ventured to introduce the reader into a society so exclusive.

CHAPTER XXIII

THE WAY OF THE WORLD

A short time after the piece of good fortune which befel Colonel Altamont at Epsom, that gentleman put into execution his projected foreign tour, and the chronicler of the polite world who goes down to London-bridge for the purpose of taking leave of the people of fashion who quit this country, announced that among the company on board the Soho to Antwerp last Saturday, were "Sir Robert, Lady, and the Misses Hodge; Mr. Sergeant Kewsy, and Mrs. and Miss Kewsy; Colonel Altamont, Major Coddy, &c." The colonel traveled in state, and as became a gentleman: he appeared in a rich traveling costume: he drank brandy-and-water freely during the passage, and was not sick, as some of the other passengers were; and he was attended by his body servant, the faithful Irish legionary who had been for some time in waiting upon himself and Captain Strong in their chambers of Shepherd's Inn.

The chevalier partook of a copious dinner at Blackwall with his departing friend the colonel, and one or two others, who drank many healths to Altamont at that liberal gentleman's expense. "Strong, old boy," the chevalier's worthy chum said, "if you want a little money, now's your time. I'm your man. You're a good feller, and have been a good feller to me, and a twenty pound note, more or less, will make no odds to me." But Strong said, no, he didn't want any money; he was flush, quite flush—"that is, not flush enough to pay you back your last loan, Altamont, but quite able to carry on for some time to come"— and so, with a not uncordial greeting between them, the two parted. Had the possession of money really made Altamont more honest and amiable than he had hitherto been, or only caused him to seem more amiable in Strong's eyes? Perhaps he really was better; and money improved him. Perhaps it was the beauty of wealth Strong saw and respected. But he argued within himself "This poor devil, this unlucky outcast of a returned convict, is ten times as good a fellow as my friend Sir Francis Clavering, Bart. He has pluck and honesty, in his way. He will stick to a friend, and face an enemy. The other never had courage to do either. And what is it that has put the poor devil under a cloud? He was only a little wild, and signed his father-in-law's name. Many a man has done worse, and come to no wrong, and holds his head up. Clavering does. No, he don't hold his head up: he never did in his best days." And Strong, perhaps, repented him of the falsehood which he had told to the free-handed colonel, that he was not in want of money; but it was a falsehood on the side of honesty, and the chevalier could not bring down his stomach to borrow a second time from his outlawed friend. Besides, he could get on. Clavering had promised him some: not that Clavering's promises were much to be believed, but the chevalier was of a hopeful turn, and trusted in many chances of catching his patron, and waylaying some of those stray remittances and supplies, in the procuring of which for his principal lay Mr. Strong's chief business.

He had grumbled about Altamont's companionship in the Shepherd's Inn chambers; but he found those lodgings more glum now without his partner than with him. The solitary life was not agreeable to his social soul; and he had got into extravagant and luxurious habits, too, having a servant at his command to run his errands, to arrange his toilet, and to cook his meal. It was rather a grand and touching sight now to see the portly and handsome gentleman painting his own boots, and broiling his own mutton chop. It has been before stated that the chevalier had a wife, a Spanish lady of Vittoria, who had gone back to her friends, after a few months' union with the captain, whose head she broke with a dish. He began to think whether he should not go back and see his Juanita. The chevalier was growing melancholy after the departure of his friend the colonel; or, to use his own picturesque expression, was "down on his luck." These moments of depression and intervals of ill-fortune occur constantly in the lives of heroes; Marius at Minturnae, Charles Edward in the Highlands, Napoleon before Elba. What great man has not been called upon to face evil fortune? From Clavering no supplies were to be had for some time. The five-and-twenty pounds, or "pony" which the exemplary baronet had received from Mr. Altamont, had fled out of Clavering's keeping as swiftly as many previous ponies. He had been down the river with a choice party of sporting gents, who dodged the police and landed in Essex, where they put up Billy Bluck to fight Dick the cabman, whom the baronet backed, and who had it all his own way for thirteen rounds, when, by an unluckly blow in the windpipe, Billy killed him. "It's always my luck, Strong," Sir Francis said; "the betting was three to one on the cabman, and I thought myself as sure of thirty pounds, as if I had it in my pocket. And dammy, I owe my man Lightfoot fourteen pound now which he's lent and paid for me: and he duns me—the confounded impudent blackguard: and I wish to Heaven I knew any way of getting a bill done, or of screwing a little out of my lady! I'll give you half, Ned, upon my soul and honor, I'll give you half if you can get any body to do us a little fifty."

But Ned said sternly that he had given his word of honor, as a gentleman, that he would be no party to any future bill-transactions in which her husband might engage (who had given his word of honor too), and the chevalier said that he, at least, would keep his word, and Would black his own boots all his life rather than break his promise. And what is more, he vowed he would advise Lady Clavering that Sir Francis was about to break his faith toward her, upon the very first hint which he could get that such was Clavering's intention. Upon this information Sir Francis Clavering, according to his custom, cried and cursed very volubly. He spoke of death as his only resource. He besought and implored his dear Strong, his best friend, his dear old Ned, not to throw him over; and when he quitted his dearest Ned, as he went down the stairs of Shepherd's Inn, swore and blasphemed at Ned as the most infernal villain, and traitor, and blackguard, and coward under the sun, and wished Ned was in his grave, and in a worse place, only he would like the confounded ruffian to live, until Frank Clavering had had his revenge out of him.

In Strong's chambers the baronet met a gentleman whose visits were now, as it has been shown, very frequent in Shepherd's Inn, Mr. Samuel Huxter, of Clavering. That young fellow, who had poached the walnuts in Clavering Park in his youth, and had seen the baronet drive through the street at home with four horses, and prance up to church with powdered footmen, had an immense respect for his member, and a prodigious delight in making his acquaintance. He introduced himself, with much blushing and trepidation, as a Clavering man—son of Mr. Huxter, of the market-place—father attended Sir Francis's keeper, Coxwood, when his gun burst and took off three fingers—proud to make Sir Francis's acquaintance. All of which introduction Sir Francis received affably. And honest Huxter talked about Sir Francis to the chaps at Bartholomew's; and told Fanny, in the lodge, that, after all, there was nothing like a thorough-bred un, a regular good old English gentleman, one of the olden time! To which Fanny replied, that she thought Sir Francis was an ojous creature—she didn't know why—but she couldn't a-bear him—she was sure he was wicked, and low, and mean—she knew he was; and when Sam to this replied that Sir Francis was very affable, and had borrowed half a sov' of him quite kindly, Fanny burst into a laugh, pulled Sam's long hair (which was not yet of irreproachable cleanliness), patted his chin, and called him a stoopid, stoopid, old foolish stoopid, and said that Sir Francis was always borrering money of every body, and that Mar had actially refused him twice, and had to wait three months to get seven shillings which he had borrered of 'er.

"Don't say 'er but her, borrer but borrow, actially but actually, Fanny," Mr. Huxter replied—not to a fault in her argument, but to grammatical errors in her statement.

"Well then, her, and borrow, and hactually—there then, you stoopid," said the other; and the scholar made such a pretty face that the grammar master was quickly appeased, and would have willingly given her a hundred more lessons on the spot at the price which he took for that one.

Of course Mrs. Bolton was by, and I suppose that Fanny and Mr. Sam were on exceedingly familiar and confidential terms by this time, and that time had brought to the former certain consolations, and soothed certain regrets, which are deucedly bitter when they occur, but which are, no more than tooth-pulling, or any other pang, eternal.

As you sit, surrounded by respect and affection; happy, honored, and flattered in your old age; your foibles gently indulged; your least words kindly cherished; your garrulous old stories received for the hundredth time with dutiful forbearance, and never-failing hypocritical smiles; the women of your house constant in their flatteries; the young men hushed and attentive when you begin to speak; the servants awe-stricken; the tenants cap in hand, and ready to act in the place of your worship's horses when your honor takes a drive—it has often struck you, O thoughtful Dives! that this respect, and these glories, are for the main part transferred, with your fee-simple, to your successor—that the servants will bow, and the tenants shout, for your son as for you; that the butler will fetch him the wine (improved by a little keeping) that's now in your cellar; and that, when your night is come, and the light of your life is gone down, as sure as the morning rises after you and without you, the sun of prosperity and flattery shines on your heir. Men come and bask in the halo of consols and acres that beams round about him: the reverence is transferred with the estate; of which, with all its advantages, pleasures, respect, and good-will, he in turn becomes the life-tenant. How long do you wish or expect that your people will regret you? How much time does a man devote to grief before he begins to enjoy? A great man must keep his heir at his feast like a living memento mori. If he holds very much by life, the presence of the other must be a constant sting and warning. "Make ready to go," says the successor to your honor; "I am waiting: and I could hold it as well as you."

What has this reference to the possible reader, to do with any of the characters of this history? Do we wish to apologize for Pen because he has got a white hat, and because his mourning for his mother is fainter? All the lapse of years, all the career of fortune, all the events of life, however strongly they may move or eagerly excite him, never can remove that sainted image from his heart, or banish that blessed love from its sanctuary. If he yields to wrong, the dear eyes will look sadly upon him when he dares to meet them; if he does well, endures pain, or conquers temptation, the ever present love will greet him, he knows, with approval and pity; if he falls, plead for him; if he suffers, cheer him;—be with him and accompany him always until death is past, and sorrow and sin are no more. Is this mere dreaming or, on the part of an idle storyteller, useless moralizing? May not the man of the world take his moment, too, to be grave and thoughtful? Ask of your own hearts and memories, brother and sister, if we do not live in the dead; and (to speak reverently) prove God by love?

Of these matters Pen and Warrington often spoke in many a solemn and friendly converse in after days; and Pendennis's mother was worshiped in his memory, and canonized there, as such a saint ought to be. Lucky he in life who knows a few such women! A kind provision of Heaven it was, that sent us such; and gave us to admire that touching and wonderful spectacle of innocence, and love, and beauty.

But as it is certain that if, in the course of these sentimental conversations, any outer stranger, Major Pendennis for instance, had walked into Pen's chambers, Arthur and Warrington would have stopped their talk, and chosen another subject, and discoursed about the Opera, or the last debate in Parliament, or Miss Jones's marriage with Captain Smith, or what not—so let us imagine that the public steps in at this juncture, and stops the confidential talk between author and reader, and begs us to resume our remarks about this world, with which both are certainly better acquainted than with that other one into which we have just been peeping.

On coming into his property, Arthur Pendennis at first comported himself with a modesty and equanimity which obtained his friend Warrington's praises, though Arthur's uncle was a little inclined to quarrel with his nephew's meanness of spirit, for not assuming greater state and pretensions now that he had entered on the enjoyment of his kingdom. He would have had Arthur installed in handsome quarters, and riding on showy park hacks, or in well-built cabriolets, every day. "I am too absent," Arthur said, with a laugh, "to drive a cab in London; the omnibuses would cut me in two, or I should send my horse's head into the ladies' carriage windows; and you wouldn't have me driven about by my servant like an apothecary, uncle?" No, Major Pendennis would on no account have his nephew appear like an apothecary; the august representative of the house of Pendennis must not so demean himself. And when Arthur, pursuing his banter, said, "And yet, I daresay, sir, my father was proud enough when he first set up his gig," the old major hemmed and ha'd, and his wrinkled face reddened with a blush as he answered, "You know what Bonaparte said, sir, 'Il faut laver son linge sale en famille.' There is no need, sir, for you to brag that your father was a—a medical man. He came of a most ancient but fallen house, and was obliged to reconstruct the family fortunes as many a man of good family has done before him. You are like the fellow in Sterne, sir—the marquis who came to demand his sword again. Your father got back yours for you. You are a man of landed estate, by Gad, sir, and a gentleman—never forget you are a gentleman."

Then Arthur slily turned on his uncle the argument which he had heard the old gentleman often use regarding himself. "In the society which I have the honor of frequenting through your introduction, who cares to ask about my paltry means or my humble gentility, uncle?" he asked. "It would be absurd of me to attempt to compete with the great folks; and all that thay can ask from us is, that we should have a decent address and good manners."

"But for all that, sir, I should belong to a better Club or two," the uncle answered: "I should give an occasional dinner, and select my society well; and I should come out of that horrible garret in the Temple, sir." And so Arthur compromised by descending to the second floor in Lamb-court: Warrington still occupying his old quarters, and the two friends being determined not to part one from the other. Cultivate kindly, reader, those friendships of your youth: it is only in that generous time that they are formed. How different the intimacies of after days are, and how much weaker the grasp of your own hand after it has been shaken about in twenty years' commerce with the world, and has squeezed and dropped a thousand equally careless palms! As you can seldom fashion your tongue to speak a new language after twenty, the heart refuses to receive friendship pretty soon: it gets too hard to yield to the impression.

So Pen had many acquaintances, and being of a jovial and easy turn, got more daily: but no friend like Warrington; and the two men continued to live almost as much in common as the Knights of the Temple, riding upon one horse (for Pen's was at Warrington's service), and having their chambers and their servitor in common.

Mr. Warrington had made the acquaintance of Pen's friends of Grosvenor-place during their last unlucky season in London, and had expressed himself no better satisfied with Sir Francis and Lady Clavering and her ladyship's daughter than was the public in general. "The world is right," George said, "about those people. The young men laugh and talk freely before those ladies, and about them. The girl sees people whom she has no right to know, and talks to men with whom no girl should have an intimacy. Did you see those two reprobates leaning over Lady Clavering's carriage in the Park the other day, and leering under Miss Blanche's bonnet? No good mother would let her daughter know those men, or admit them within her doors."

"The Begum is the most innocent and good-natured soul alive," interposed Pen. "She never heard any harm of Captain Blackball, or read that trial in which Charley Lovelace figures. Do you suppose that honest ladies read and remember the Chronique Scandaleuse as well as you, you old grumbler?"

"Would you like Laura Bell to know those fellows?" Warrington asked, his face turning rather red. "Would you let any woman you loved be contaminated by their company? I have no doubt that poor Begum is ignorant of their histories. It seems to me she is ignorant of a great number of better things. It seems to me that your honest Begum is not a lady, Pen. It is not her fault, doubtless, that she has not had the education, or learned the refinements of a lady."

"She is as moral as Lady Portsea, who has all the world at her balls, and as refined as Mrs. Bull, who breaks the king's English, and has half-a-dozen dukes at her table," Pen answered, rather sulkily. "Why should you and I be more squeamish than the rest of the world? Why are we to visit the sins of her fathers on this harmless, kind creature? She never did any thing but kindness to you or any mortal soul. As far as she knows she does her best. She does not set up to be more than she is. She gives you the best dinners she can buy, and the best company she can get. She pays the debts of that scamp of a husband of hers. She spoils her boy like the most virtuous mother in England. Her opinion about literary matters, to be sure, is not much; and I daresay she never read a line of Wordsworth, or heard of Tennyson in her life."

"No more has Mrs. Flanagan the laundress," growled out Pen's Mentor; "no more has Betty the housemaid; and I have no word of blame against them. But a high-souled man doesn't make friends of these. A gentleman doesn't choose these for his companions, or bitterly rues it afterward if he do. Are you, who are setting up to be a man of the world and philosopher, to tell me that the aim of life is to guttle three courses and dine off silver? Do you dare to own to yourself that your ambition in life is good claret, and that you'll dine with any, provided you get a stalled ox to feed on? You call me a Cynic—why, what a monstrous Cynicism it is, which you and the rest of you men of the world admit. I'd rather live upon raw turnips and sleep in a hollow tree, or turn backwoodsman or savage, than degrade myself to this civilization, and own that a French cook was the thing in life best worth living for."

"Because you like a raw beef-steak and a pipe afterward," broke out Pen, "you give yourself airs of superiority over people, whose tastes are more dainty, and are not ashamed of the world they live in. Who goes about professing particular admiration, or esteem, or friendship, or gratitude, even for the people one meets every day? If A. asks me to his house, and gives me his best, I take his good things for what they are worth, and no more. I do not profess to pay him back in friendship, but in the convention's money of society. When we part, we part without any grief. When we meet, we are tolerably glad to see one another. If I were only to live with my friends, your black muzzle, old George, is the only face I should see."

"You are your uncle's pupil," said Warrington, rather sadly; "and you speak like a worldling."

"And why not?" asked Pendennis; "why not acknowledge the world I stand upon, and submit to the conditions of the society which we live in and live by? I am older than you, George, in spite of your grizzled whiskers, and have seen much more of the world than you have in your garret here, shut up with your books and your reveries and your ideas of one-and-twenty. I say, I take the world as it is, and being of it, will not be ashamed of it. If the time is out of joint, have I any calling or strength to set it right?"

"Indeed, I don't think you have much of either," growled Pen's interlocutor.

"If I doubt whether I am better than my neighbor," Arthur continued—"if I concede that I am no better—I also doubt whether he is better than I. I see men who begin with ideas of universal reform, and who, before their beards are grown, propound their loud plans for the regeneration of mankind, give up their schemes after a few years of bootless talking and vain-glorious attempts to lead their fellows; and after they have found that men will no longer hear them, as indeed they never were in the least worthy to be heard, sink quietly into the rank and file—acknowledging their aims impracticable, or thankful that they were never put into practice. The fiercest reformers grow calm, and are fain to put up with things as they are: the loudest Radical orators become dumb, quiescent placemen: the most fervent Liberals, when out of power, become humdrum Conservatives, or downright tyrants or despots in office. Look at Thiers, look at Guizot, in opposition and in place! Look at the Whigs appealing to the country, and the Whigs in power! Would you say that the conduct of these men is an act of treason, as the Radicals bawl—who would give way in their turn, were their turn ever to come? No, only that they submit to circumstances which are stronger than they—march as the world marches toward reform, but at the world's pace (and the movements of the vast body of mankind must needs be slow)—forego this scheme as impracticable, on account of opposition—that as immature, because against the sense of the majority—are forced to calculate drawbacks and difficulties, as well as to think of reforms and advances—and compelled finally to submit, and to wait, and to compromise."

"The Right Honorable Arthur Pendennis could not speak better, or be more satisfied with himself, if he was First Lord of the Treasury and Chancellor of the Exchequer," Warrington said.

"Self-satisfied? Why self-satisfied?" continued Pen. "It seems to me that my skepticism is more respectful and more modest than the revolutionary ardor of other folks. Many a patriot of eighteen, many a spouting-club orator, would turn the bishops out of the House of Lords to-morrow, and throw the lords out after the bishops, and throw the throne into the Thames after the peers and the bench. Is that man more modest than I, who take these institutions as I find them, and wait for time and truth to develop, or fortify, or (if you like) destroy them? A college tutor, or a nobleman's toady, who appears one fine day as my right reverend lord, in a silk apron and a shovel-hat, and assumes benedictory airs over me, is still the same man we remember at Oxbridge, when he was truckling to the tufts, and bullying the poor under-graduates in the lecture-room. An hereditary legislator, who passes his time with jockeys and blacklegs and ballet-girls, and who is called to rule over me and his other betters, because his grandfather made a lucky speculation in the funds, or found a coal or tin-mine on his property, or because his stupid ancestor happened to be in command of ten thousand men as brave as himself, who overcame twelve thousand Frenchmen, or fifty thousand Indians—such a man, I say, inspires me with no more respect than the bitterest democrat can feel toward him. But, such as he is, he is a part of the old society to which we belong: and I submit to his lordship with acquiescence; and he takes his place above the best of us at all dinner parties, and there bides his time. I don't want to chop his head off with a guillotine, or to fling mud at him in the streets. When they call such a man a disgrace to his order; and such another, who is good and gentle, refined and generous, who employs his great means in promoting every kindness and charity, and art and grace of life, in the kindest and most gracious manner, an ornament to his rank—the question as to the use and propriety of the order is not in the least affected one way or other. There it is, extant among us, a part of our habits, the creed of many of us, the growth of centuries, the symbol of a most complicated tradition—there stand my lord the bishop and my lord the hereditary legislator—what the French call transactions both of them—representing in their present shape mail-clad barons and double-sworded chiefs (from whom their lordships the hereditaries, for the most part, don't descend), and priests, professing to hold an absolute truth and a divinely inherited power, the which truth absolute our ancestors burned at the stake, and denied there; the which divine transmissible power still exists in print—to be believed, or not, pretty much at choice; and of these, I say, I acquiesce that they exist, and no more. If you say that these schemes, devised before printing was known, or steam was born; when thought was an infant, scared and whipped; and truth under its guardians was gagged, and swathed, and blindfolded, and not allowed to lift its voice, or to look out or to walk under the sun; before men were permitted to meet, or to trade, or to speak with each other—if any one says (as some faithful souls do) that these schemes are for ever, and having been changed, and modified constantly are to be subject to no farther development or decay, I laugh, and let the man speak. But I would have toleration for these, as I would ask it for my own opinions; and if they are to die, I would rather they had a decent and natural than an abrupt and violent death."

"You would have sacrificed to Jove," Warrington said, "had you lived in the time of the Christian persecutions."

"Perhaps I would," said Pen, with some sadness. "Perhaps I am a coward—perhaps my faith is unsteady; but this is my own reserve. What I argue here is that I will not persecute. Make a faith or a dogma absolute, and persecution becomes a logical consequence; and Dominic burns a Jew, or Calvin an Arian, or Nero a Christian, or Elizabeth or Mary a Papist or Protestant; or their father both or either, according to his humor; and acting without any pangs of remorse—but, on the contrary, with strict notions of duty fulfilled. Make dogma absolute, and to inflict or to suffer death becomes easy and necessary; and Mahomet's soldiers shouting 'Paradise! Paradise!' and dying on the Christian spears, are not more or less praiseworthy than the same men slaughtering a townful of Jews, or cutting off the heads of all prisoners who would not acknowledge that there was but one prophet of God."

"A little while since, young one," Warrington said, who had been listening to his friend's confessions neither without sympathy nor scorn, for his mood led him to indulge in both, "you asked me why I remained out of the strife of the world, and looked on at the great labor of my neighbor without taking any part in the struggle. Why, what a mere dilettante you own yourself to be, in this confession of general skepticism, and what a listless spectator yourself! You are six-and-twenty years old, and as blasé as a rake of sixty. You neither hope much, nor care much, nor believe much. You doubt about other men as much as about yourself. Were it made of such pococuranti as you, the world would be intolerable; and I had rather live in a wilderness of monkeys, and listen to their chatter, than in a company of men who denied every thing."

"Were the world composed of Saint Bernards or Saint Dominics, it would be equally odious," said Pen, "and at the end of a few scores of years would cease to exist altogether. Would you have every man with his head shaved, and every woman in a cloister—carrying out to the full the ascetic principle? Would you have conventicle hymns twanging from every lane in every city in the world? Would you have all the birds of the forest sing one note and fly with one feather? You call me a skeptic because I acknowledge what is; and in acknowledging that, be it linnet or lark, a priest or parson, be it, I mean, any single one of the infinite varieties of the creatures of God (whose very name I would be understood to pronounce with reverence, and never to approach but with distant awe), I say that the study and acknowledgment of that variety among men especially increases our respect and wonder for the Creator, Commander, and Ordainer of all these minds, so different and yet so united—meeting in a common adoration, and offering up each according to his degree and means of approaching the Divine centre, his acknowledgment of praise and worship, each singing (to recur to the bird simile) his natural song."

"And so, Arthur, the hymn of a saint, or the ode of a poet, or the chant of a Newgate thief, are all pretty much the same in your philosophy," said George.

"Even that sneer could be answered were it to the point," Pendennis replied; "but it is not; and it could be replied to you, that even to the wretched outcry of the thief on the tree, the wisest and the best of all teachers we know of, the untiring Comforter and Consoler, promised a pitiful hearing and a certain hope. Hymns of saints! Odes of poets! who are we to measure the chances and opportunities, the means of doing, or even judging, right and wrong, awarded to men; and to establish the rule for meting out their punishments and rewards? We are as insolent and unthinking in judging of men's morals as of their intellects. We admire this man as being a great philosopher, and set down the other as a dullard, not knowing either, or the amount of truth in either, or being certain of the truth any where. We sing Te Deum for this hero who has won a battle, and De Profundis for that other one who has broken out of prison, and has been caught afterward by the policemen. Our measure of rewards and punishments is most partial and incomplete, absurdly inadequate, utterly worldly, and we wish to continue it into the next world. Into that next and awful world we strive to pursue men, and send after them our impotent party verdicts of condemnation or acquittal. We set up our paltry little rods to measure Heaven immeasurable, as if, in comparison to that, Newton's mind or Pascal's or Shakspeare's was any loftier than mine; as if the ray which travels from the sun would reach me sooner than the man who blacks my boots. Measured by that altitude, the tallest and the smallest among us are so alike diminutive and pitifully base, that I say we should take no count of the calculation, and it is a meanness to reckon the difference."

"Your figure fails there, Arthur," said the other, better pleased; "if even by common arithmetic we can multiply as we can reduce almost infinitely, the Great Reckoner must take count of all; and the small is not small, or the great great, to his infinity."

"I don't call those calculations in question," Arthur said: "I only say that yours are incomplete and premature; false in consequence, and, by every operation, multiplying into wider error. I do not condemn the man who murdered Socrates and damned Galileo. I say that they damned Galileo and murdered Socrates."

"And yet but a moment since you admitted the propriety of acquiescence in the present, and, I suppose, all other tyrannies?"

"No: but that if an opponent menaces me, of whom and without cost of blood and violence I can get rid, I would rather wait him out, and starve him out, than fight him out. Fabius fought Hannibal skeptically. Who was his Roman coadjutor, whom we read of in Plutarch when we were boys, who scoffed at the other's procrastination and doubted his courage, and engaged the enemy and was beaten for his pains?"

In these speculations and confessions of Arthur, the reader may perhaps see allusions to questions which, no doubt, have occupied and discomposed himself, and which he has answered by very different solutions to those come to by our friend. We are not pledging ourselves for the correctness of his opinions, which readers will please to consider are delivered dramatically, the writer being no more answerable for them, than for the sentiments uttered by any other character of the story: our endeavor is merely to follow out, in its progress, the development of the mind of a worldly and selfish, but not ungenerous or unkind, or truth-avoiding man. And it will be seen that the lamentable stage to which his logic at present has brought him, is one of general skepticism and sneering acquiescence in the world as it is; or if you like so to call it, a belief qualified with scorn in all things extant. The tastes and habits of such a man prevent him from being a boisterous demagogue, and his love of truth and dislike of cant keep him from advancing crude propositions, such as many loud reformers are constantly ready with; much more of uttering downright falsehoods in arguing questions or abusing opponents, which he would die or starve rather than use. It was not in our friend's nature to be able to utter certain lies; nor was he strong enough to protest against others, except with a polite sneer; his maxim being, that he owed obedience to all Acts of Parliament, as long as they were not repealed.

And to what does this easy and skeptical life lead a man? Friend Arthur was a Sadducee, and the Baptist might be in the Wilderness shouting to the poor, who were listening with all their might and faith to the preacher's awful accents and denunciations of wrath or woe or salvation; and our friend the Sadducee would turn his sleek mule with a shrug and a smile from the crowd, and go home to the shade of his terrace, and muse over preacher and audience, and turn to his roll of Plato, or his pleasant Greek song-book babbling of honey and Hybla, and nymphs and fountains and love. To what, we say, does this skepticism lead? It leads a man to a shameful loneliness and selfishness, so to speak—the more shameful, because it is so good-humored and conscienceless and serene. Conscience! What is conscience? Why accept remorse? What is public or private faith? Mythuses alike enveloped in enormous tradition. If seeing and acknowledging the lies of the world, Arthur, as see them you can with only too fatal a clearness, you submit to them without any protest farther than a laugh: if plunged yourself in easy sensuality, you allow the whole wretched world to pass groaning by you unmoved: if the fight for the truth is taking place, and all men of honor are on the ground armed on the one side or the other, and you alone are to lie on your balcony and smoke your pipe out of the noise and the danger, you had better have died, or never have been at all, than such a sensual coward.

"The truth, friend!" Arthur said, imperturbably; "where is the truth? Show it me. That is the question between us. I see it on both sides. I see it in the Conservative side of the house, and among the Radicals, and even on the ministerial benches. I see it in this man who worships by act of Parliament, and is rewarded with a silk apron and five thousand a year; in that man, who, driven fatally by the remorseless logic of his creed, gives up every thing, friends, fame, dearest ties, closest vanities, the respect of an army of churchmen, the recognized position of a leader, and passes over, truth-impelled, to the enemy, in whose ranks he will serve henceforth as a nameless private soldier:—I see the truth in that man, as I do in his brother, whose logic drives him to quite a different conclusion, and who, after having passed a life in vain endeavors to reconcile an irreconcileable book, flings it at last down in despair, and declares, with tearful eyes, and hands up to heaven, his revolt and recantation. If the truth is with all these, why should I take side with any one of them? Some are called upon to preach: let them preach. Of these preachers there are somewhat too many, methinks, who fancy they have the gift. But we can not all be parsons in church, that is clear. Some must sit silent and listen, or go to sleep mayhap. Have we not all our duties? The head charity-boy blows the bellows; the master canes the other boys in the organ-loft; the clerk sings out Amen from the desk; and the beadle with the staff opens the door for his Reverence, who rustles in silk up to the cushion. I won't cane the boys, nay, or say Amen always, or act as the church's champion and warrior, in the shape of the beadle with the staff; but I will take off my hat in the place, and say my prayers there too, and shake hands with the clergyman as he steps on the grass outside. Don't I know that his being there is a compromise, and that he stands before me an Act of Parliament? That the church he occupies was built for other worship? That the Methodist chapel is next door; and that Bunyan the tinker is bawling out the tidings of damnation on the common hard by? Yes, I am a Sadducee; and I take things as I find them, and the world, and the Acts of Parliament of the world, as they are; and as I intend to take a wife, if I find one—not to be madly in love and prostrate at her feet like a fool—not to worship her as an angel, or to expect to find her as such—but to be good-natured to her, and courteous, expecting good-nature and pleasant society from her in turn. And so, George, if ever you hear of my marrying, depend on it, it won't be a romantic attachment on my side: and if you hear of any good place under Government, I have no particular scruples that I know of, which would prevent me from accepting your offer."

"O Pen, you scoundrel! I know what you mean," here Warrington broke out. "This is the meaning of your skepticism, of your quietism, of your atheism, my poor fellow. You're going to sell yourself, and Heaven help you! You're going to make a bargain which will degrade you and make you miserable for life, and there's no use talking of it. If you are once bent on it, the devil won't prevent you."

"On the contrary, he's on my side, isn't he, George?" said Pen with a laugh. "What good cigars these are! Come down and have a little dinner at the Club; the chef's in town, and he'll cook a good one for me. No, you won't? Don't be sulky, old boy, I'm going down to—to the country to-morrow."

CHAPTER XXIV

WHICH ACCOUNTS PERHAPS FOR CHAPTER XXIII

The information regarding the affairs of the Clavering family, which Major Pendennis had acquired through Strong, and by his own personal interference as the friend of the house, was such as almost made the old gentleman pause in any plans which he might have once entertained for his nephew's benefit. To bestow upon Arthur a wife with two such fathers-in-law as the two worthies whom the guileless and unfortunate Lady Clavering had drawn in her marriage ventures, was to benefit no man. And though the one, in a manner, neutralized the other, and the appearance of Amory or Altamont in public would be the signal for his instantaneous withdrawal and condign punishment—for the fugitive convict had cut down the officer in charge of him—and a rope would be inevitably his end, if he came again under British authorities; yet, no guardian would like to secure for his ward a wife, whose parent was to be got rid of in such a way; and the old gentleman's notion always had been that Altamont, with the gallows before his eyes, would assuredly avoid recognition; while, at the same time, by holding the threat of his discovery over Clavering, the latter, who would lose every thing by Amory's appearance, would be a slave in the hands of the person who knew so fatal a secret.

But if the Begum paid Clavering's debts many times more, her wealth would be expended altogether upon this irreclaimable reprobate: and her heirs, whoever they might be, would succeed but to an emptied treasury; and Miss Amory, instead of bringing her husband a good income and a seat in

Parliament, would bring to that individual her person only, and her pedigree with that lamentable note of sus per coll at the name of the last male of her line.

There was, however, to the old schemer revolving these things in his mind, another course yet open; the which will appear to the reader who may take the trouble to peruse a conversation, which presently ensued, between Major Pendennis and the honorable baronet, the member for Clavering.

When a man, under pecuniary difficulties, disappears from among his usual friends and equals—dives out of sight, as it were, from the flock of birds in which he is accustomed to sail, it is wonderful at what strange and distant nooks he comes up again for breath. I have known a Pall Mall lounger and Rotten Row buck, of no inconsiderable fashion, vanish from among his comrades of the Clubs and the Park, and be discovered, very happy and affable, at an eighteenpenny ordinary in Billingsgate: another gentleman, of great learning and wit, when out running the constables (were I to say he was a literary man, some critics would vow that I intended to insult the literary profession), once sent me his address at a little public-house called the "Fox under the Hill," down a most darksome and cavernous archway in the Strand. Such a man, under such misfortunes, may have a house, but he is never in his house; and has an address where letters may be left; but only simpletons go with the hopes of seeing him. Only a few of the faithful know where he is to be found, and have the clew to his hiding-place. So, after the disputes with his wife, and the misfortunes consequent thereon, to find Sir Francis Clavering at home was impossible. "Ever since I hast him for my book, which is fourteen pound, he don't come home till three o'clock, and purtends to be asleep when I bring his water of a mornin', and dodges hout when I'm down stairs," Mr. Lightfoot remarked to his friend Morgan; and announced that he should go down to my Lady, and be butler there, and marry his old woman. In like manner, after his altercations with Strong, the baronet did not come near him, and fled to other haunts, out of the reach of the chevalier's reproaches; out of the reach of conscience, if possible, which many of us try to dodge and leave behind us by changes of scenes and other fugitive stratagems.

So, though the elder Pendennis, having his own ulterior object, was bent upon seeing Pen's country neighbor and representative in Parliament, it took the major no inconsiderable trouble and time before he could get him into such a confidential state and conversation, as were necessary for the ends which the major had in view. For since the major had been called in as family friend, and had cognizance of Clavering's affairs, conjugal and pecuniary, the baronet avoided him: as he always avoided all his lawyers and agents when there was an account to be rendered, or an affair of business to be discussed between them; and never kept any appointment but when its object was the raising of money. Thus, previous to catching this most shy and timorous bird, the major made more than one futile attempt to hold him; on one day it was a most innocent-looking invitation to dinner at Greenwich, to meet a few friends; the baronet accepted, suspected something, and did not come; leaving the major (who indeed proposed to represent in himself the body of friends) to eat his whitebait done: on another occasion the major wrote and asked for ten minutes' talk, and the baronet instantly acknowledged the note, and made the appointment at four o'clock the next day at Bays's precisely (he carefully underlined the "precisely"); but though four o'clock came, as in the course of time and destiny it could not do otherwise, no Clavering made his appearance. Indeed, if he had borrowed twenty pounds of Pendennis, he could not have been more timid, or desirous of avoiding the major; and the latter found that it was one thing to seek a man, and another to find him.

Before the close of that day in which Strong's patron had given the chevalier the benefit of so many blessings before his face and curses behind his back, Sir Francis Clavering who had pledged his word and his oath to his wife's advisers to draw or accept no more bills of exchange, and to be content with the allowance which his victimized wife still awarded him, had managed to sign his respectable name to a piece of stamped paper, which the baronet's friend, Mr. Moss Abrams, had carried off, promising to have the bill "done" by a party with whose intimacy Mr. Abrams was favored. And it chanced that Strong heard of this transaction at the place where the writings had been drawn—in the back parlor, namely, of Mr. Santiago's cigar-shop, where the chevalier was constantly in the habit of spending an hour in the evening.

"He is at his old work again," Mr. Santiago told his customer. "He and Moss Abrams were in my parlor. Moss sent out my boy for a stamp. It must have been a bill for fifty pound. I heard the baronet tell Moss to date it two months back. He will pretend that it is an old bill, and that he forgot it when he came to a settlement with his wife the other day. I daresay they will give him some more money now he is clear." A man who has the habit of putting his unlucky name to "promises to pay" at six months, has the satisfaction of knowing, too, that his affairs are known and canvassed, and his signature handed round among the very worst knaves and rogues of London.

Mr. Santiago's shop was close by St. James's-street and Bury-street, where we have had the honor of visiting our friend Major Pendennis in his lodgings. The major was walking daintily toward his apartment, as Strong, burning with wrath and redolent of Havanna, strode along the same pavement opposite to him.

"Confound these young men: how they poison every thing with their smoke," thought the major. "Here comes a fellow with mustaches and a cigar. Every fellow who smokes and wears mustaches is a low fellow. Oh! it's Mr. Strong—I hope you are well, Mr. Strong?" and the old gentleman, making a dignified bow to the chevalier, was about to pass into his house; directing toward the lock of the door, with trembling hand, the polished door-key.

We have said, that, at the long and weary disputes and conferences regarding the payment of Sir Francis Clavering's last debts, Strong and Pendennis had both been present as friends and advisers of the baronet's unlucky family. Strong stopped and held out his hand to his brother negotiator, and old Pendennis put out toward him a couple of ungracious fingers.

"What is your good news?" said Major Pendennis, patronizing the other still farther, and condescending to address to him an observation, for old Pendennis had kept such good company all his life, that he vaguely imagined he honored common men by speaking to them. "Still in town, Mr. Strong? I hope I see you well."

"My news is bad news, sir," Strong answered; "it concerns our friends at Tunbridge Wells, and I should like to talk to you about it. Clavering is at his old tricks again, Major Pendennis."

"Indeed! Pray do me the favor to come into my lodging," cried the major with awakened interest; and the pair entered and took possession of his drawing-room. Here seated, Strong unburdened himself of his indignation to the major, and spoke at large of Clavering's recklessness and treachery. "No promises will bind him sir," he said. "You remember when we met, sir, with my lady's lawyer, how he wouldn't be satisfied with giving his honor, but wanted to take his oath on his knees to his wife, and rang the bell for a Bible, and swore perdition on his soul if he ever would give another bill. He has been signing one this very day, sir: and will sign as many more as you please for ready money: and will deceive any body, his wife or his child, or his old friend, who has backed him a hundred times. Why, there's a bill of his and mine will be due next week—"

"I thought we had paid all—"

"Not that one," Strong said, blushing. "He asked me not to mention it, and—and—I had half the money for that, major. And they will be down on me. But I don't care for it; I'm used to it. It's Lady Clavering that riles me. It's a shame that that good-natured woman, who has paid him out of jail a score of times, should be ruined by his heartlessness. A parcel of bill-stealers, boxers, any rascals, get his money; and he don't scruple to throw an honest fellow over. Would you believe it, sir, he took money of Altamont—you know whom I mean."

"Indeed? of that singular man, who I think came tipsy once to Sir Francis's house?" Major Pendennis said, with impenetrable countenance. "Who is Altamont, Mr. Strong?"

"I am sure I don't know, if you don't know," the chevalier answered, with a look of surprise and suspicion.

"To tell you frankly," said the major, "I have my suspicions. I suppose—mind, I only suppose—that in our friend Clavering's life— who, between you and me, Captain Strong, we must own is about as loose a fish as any in my acquaintance—there are, no doubt, some queer secrets and stories which he would not like to have known: none of us would. And very likely this fellow, who calls himself Altamont, knows some story against Clavering, and has some hold on him, and gets money out of him on the strength of his information. I know some of the best men of the best families in England who are paying through the nose in that way. But their private affairs are no business of mine, Mr. Strong; and it is not to be supposed that because I go and dine with a man, I pry into his secrets, or am answerable for all his past life. And so with our friend Clavering, I am most interested for his wife's sake, and her daughter's, who is a most charming creature: and when her ladyship asked me, I looked into her affairs, and tried to set them straight; and shall do so again, you understand, to the hest of my humble power and ability, if I can make myself useful. And if I am called upon—you understand, if I am called upon—and—by-the-way, this Mr. Altamont, Mr. Strong? How is this Mr. Altamont? I believe you are acquainted with him. Is he in town?"

"I don't know that I am called upon to know where he is, Major Pendennis," said Strong, rising and taking up his hat in dudgeon, for the major's patronizing manner and impertinence of caution offended the honest gentleman not a little.

Pendennis's manner altered at once from a tone of hauteur to one of knowing good-humor. "Ah, Captain Strong, you are cautious too, I see; and quite right, my good sir, quite right. We don't know what ears walls may have, sir, or to whom we may be talking; and as a man of the world, and an old soldier—an old and distinguished soldier, I have been told, Captain Strong—you know very well that there is no use in throwing away your fire; you may have your ideas, and I may put two and two together and have mine. But there are things which don't concern him that many a man had better not know, eh, captain? and which I, for one, won't know until I have reason for knowing them: and that I believe is your maxim too. With regard to our friend the baronet, I think with you, it would be most advisable that he should be checked in his imprudent courses; and most strongly reprehend any man's departure from his word, or any conduct of his which can give any pain to his family, or cause them annoyance in any way. That is my full and frank opinion, and I am sure it is yours."

"Certainly," said Mr. Strong, drily.

"I am delighted to hear it; delighted, that an old brother soldier should agree with me so fully. And I am exceedingly glad of the lucky meeting which has procured me the good fortune of your visit. Good evening. Thank you. Morgan, show the door to Captain Strong."

And Strong, preceded by Morgan, took his leave of Major Pendennis; the chevalier not a little puzzled at the old fellow's prudence; and the valet, to say the truth, to the full as much perplexed at his master's reticence. For Mr. Morgan, in his capacity of accomplished valet, moved here and there in a house as silent as a shadow; and, as it so happened, during the latter part of his master's conversation with his visitor, had been standing very close to the door, and had overheard not a little of the talk between, the two gentlemen, and a great deal more than he could understand.

"Who is that Altamont? know any thing about him and Strong?" Mr. Morgan asked of Mr. Lightfoot, on the next convenient occasion when they met at the Club.

"Strong's his man of business, draws the governor's bills, and indosses 'em, and does his odd jobs and that; and I suppose Altamont's in it too," Mr. Lightfoot replied. "That kite-flying, you know, Mr. M. always takes two or three on 'em to set the paper going. Altamont put the pot on at the Derby, and won a good bit of money. I wish the governor could get some somewhere, and I could get my book paid up."

"Do you think my lady would pay his debts again?" Morgan asked "Find out that for me, Lightfoot, and I'll make it worth your while my boy."

Major Pendennis had often said with a laugh, that his valet Morgan was a much richer man than himself: and, indeed, by a long course of careful speculation, this wary and silent attendant had been amassing a considerable sum of money, during the years which he had passed in the major's service, where he had made the acquaintance of many other valets of distinction, from whom he had learned the affairs of their principals. When Mr. Arthur came into his property, but not until then, Morgan had surprised the young gentleman, by saying that he had a little sum of money, some fifty or a hundred pound, which he wanted to lay out to advantage; perhaps the gentlemen in the Temple, knowing about affairs and business and that, could help a poor fellow to a good investment? Morgan would be very much obliged to Mr. Arthur, most grateful and obliged indeed, if Arthur could tell him of one. When Arthur laughingly replied, that he knew nothing about money matters, and knew no earthly way of helping Morgan, the latter, with the utmost simplicity, was very grateful, very grateful indeed, to Mr. Arthur, and if Mr. Arthur should want a little money before his rents was paid perhaps he would kindly remember that his uncle's old and faithful servant had some as he would like to put out: and be most proud if he could be useful anyways to any of the family.

The Prince of Fairoaks, who was tolerably prudent and had no need of ready money, would as soon have thought of borrowing from his uncle's servant as of stealing the valet's pocket-handkerchief, and was on the point of making some haughty reply to Morgan's offer, but was checked by the humor of the transaction. Morgan a capitalist! Morgan offering to lend to him! The joke was excellent. On the other hand, the man might be quite innocent, and the proposal of money a simple offer of good-will. So Arthur withheld the sarcasm that was rising to his lips, and contented himself by declining Mr. Morgan's kind proposal. He mentioned the matter to his uncle, however, and congratulated the latter on having such a treasure in his service.

It was then that the major said that he believed Morgan had been getting devilish rich for a devilish long time; in fact he had bought the house in Bury-street, in which his master was a lodger; and had actually made a considerable sum of money, from his acquaintance with the Clavering family and his knowledge obtained through his master that the Begum would pay all her husband's debts, by buying up as many of the baronet's acceptances as he could raise money to purchase. Of these transactions the major, however, knew no more than most gentlemen do of their servants, who live with us all our days and are strangers to us, so strong custom is, and so pitiless the distinction between class and class.

"So he offered to lend you money, did he?" the elder Pendennis remarked to his nephew. "He's a dev'lish sly fellow, and a dev'lish rich fellow; and there's many a nobleman would like to have such a valet in his service, and borrow from him too. And he ain't a bit changed, Monsieur Morgan. He does his work just as well as ever—he's always ready to my bell—steals about the room like a cat—he's so dev'lishly attached to me, Morgan!"

On the day of Strong's visit, the major bethought him of Pen's story, and that Morgan might help him, and rallied the valet regarding his wealth with that free and insolent way which so high-placed a gentleman might be disposed to adopt toward so unfortunate a creature.

"I hear that you have got some money to invest, Morgan," said the major.

It's Mr. Arthur has been telling, hang him, thought the valet.

"I'm glad my place is such a good one."

"Thank you, sir—I've no reason to complain of my place, nor of my master," replied Morgan, demurely.

"You're a good fellow: and I believe you are attached to me; and I'm glad you get on well. And I hope you'll be prudent, and not be taking a public-house or that kind of thing."

A public-house, thought Morgan—me in a public-house!—the old fool!—Dammy, if I was ten years younger I'd set in Parlyment before I died, that I would. "No, thank you kindly, sir. I don't think of the public line, sir. And I've got my little savings pretty well put out, sir."

"You do a little in the discounting way, eh, Morgan?"

"Yes, sir, a very little—I—I beg your pardon, sir—might I be so free as to ask a question—"

"Speak on, my good fellow," the elder said, graciously.

"About Sir Francis Clavering's paper, sir? Do you think he's any longer any good, sir? Will my lady pay on 'em, any more, sir?"

"What, you've done something in that business already?"

"Yes, sir, a little," replied Morgan, dropping down his eyes. "And I don't mind owning, sir, and I hope I may take the liberty of saying, sir, that a little more would make me very comfortable if it turned out as well as the last."

"Why, how much have you netted by him, in Gad's name?" asked the major.

"I've done a good bit, sir, at it: that I own, sir. Having some information, and made acquaintance with the fam'ly through your kindness, I put on the pot, sir."

"You did what?"

"I laid my money on, sir—I got all I could, and borrowed, and bought Sir Francis's bills; many of 'em had his name, and the gentleman's as is just gone out, Edward Strong, Esquire, sir: and of course I know of the blow hup and shindy as is took place in Grosvenor-place, sir: and as I may as well make my money as another, I'd be very much obleeged to you if you'd tell me whether my lady will come down any more."

Although Major Pendennis was as much surprised at this intelligence regarding his servant, as if he had heard that Morgan was a disguised marquis, about to throw off his mask and assume his seat in the House of Peers; and although he was of course indignant at the audacity of the fellow who had dared to grow rich under his nose, and without his cognizance; yet he had a natural admiration for every man who represented money and success, and found himself respecting Morgan, and being rather afraid of that worthy, as the truth began to dawn upon him.

"Well, Morgan," said he, "I mustn't ask how rich you are; and the richer the better for your sake, I'm sure. And if I could give you any information that could serve you, I would speedily help you. But frankly, if Lady Clavering asks me whether she shall pay any more of Sir Francis's debts, I shall advise and I hope she won't, though I fear she will—and that is all I know. And so you are aware that Sir Francis is beginning again in his—eh—reckless and imprudent course?"

"At his old games, sir—can't prevent that gentleman. He will do it."

"Mr. Strong was saying that a Mr. Moss Abrams was the holder of one of Sir Francis Covering's notes. Do you know any thing of this Mr. Abrams, or the amount of the bill?"

"Don't know the bill—know Abrams quite well, sir."

"I wish you would find out about it for me. And I wish you would find out where I can see Sir Francis Clavering, Morgan."

And Morgan said, "thank you, sir, yes, sir, I will, sir;" and retired from the room, as he had entered it, with his usual stealthy respect and quiet humility; leaving the major to muse and wonder over what he had just heard.

The next morning the valet informed Major Pendennis that he had seen Mr. Abrams; what was the amount of the bill that gentleman was desirous to negotiate; and that the baronet would be sure to be in the back parlor of the Wheel of Fortune Tavern that day at one o'clock.

To this appointment Sir Francis Clavering was punctual, and as at one o'clock he sat in the parlor of the tavern in question, surrounded by spittoons, Windsor chairs, cheerful prints of boxers, trotting horses, and pedestrians, and the lingering of last night's tobacco fumes—as the descendant of an ancient line sate in this delectable place, accommodated with an old copy of Bell's Life in London, much blotted with beer, the polite Major Pendennis walked into the apartment.

"So it's you, old boy?" asked the baronet, thinking that Mr. Moss Abrams had arrived with the money.

"How do you do, Sir Francis Clavering? I wanted to see you, and followed you here," said the major, at sight of whom the other's countenance fell. Now that he had his opponent before him, the major was determined to make a brisk and sudden attack upon him, and went into action at once. "I know," he continued, "who is the exceedingly disreputable person for whom you took me, Clavering; and the errand which brought you here."

"It ain't your business, is it?" asked the baronet, with a sulky and deprecatory look. "Why are you following me about and taking the command, and meddling in my affairs, Major Pendennis? I've never done you any harm, have I? I've never had your money. And I don't choose to be dodged about in this way, and domineered over. I don't choose it, and I won't have it. If Lady Clavering has any proposal to make to me, let it be done in the regular way, and through the lawyers. I'd rather not have you."

"I am not come from Lady Clavering," the major said, "but of my own accord, to try and remonstrate with you, Clavering, and see if you can be kept from ruin. It is but a month ago that you swore on your honor, and wanted to get a Bible to strengthen the oath, that you would accept no more bills, but content yourself with the allowance which Lady Clavering gives you. All your debts were paid with that proviso, and you have broken it; this Mr. Abrams has a bill of yours for sixty pounds."

"It's an old bill. I take my solemn oath it's an old bill," shrieked out the baronet.

"You drew it yesterday, and you dated three months back purposely. By Gad, Clavering, you sicken me with lies, I can't help telling you so. I've no patience with you, by Gad. You cheat every body, yourself included. I've seen a deal of the world, but I never met your equal at humbugging. It's my belief you had rather lie than not."

"Have you come here, you old, old beast, to tempt me to—to pitch into you, and—and knock your old head off?" said the baronet, with a poisonous look of hatred at the major.

"What, sir?" shouted out the old major, rising to his feet and clasping his cane, and looking so fiercely, that the baronet's tone instantly changed toward him.

"No, no," said Clavering piteously, "I beg your pardon. I didn't mean to be angry, or say any thing unkind, only you're so damned harsh to me, Major Pendennis. What is it you want of me? Why have you been hunting me so? Do you want money out of me too? By Jove, you know I've not got a shilling,"—and so Clavering, according to his custom, passed from a curse into a whimper.

Major Pendennis saw from the other's tone, that Clavering knew his secret was in the major's hands.

"I've no errand from any body, or no design upon you," Pendennis said, "but an endeavor, if it's not too late, to save you and your family from utter ruin, through the infernal recklessness of your courses. I knew your secret—"

"I didn't know it when I married her; upon my oath I didn't know it till the d—d scoundrel came back and told me himself; and it's the misery about that which makes me so reckless, Pendennis; indeed it is;" the baronet cried, clasping his hands.

"I knew your secret from the very first day when I saw Amory come drunk into your dining-room in Grosvenor-place. I never forget faces. I remember that fellow in Sidney a convict, and he remembers me. I know his trial, the date of his marriage, and of his reported death in the bush. I could swear to him. And I know that you are no more married to Lady Clavering than I am. I've kept your secret well enough, for I've not told a single soul that I know it—not your wife, not yourself till now."

"Poor Lady C., it would cut her up dreadfully," whimpered Sir Francis; "and it wasn't my fault, major; you know it wasn't."

"Rather than allow you to go on ruining her as you do, I will tell her, Clavering, and tell all the world too; that is what I swear I will do, unless I can come to some terms with you, and put some curb on your infernal folly. By play, debt, and extravagance of all kind, you've got through half your wife's fortune, and that of her legitimate heirs, mind—her legitimate heirs. Here it must stop. You can't live together. You're not fit to live in a great house like Clavering; and before three years more were over would not leave a shilling to carry on. I've settled what must be done. You shall have six hundred a year; you shall go abroad and live on that. You must give up Parliament, and get on as well as you can. If you refuse, I give you my word I'll make the real state of things known to-morrow; I'll swear to Amory, who, when identified, will go back to the country from whence he came, and will rid the widow of you and himself together. And so that boy of yours loses at once all title to old Snell's property, and it goes to your wife's daughter. Ain't I making myself pretty clearly understood?"

"You wouldn't be so cruel to that poor boy, would you, Pendennis?" asked the father, pleading piteously; "hang it, think about him. He's a nice boy: though he's dev'lish wild, I own—he's dev'lish wild."

"It's you who are cruel to him," said the old moralist. "Why, sir, you'll ruin him yourself inevitably in three years."

"Yes, but perhaps I won't have such dev'lish bad luck, you know; the luck must turn: and I'll reform, by Gad, I'll reform. And if you were to split on me, it would cut up my wife so; you know it would, most infernally."

"To be parted from you," said the old major, with a sneer; "you know she won't live with you again."

"But why can't Lady C. live abroad, or at Bath, or at Tunbridge, or at the doose, and I go on here?" Clavering continued. "I like being here better than abroad, and I like being in Parliament. It's dev'lish convenient being in Parliament. There's very few seats like mine left; and if I gave it to 'em, I should not wonder the ministry would give me an island to govern, or some dev'lish good thing; for you know I'm a gentleman of dev'lish good family, and have a handle to my name, and—and that sort of thing, Major Pendennis. Eh, don't you see? Don't you think they'd give me something dev'lish good if I was to play my cards well? And then, you know, I'd save money, and be kept out of the way of the confounded hells and rouge et noir—and—and so I'd rather not give up Parliament, please." For at one instant to hate and defy a man, at the next to weep before him, and at the next to be perfectly confidential and friendly with him, was not an unusual process with our versatile-minded baronet.

"As for your seat in Parliament," the major said, with something of a blush on his cheek, and a certain tremor, which the other did not see "you must part with that, Sir Francis Clavering, to—to me."

"What! are you going into the House, Major Pendennis?"

"No—not I; but my nephew, Arthur, is a very clever fellow, and would make a figure there: and when Clavering had two members, his father might very likely have been one; and—and I should like Arthur to be there," the major said.

"Dammy, does he know it, too?" cried out Clavering.

"Nobody knows any thing out of this room," Pendennis answered; "and if you do this favor for me, I hold my tongue. If not, I'm a man of my word, and will do what I have said."

"I say, major," said Sir Francis, with a peculiarly humble smile, "you—you couldn't get me my first quarter in advance, could you, like the best of fellows? You can do any thing with Lady Clavering; and, upon my oath, I'll take up that bill of Abrams. The little dam scoundrel, I know he'll do me in the business—he always does; and if you could do this for me, we'd see, major."

"And I think your best plan would be to go down in September to Clavering to shoot, and take my nephew with you, and introduce him. Yes, that will be the best time. And we will try and manage about the advance." (Arthur may lend him that, thought old Pendennis. Confound him, a seat in Parliament is worth a hundred and fifty pounds.) "And, Clavering, you understand, of course, my nephew knows nothing about this business. You have a mind to retire: he is a Clavering man, and a good representative for the borough; you introduce him, and your people vote for him—you see."

"When can you get me the hundred and fifty, major? When shall I come and see you? Will you be at home this evening or to-morrow morning? Will you have any thing here? They've got some dev'lish good bitters in the bar. I often have a glass of bitters, it sets one up so."

The old major would take no refreshment; but rose and took his leave of the baronet, who walked with him to the door of the Wheel of Fortune, and then strolled into the bar, where he took a glass of gin and bitters with the landlady there: and a gentleman connected with the ring (who boarded at the Wheel of F.) coming in, he and Sir Francis Clavering and the landlord talked about the fights and the news of the sporting world in general; and at length Mr. Moss Abrams arrived with the proceeds of the baronet's bill, from which his own handsome commission was deducted, and out of the remainder Sir Francis "stood" a dinner at Greenwich to his distinguished friend, and passed the evening gayly at Vauxhall. Meanwhile Major Pendennis, calling a cab in Piccadilly, drove to Lamb-court, Temple, where he speedily was closeted with his nephew in deep conversation.

After their talk they parted on very good terms, and it was in consequence of that unreported conversation, whereof the reader nevertheless can pretty well guess the bearing, that Arthur expressed himself as we have heard in the colloquy with Warrington, which is reported in the last chapter.

When a man is tempted to do a tempting thing, he can find a hundred ingenious reasons for gratifying his liking; and Arthur thought very much that he would like to be in Parliament, and that he would like to distinguish himself there, and that he need not care much what side he took, as there was falsehood and truth on every side. And on this and on other matters he thought he would compromise with his conscience, and that Sadduceeism was a very convenient and good-humored profession of faith.

CHAPTER XXV

PHILLIS AND CORYDON

On a picturesque common in the neighborhood of Tunbridge Wells, Lady Clavering had found a pretty villa, whither she retired after her conjugal disputes at the end of that unlucky London season. Miss Amory, of course, accompanied her mother, and Master Clavering came home for the holidays, with whom Blanche's chief occupation was to fight and quarrel. But this was only a home pastime, and the young school-boy was not fond of home sports. He found cricket, and horses, and plenty of friends at Tunbridge. The good-natured Begum's house was filled with a constant society of young gentlemen of thirteen, who ate and drank much too copiously of tarts and Champagne, who rode races on the lawn, and frightened the fond mother; who smoked and made themselves sick, and the dining-room unbearable to Miss Blanche. She did not like the society of young gentlemen of thirteen.

As for that fair young creature, any change, as long as it was change, was pleasant to her; and for a week or two she would have liked poverty and a cottage, and bread and cheese; and, for a night, perhaps, a dungeon and bread and water, and so the move to Tunbridge was by no means unwelcome to her. She wandered in the woods, and sketched trees and farm-houses; she read French novels habitually; she drove into Tunbridge Wells pretty often, and to any play, or ball, or conjuror, or musician who might happen to appear in the place; she slept a great deal; she quarreled with mamma and Frank during the morning; she found the little village school and attended it, and first fondled the girls and thwarted the mistress, then scolded the girls and laughed at the teacher; she was constant at church, of course. It was a pretty little church, of immense antiquity—a little Anglo-Norman bijou, built the day before yesterday, and decorated with all sorts of painted windows, carved saints' heads, gilt Scripture texts, and open pews. Blanche began forthwith to work a most correct high-church altar-cover for the church. She passed for a saint with the clergyman for a while, whom she quite took in, and whom she coaxed, and wheedled, and fondled so artfully, that poor Mrs. Smirke, who at first was charmed with her, then bore with her, then would hardly speak to her, was almost mad with jealousy. Mrs. Smirke was the wife of our old friend Smirke, Pen's tutor and poor Helen's suitor. He had consoled himself for her refusal with a young lady from Clapham whom his mamma provided. When the latter died, our friend's views became every day more and more pronounced. He cut off his coat collar, and let his hair grow over his back. He rigorously gave up the curl which he used to sport on his forehead, and the tie of his neckcloth of which he was rather proud. He went without any tie at all. He went without dinner on Fridays. He read the Roman Hours, and intimated that he was ready to receive confessions in the vestry. The most harmless creature in the world, he was denounced as a black and a most dangerous Jesuit and Papist, by Muffin of the Dissenting chapel, and Mr. Simeon Knight at the old church. Mr. Smirke had built his chapel of ease with the money left him by his mother at Clapham. Lord! lord! what would she have said to hear a table called an altar! to see candlesticks on it! to get letters signed on the Feast of Saint So-and-so, or the Vigil of Saint What-do-you-call-'em! All these things did the boy of Clapham practice; his faithful wife following him. But when Blanche had a conference of near two hours in the vestry with Mr. Smirke, Belinda paced up and down on the grass, where there were only two little grave-stones as yet; she wished that she had a third there: only, only he would offer very likely to that creature, who had infatuated him, in a fortnight. No, she would retire; she would go into a convent, and profess, and leave him. Such bad thoughts had Smirke's wife and his neighbors regarding him; these, thinking him in direct correspondence with the bishop of Rome; that, bewailing errors to her even more odious and fatal; and yet our friend meant no earthly harm. The post-office never brought him any letters from the Pope; he thought Blanche, to be sure, at first, the most pious, gifted, right-thinking, fascinating person he had ever met; and her manner of singing the chants delighted him—but after a while he began to grow rather tired of Miss Amory, her ways and graces grew stale somehow; then he was doubtful about Miss Amory; then she made a disturbance in his school, lost her temper, and rapped the children's fingers. Blanche inspired this admiration and satiety, somehow, in many men. She tried to please them, and flung out all her graces at once; came down to them with all her jewels on, all her smiles, and cajoleries, and coaxings, and ogles. Then she grew tired of them and of trying to please them, and never having cared about them, dropped them: and the men grew tired of her, and dropped her too. It was a happy night for Belinda when Blanche went away; and her husband, with rather a blush and a sigh, said "he had been deceived in her; he had thought her endowed with many precious gifts, he feared they were mere tinsel; he thought she had been a right-thinking person, he feared she had merely made religion an amusement—she certainly had quite lost her temper to the schoolmistress, and beat Polly Rucker's knuckles cruelly." Belinda flew to his arms, there was no question about the grave or the veil any more. He tenderly embraced her on the forehead. "There is none like thee, my Belinda," he said, throwing his fine eyes up to the ceiling, "precious among women!" As for Blanche, from the instant she lost sight of him and Belinda, she never thought or cared about either any more.

But when Arthur went down to pass a few days at Tunbridge Wells with the Begum, this stage of indifference had not arrived on Miss Blanche's part or on that of the simple clergyman. Smirke believed her to be an angel and wonder of a woman. Such a perfection he had never seen, and sate listening to her music in the summer evenings, open-mouthed, rapt in wonder, tea-less, and bread-and-butterless. Fascinating as he had heard the music of the opera to be—he had never but once attended an exhibition of that nature (which he mentioned with a blush and a sigh—it was on that day when he had accompanied Helen and her son to the play at Chatteris)—he could not conceive any thing more delicious, more celestial, he had almost said, than Miss Amory's music. She was a most gifted being: she had a precious soul: she had the most remarkable talents—to all outward seeming, the most heavenly disposition, &c. It was in this way that, being then at the height of his own fever and bewitchment for Blanche, Smirke discoursed to Arthur about her.

The meeting between the two old acquaintances had been very cordial. Arthur loved any body who loved his mother; Smirke could speak on that theme with genuine feeling and emotion. They had a hundred things to tell each other of what had occurred in their lives. "Arthur would perceive," Smirke said, "that his—his views on Church matters had developed themselves since their acquaintance." Mrs. Smirke, a most exemplary person, seconded them with all her endeavors. He had built this little church on his mother's demise, who had left him provided with a sufficiency of worldly means. Though in the cloister himself, he had heard of Arthur's reputation. He spoke in the kindest and most saddened tone; he held his eyelids down, and bowed his fair head on one side. Arthur was immensely amused with him; with his airs; with his follies and simplicity; with his blank stock and long hair; with his real goodness, kindness, friendliness of feeling. And his praises of Blanche pleased and surprised our friend not a little, and made him regard her with eyes of particular favor.

The truth is, Blanche was very glad to see Arthur; as one is glad to see an agreeable man in the country, who brings down the last news and stories from the great city; who can talk better than most country folks, at least can talk that darling London jargon, so dear and indispensable to London people, so little understood by persons out of the world. The first day Pen came down, he kept Blanche laughing for hours after dinner. She sang her songs with redoubled spirit. She did not scold her mother; she fondled and kissed her to the honest Begum's surprise. When it came to be bed-time, she said, "Déjà!" with the prettiest air of regret possible; and was really quite sorry to go to bed, and squeezed Arthur's hand quite fondly. He on his side gave her pretty palm a very cordial pressure. Our young gentleman was of that turn, that eyes very moderately bright dazzled him.

"She is very much improved," thought Pen, looking out into the night, "very much. I suppose the Begum won't mind my smoking with the window open. She's a jolly good old woman, and Blanche is immensely improved. I liked her manner with her mother to-night. I liked her laughing way with that stupid young cub of a boy, whom they oughtn't to allow to get tipsy. She sang those little verses very prettily; they were devilish pretty verses too, though I say it who shouldn't say it." And he hummed a tune which Blanche had put to some verses of his own. "Ah! what a fine night! How jolly a cigar is at night! How pretty that little Saxon church looks in the moonlight! I wonder what old Warrington's doing? Yes, she's a dayvlish nice little thing, as my uncle says."

"O heavenly!" here broke out a voice from a clematis-covered casement near—a girl's voice: it was the voice of the author of Mes Larmes.

Pen burst into a laugh. "Don't tell about my smoking," he said, leaning out of his own window.

"O! go on! I adore it," cried the lady of Mes Larmes. "Heavenly night! Heavenly, heavenly moon! but I most shut my window, and not talk to you on account of les moeurs. How droll they are, les moeurs! Adieu." And Pen began to sing the good night to Don Basilio.

The next day they were walking in the fields together, laughing and chattering—the gayest pair of friends. They talked about the days of their youth, and Blanche was prettily sentimental. They talked about Laura, dearest Laura—Blanche had loved her as a sister: was she happy with that odd Lady Rockminster? Wouldn't she come and stay with them at Tunbridge? O, what walks they would take together! What songs they would sing—the old, old songs. Laura's voice was splendid. Did Arthur—she must call him Arthur—remember the songs they sang in the happy old days, now he was grown such a great man, and had such a succès? &c. &c.

And the day after, which was enlivened with a happy ramble through the woods to Penshurst, and a sight of that pleasant Park and Hall, came that conversation with the curate which we have narrated, and which made our young friend think more and more.

"Is she all this perfection?" he asked himself. "Has she become serious and religious? Does she tend schools, and visit the poor? Is she kind to her mother and brother? Yes, I am sure of that, I have seen her." And walking with his old tutor over his little parish, and going to visit his school, it was with inexpressible delight that Pen found Blanche seated instructing the children, and fancied to himself how patient she must be, how good-natured, how ingenuous, how really simple in her tastes, and unspoiled by the world.

"And do you really like the country?" he asked her, as they walked together.

"I should like never to see that odious city again. O Arthur—that is, Mr.—well, Arthur, then—one's good thoughts grow up in these sweet woods and calm solitudes, like those flowers which won't bloom in London, you know. The gardener comes and changes our balconies once a week. I don't think I shall bear to look London in the face again—its odious, smoky, brazen face! But, heigho!"

"Why that sigh, Blanche?" "Never mind why."

"Yes, I do mind why. Tell me, tell me every thing."

"I wish you hadn't come down;" and a second edition of Mes Soupirs came out.

"You don't want me, Blanche?"

"I don't want you to go away. I don't think this house will be very happy without you, and that's why I wish that you never had come."

Mes Soupirs were here laid aside, and Mes Larmes had begun.

Ah! What answer is given to those in the eyes of a young woman? What is the method employed for drying them? What took place? O ringdoves and roses, O dews and wildflowers, O waving greenwoods and balmy airs of summer! Here were two battered London rakes, taking themselves in for a moment, and fancying that they were in love with each other, like Phillis and Corydon!

When one thinks of country houses and country walks, one wonders that any man is left unmarried.

CHAPTER XXVI

TEMPTATION

Easy and frank-spoken as Pendennis commonly was with Warrington, how came it that Arthur did not inform the friend and depository of all his secrets, of the little circumstances which had taken place at the villa near Tunbridge Wells? He talked about the discovery of his old tutor Smirke, freely enough, and of his wife, and of his Anglo-Norman church, and of his departure from Clapham to Rome; but, when asked about Blanche, his answers were evasive or general; he said she was a good-natured, clever little thing—that, rightly guided, she might make no such bad wife after all; but that he had for the moment no intention of marriage, that his days of romance were over, that he was contented with his present lot, and so forth.

In the mean time there came occasionally to Lamb Court, Temple, pretty little satin envelopes, superscribed in the neatest handwriting, and sealed with one of those admirable ciphers, which, if Warrington had been curious enough to watch his friend's letters, or indeed if the cipher had been decipherable, would have shown George that Mr. Arthur was in correspondence with a young lady whose initials were B. A. To these pretty little compositions Mr. Pen replied in his best and gallantest manner; with jokes, with news of the town, with points of wit, nay, with pretty little verses very likely, in reply to the versicles of the Muse of "Mes Larmes." Blanche we know rhymes with "branch," and "stanch," and "launch," and no doubt a gentleman of Pen's ingenuity would not forego these advantages of position, and would ring the pretty little changes upon these pleasing notes. Indeed we believe that those love-verses of Mr. Pen's, which had such a pleasing success in the "Roseleaves," that charming Annual edited by Lady Violet Lebas, and illustrated by portraits of the female nobility by the famous artist Pinkney, were composed at this period of our hero's life; and were first addressed to Blanche, per post, before they figured in print, cornets as it were to Pinkney's pictorial garland.

"Verses are all very well," the elder Pendennis said, who found Pen scratching down one of these artless effusions at the Club as he was waiting for his dinner; "and letter-writing if mamma allows it, and between such old country friends of course there may be a correspondence, and that sort of thing—but mind, Pen, and don't commit yourself, my boy. For who knows what the doose may happen? The best way is to make your letters safe. I never wrote a letter in all my life that would commit me, and demmy, sir, I have had some experience of women." And the worthy gentleman, growing more garrulous and confidential with his nephew as he grew older, told many affecting instances of the evil results consequent upon this want of caution to many persons in "society;"—how from using too ardent expressions in some poetical notes to the widow Naylor, young Spoony had subjected himself to a visit of remonstrance from the widow's brother, Colonel Flint; and thus had been forced into a marriage with a woman old enough to be his mother: how when Louisa Salter had at length succeeded in securing young Sir John Bird, Hopwood, of the Blues, produced some letters which Miss S. had written to him, and caused a withdrawal on Bird's part, who afterward was united to Miss Stickney, of Lyme Regis, &c. The major, if he had not reading, had plenty of observation, and could back his wise saws with a multitude of modern instances, which he had acquired in a long and careful perusal of the great book of the world.

Pen laughed at the examples, and blushing a little at his uncle's remonstrances, said that he would bear them in mind and be cautious. He blushed, perhaps, because he had borne them in mind; because he was cautious: because in his letters to Miss Blanche he had from instinct or honesty perhaps refrained from any avowals which might compromise him. "Don't you remember the lesson I had, sir, in Lady Mirabel's—Miss Fotheringay's affair? I am not to be caught again, uncle," Arthur said with mock frankness and humility. Old Pendennis congratulated himself and his nephew heartily on the latter's prudence and progress, and was pleased at the position which Arthur was taking as a man of the world.

No doubt, if Warrington had been consulted, his opinion would have been different; and he would have told Pen that the boy's foolish letters were better than the man's adroit compliments and slippery gallantries; that to win the woman he loves, only a knave or a coward advances under cover, with subterfuges, and a retreat secured behind him: but Pen spoke not on this matter to Mr. Warrington, knowing pretty well that he was guilty, and what his friend's verdict would be.

Colonel Altamont had not been for many weeks absent on his foreign tour, Sir Francis Clavering having retired meanwhile into the country pursuant to his agreement with Major Pendennis, when the ills of fate began to fall rather suddenly and heavily upon the sole remaining partner of the little firm of Shepherd's Inn. When Strong, at parting with Altamont, refused the loan proffered by the latter in the fullness of his purse and the generosity of his heart, he made such a sacrifice to conscience and delicacy as caused him many an after-twinge and pang; and he felt—it was not very many hours in his life he had experienced the feeling—that in this juncture of his affairs he had been too delicate and too scrupulous. Why should a fellow in want refuse a kind offer kindly made? Why should a thirsty man decline a pitcher of water from a friendly hand, because it was a little soiled? Strong's conscience smote him for refusing what the other had fairly come by, and generously proffered: and he thought ruefully, now it was too late, that Altamont's cash would have been as well in his pocket as in that of the gambling-house proprietor at Baden or Ems, with whom his Excellency would infallibly leave his Derby winnings. It was whispered among the tradesmen, bill-discounters, and others who had commercial dealings with Captain Strong, that he and the baronet had parted company, and that the captain's "paper" was henceforth of no value. The tradesmen, who had put a wonderful confidence in him hitherto—for who could resist Strong's jolly face and frank and honest demeanor?—now began to pour in their bills with a cowardly mistrust and unanimity. The knocks at the Shepherd's Inn Chambers' door were constant, and tailors, bootmakers, pastrycooks who had furnished dinners, in their own persons, or by the boys their representatives, held levees on Strong's stairs. To these were added one or two persons of a less clamorous but far more sly and dangerous sort—the young clerks of lawyers, namely, who lurked about the Inn, or concerted with Mr. Campion's young man in the chambers hard by, having in their dismal pocketbooks copies of writs to be served on Edward Strong, requiring him to appear on an early day next term before our Sovereign Lady the Queen, and answer to, &c., &c.

From this invasion of creditors, poor Strong, who had not a guinea in his pocket, had, of course, no refuge but that of the Englishman's castle, into which he retired, shutting the outer and inner door upon the enemy, and not quitting his stronghold until after nightfall. Against this outer barrier the foe used to come and knock and curse in vain, while the chevalier peeped at them from behind the little curtain which he had put over the orifice of his letter-box; and had the dismal satisfaction of seeing the faces of furious clerk and fiery dun, as they dashed up against the door and retreated from it. But as they could not be always at his gate, or sleep on his staircase, the enemies of the chevalier sometimes left him free.

Strong, when so pressed by his commercial antagonists, was not quite alone in his defense against them, but had secured for himself an ally or two. His friends were instructed to communicate with him by a system of private signals: and they thus kept the garrison from starving by bringing in necessary supplies, and kept up Strong's heart and prevented him from surrendering, by visiting him and cheering him in his retreat. Two of Ned's most faithful allies were Huxter and Miss Fanny Bolton: when hostile visitors were prowling about the Inn, Fanny's little sisters were taught a particular cry or jödel, which they innocently whooped in the court: when Fanny and Huxter came up to visit Strong, they archly sang this same note at his door; when that barrier was straightway opened, the honest garrison came out smiling, the provisions and the pot of porter were brought in, and, in the society of his faithful friends, the beleaguered one passed a comfortable night. There are some men who could not live under this excitement, but Strong was a brave man, as we have said, who had seen service and never lost heart in peril.

But besides allies, our general had secured for himself, under difficulties, that still more necessary aid—a retreat. It has been mentioned in a former part of this history, how Messrs. Costigan and Bows lived in the house next door to Captain Strong, and that the window of one of their rooms was not very far off the kitchen-window which was situated in the upper story of Strong's chambers. A leaden water-pipe and gutter served for the two; and Strong, looking out from his kitchen one day, saw that he could spring with great ease up to the sill of his neighbor's window, and clamber up the pipe which communicated from one to the other. He had laughingly shown this refuge to his chum, Altamont; and they had agreed that it would be as well not to mention the circumstance to Captain Costigan, whose duns were numerous, and who would be constantly flying down the pipe into their apartments if this way of escape were shown to him.

But now that the evil days were come, Strong made use of the passage, and one afternoon burst in upon Bows and Costigan with his jolly face, and explained that the enemy was in waiting on his staircase, and that he had taken this means of giving them the slip. So while Mr. Marks's aid-de-camps were in waiting in the passage of No. 3, Strong walked down the steps of No. 4, dined at the Albion, went to the play, and returned home at midnight, to the astonishment of Mrs. Bolton and Fanny, who had not seen him quit his chambers and could not conceive how he could have passed the line of sentries.

Strong bore this siege for some weeks with admirable spirit and resolution, and as only such an old and brave soldier would, for the pains and privations which he had to endure were enough to depress any man of ordinary courage; and what vexed and "riled" him (to use his own expression) was the infernal indifference and cowardly ingratitude of Clavering, to whom he wrote letter after letter, which the baronet never acknowledged by a single word, or by the smallest remittance, though a five-pound note, as Strong said, at that time would have been a fortune to him.

But better days were in store for the chevalier, and in the midst of his despondency and perplexities there came to him a most welcome aid, "Yes, if it hadn't been for this good fellow here," said Strong; "for a good fellow you are, Altamont, my boy, and hang me if I don't stand by you as long as I live; I think, Pendennis, it would have been all up with Ned Strong. It was the fifth week of my being kept a prisoner, for I couldn't be always risking my neck across that water-pipe, and taking my walks abroad through poor old Cos's window, and my spirit was quite broken, sir—dammy, quite beat, and I was thinking of putting an end to myself, and should have done it in another week, when who should drop down from heaven but Altamont!"

"Heaven ain't exactly the place, Ned," said Altamont. "I came from Baden-Baden," said he, "and I'd had a deuced lucky month there, that's all."

"Well, sir, he took up Marks's bill, and he paid the other fellows that were upon me, like a man, sir, that he did," said Strong, enthusiastically.

"And I shall be very happy to stand a bottle of claret for this company, and as many more as the company chooses," said Mr. Altamont, with a blush. "Hallo! waiter, bring us a magnum of the right sort, do you hear? And we'll drink our healths all round, sir—and may every good fellow like Strong find another good fellow to stand by him at a pinch. That's my sentiment, Mr. Pendennis, though I don't like your name." "No! And why?" asked Arthur.

Strong pressed the colonel's foot under the table here; and Altamont, rather excited, filled up another bumper, nodded to Pen, drank off his wine, and said, "He was a gentleman, and that was sufficient, and they were all gentlemen."

The meeting between these "all gentlemen" took place at Richmond, whither Pendennis had gone to dinner, and where he found the chevalier and his friend at table in the coffee-room. Both of the latter were exceedingly hilarious, talkative, and excited by wine; and Strong, who was an admirable story-teller, told the story of his own siege, and adventures, and escapes with great liveliness and humor, and described the talk of the sheriff's officers at his door, the pretty little signals of Fanny, the grotesque exclamations of Costigan when the chevalier burst in at his window, and his final rescue by Altamont, in a most graphic manner, and so as greatly to interest his hearers.

"As for me, it's nothing," Altamont said. "When a ship's paid off, a chap spends his money, you know. And it's the fellers at the black and red at Baden-Baden that did it. I won a good bit of money there, and intend to win a good bit more, don't I, Strong? I'm going to take him with me. I've got a system. I'll make his fortune, I tell you. I'll make your fortune, if you like—dammy, every body's fortune. But what I'll do, and no mistake, boys, I promise you. I'll put in for that little Fanny. Dammy, sir, what do you think she did? She had two pound, and I'm blest if she didn't go and lend it to Ned Strong! Didn't she, Ned? Let's drink her health."

"With all my heart," said Arthur, and pledged this toast with the greatest cordiality.

Mr. Altamont then began, with the greatest volubility, and at great length, to describe his system. He said that it was infallible, if played with coolness; that he had it from a chap at Baden, who had lost by it, it was true, but because he had not capital enough; if he could have stood one more turn of the wheel, he would have all his money back; that he and several more chaps were going to make a bank, and try it; and that he would put every shilling he was worth into it, and had come back to this country for the express purpose of fetching away his money, and Captain Strong; that Strong should play for him; that he could trust Strong and his temper much better than he could his own, and much better than Bloundell-Bloundell or the Italian that "stood in." As he emptied his bottle, the colonel described at full length all his plans and prospects to Pen, who was interested in listening to his story, and the confessions of his daring and lawless good-humor.

"I met that queer fellow Altamont the other day," Pen said to his uncle, a day or two afterward.

"Altamont? What Altamont? There's Lord Westport's son," said the major.

"No, no; the fellow who came tipsy into Clavering's dining-room one day when we were there," said the nephew, laughing; "and he said he did not like the name of Pendennis, though he did me the honor to think that I was a good fellow."

"I don't know any man of the name of Altamont, I give you my honor," said the impenetrable major; "and as for your acquaintance, I think the less you have to do with him the better, Arthur."

Arthur laughed again. "He is going to quit the country, and make his fortune by a gambling system. He and my amiable college acquaintance, Bloundell, are partners, and the colonel takes out Strong with him as aid-de-camp. What is it that binds the chevalier and Clavering, I wonder?"

"I should think, mind you, Pen, I should think, but of course I have only the idea, that there has been something in Clavering's previous life which gives these fellows, and some others, a certain power over him; and if there should be such a secret, which is no affair of ours, my boy, dammy, I say, it ought to be a lesson to a man to keep himself straight in life, and not to give any man a chance over him."

"Why, I think you have some means of persuasion over Clavering, uncle, or why should he give me that seat in Parliament?"

"Clavering thinks he ain't fit for Parliament!" the major answered. "No more he is. What's to prevent him from putting you or any body else into his place if he likes? Do you think that the Government or the Opposition would make any bones about accepting the seat if he offered it to them? Why should you be more squeamish than the first men, and the most honorable men, and men of the highest birth and position in the country, begad?" The major had an answer of this kind to most of Pen's objections, and Pen accepted his uncle's replies, not so much because he believed them, but because he wished to believe them. We do a thing—which of us has not? not because "every body does it," but because we like it; and our acquiescence, alas! proves not that every body is right, but that we and the rest of the world are poor creatures alike.

At his next visit to Tunbridge, Mr. Pen did not forget to amuse Miss Blanche with the history which he had learned at Richmond of the chevalier's imprisonment, and of Altamont's gallant rescue. And after he had told his tale in his usual satirical way, he mentioned with praise and emotion little Fanny's generous behavior to the chevalier, and Altamont's enthusiasm in her behalf.

Miss Blanche was somewhat jealous, and a good deal piqued and curious about Fanny. Among the many confidential little communications which Arthur made to Miss Amory in the course of their delightful rural drives and their sweet evening walks, it may be supposed that our hero would not forget a story so interesting to himself and so likely to be interesting to her, as that of the passion and care of the poor little Ariadne of Shepherd's Inn. His own part in that drama he described, to do him justice, with becoming modesty; the moral which he wished to draw from the tale being one in accordance with his usual satirical mood, viz., that women get over their first loves quite as easily as men do (for the fair Blanche, in their intimes conversations, did not cease to twit Mr. Pen about his notorious failure in his own virgin attachment to the Fotheringay), and, number one being withdrawn, transfer themselves to number two without much difficulty. And poor little Fanny was offered up in sacrifice as an instance to prove this theory. What griefs she had endured and surmounted, what bitter pangs of hopeless attachment she had gone through, what time it had taken to heal those wounds of the tender little bleeding heart, Mr. Pen did not know, or perhaps did not choose to know; for he was at once modest and doubtful about his capabilities as a conqueror of hearts, and averse to believe that he had executed any dangerous ravages on that particular one, though his own instance and argument told against himself in this case; for if, as he said, Miss Fanny was by this time in love with her surgical adorer, who had neither good looks, nor good manners, nor wit, nor any thing but ardor and fidelity to recommend him, must she not in her first sickness of the love-complaint, have had a serious attack, and suffered keenly for a man, who had certainly a number of the showy qualities which Mr. Huxter wanted?

"You wicked, odious creature," Miss Blanche said, "I believe that you are enraged with Fanny for being so impudent as to forget you, and that you are actually jealous of Mr. Huxter." Perhaps Miss Amory was right, as the blush which came in spite of himself and tingled upon Pendennis's cheek (one of those blows with which a man's vanity is constantly slapping his face), proved to Pen that he was angry to think he had been superseded by such a rival. By such a fellow as that! without any conceivable good quality! Oh, Mr. Pendennis! (although this remark does not apply to such a smart fellow as you) if Nature had not made that provision for each sex in the credulity of the other, which sees good qualities where none exist, good looks in donkeys' ears, wit in their numskulls, and music in their bray, there would not have been near so much marrying and giving in marriage as now obtains, and as is necessary for the due propagation and continuance of the noble race to which we belong!

"Jealous or not," Pen said, "and, Blanche, I don't say no, I should have liked Fanny to have come to a better end than that. I don't like histories that end in that cynical way; and when we arrive at the conclusion of the story of a pretty girl's passion, to find such a figure as Huxter's at the last page of the tale. Is all life a compromise, my lady fair, and the end of the battle of love an ignoble surrender? Is the search for the Cupid which my poor little Psyche pursued in the darkness—the god of her soul's longing—the God of the blooming cheek and rainbow pinions—to result in Huxter, smelling of tobacco and gallypots? I wish, though I don't see it in life, that people could be like Jenny and Jessamy, or my lord and lady Clementina in the storybook and fashionable novels, and at once under the ceremony, and, as it were, at the parson's benediction, become perfectly handsome and good and happy ever after."

"And don't you intend to be good and happy, pray, Monsieur le Misanthrope—and are you very discontented with your lot—and will your marriage be a compromise "—(asked the author of "Mes Larmes," with a charming moue)—"and is your Psyche an odious vulgar wretch? You wicked, satirical creature, I can't abide you! You take the hearts of young things, play with them, and fling them away with scorn. You ask for love and trample on it. You—you make me cry, that you do, Arthur, and—and don't—and I won't be consoled in that way—and I think Fanny was quite right in leaving such a heartless creature."

"Again, I don't say no," said Pen, looking very gloomily at Blanche, and not offering by any means to repeat the attempt at consolation, which had elicited that sweet monosyllable "don't" from the young lady. "I don't think I have much of what people call heart; but I don't profess it. I made my venture when I was eighteen, and lighted my lamp and went in search of Cupid. And what was my discovery of love!— a vulgar dancing woman. I failed, as every body does, almost every body; only it is luckier to fail before marriage than after."

"Merci du choix, Monsieur" said the Sylphide, making a courtesy.

"Look, my little Blanche," said Pen, taking her hand, and with his voice of sad good-humor; "at least I stoop to no flatteries."

"Quite the contrary," said Miss Blanche.

"And tell you no foolish lies, as vulgar men do. Why should you and I, with our experience, ape romance and dissemble passion? I do not believe Miss Blanche Amory to be peerless among the beautiful, nor the greatest poetess, nor the most surpassing musician, any more than I believe you to be the tallest woman in the whole world—like the giantess whose picture we saw as we rode through the fair yesterday. But if I don't set you up as a heroine, neither do I offer you your very humble servant as a hero. But I think you are—well, there, I think you are very sufficiently good-looking."

"Merci," Miss Blanche said, with another courtesy.

"I think you sing charmingly. I'm sure you're clever. I hope and believe that you are good-natured, and that you will be companionable."

"And so, provided I bring you a certain sum of money and a seat in Parliament, you condescend to fling to me your royal pocket-handkerchief," said Blanche. "Que dhonneur! We used to call your Highness the Prince of Fairoaks. What an honor to think that I am to be elevated to the throne, and to bring the seat in Parliament as backsheesh to the sultan! I am glad I am clever, and that I can play and sing to your liking; my songs will amuse my lord's leisure."

"And if thieves are about the house," said Pen, grimly pursuing the simile, "forty besetting thieves in the shape of lurking cares and enemies in ambush and passions in arms, my Morgiana will dance round me with a tambourine, and kill all my rogues and thieves with a smile. Won't she?" But Pen looked as if he did not believe that she would. "Ah, Blanche," he continued after a pause, "don't be angry; don't be hurt at my truth-telling. Don't you see that I always take you at your word? You say you will be a slave and dance—I say, dance. You say, 'I take you with what you bring;' I say, 'I take you with what you bring.' To the necessary deceits and hypocrisies of our life, why add any that are useless and unnecessary? If I offer myself to you because I think we have a fair chance of being happy together, and because by your help I may get for both of us a good place and a not undistinguished name, why ask me to feign raptures and counterfeit romance, in which neither of us believe? Do you want me to come wooing in a Prince Prettyman's dress from the masquerade warehouse, and to pay you compliments like Sir Charles Grandison? Do you want me to make you verses as in the days when we were—when we were children?

I will if you like, and sell them to Bacon and Bungay afterward. Shall I feed my pretty princess with bonbons."

"Mais j'adore les bonbons, moi," said the little Sylphide, with a queer, piteous look.

"I can buy a hatful at Fortnum and Mason's for a guinea. And it shall have its bonbons, its pootty little sugar-plums, that it shall," Pen said, with a bitter smile. "Nay, my dear, nay my dearest little Blanche, don't cry. Dry the pretty eyes, I can't bear that;" and he proceeded to offer that consolation which the circumstance required, and which the tears, the genuine tears of vexation, which now sprang from the angry eyes of the author of "Mes Larmes" demanded.

The scornful and sarcastic tone of Pendennis quite frightened and overcame the girl. "I—I don't want your consolation. I—I never was—so—spoken to bef—by any of my—my—by any body"—she sobbed out, with much simplicity.

"Any body!" shouted out Pen, with a savage burst of laughter, and Blanche blushed one of the most genuine blushes which her cheek had ever exhibited, and she cried out, "O, Arthur, vous êtes un homme terrible!" She felt bewildered, frightened, oppressed, the worldly little flirt who had been playing at love for the last dozen years of her life, and yet not displeased at meeting a master.

"Tell me, Arthur," she said, after a pause in this strange love-making. "Why does Sir Francis Clavering give up his seat in Parliament?"

"Au fait, why does he give it to me?" asked Arthur, now blushing in his turn.

"You always mock me, sir," she said. "If it is good to be in Parliament, why does Sir Francis go out?"

"My uncle has talked him over. He always said that you were not sufficiently provided for. In the—the family disputes, when your mamma paid his debts so liberally, it was stipulated, I suppose, that you— that is, that I—that is, upon my word, I don't know why he goes out of Parliament," Pen said, with rather a forced laugh. "You see, Blanche, that you and I are two good little children, and that this marriage has been arranged for us by our mammas and uncles, and that we must be obedient, like a good little boy and girl."

So, when Pen went to London, he sent Blanche a box of bonbons, each sugar plum of which was wrapped up in ready-made French verses, of the most tender kind; and, besides, dispatched to her some poems of his own manufacture, quite as artless and authentic; and it was no wonder that he did not tell Warrington what his conversations with Miss Amory had been, of so delicate a sentiment were they, and of a nature so necessarily private.

And if, like many a worse and better man, Arthur Pendennis, the widow's son, was meditating an apostasy, and going to sell himself to—we all know whom—at least the renegade did not pretend to be a believer in the creed to which he was ready to swear. And if every woman and man in this kingdom, who has sold her or himself for money or position, as Mr. Pendennis was about to do, would but purchase a copy of his memoirs, what tons of volumes the Publishers would sell!

CHAPTER XXVII

IN WHICH PEN BEGINS HIS CANVASS.

Melancholy as the great house at Clavering Park had been in the days before his marriage, when its bankrupt proprietor was a refugee in foreign lands, it was not much more cheerful now when Sir Francis Clavering came to inhabit it. The greater part of the mansion was shut up, and the baronet only occupied a few of the rooms on the ground floor, where his housekeeper and her assistant from the lodge gate waited upon the luckless gentleman in his forced retreat, and cooked a part of the game which he spent the dreary mornings in shooting. Lightfoot, his man, had passed over to my lady's service; and, as Pen was informed in a letter from Mr. Smirke, who performed the ceremony, had executed his prudent intention of marrying Mrs. Bonner, my lady's woman, who, in her mature years, was stricken with the charms of the youth, and endowed him with her savings and her mature person. To be landlord and landlady of the Clavering Arms was the ambition of both of them; and it was agreed that they were to remain in Lady Clavering's service until quarter-day arrived, when they were to take possession of their hotel. Pen graciously promised that he would give his election dinner there, when the baronet should vacate his seat in the young man's favor; and, as it had been agreed by his uncle, to whom Clavering seemed to be able to refuse nothing, Arthur came down in September on a visit to Clavering Park, the owner of which was very glad to have a companion who would relieve his loneliness, and perhaps would lend him a little ready money.

Pen furnished his host with the desirable supplies a couple of days after he had made his appearance at Clavering: and no sooner were these small funds in Sir Francis's pocket, than the latter found he had business at Chatteris and at the neighboring watering-places, of which——shire boasts many, and went off to see to his affairs, which were transacted, as might be supposed, at the county race-grounds and billiard-rooms. Arthur could live alone well enough, having many mental resources and amusements which did not require other persons' company: he could walk with the game-keeper of a morning, and for the evenings there was a plenty of books and occupation for a literary genius like Mr. Arthur, and who required but a cigar and a sheet of paper or two to make the night pass away pleasantly. In truth, in two or three days he had found the society of Sir Francis Clavering perfectly intolerable; and it was with a mischievous eagerness and satisfaction that he offered Clavering the little pecuniary aid which the latter according to his custom solicited; and supplied him with the means of taking flight from his own house.

Besides, our ingenious friend had to ingratiate himself with the townspeople of Clavering, and with the voters of the borough which he hoped to represent; and he set himself to this task with only the more eagerness, remembering how unpopular he had before been in Clavering, and determined to vanquish the odium which he had inspired among the simple people there. His sense of humor made him delight in this task. Naturally rather reserved and silent in public, he became on a sudden as frank, easy, and jovial, as Captain Strong. He laughed with every body who would exchange a laugh with him, shook hands right and left, with what may be certainly called a dexterous cordiality; made his appearance at the market-day and the farmers' ordinary; and, in fine, acted like a consummate hypocrite, and as gentlemen of the highest birth and most spotless integrity act when they wish to make themselves agreeable to their constituents, and have some end to gain of the country folks. How is it that we allow ourselves not to be deceived, but to be ingratiated so readily by a glib tongue, a ready laugh, and a frank manner? We know, for the most part, that it is false coin, and we take it: we know that it is flattery, which it costs nothing to distribute to every body, and we had rather have it than be without it. Friend

Pen went about at Clavering, laboriously simple and adroitly pleased, and quite a different being from the scornful and rather sulky young dandy whom the inhabitants remembered ten years ago.

The Rectory was shut up. Doctor Portman was gone, with his gout and his family, to Harrowgate—an event which Pen deplored very much in a letter to the doctor, in which, in a few kind and simple words, he expressed his regret at not seeing his old friend, whose advice he wanted and whose aid he might require some day: but Pen consoled himself for the doctor's absence by making acquaintance with Mr. Simcoe, the opposition preacher, and with the two partners of the cloth-factory at Chatteris, and with the Independent preacher there, all of whom he met at the Clavering Athenaeum, which the Liberal party had set up in accordance with the advanced spirit of the age, and perhaps in opposition to the aristocratic old reading-room, into which the Edinburgh Review had once scarcely got an admission, and where no tradesmen were allowed an entrance He propitiated the younger partner of the cloth-factory, by asking him to dine in a friendly way at the Park; he complimented the Honorable Mrs. Simcoe with hares and partridges from the same quarter, and a request to read her husband's last sermon; and being a little unwell one day, the rascal took advantage of the circumstance to show his tongue to Mr. Huxter, who sent him medicines and called the next morning. How delighted old Pendennis would have been with his pupil! Pen himself was amused with the sport in which he was engaged, and his success inspired him with a wicked good-humor.

And yet, as he walked out of Clavering of a night, after "presiding" at a meeting of the Athenaeum, or working through an evening with Mrs. Simcoe, who, with her husband, was awed by the young Londoner's reputation, and had heard of his social successes; as he passed over the old familiar bridge of the rushing Brawl, and heard that well-remembered sound of waters beneath, and saw his own cottage of Fairoaks among the trees, their darkling outlines clear against the starlit sky, different thoughts no doubt came to the young man's mind, and awakened pangs of grief and shame there. There still used to be a light in the windows of the room which he remembered so well, and in which the saint who loved him had passed so many hours of care and yearning and prayer. He turned away his gaze from the faint light which seemed to pursue him with its wan reproachful gaze, as though it was his mother's spirit watching and warning. How clear the night was! How keen the stars shone; how ceaseless the rush of the flowing waters; the old home trees whispered, and waved gently their dark heads and branches over the cottage roof. Yonder, in the faint starlight glimmer, was the terrace where, as a boy, he walked of summer evenings, ardent and trustful, unspotted, untried, ignorant of doubts or passions; sheltered as yet from the world's contamination in the pure and anxious bosom of love.... The clock of the near town tolling midnight, with a clang disturbs our wanderer's reverie, and sends him onward toward his night's resting-place, through the lodge into Clavering avenue, and under the dark arcades of the rustling limes.

When he sees the cottage the next time, it is smiling in sunset; those bedroom windows are open where the light was burning the night before; and Pen's tenant, Captain Stokes, of the Bombay Artillery, (whose mother, old Mrs. Stokes, lives in Clavering), receives his landlord's visit with great cordiality: shows him over the grounds and the new pond he has made in the back-garden from the stables; talks to him confidentially about the roof and chimneys, and begs Mr. Pendennis to name a day when he will do himself and Mrs. Stokes the pleasure to, &c. Pen, who has been a fortnight in the country, excuses himself for not having called sooner upon the captain by frankly owning that he had not the heart to do it. "I understand you, sir," the captain says; and Mrs. Stokes who had slipped away at the ring of the bell (how odd it seemed to Pen to ring the bell!) comes down in her best gown, surrounded by her children. The young ones clamber about Stokes: the boy jumps into an arm-chair. It was Pen's father's arm-chair; and Arthur remembers the days when he would as soon have thought of mounting the king's throne as of seating himself in that arm-chair. He asks if Miss Stokes—she is the very image of her mamma—if she can play? He should like to hear a tune on that piano. She plays. He hears the notes of the old piano once more, enfeebled by age, but he does not listen to the player. He is listening to Laura singing as in the days of their youth, and sees his mother bending and beating time over the shoulder of the girl.

The dinner at Fairoaks given in Pen's honor by his tenant, and at which old Mrs. Stokes, Captain Glanders, Squire Hobnell, and the clergyman and his lady, from Tinckleton, were present, was very stupid and melancholy for Pen, until the waiter from Clavering (who aided the captain's stable-boy and Mrs. Stokes's butler) whom Pen remembered as a street boy, and who was now indeed barber in that place, dropped a plate over Pen's shoulder, on which Mr. Hobnell (who also employed him) remarked, "I suppose, Hodson, your hands are slippery with bear's-grease. He's always dropping the crockery about, that Hodson is—haw, haw!" On which Hodson blushed, and looked so disconcerted, that Pen burst out laughing; and good humor and hilarity were the order of the evening. For the second course there was a hare and partridges top and bottom, and when after the withdrawal of the servants, Pen said to the Vicar of Tinckleton, "I think, Mr. Stooks, you should have asked Hodson to cut the hare," the joke was taken instantly by the clergyman, who was followed in the course of a few minutes by Captains Stokes and Glanders, and by Mr. Hobnell, who arrived rather late, but with an immense guffaw.

While Mr. Pen was engaged in the country in the above schemes, it happened that the lady of his choice, if not of his affections, came up to London from the Tunbridge villa, bound upon shopping expeditions or important business, and in company of old Mrs. Bonner, her mother's maid, who had lived and quarreled with Blanche many times since she was an infant, and who now being about to quit Lady Clavering's service for the hymeneal state, was anxious like a good soul to bestow some token of respectful kindness upon her old and young mistress before she quitted them altogether, to take her post as the wife of Lightfoot, and landlady of the Clavering Arms.

The honest woman took the benefit of Miss Amory's taste to make the purchase which she intended to offer her ladyship; and requested the fair Blanche to choose something for herself that should be to her liking, and remind her of her old nurse who had attended her through many a wakeful night, and eventful teething, and childish fever, and who loved her like a child of her own a'most. These purchases were made, and as the nurse insisted on buying an immense Bible for Blanche, the young lady suggested that Bonner should purchase a large Johnson's Dictionary for her mamma. Each of the two women might certainly profit by the present made to her.

Then Mrs. Bonner invested money in some bargains in linendrapery, which might be useful at the Clavering Arms, and bought a red and yellow neck-handkerchief, which Blanche could see at once was intended for Mr. Lightfoot. Younger than herself by at least five-and-twenty years, Mrs. Bonner regarded that youth with a fondness at once parental and conjugal, and loved to lavish ornaments on his person, which already glittered with pins, rings, shirt-studs, and chains and seals, purchased at the good creature's expense.

It was in the Strand that Mrs. Bonner made her purchases, aided by Miss Blanche, who liked the fun very well, and when the old lady had bought every thing that she desired, and was leaving the shop, Blanche, with a smiling face, and a sweet bow to one of the shop, said, "Pray, sir, will you have the kindness to show us the way to Shepherd's Inn."

Shepherd's Inn was but a few score of yards off, Old Castle Street was close by, the elegant young shopman pointed out the turning which the young lady was to take, and she and her companion walked off together. "Shepherd's Inn! what can you want in Shepherd's Inn, Miss Blanche?" Bonner inquired. "Mr. Strong lives there. Do you want to go and see the captain?"

"I should like to see the captain very well. I like the captain; but it is not him I want. I want to see a dear little good girl, who was very kind to—to Mr. Arthur when he was so ill last year, and saved his life almost; and I want to thank her, and ask her if she would like any thing. I looked out several of my dresses on purpose this morning, Bonner!" and she looked at Bonner as if she had a right to admiration, and had performed an act of remarkable virtue. Blanche, indeed, was very fond of sugar-plums; she would have fed the poor upon them, when she had had enough, and given a country girl a ball dress when she had worn it and was tired of it.

"Pretty girl, pretty young woman!" mumbled Mrs. Bonner. "I know I want no pretty young women come about Lightfoot," and in imagination she peopled the Clavering Arms with a Harem of the most hideous chambermaids and barmaids.

Blanche, with pink and blue, and feathers, and flowers, and trinkets (that wondrous invention, a châtelaine, was not extant yet, or she would have had one, we may be sure), and a shot silk dress, and a wonderful mantle, and a charming parasol, presented a vision of elegance and beauty such as bewildered the eyes of Mrs. Bolton, who was scrubbing the lodge-floor of Shepherd's Inn, and caused Betsy-Jane, and Ameliar-Ann to look with delight.

Blanche looked on them with a smile of ineffable sweetness and protection; like Rowena going to see Ivanhoe; like Marie Antoinette visiting the poor in the famine; like the Marchioness of Carabas alighting from her carriage and four at a pauper-tenant's door, and taking from John No. II., the packet of Epsom salts for the invalid's benefit, carrying it with her own imperial hand into the sick room—Blanche felt a queen stepping down from her throne to visit a subject, and enjoyed all the bland consciousness of doing a good action.

"My good woman! I want to see Fanny—Fanny Bolton; is she here?"

Mrs. Bolton had a sudden suspicion, from the splendor of Blanche's appearance, that it must be a play-actor, or something worse.

"What do you want with Fanny, pray?" she asked.

"I am Lady Clavering's daughter—you have heard of Sir Francis Clavering? And I wish very much indeed to see Fanny Bolton."

"Pray step in, Miss—Betsy-Jane, where's Fanny?"

Betsy-Jane said Fanny had gone into No. 3 staircase, on which Mrs. Bolton said she was probably in Strong's rooms, and bade the child go and see if she was there.

"In Captain Strong's rooms! oh, let us go to Captain Strong's rooms," cried out Miss Blanche. "I know him very well. You dearest little girl, show us the way to Captain Strong!" cried out Miss Blanche, for the floor reeked with the recent scrubbing, and the goddess did not like the smell of brown soap. And as they passed up the stairs, a gentleman by the name of Costigan, who happened to be swaggering about the court, and gave a very knowing look with his "oi" under Blanche's bonnet, remarked to himself,

"That's a devilish foine gyurll, bedad, goan up to Sthrong and Altamont: they're always having foine gyurlls up their stairs."

"Halloo—hwhat's that?" he presently said, looking up at the windows: from which some piercing shrieks issued.

At the sound of the voice of a distressed female the intrepid Cos rushed up the stairs as fast as his old legs would carry him, being nearly overthrown by Strong's servant, who was descending the stair. Cos found the outer door of Strong's chambers opened, and began to thunder at the knocker. After many and fierce knocks, the inner door was partially unclosed, and Strong's head appeared.

"It's oi, me boy. Hwhat's that noise, Sthrong?" asked Costigan.

"Go to the d—" was the only answer, and the door was shut on Cos's venerable red nose, and he went down stairs muttering threats at the indignity offered to him, and vowing that he would have satisfaction. In the meanwhile the reader, more lucky than Captain Costigan, will have the privilege of being made acquainted with the secret which was withheld from that officer.

It has been said of how generous a disposition Mr. Altamont was, and when he was well supplied with funds, how liberally he spent them. Of a hospitable turn, he had no greater pleasure than drinking in company with other people; so that there was no man more welcome at Greenwich and Richmond than the Emissary of the Nawaub of Lucknow.

Now it chanced that on the day when Blanche and Mrs. Bonner ascended the staircase to Strong's room in Shepherd's Inn, the colonel had invited Miss Delaval of the——Theatre Royal, and her mother, Mrs. Hodge, to a little party down the river, and it had been agreed that they were to meet at Chambers, and thence walk down to a port in the neighboring Strand to take water. So that when Mrs. Bonner and Mes Larmes came to the door, where Grady, Altamont's servant, was standing, the domestic said, "Walk in, ladies," with the utmost affability, and led them into the room, which was arranged as if they had been expected there. Indeed, two bouquets of flowers, bought at Covent Garden that morning, and instances of the tender gallantry of Altamont, were awaiting his guests upon the table. Blanche smelt at the bouquet, and put her pretty little dainty nose into it, and tripped about the room, and looked behind the curtains, and at the books and prints, and at the plan of Clavering estate hanging up on the wall; and had asked the servant for Captain Strong, and had almost forgotten his existence and the errand about which she had come, namely, to visit Fanny Bolton; so pleased was she with the new adventure, and the odd, strange, delightful, droll little idea of being in a bachelor's chambers in a queer old place in the city!

Grady meanwhile, with a pair of ample varnished boots, had disappeared into his master's room. Blanche had hardly the leisure to remark how big the boots were, and how unlike Mr. Strong's.

"The women's come," said Grady, helping his master to the boots.

"Did you ask 'em if they would take a glass of any thing?" asked Altamont.

Grady came out—"He says, will you take any thing to drink?" the domestic asked of them; at which Blanche, amused with the artless question, broke out into a pretty little laugh, and asked of Mrs. Bonner, "Shall we take any thing to drink?"

"Well, you may take it or lave it," said Mr. Grady, who thought his offer slighted, and did not like the contemptuous manners of the newcomers, and so left them.

"Will we take any thing to drink?" Blanche asked again: and again began to laugh.

"Grady," bawled out a voice from the chamber within:—a voice that made Mrs. Bonner start.

Grady did not answer: his song was heard from afar off, from the kitchen, his upper room, where Grady was singing at his work.

"Grady, my coat!" again roared the voice from within.

"Why, that is not Mr. Strong's voice," said the Sylphide, still half laughing. "Grady my coat!—Bonner, who is Grady my coat? We ought to go away."

Bonner still looked quite puzzled at the sound of the voice which she had heard.

The bedroom door here opened and the individual who had called out "Grady, my coat," appeared without the garment in question.

He nodded to the women, and walked across the room. "I beg your pardon, ladies. Grady, bring my coat down, sir! Well, my dears, it's a fine day, and we'll have a jolly lark at—"

He said no more; for here Mrs. Bonner, who had been looking at him with scared eyes, suddenly shrieked out, "Amory! Amory!" and fell back screaming and fainting in her chair.

The man, so apostrophized, looked at the woman an instant, and, rushing up to Blanche, seized her and kissed her. "Yes, Betsy," he said, "by G—it is me. Mary Bonner knew me. What a fine gal we've grown! But it's a secret, mind. I'm dead, though I'm your father. Your poor mother don't know it. What a pretty gal we've grown! Kiss me—kiss me close, my Betsy! D—it, I love you: I'm your old father."

Betsy or Blanche looked quite bewildered, and began to scream too —once, twice, thrice; and it was her piercing shrieks which Captain Costigan heard as he walked the court below.

At the sound of these shrieks the perplexed parent clasped his hands (his wristbands were open, and on one brawny arm you could see letters tattooed in blue), and, rushing to his apartment, came back with an eau de Cologne bottle from his grand silver dressing-case, with the fragrant contents of which he began liberally to sprinkle Bonner and Blanche.

The screams of these women brought the other occupants of the chamber into the room: Grady from his kitchen, and Strong from his apartment in the upper story. The latter at once saw from the aspect of the two women what had occurred.

"Grady, go and wait in the court," he said, "and if any body comes —you understand me."

"Is it the play-actress and her mother?" said Grady.

"Yes—confound you—say that there's nobody in Chambers, and the party's off for to-day."

"Shall I say that, sir? and after I bought them bokays?" asked Grady of his master.

"Yes," said Amory, with a stamp of his foot; and Strong going to the door, too, reached it just in time to prevent the entrance of Captain Costigan, who had mounted the stair.

The ladies from the theatre did not have their treat to Greenwich, nor did Blanche pay her visit to Fanny Bolton on that day. And Cos, who took occasion majestically to inquire of Grady what the mischief was, and who was crying?—had for answer that 'twas a woman, another of them, and that they were, in Grady's opinion, the cause of 'most all the mischief in the world.

CHAPTER XXVIII

IN WHICH PEN BEGINS TO DOUBT ABOUT HIS ELECTION

While Pen, in his own county, was thus carrying on his selfish plans and parliamentary schemes, news came to him that Lady Rockminster had arrived at Baymouth, and had brought with her our friend Laura. At the announcement that Laura his sister was near him, Pen felt rather guilty. His wish was to stand higher in her esteem, perhaps, than in that of any other person in the world. She was his mother's legacy to him. He was to be her patron and protector in some sort. How would she brave the news which he had to tell her; and how should he explain the plans which he was meditating? He felt as if neither he nor Blanche could bear Laura's dazzling glance of calm scrutiny, and as if he would not dare to disclose his worldly hopes and ambitions to that spotless judge. At her arrival at Baymouth, he wrote a letter thither which contained a great number of fine phrases and protests of affection, and a great deal of easy satire and raillery; in the midst of all which Mr. Pen could not help feeling that he was in a panic, and that he was acting like a rogue and hypocrite.

How was it that a single country-girl should be the object of fear and trembling to such an accomplished gentleman as Mr. Pen? His worldly tactics and diplomacy, his satire and knowledge of the world, could not bear the test of her purity, he felt somehow. And he had to own to himself that his affairs were in such a position, that he could not tell the truth to that honest soul. As he rode from Clavering to Baymouth he felt as guilty as a school-boy, who doesn't know his lesson and is about to face the awful master. For is not truth the master always, and does she not have the power and hold the book?

Under the charge of her kind, though somewhat wayward and absolute, patroness, Lady Rockminster, Laura had seen somewhat of the world in the last year, had gathered some accomplishments, and profited by the lessons of society. Many a girl who had been accustomed to that too great tenderness in which Laura's early life had been passed, would have been unfitted for the changed existence which she now had to lead. Helen worshiped her two children, and thought, as home-bred women will, that all the world was made for them, or to be considered after them. She tended Laura with a watchfulness of affection which never left her. If she had a headache, the widow was as alarmed as if there had never been an aching head before in the world. She slept and woke, read, and moved under her mother's fond superintendence, which was now withdrawn from her, along with the tender creature whose anxious heart would beat no more. And painful moments of grief and depression no doubt Laura had, when she stood in the great careless world alone. Nobody heeded her griefs or her solitude. She was not quite the equal, in social rank, of the lady whose companion she was, or of the friends and relatives of the imperious, but kind old dowager.

Some, very likely, bore her no good-will—some, perhaps, slighted her: it might have been that servants were occasionally rude; their mistress certainly was often. Laura not seldom found herself in family meetings, the confidence and familiarity of which she felt were interrupted by her intrusion; and her sensitiveness of course was wounded at the idea that she should give or feel this annoyance. How many governesses are there in the world, thought cheerful Laura—how many ladies, whose necessities make them slaves and companions by profession! What bad tempers and coarse unkindness have not these to encounter! How infinitely better my lot is with these really kind and affectionate people than that of thousands of unprotected girls! It was with this cordial spirit that our young lady adapted herself to her new position; and went in advance of her fortune with a trustful smile.

Did you ever know a person who met Fortune in that way, whom the goddess did not regard kindly? Are not even bad people won by a constant cheerfulness and a pure and affectionate heart? When the babes in the wood, in the ballad, looked up fondly and trustfully at those notorious rogues whom their uncle had set to make away with the little folks, we all know how one of the rascals relented, and made away with the other—not having the heart to be unkind to so much innocence and beauty. Oh happy they who have that virgin, loving trust and sweet smiling confidence in the world, and fear no evil because they think none! Miss Laura Bell was one of these fortunate persons; and besides the gentle widow's little cross, which, as we have seen, Pen gave her, had such a sparkling and brilliant koh-i-noor in her bosom, as is even more precious than that famous jewel; for it not only fetches a price, and is retained by its owner in another world where diamonds are stated to be of no value, but here, too, is of inestimable worth to its possessor; is a talisman against evil, and lightens up the darkness of life, like Cogia Hassan's famous stone.

So that before Miss Bell had been a year in Lady Rockminster's house, there was not a single person in it whose love she had not won by the use of this talisman. From the old lady to the lowest dependent of her bounty, Laura had secured the good-will and kindness of every body. With a mistress of such a temper, my lady's woman (who had endured her mistress for forty years, and had been clawed and scolded and jibed every day and night in that space of time), could not be expected to have a good temper of her own; and was at first angry against Miss Laura, as she had been against her ladyship's fifteen preceding companions. But when Laura was ill at Paris, this old woman nursed her in spite of her mistress, who was afraid of catching the fever, and absolutely fought for her medicine with Martha from Fairoaks, now advanced to be Miss Laura's own maid. As she was recovering, Grandjean the chef wanted to kill her by the numbers of delicacies which he dressed for her, and wept when she ate her first slice of chicken. The Swiss major-domo of the house celebrated Miss Bell's praises in almost every European language, which he spoke with indifferent incorrectness; the coachman was happy to drive her out; the page cried when he heard she was ill; and Calverley and Coldstream (those two footmen, so large, so calm ordinarily, and so difficult to move), broke out into extraordinary hilarity at the news of her convalescence, and intoxicated the page at a wine shop, to fete Laura's recovery. Even Lady Diana Pynsent (our former acquaintance Mr. Pynsent had married by this time), Lady Diana, who had had a considerable dislike to Laura for some time, was so enthusiastic as to say that she thought Miss Bell was a very agreeable person, and that grandmamma had found a great trouvaille in her. All this good-will and kindness Laura had acquired, not by any arts, not by any flattery, but by the simple force of good-nature, and by the blessed gift of pleasing and being pleased.

On the one or two occasions when he had seen Lady Rockminster, the old lady, who did not admire him, had been very pitiless and abrupt with our young friend, and perhaps Pen expected when he came to Baymouth to find Laura installed in her house in the quality of humble companion, and treated no better than himself. When she heard of his arrival she came running down stairs, and I am not sure that she did not embrace him in the presence of Calverley and Coldstream: not that those gentleman ever told: if the fractus orbis had come to a smash, if Laura, instead of kissing Pen, had taken her scissors and snipped off his head—Calverly and Coldstream would have looked on impavidly, without allowing a grain of powder to be disturbed by the calamity.

Laura had so much improved in health and looks that Pen could not but admire her. The frank and kind eyes which met his, beamed with good health; the cheek which he kissed blushed with beauty. As he looked at her, artless and graceful, pure and candid, he thought he had never seen her so beautiful. Why should he remark her beauty now so much, and remark too to himself that he had not remarked it sooner? He took her fair trustful hand and kissed it fondly: he looked in her bright clear eyes, and read in them that kindling welcome which he was always sure to find there. He was affected and touched by the tender tone and the pure sparkling glance; their innocence smote him somehow and moved him.

"How good you are to me, Laura—sister!" said Pen, "I don't deserve that you should—that you should be so kind to me."

"Mamma left you to me," she said, stooping down and brushing his forehead with her lips hastily. "You know you were to come to me when you were in trouble, or to tell me when you were very happy: that was our compact, Arthur, last year, before we parted. Are you very happy now, or are you in trouble, which is it?" and she looked at him with an arch glance of kindness. "Do you like going into Parliament? Do you intend to distinguish yourself there? How I shall tremble for your first speech!"

"Do you know about the Parliament plan, then?" Pen asked.

"Know?—all the world knows! I have heard it talked about many times. Lady Rockminster's doctor talked about it to-day. I daresay it will be in the Chatteris paper to-morrow. It is all over the county that Sir Francis Clavering, of Clavering, is going to retire, in behalf of Mr. Arthur Pendennis, of Fairoaks; and that the young and beautiful Miss Blanche Amory is—"

"What! that too?" asked Pendennis.

"That, too, dear Arthur. Tout se sait, as somebody would say, whom I intend to be very fond of; and who I am sure is very clever and pretty. I have had a letter from Blanche. The kindest of letters. She speaks so warmly of you, Arthur! I hope—I know she feels what she writes. When is it to be, Arthur? Why did you not tell me? I may come and live with you then, mayn't I?"

"My home is yours, dear Laura, and every thing I have," Pen said. "If I did not tell you, it was because—because—I do not know: nothing is decided as yet. No words have passed between us. But you think Blanche could be happy with me—don't you? Not a romantic fondness, you know. I have no heart, I think; I've told her so: only a sober-sided attachment: and want my wife on one side of the fire and my sister on the other, Parliament in the session and Fairoaks in the holidays, and my Laura never to leave me until somebody who has a right comes to take her away."

Somebody who has a right—somebody with a right! Why did Pen as he looked at the girl and slowly uttered the words, begin to feel angry and jealous of the invisible somebody with the right to take her away? Anxious, but a minute ago, how she would take the news regarding his probable arrangements with Blanche, Pen was hurt somehow that she received the intelligence so easily, and took his happiness for granted.

"Until somebody comes," Laura said, with a laugh, "I will stay at home and be aunt Laura, and take care of the children when Blanche is in the world. I have arranged it all. I am an excellent house-keeper. Do you know I have been to market at Paris with Mrs. Beck, and have taken some lessons from M. Grandjean. And I have had some lessons in Paris in singing too, with the money which you sent me, you kind boy: and I can sing much better now: and I have learned to dance, though not so well as Blanche, and when you become a minister of state, Blanche shall present me:" and with this, and with a provoking good-humor, she performed for him the last Parisian courtesy.

Lady Rockminster came in while this courtesy was being performed, and gave to Arthur one finger to shake; which he took, and over which he bowed as well as he could, which, in truth, was very clumsily.

"So you are going to be married, sir," said the old lady.

"Scold him, Lady Rockminster, for not telling us," Laura said, going away: which, in truth, the old lady began instantly to do. "So you are going to marry, and to go into Parliament in place of that good-for-nothing Sir Francis Clavering. I wanted him to give my grandson his seat—why did he not give my grandson his seat? I hope you are to have a great deal of money with Miss Amory. I wouldn't take her without a great deal."

"Sir Francis Clavering is tired of Parliament," Pen said, wincing, "and—and I rather wish to attempt that career. The rest of the story is at least premature."

"I wonder, when you had Laura at home, you could take up with such an affected little creature as that," the old lady continued.

"I am very sorry Miss Amory does not please your ladyship," said Pen, smiling.

"You mean—that it is no affair of mine, and that I am not going to marry her. Well I'm not, and I'm very glad I am not—a little odious thing—when I think that a man could prefer her to my Laura, I've no patience with him, and so I tell you, Mr. Arthur Pendennis."

"I am very glad you see Laura with such favorable eyes," Pen said.

"You are very glad, and you are very sorry. What does it matter, sir, whether you are very glad or very sorry? A young man who prefers Miss Amory to Miss Bell has no business to be sorry or glad. A young man who takes up with such a crooked lump of affectation as that little Amory—for she is crooked, I tell you she is—after seeing my Laura, has no right to hold up his head again. Where is your friend Bluebeard? The tall young man, I mean—Warrington, isn't his name? Why does he not come down, and marry Laura? What do the young men mean by not marrying such a girl as that? They all marry for money now. You are all selfish and cowards. We ran away with each other and made foolish matches in my time. I have no patience with the young men! When I was at Paris in the winter, I asked all the three attaches at the Embassy why they did not fall in love with Miss Bell? They laughed—they said they wanted money. You are all selfish—you are all cowards."

"I hope before you offered Miss Bell to the attaches," said Pen, with some heat, "you did her the favor to consult her?"

"Miss Bell has only a little money. Miss Bell must marry soon. Somebody must make a match for her, sir; and a girl can't offer herself," said the old dowager, with great state. "Laura, my dear, I've been telling your cousin that all the young men are selfish; and that there is not a pennyworth of romance left among them. He is as bad as the rest."

"Have you been asking Arthur why he won't marry me?" said Laura, with a kindling smile, coming back and taking her cousin's hand. (She had been away, perhaps, to hide some traces of emotion, which she did not wish others to see). "He is going to marry somebody else; and I intend to be very fond of her, and to go and live with them, provided he then does not ask every bachelor who comes to his house, why he does not marry me?"

The terrors of Pen's conscience being thus appeased, and his examination before Laura over without any reproaches on the part of the latter, Pen began to find that his duty and inclination led him constantly to Baymouth, where Lady Rockminster informed him that a place was always reserved for him at her table. "And I recommend you to come often," the old lady said, "for Grandjean is an excellent cook, and to be with Laura and me will do your manners good. It is easy to see that you are always thinking about yourself. Don't blush and stammer—almost all young men are always thinking about themselves. My sons and grandsons always were until I cured them. Come here, and let us teach you to behave properly; you will not have to carve, that is done at the side-table. Hecker will give you as much wine as is good for you; and on days when you are very good and amusing you shall have some Champagne. Hecker, mind what I say, Mr. Pendennis is Miss Laura's brother; and you will make him comfortable, and see that he does not have too much wine, or disturb me while I am taking my nap after dinner. You are selfish; I intend to cure you of being selfish. You will dine here when you have no other engagements; and if it rains you had better put up at the hotel." As long as the good lady could order every body round about her, she was not hard to please; and all the slaves and subjects of her little dowager court trembled before her, but loved her.

She did not receive a very numerous or brilliant society. The doctor, of course, was admitted as a constant and faithful visitor; the vicar and his curate; and on public days the vicar's wife and daughters, and some of the season visitors at Baymouth were received at the old lady's entertainments: but generally the company was a small one, and Mr. Arthur drank his wine by himself, when Lady Rockminster retired to take her doze, and to be played and sung to sleep by Laura after dinner.

"If my music can give her a nap," said the good-natured girl, "ought I not to be very glad that I can do so much good? Lady Rockminster sleeps very little of nights: and I used to read to her until I fell ill at Paris, since when she will not hear of my sitting up."

"Why did you not write to me when you were ill?" asked Pen, with a blush.

"What good could you do me? I had Martha to nurse me; and the doctor every day. You are too busy to write to women or to think about them. You have your books and your newspapers, and your politics and your railroads to occupy you. I wrote when I was well."

And Pen looked at her, and blushed again, as he remembered that, during all the time of her illness, he had never written to her, and had scarcely thought about her.

In consequence of his relationship, Pen was free to walk and ride with his cousin constantly, and in the course of those walks and rides, could appreciate the sweet frankness of her disposition, and the truth, simplicity, and kindliness, of her fair and spotless heart. In their mother's life-time, she had never spoken so openly or so cordially as now. The desire of poor Helen to make an union between her two children, had caused a reserve on Laura's part toward Pen; for which, under the altered circumstances of Arthur's life, there was now no necessity. He was engaged to another woman; and Laura became his sister at once—hiding, or banishing from herself, any doubts which she might have as to his choice; striving to look cheerfully forward, and hope for his prosperity; promising herself to do all that affection might do to make her mother's darling happy.

Their talk was often about the departed mother. And it was from a thousand stories which Laura told him that Arthur was made aware how constant and absorbing that silent maternal devotion had been, which had accompanied him, present and absent, through life, and had only ended with the fond widow's last breath. One day the people in Clavering saw a lad in charge of a couple of horses at the church-yard-gate: and it was told over the place that Pen and Laura had visited Helen's grave together. Since Arthur had come down into the country, he had been there once or twice: but the sight of the sacred stone had brought no consolation to him. A guilty man doing a guilty deed: a mere speculator, content to lay down his faith and honor for a fortune and a worldly career; and owning that his life was but a contemptible surrender—what right had he in the holy place? what booted it to him in the world he lived in, that others were no better than himself? Arthur and Laura rode by the gates of Fairoaks; and he shook hands with his tenant's children, playing on the lawn and the terrace—Laura looked steadily at the cottage wall, at the creeper on the porch and the magnolia growing up to her window. "Mr. Pendennis rode by to-day," one of the boys told his mother, "with a lady, and he stopped and talked to us, and he asked for a bit of honeysuckle off the porch, and gave it the lady. I couldn't see if she was pretty; she had her veil down. She was riding one of Cramp's horses, out of Baymouth."

As they rode over the downs between home and Baymouth, Pen did not speak much, though they rode very close together. He was thinking what a mockery life was, and how men refuse happiness when they may have it; or, having it, kick it down; or barter it, with their eyes open, for a little worthless money or beggarly honor. And then the thought came, what does it matter for the little space? The lives of the best and purest of us are consumed in a vain desire, and end in a disappointment: as the dear soul's who sleeps in her grave yonder. She had her selfish ambition, as much as Caesar had; and died, balked of her life's longing. The stone covers over our hopes and our memories. Our place knows us not. "Other people's children are playing on the grass," he broke out, in a hard voice, "where you and I used to play, Laura. And you see how the magnolia we planted has grown up since our time. I have been round to one or two of the cottages where my mother used to visit. It is scarcely more than a year that she is gone, and the people whom she used to benefit care no more for her death than for Queen Anne's. We are all selfish: the world is selfish: there are but a few exceptions, like you, my dear, to shine like good deeds in a naughty world, and make the blackness more dismal."

"I wish you would not speak in that way, Arthur," said Laura, looking down and bending her head to the honeysuckle on her breast. "When you told the little boy to give me this, you were not selfish."

"A pretty sacrifice I made to get it for you!" said the sneerer.

"But your heart was kind and full of love when you did so. One can not ask for more than love and kindness; and if you think humbly of yourself, Arthur, the love and kindness are not diminished—are they? I often thought our dearest mother spoiled you at home, by worshiping you; and that if you are—I hate the word—what you say, her too great fondness helped to make you so. And as for the world, when men go out into it, I suppose they can not be otherwise than selfish. You have to fight for yourself, and to get on for yourself, and to make a name for yourself. Mamma and your uncle both encouraged you in this ambition. If it is a vain thing, why pursue it? I suppose such a clever man as you intend to do a great deal of good to the country, by going into Parliament, or you would not wish to be there. What are you going to do when you are in the House of Commons?"

"Women don't understand about politics, my dear," Pen said, sneering at himself as he spoke.

"But why don't you make us understand? I could never tell about Mr. Pynsent why he should like to be there so much. He is not a clever man—"

"He certainly is not a genius, Pynsent," said Pen.

"Lady Diana says that he attends Committees all day; that then again he is at the House all night; that he always votes as he is told; that he never speaks; that he will never get on beyond a subordinate place, and as his grandmother tells him, he is choked with red-tape. Are you going to follow the same career, Arthur? What is there in it so brilliant that you should be so eager for it? I would rather that you should stop at home, and write books—good books, kind books, with gentle kind thoughts, such as you have, dear Arthur, and such as might do people good to read. And if you do not win fame, what then? You own it is vanity, and you can live very happily without it. I must not pretend to advise; but I take you at your own word about the world; and as you own it is wicked, and that it tires you, ask you why you don't leave it?"

"And what would you have me do?" asked Arthur.

"I would have you bring your wife to Fairoaks to live there, and study, and do good round about you. I would like to see your own children playing on the lawn, Arthur, and that we might pray in our mother's church again once more, dear brother. If the world is a temptation, are we not told to pray that we may not be led into it?"

"Do you think Blanche would make a good wife for a petty country gentleman? Do you think I should become the character very well, Laura?" Pen asked. "Remember temptation walks about the hedgerows as well as the city streets: and idleness is the greatest tempter of all."

"What does—does Mr. Warrington say?" said Laura, as a blush mounted up to her cheek, and of which Pen saw the fervor, though Laura's veil fell over her face to hide it.

Pen rode on by Laura's side silently for a while. George's name, so mentioned, brought back the past to him, and the thoughts which he had once had regarding George and Laura. Why should the recurrence of the thought agitate him, now that he knew the union was impossible? Why should he be curious to know if, during the months of their intimacy, Laura had felt a regard for Warrington? From that day until the present time George had never alluded to his story, and Arthur remembered now that since then George had scarcely ever mentioned Laura's name.

At last he came close to her. "Tell me something, Laura," he said.

She put back her veil and looked at him. "What is it, Arthur?" she asked—though from the tremor of her voice she guessed very well.

"Tell me—but for George's misfortune—I never knew him speak of it before or since that day—would you—would you have given him—what you refused me?"

"Yes, Pen," she said, bursting into tears.

"He deserved you better than I did," poor Arthur groaned forth, with an indescribable pang at his heart. "I am but a selfish wretch, and George is better, nobler, truer, than I am. God bless him!"

"Yes, Pen," said Laura, reaching out her hand to her cousin, and he put his arm round her, and for a moment she sobbed on his shoulder.

The gentle girl had had her secret, and told it. In the widow's last journey from Fairoaks, when hastening with her mother to Arthur's sick bed, Laura had made a different confession; and it was only when Warrington told his own story, and described the hopeless condition of his life, that she discovered how much her feelings had changed, and with what tender sympathy, with what great respect, delight, and admiration she had grown to regard her cousin's friend. Until she knew that some plans she might have dreamed of were impossible, and that Warrington reading in her heart, perhaps, had told his melancholy story to warn her, she had not asked herself whether it was possible that her affections could change; and had been shocked and scared by the discovery of the truth. How should she have told it to Helen, and confessed her shame? Poor Laura felt guilty before her friend, with the secret which she dared not confide to her; felt as if she had been ungrateful for Helen's love and regard; felt as if she had been wickedly faithless to Pen in withdrawing that love from him which he did not even care to accept; humbled even and repentant before Warrington, lest she should have encouraged him by undue sympathy, or shown the preference which she began to feel.

The catastrophe which broke up Laura's home, and the grief and anguish which she felt for her mother's death, gave her little leisure for thoughts more selfish; and by the time she rallied from that grief the minor was also almost cured. It was but for a moment that she had indulged a hope about Warrington. Her admiration and respect for him remained as strong as ever. But the tender feeling with which she knew she had regarded him, was schooled into such calmness, that it may be said to have been dead and passed away. The pang which it left behind was one of humility and remorse. "O how wicked and proud I was about Arthur," she thought, "how self-confident and unforgiving! I never forgave from my heart this poor girl, who was fond of him, or him for encouraging her love; and I have been more guilty than she, poor, little artless creature! I, professing to love one man, could listen to another only too eagerly; and would not pardon the change of feelings in Arthur, while I myself was changing and unfaithful." And so humiliating herself, and acknowledging her weakness, the poor girl sought for strength and refuge in the manner in which she had been accustomed to look for them.

She had done no wrong: but there are some folks who suffer for a fault ever so trifling as much as others whose stout consciences can walk under crimes of almost any weight; and poor Laura chose to fancy that she had acted in this delicate juncture of her life as a very great criminal. She determined that she had done Pen a great injury by withdrawing that love which, privately in her mother's hearing, she had bestowed upon him; that she had been ungrateful to her dead benefactress by ever allowing herself to think of another or of violating her promise; and that, considering her own enormous crimes, she ought to be very gentle in judging those of others, whose temptations were much greater, very likely; and whose motives she could not understand.

A year back Laura would have been indignant at the idea that Arthur should marry Blanche: and her high spirit would have risen, as she thought that from worldly motives he should stoop to one so unworthy. Now when the news was brought to her of such a chance (the intelligence was given to her by old Lady Rockminster, whose speeches were as direct and rapid as a slap on the face), the humbled girl winced a little at the blow, but bore it meekly, and with a desperate acquiescence. "He has a right to marry, he knows a great deal more of the world than I do," she argued with herself. "Blanche may not be so light-minded as she seemed, and who am I to be her judge? I daresay it is very good that Arthur should go into Parliament and distinguish himself, and my duty is to do every thing that lies in my power to aid him and Blanche, and to make his home happy. I daresay I shall live with them. If I am godmother to one of their children, I will leave her my three thousand pounds!" And forthwith she began to think what she could give Blanche out of her small treasures, and how best to conciliate her affection. She wrote her forthwith a kind letter, in which, of course, no mention was made of the plans in contemplation, but in which Laura recalled old times, and spoke her good-will, and in reply to this she received an eager answer from Blanche: in which not a word about marriage was said, to be sure, but Mr. Pendennis was mentioned two or three times in the letter, and they were to be henceforth, dearest Laura, and dearest Blanche, and loving sisters, and so forth.

When Pen and Laura reached home, after Laura's confession (Pen's noble acknowledgment of his own inferiority, and generous expression of love for Warrington, causing the girl's heart to throb, and rendering doubly keen those tears which she sobbed on his shoulder), a little slim letter was awaiting Miss Bell in the hall, which she trembled rather guiltily as she unsealed, and which Pen blushed as he recognized; for he saw instantly that it was from Blanche.

Laura opened it hastily, and cast her eyes quickly over it, as Pen kept his fixed on her, blushing.

"She dates from London," Laura said. "She has been with old Bonner, Lady Clavering's maid. Bonner is going to marry Lightfoot the butler. Where do you think Blanche has been?" she cried out eagerly.

"To Paris, to Scotland, to the Casino?"

"To Shepherd's Inn, to see Fanny; but Fanny wasn't there, and Blanche is going to leave a present for her. Isn't it kind of her and thoughtful?" And she handed the letter to Pen who read—

"'I saw Madame Mère who was scrubbing the room, and looked at me with very scrubby looks; but la belle Fanny was not au logis; and as I heard that she was in Captain Strong's apartments, Bonner and I mounted au troisième to see this famous beauty. Another disappointment—only the Chevalier Strong and a friend of his in the room: so we came away, after all, without seeing the enchanting Fanny.

"'Je t'envoie mille et mille baisers. When will that horrid canvassing be over? Sleeves are worn, &c. &c. &c.'"

After dinner the doctor was reading the Times, "A young gentleman I attended when he was here some eight or nine years ago, has come into a fine fortune," the doctor said. "I see here announced the death of John Henry Foker, Esq., of Logwood Hall, at Pau, in the Pyrenees, on the 15th ult."

CHAPTER XXIX

IN WHICH THE MAJOR IS BIDDEN TO STAND AND DELIVER

Any gentleman who has frequented the Wheel of Fortune public-house, where it may be remembered that Mr. James Morgan's Club was held, and where Sir Francis Clavering had an interview with Major Pendennis, is aware that there are three rooms for guests upon the ground floor, besides the bar where the landlady sits. One is a parlor frequented by the public at large; to another room gentlemen in livery resort; and the third apartment, on the door of which "Private" is painted, is that hired by the Club of "The Confidentials," of which Messrs. Morgan and Lightfoot were members.

The noiseless Morgan had listened to the conversation between Strong and Major Pendennis at the latter's own lodgings, and had carried away from it matter for much private speculation; and a desire of knowledge had led him to follow his master when the major came to the Wheel of Fortune, and to take his place quietly in the confidential room, while Pendennis and Clavering had their discourse in the parlor. There was a particular corner in the confidential room from which you could hear almost all that passed in the next apartment; and as the conversation between the two gentlemen there was rather angry, and carried on in a high key, Morgan had the benefit of overhearing almost the whole of it: and what he heard, strengthened the conclusions which his mind had previously formed.

"He knew Altamont at once, did he, when he saw him in Sidney? Clavering ain't no more married to my lady than I am! Altamont's the man: Altamont's a convick; young Harthur comes into Parlyment, and the Gov'nor promises not to split. By Jove, what a sly old rogue it is, that old Gov'nor! No wonder he's anxious to make the match between Blanche and Harthur; why, she'll have a hundred thousand if she's a penny, and bring her man a seat in Parlyment into the bargain." Nobody saw, but a physiognomist would have liked to behold, the expression of Mr. Morgan's countenance, when this astounding intelligence was made clear to him. "But for my hage, and the confounded prejudices of society," he said, surveying himself in the glass, "dammy, James Morgan, you might marry her yourself," But if he could not marry Miss Blanche and her fortune, Morgan thought he could mend his own by the possession of this information, and that it might be productive of benefit to him from very many sources. Of all the persons whom the secret affected, the greater number would not like to have it known. For instance, Sir Francis Clavering, whose fortune it involved, would wish to keep it quiet; Colonel Altamont, whose neck it implicated, would naturally be desirous to hush it; and that young hupstart beast, Mr. Harthur, who was for gettin' into Parlyment on the strenth of it, and was as proud as if he was a duke with half a million a year (such, we grieve to say, was Morgan's opinion of his employer's nephew), would pay any think sooner than let the world know that he was married to a convick's daughter, and had got his seat in Parlyment by trafficking with this secret. As for Lady C., Morgan thought, if she's tired of Clavering, and wants to get rid of him, she'll pay: if she's frightened about her son, and fond of the little beggar, she'll pay all the same: and Miss Blanche will certainly come down handsome to the man who will put her into her rights, which she was unjustly defrauded of them, and no mistake. "Dammy," concluded the valet, reflecting upon this wonderful hand which luck had given him to play, "with such cards as these, James Morgan, you are a made man. It may be a reg'lar enewity to me. Every one of 'em must susscribe. And with what I've made already, I may cut business, give my old Gov'nor warning, turn gentleman, and have a servant of my own, begad." Entertaining himself with calculations such as these, that were not a little likely to perturb a man's spirit, Mr. Morgan showed a very great degree of self-command by appearing and being calm, and by not allowing his future prospects in any way to interfere with his present duties.

One of the persons whom the story chiefly concerned, Colonel Altamont, was absent from London, when Morgan was thus made acquainted with his history. The valet knew of Sir Francis Clavering's Shepherd's Inn haunt, and walked thither an hour or two after the baronet and Pendennis had had their conversation together. But that bird was flown; Colonel Altamont had received his Derby winnings and was gone to the Continent. The fact of his absence was exceedingly vexatious to Mr. Morgan. "He'll drop all that money at the gambling-shops on the Rhind," thought Morgan, "and I might have had a good bit of it. It's confounded annoying to think he's gone and couldn't have waited a few days longer." Hope, triumphant or deferred, ambition or disappointment, victory or patient ambush, Morgan bore all alike, with similar equable countenance. Until the proper day came, the major's boots were varnished and his hair was curled, his early cup of tea was brought to his bedside, his oaths, rebukes, and senile satire borne, with silent, obsequious fidelity. Who would think, to see him waiting upon his master, packing and shouldering his trunks, and occasionally assisting at table, at the country-houses where he might be staying, that Morgan was richer than his employer, and knew his secrets and other people's? In the profession Mr. Morgan was greatly respected and admired, and his reputation for wealth and wisdom got him much renown at most supper-tables: the younger gentlemen voted him stoopid, a feller of no idears, and a fogey, in a word: but not one of them would not say amen to the heartfelt prayer which some of the most serious-minded among the gentlemen uttered, "When I die may I cut up as well as Morgan Pendennis!"

As became a man of fashion, Major Pendennis spent the autumn passing from house to house of such country friends as were at home to receive him, and if the duke happened to be abroad, or the marquis in Scotland, condescending to sojourn with Sir John or the plain squire. To say the truth, the old gentleman's reputation was somewhat on the wane: many of the men of his time had died out, and the occupants of their halls and the present wearers of their titles knew not Major Pendennis: and little cared for his traditions "of the wild Prince and Poyns," and of the heroes of fashion passed away. It must have struck the good man with melancholy as he walked by many a London door, to think how seldom it was now opened for him, and how often he used to knock at it—to what banquets and welcome he used to pass through it—a score of years back. He began to own that he was no longer of the present age, and dimly to apprehend that the young men laughed at him. Such melancholy musings must come across many a Pall Mall philosopher. The men, thinks he, are not such as they used to be in his time: the old grand manner and courtly grace of life are gone: what is Castlewood House and the present Castlewood, compared to the magnificence of the old mansion and owner? The late lord came to London with four post-chaises and sixteen horses: all the North Road hurried out to look at his cavalcade: the people in London streets even stopped as his procession passed them. The present lord travels with five bagmen in a railway carriage, and sneaks away from the station, smoking a cigar in a brougham. The late lord in autumn filled Castlewood with company, who drank claret till midnight: the present man buries himself in a hut on a Scotch mountain, and passes November in two or three closets in an entresol at Paris, where his amusements are a dinner at a café and a box at a little theatre. What a contrast there is between his Lady Lorraine, the Regent's Lady Lorraine, and her little ladyship of the present era! He figures to himself the first, beautiful, gorgeous, magnificent in diamonds and velvets, daring in rouge, the wits of the world (the old wits, the old polished gentlemen—not the canaille of to-day with their language of the cab-stand, and their coats smelling of smoke) bowing at her feet; and then thinks of to-day's Lady Lorraine—a little woman in a black silk gown, like a governess, who talks astronomy, and laboring classes, and emigration, and the deuce knows what, and lurks to church at eight o'clock in the morning. Abbots-Lorraine, that used to be the noblest house in the county, is turned into a monastery—a regular La Trappe. They don't drink two glasses of wine after dinner, and every other man at table is a country curate, with a white neckcloth, whose talk is about Polly Higson's progress at school, or widow Watkins's lumbago. "And the other young men, those lounging guardsmen and great lazy dandies—sprawling over sofas and billiard-tables, and stealing off to smoke pipes in each other's bedrooms, caring for nothing, reverencing nothing, not even an old gentleman who has known their fathers and their betters, not even a pretty woman—what a difference there is between these men who poison the very turnips and stubble-fields with their tobacco, and the gentlemen of our time!" thinks the major; "the breed is gone—there's no use for 'em; they're replaced by a parcel of damned cotton-spinners and utilitarians, and young sprigs of parsons with their hair combed down their backs. I'm getting old: they're getting past me: they laugh at us old boys," thought old Pendennis. And he was not far wrong; the times and manners which he admired were pretty nearly gone—the gay young men 'larked' him irreverently, while the serious youth had a grave pity and wonder at him, which would have been even more painful to bear, had the old gentleman been aware of its extent. But he was rather simple: his examination of moral questions had never been very deep; it had never struck him perhaps, until very lately, that he was otherwise than a most respectable and rather fortunate man. Is there no old age but his without reverence? Did youthful folly never jeer at other bald pates? For the past two or three years, he had begun to perceive that his day was well nigh over, and that the men of the new time had begun to reign.

After a rather unsuccessful autumn season, then, during which he was faithfully followed by Mr. Morgan, his nephew Arthur being engaged, as we have seen, at Clavering, it happened that Major Pendennis came back for awhile to London, at the dismal end of October, when the fogs and the lawyers come to town. Who has not looked with interest at those loaded cabs, piled boxes, and crowded children, rattling through the streets on the dun October evenings; stopping at the dark houses, where they discharge nurse and infant, girls, matron, and father, whose holidays are over? Yesterday it was France and sunshine, or Broadstairs and liberty; to-day comes work and a yellow fog; and, ye gods! what a heap of bills there lies in master's study. And the clerk has brought the lawyer's papers from Chambers; and in half an hour the literary man knows that the printer's boy will be in the passage; and Mr. Smith with that little account (that particular little account) has called presentient of your arrival, and has left word that he will call to-morrow morning at ten. Who among us has not said good-by to his holiday; returned to dun London, and his fate; surveyed his labors and liabilities laid out before him, and been aware of that inevitable little account to settle? Smith and his little account, in the morning, symbolize duty, difficulty, struggle, which you will meet, let us hope, friend, with a manly and honest heart. And you think of him, as the children are slumbering once more in their own beds, and the watchful housewife tenderly pretends to sleep.

Old Pendennis had no special labors or bills to encounter on the morrow, as he had no affection at home to soothe him. He had always money in his desk sufficient for his wants; and being by nature and habit tolerably indifferent to the wants of other people, these latter were not likely to disturb him. But a gentleman may be out of temper though he does not owe a shilling: and though he may be ever so selfish, he must occasionally feel dispirited and lonely. He had had two or three twinges of gout in the country-house where he had been staying: the birds were wild and shy, and the walking over the plowed fields had fatigued him deucedly: the young men had laughed at him, and he had been peevish at table once or twice: he had not been able to get his whist of an evening: and, in fine, was glad to come away. In all his dealings with Morgan, his valet, he had been exceedingly sulky and discontented.

He had sworn at him and abused him for many days past. He had scalded his mouth with bad soup at Swindon. He had left his umbrella in the rail-road carriage: at which piece of forgetfulness, he was in such a rage, that he cursed Morgan more freely than ever. Both the chimneys smoked furiously in his lodgings; and when he caused the windows to be flung open, he swore so acrimoniously, that Morgan was inclined to fling him out of window, too, through that opened casement. The valet swore after his master, as Pendennis went down the street on his way to the Club.

Bays's was not at all pleasant. The house had been new painted, and smelt of varnish and turpentine, and a large streak of white paint inflicted itself on the back of the old boy's fur-collared surtout. The dinner was not good: and the three most odious men in all London— old Hawkshaw, whose cough and accompaniments are fit to make any man uncomfortable; old Colonel Gripley, who seizes on all the newspapers; and that irreclaimable old bore Jawkins, who would come and dine at the next table to Pendennis, and describe to him every inn-bill which he had paid in his foreign tour: each and all of these disagreeable personages and incidents had contributed to make Major Pendennis miserable; and the Club waiter trod on his toe as he brought him his coffee. Never alone appear the Immortals. The Furies always hunt in company: they pursued Pendennis from home to the Club, and from the Club home.

While the major was absent from his lodgings, Morgan had been seated in the landlady's parlor, drinking freely of hot brandy-and-water, and pouring out on Mrs. Brixham some of the abuse which he had received from his master up-stairs. Mrs. Brixham was Morgan's slave. He was his landlady's landlord. He had bought the lease of the house which she rented; he had got her name and her son's to acceptances, and a bill of sale which made him master of the luckless widow's furniture. The young Brixham was a clerk in an insurance office, and Morgan could put him into what he called quod any day. Mrs. Brixham was a clergyman's widow, and Mr. Morgan, after performing his duties on the first floor, had a pleasure in making the old lady fetch him his boot-jack and his slippers. She was his slave. The little black profiles of her son and daughter; the very picture of Tiddlecot church, where she was married, and her poor dear Brixham lived and died, was now Morgan's property, as it hung there over the mantle-piece of his back-parlor. Morgan sate in the widow's back-room, in the ex-curate's old horse-hair study-chair, making Mrs. Brixham bring supper for him, and fill his glass again and again.

The liquor was bought with the poor woman's own coin, and hence Morgan indulged in it only the more freely; and he had eaten his supper and was drinking a third tumbler, when old Pendennis returned from the Club, and went up-stairs to his rooms. Mr. Morgan swore very savagely at him and his bell, when he heard the latter, and finished his tumbler of brandy before he went up to answer the summons.

He received the abuse consequent on this delay in silence, nor did the major condescend to read in the flushed face and glaring eyes of the man, the anger under which he was laboring. The old gentleman's foot-bath was at the fire; his gown and slippers awaiting him there. Morgan knelt down to take his boots off with due subordination: and as the major abused him from above, kept up a growl of maledictions below at his feet. Thus, when Pendennis was crying "Confound you, sir; mind that strap—curse you, don't wrench my foot off," Morgan sotto voce below was expressing a wish to strangle him, drown him, and punch his head off.

The boots removed, it became necessary to divest Mr. Pendennis of his coat: and for this purpose the valet had necessarily to approach very near to his employer; so near that Pendennis could not but perceive what Mr. Morgan's late occupation had been; to which he adverted in that simple and forcible phraseology which men are sometimes in the habit of using to their domestics; informing Morgan that he was a drunken beast, and that he smelt of brandy.

At this the man broke out, losing patience, and flinging up all subordination? "I'm drunk, am I? I'm a beast, am I? I'm d——d, am I? you infernal old miscreant. Shall I wring your old head off, and drownd yer in that pail of water? Do you think I'm a-goin' to bear your confounded old harrogance, you old Wigsby! Chatter your old hivories at me, do you, you grinning old baboon! Come on, if you are a man, and can stand to a man. Ha! you coward, knives, knives!"

"If you advance a step, I'll send it into you," said the major, seizing up a knife that was on the table near him. "Go down stairs, you drunken brute, and leave the house; send for your book and your wages in the morning, and never let me see your insolent face again. This d——d impertinence of yours has been growing for some months past. You have been growing too rich. You are not fit for service. Get out of it, and out of the house."

"And where would you wish me to go, pray, out of the ouse?" asked the man, "and won't it be equal convenient to-morrow mornin'?—tooty-fay mame shose, sivvaplay, munseer?"

"Silence, you beast, and go!" cried out the major.

Morgan began to laugh, with rather a sinister laugh. "Look yere, Pendennis," he said, seating himself; "since I've been in this room you've called me beast, brute, dog: and d—d me, haven't you? How do you suppose one man likes that sort of talk from another? How many years have I waited on you, and how many damns and cusses have you given me, along with my wages? Do you think a man's a dog, that you can talk to him in this way? If I choose to drink a little, why shouldn't I? I've seen many a gentleman drunk formly, and peraps have the abit from them. I ain't a-goin' to leave this house, old feller, and shall I tell you why? The house is my house, every stick of furnitur' in it is mine, excep' your old traps, and your shower-bath, and your wig-box. I've bought the place, I tell you, with my own industry and perseverance. I can show a hundred pound, where you can show a fifty, or your damned supersellious nephew either. I've served you honorable, done every thing for you these dozen years, and I'm a dog, am I? I'm a beast, am I? That's the language for gentlemen, not for our rank. But I'll bear it no more. I throw up your service; I'm tired on it; I've combed your old wig and buckled your old girths and waistbands long enough, I tell you. Don't look savage at me, I'm sitting in my own chair, in my own room, a-telling the truth to you. I'll be your beast, and your brute, and your dog, no more, Major Pendennis AlfPay."

The fury of the old gentleman, met by the servant's abrupt revolt, had been shocked and cooled by the concussion, as much as if a sudden shower-bath or a pail of cold water had been flung upon him. That effect produced, and his anger calmed, Morgan's speech had interested him, and he rather respected his adversary, and his courage in facing him, as of old days, in the fencing-room, he would have admired the opponent who hit him.

"You are no longer my servant," the major said, "and the house may be yours; but the lodgings are mine, and you will have the goodness to leave them. To-morrow morning, when we have settled our accounts, I shall remove into other quarters. In the mean time, I desire to go to bed, and have not the slightest wish for your farther company."

"We'll have a settlement, don't you be afraid," Morgan said, getting up from his chair. "I ain't done with you yet; nor with your family, nor with the Clavering family, Major Pendennis; and that you shall know."

"Have the goodness to leave the room, sir;—I'm tired," said the major.

"Hah! you'll be more tired of me afore you've done," answered the man, with a sneer, and walked out of the room; leaving the major to compose himself, as best he might, after the agitation of this extraordinary scene.

He sate and mused by his fire-side over the past events, and the confounded impudence and ingratitude of servants; and thought how he should get a new man: how devilish unpleasant it was for a man of his age, and with his habits, to part with a fellow to whom he had been accustomed: how Morgan had a receipt for boot-varnish, which was incomparably better and more comfortable to the feet than any he had ever tried; how very well he made mutton-broth, and tended him when he was unwell. "Gad, it's a hard thine: to lose a fellow of that sort: but he must go," thought the major. "He has grown rich, and impudent since he has grown rich. He was horribly tipsy and abusive tonight. We must part, and I must go out of the lodgings. Dammy, I like the lodgings; I'm used to 'em. It's very unpleasant, at my time of life, to change my quarters." And so on, mused the old gentleman. The shower-bath had done him good: the testiness was gone: the loss of the umbrella, the smell of paint at the Club, were forgotten under the superior excitement. "Confound the insolent villain!" thought the old gentleman. "He understood my wants to a nicety: he was the best servant in England." He thought about his servant as a man thinks of a horse that has carried him long and well, and that has come down with him, and is safe no longer. How the deuce to replace him? Where can he get such another animal?

In these melancholy cogitations the major, who had donned his own dressing gown and replaced his head of hair (a little gray had been introduced into the coiffure of late by Mr. Truefitt, which had given the major's head the most artless and respectable appearance); in these cogitations, we say, the major, who had taken off his wig and put on his night-handkerchief, sate absorbed by the fire-side, when a feeble knock came at his door, which was presently opened by the landlady of the lodgings.

"God bless my soul, Mrs. Brixham!" cried out the major, startled that a lady should behold him in the simple appareil of his night-toilet. "It—it's very late, Mrs. Brixham."

"I wish I might speak to you, sir," said the landlady, very piteously. "About Morgan, I suppose? He has cooled himself at the pump. Can't take him back, Mrs. Brixham. Impossible. I'd determined to part with him before, when I heard of his dealings in the discount business—I suppose you've heard of them, Mrs. Brixham? My servant's a capitalist, begad."

"O sir," said Mrs. Brixham, "I know it to my cost. I borrowed from him a little money five years ago; and though I have paid him many times over, I am entirely in his power. I am ruined by him, sir. Every thing I had is his. He's a dreadful man." "Eh, Mrs. Brixham? tant pis—dev'lish sorry for you, and that I must quit your house after lodging here so long: there's no help for it. I must go."

"He says we must all go, sir," sobbed out the luckless widow. "He came down stairs from you just now— he had been drinking, and it always makes him very wicked—and he said that you had insulted him, sir, and treated him like a dog, and spoken to him unkindly; and he swore he would be revenged, and—and I owe him a hundred and twenty pounds, sir—and he has a bill of sale of all my furniture—and says he will turn me out of my house, and send my poor George to prison. He has been the ruin of my family, that man."

"Dev'lish sorry, Mrs. Brixham; pray take a chair. What can I do?"

"Could you not intercede with him for us? George will give half his allowance; my daughter can send something. If you will but stay on, sir, and pay a quarter's rent in advance—"

"My good madam, I would as soon give you a quarter in advance as not, if I were going to stay in the lodgings. But I can't; and I can't afford to fling away twenty pounds, my good madam. I'm a poor half-pay officer, and want every shilling I have, begad. As far as a few pounds goes—say five pounds—I don't say—and shall be most happy, and that sort of thing: and I'll give it you in the morning with pleasure: but—but it's getting late, and I have made a railroad journey."

"God's will be done, sir," said the poor woman, drying her tears. "I must bear my fate."

"And a dev'lish hard one it is, and most sincerely I pity you, Mrs. Brixham. I—I'll say ten pounds, if you will permit me. Good night."

"Mr. Morgan, sir, when he came down stairs, and when—when I besought him to have pity on me, and told him he had been the ruin of my family, said something which I did not well understand—that he would ruin every family in the house—that he knew something would bring you down too—and that you should pay him for your—your insolence to him. I—I must own to you, that I went down on my knees to him, sir; and he said, with a dreadful oath against you, that he would have you on your knees."

"Me?—by Gad, that is too pleasant! Where is the confounded fellow?"

"He went away, sir. He said he should see you in the morning. O, pray try and pacify him, and save me and my poor boy." And the widow went away with this prayer, to pass her night as she might, and look for the dreadful morrow.

The last words about himself excited Major Pendennis so much, that his compassion for Mrs. Brixham's misfortunes was quite forgotten in the consideration of his own case.

"Me on my knees?" thought he, as he got into bed: "confound his impudence. Who ever saw me on my knees? What the devil does the fellow know? Gad, I've not had an affair these twenty years. I defy him." And the old campaigner turned round and slept pretty sound, being rather excited and amused by the events of the day—the last day in Bury-street, he was determined it should be. "For it's impossible to stay on with a valet over me and a bankrupt landlady. What good can I do this poor devil of a woman? I'll give her twenty pound—there's Warrington's twenty pound, which he has just paid—but what's the use? She'll want more, and more, and more, and that cormorant Morgan will swallow all. No, dammy, I can't afford to know poor people; and to-morrow I'll say good-by—to Mrs. Brixham and Mr. Morgan."

CHAPTER XXX

IN WHICH THE MAJOR NEITHER YIELDS HIS MONEY NOR HIS LIFE

Early next morning Pendennis's shutters were opened by Morgan, who appeared as usual, with a face perfectly grave and respectful, bearing with him the old gentleman's clothes, cans of water, and elaborate toilet requisites.

"It's you, is it?" said the old fellow from his bed. "I shan't take you back again, you understand."

"I ave not the least wish to be took back agin, Major Pendennis," Mr. Morgan said, with grave dignity, "nor to serve you nor hany man. But as I wish you to be comftable as long as you stay in my house, I came up to do what's nessary." And once more, and for the last time, Mr. James Morgan laid out the silver dressing-case, and strapped the shining razor.

These offices concluded, he addressed himself to the major with an indescribable solemnity, and said: "Thinkin' that you would most likely be in want of a respectable pusson, until you suited yourself, I spoke to a young man last night, who is 'ere."

"Indeed," said the warrior in the tent-bed.

"He ave lived in the fust families, and I can vouch for his respectability."

"You are monstrous polite," grinned the old major. And the truth is that after the occurrences of the previous evening, Morgan had gone out to his own Club at the Wheel of Fortune, and there finding Frosch, a courier and valet just returned from a foreign tour with young Lord Cubley, and for the present disposable, had represented to Mr. Frosch, that he, Morgan, had "a devil of a blow hup with his own Gov'ner and was goin' to retire from the business haltogether, and that if Frosch wanted a tempory job, he might probbly have it by applying in Bury street."

"You are very polite," said the major, "and your recommendation, I am sure, will have every weight."

Morgan blushed, he felt his master was "a-chaffin' of him." "The man have waited on you before, sir," he said with great dignity. "Lord De la Pole, sir, gave him to his nephew young Lord Cubley, and he have been with him on his foring tour, and not wishing to go to Fitzurse Castle, which Frosch's chest is delicate, and he can not bear the cold in Scotland, he is free to serve you or not, as you choose."

"I repeat, sir, that you are exceedingly polite," said the major. "Come in, Frosch—you will do very well—Mr. Morgan, will you have the great kindness to—"

"I shall show him what is nessary, sir, and what is customry for you to wish to ave done. Will you please to take breakfast 'ere or at the Club, Major Pendennis?"

"With your kind permission, I will breakfast here, and afterward we will make our little arrangements."

"If you please, sir."

"Will you now oblige me by leaving the room?"

Morgan withdrew; the excessive politeness of his ex-employer made him almost as angry as the major's bitterest words. And while the old gentleman is making his mysterious toilet, we will also modestly retire.

After breakfast, Major Pendennis and his new aid-de-camp occupied themselves in preparing for their departure. The establishment of the old bachelor was not very complicated. He encumbered himself with no useless wardrobe. A Bible (his mother's), a road-book, Pen's novel (calf elegant), and the Duke of Wellington's Dispatches, with a few prints, maps, and portraits of that illustrious general, and of various sovereigns and consorts of this country, and of the general under whom Major Pendennis had served in India, formed his literary and artistical collection; he was always ready to march at a few hours' notice, and the cases in which he had brought his property into his lodgings some fifteen years before, were still in the lofts amply sufficient to receive all his goods. These, the young woman who did the work of the house, and who was known by the name of Betty to her mistress, and of 'Slavey' to Mr. Morgan, brought down from their resting place, and obediently dusted and cleaned under the eyes of the terrible Morgan. His demeanor was guarded and solemn; he had spoken no word as yet to Mrs. Brixham respecting his threats of the past night, but he looked as if he would execute them, and the poor widow tremblingly awaited her fate.

Old Pendennis, armed with his cane, superintended the package of his goods and chattels under the hands of Mr. Frosch, and the Slavey burned such of his papers as he did not care to keep; flung open doors and closets until they were all empty; and now all boxes and chests were closed, except his desk, which was ready to receive the final accounts of Mr. Morgan.

That individual now made his appearance, and brought his books. "As I wish to speak to you in privick, peraps you will ave the kindness to request Frosch to step down stairs," he said, on entering.

"Bring a couple of cabs, Frosch, if you please—and wait down stairs until I ring for you," said the major. Morgan saw Frosch down stairs, watched him go along the street upon his errand and produced his books and accounts, which were simple and very easily settled.

"And now, sir," said he, having pocketed the check which his ex-employer gave him, and signed his name to his book with a flourish, "and now that accounts is closed between us, sir," he said, "I porpose to speak to you as one man to another" (Morgan liked the sound of his own voice; and, as an individual, indulged in public speaking whenever he could get an opportunity, at the Club, or the housekeeper's room), "and I must tell you, that I'm in possussion of certing information."

"And may I inquire of what nature, pray?" asked the major.

"It's valuble information, Major Pendennis, as you know very well I know of a marriage as is no marriage—of a honorable baronet as is no more married than I am; and which his wife is married to somebody else, as you know too, sir."

Pendennis at once understood all. "Ha! this accounts for your behavior. You have been listening at the door, sir, I suppose," said the major, looking very haughty; "I forgot to look at the key-hole when I went to that public-house, or I might have suspected what sort of person was behind it."

"I may have my schemes as you may have yours, I suppose," answered Morgan. "I may get my information, and I may act on that information, and I may find that information valuble as any body else may. A poor servant may have a bit of luck as well as a gentleman, mayn't he? Don't you be putting on your aughty looks, sir, and comin' the aristocrat over me. That's all gammon with me. I'm an Englishman, I am, and as good as you."

"To what the devil does this tend, sir? and how does the secret which you have surprised concern me, I should like to know?" asked Major Pendennis, with great majesty.

"How does it concern me, indeed? how grand we are! how does it concern my nephew, I wonder? How does it concern my nephew's seat in Parlyment: and to subornation of bigamy? How does it concern that? What, are you to be the only man to have a secret, and to trade on it? Why shouldn't I go halves, Major Pendennis? I've found it out too. Look here! I ain't goin' to be unreasonable with you. Make it worth my while, and I'll keep the thing close. Let Mr. Arthur take his seat, and his rich wife, if you like; I don't want to marry her. But I will have my share as sure as my name's James Morgan. And if I don't—"

"And if you don't, sir—what?" Pendennis asked. "If I don't, I split, and tell all. I smash Clavering, and have him and his wife up for bigamy—so help me, I will! I smash young Hopeful's marriage, and I show up you and him as makin' use of this secret, in order to squeeze a seat in Parlyment out of Sir Francis, and a fortune out of his wife."

"Mr. Pendennis knows no more of this business than the babe unborn, sir," cried the major, aghast. "No more than Lady Clavering, than Miss Amory does."

"Tell that to the marines, major," replied the valet; "that cock won't fight with me."

"Do you doubt my word, you villain?"

"No bad language. I don't care one twopence'a'p'ny whether your word's true or not. I tell you, I intend this to be a nice little annuity to me, major: for I have every one of you; and I ain't such a fool as to let you go. I should say that you might make it five hundred a year to me among you, easy. Pay me down the first quarter now, and I'm as mum as a mouse. Just give me a note for one twenty-five. There's your check-book on your desk."

"And there's this, too, you villain," cried the old gentleman. In the desk to which the valet pointed was a little double-barreled pistol, which had belonged to Pendennis's old patron, the Indian commander-in-chief, and which had accompanied him in many a campaign. "One more word, you scoundrel, and I'll shoot you, like a mad dog. Stop—by Jove, I'll do it now. You'll assault me will you? You'll strike at an old man, will you, you lying coward? Kneel down and say your prayers, sir, for by the Lord you shall die."

The major's face glared with rage at his adversary, who looked terrified before him for a moment, and at the next, with a shriek of "Murder," sprang toward the open window, under which a policeman happened to be on his beat. "Murder! Police!" bellowed Mr. Morgan. To his surprise, Major Pendennis wheeled away the table and walked to the other window, which was also open. He beckoned the policeman. "Come up here, policeman," he said, and then went and placed himself against the door.

"You miserable sneak," he said to Morgan; "the pistol hasn't been loaded these fifteen years as you have known very well: if you had not been such a coward. That policeman is coming, and I will have him up, and have your trunks searched; I have reason to believe that you are a thief, sir. I know you are. I'll swear to the things."

"You gave 'em to me—you gave 'em to me!" cried Morgan.

The major laughed. "We'll see," he said; and the guilty valet remembered some fine lawn-fronted shirts—a certain gold-headed cane— an opera-glass, which he had forgotten to bring down, and of which he had assumed the use along with certain articles of his master's clothes, which the old dandy neither wore nor asked for.

Policeman X entered; followed by the scared Mrs. Brixham and her maid-of-all-work, who had been at the door and found some difficulty in closing it against the street amateurs, who wished to see the row. The major began instantly to speak.

"I have had occasion to discharge this drunken scoundrel," he said, "Both last night and this morning he insulted and assaulted me. I am an old man and took up a pistol. You see it is not loaded, and this coward cried out before he was hurt. I am glad you are come. I was charging him with taking my property, and desired to examine his trunks and his room."

"The velvet cloak you ain't worn these three years, nor the weskits, and I thought I might take the shirts, and I—I take my hoath I intended to put back the hopera-glass," roared Morgan, writhing with rage and terror.

"The man acknowledges that he is a thief," the major said, calmly, "He has been in my service for years, and I have treated him with every kindness and confidence. We will go up-stairs and examine his trunks." In those trunks Mr. Morgan had things which he would fain keep from public eyes. Mr. Morgan, the bill discounter, gave goods as well as money to his customers. He provided young spendthrifts with snuff-boxes and pins and jewels and pictures and cigars, and of a very doubtful quality those cigars and jewels and pictures were. Their display at a police-office, the discovery of his occult profession, and the exposure of the major's property, which he had appropriated, indeed, rather than stolen—would not have added to the reputation of Mr. Morgan. He looked a piteous image of terror and discomfiture.

"He'll smash me, will he?" thought the major. "I'll crush him now, and finish with him."

But he paused. He looked at poor Mrs. Brixham's scared face; and he thought for a moment to himself that the man brought to bay and in prison might make disclosures which had best be kept secret, and that it was best not to deal too fiercely with a desperate man.

"Stop," he said, "policeman. I'll speak with this man by himself." "Do you give Mr. Morgan in charge?" said the policeman.

"I have brought no charge as yet," the major said, with a significant look at his man.

"Thank you sir," whispered Morgan, very low.

"Go outside the door, and wait there, policeman, if you please—Now, Morgan, you have played one game with me, and you have not had the best of it, my good man. No, begad, you've not had the best of it, though you had the best hand; and you've got to pay, too, now, you scoundrel."

"Yes, sir," said the man.

"I've only found out, within the last week, the game which you have been driving, you villain. Young De Boots, of the Blues, recognized you as the man who came to barracks, and did business one-third in money, one-third in Eau-de-Cologne, and one-third in French prints, you confounded demure old sinner! I didn't miss any thing, or care a straw what you'd taken, you booby; but I took the shot, and it hit—hit the bull's-eye, begad. Dammy, sir, I'm an old campaigner." "What do you want with me, sir?"

"I'll tell you. Your bills, I suppose, you keep about you in that dem'd great leather pocket-book, don't you? You'll burn Mrs. Brixham's bill?"

"Sir, I ain't a-goin' to part with my property," growled the man.

"You lent her sixty pounds five years ago. She and that poor devil of an insurance clerk, her son, have paid you fifty pounds a year ever since; and you have got a bill of sale of her furniture, and her note of hand for a hundred and fifty pounds. She told me so last night. By Jove, sir, you've bled that poor woman enough."

"I won't give it up," said Morgan; "If I do I'm—"

"Policeman!" cried the major.

"You shall have the bill," said Morgan. "You're not going to take money of me, and you a gentleman?"

"I shall want you directly," said the major to X, who here entered, and who again withdrew.

"No, my good sir," the old gentleman continued; "I have not any desire to have farther pecuniary transactions with you; but we will draw out a little paper, which you will have the kindness to sign. No, stop!—you shall write it: you have improved immensely in writing of late, and have now a very good hand. You shall sit down and write, if you please—there, at that table—so—let me see—we may as well have the date. Write 'Bury-street, St. James's, October 21, 18—.'"

And Morgan wrote as he was instructed, and as the pitiless old major continued:

"I, James Morgan, having come in extreme poverty into the service of Arthur Pendennis, Esquire, of Bury-street, St. James's, a major in her Majesty's service, acknowledge that I received liberal wages and board wages from my employer, during fifteen years. You can't object to that, I am sure," said the major.

"During fifteen years," wrote Morgan.

"In which time, by my own care and prudence," the dictator resumed, "I have managed to amass sufficient money to purchase the house in which my master resides, and, besides, to effect other savings. Among other persons from whom I have had money, I may mention my present tenant, Mrs. Brixham, who, in consideration of sixty pounds advanced by me five years since, has paid back to me the sum of two hundred and fifty pounds sterling, besides giving me a note of hand for one hundred and twenty pounds, which I restore to her at the desire of my late master, Major Arthur Pendennis, and therewith free her furniture, of which I had a bill of sale. Have you written?"

"I think if this pistol was loaded, I'd blow your brains out," said Morgan.

"No, you wouldn't. You have too great a respect for your valuable life, my good man," the major answered. "Let us go on and begin a new sentence."

"And having, in return for my master's kindness, stolen his property from him, which I acknowledge to be now up-stairs in my trunks; and having uttered falsehoods regarding his and other honorable families, I do hereby, in consideration of his clemency to me, express my regret for uttering these falsehoods, and for stealing his property; and declare that I am not worthy of belief, and that I hope— yes, begad—that I hope to amend for the future. Signed, James Morgan."

"I'm d—d if I sign it," said Morgan.

"My good man, it will happen to you, whether you sign or no, begad," said the old fellow, chuckling at his own wit. "There, I shall not use this, you understand, unless—unless I am compelled to do so. Mrs. Brixham, and our friend the policeman, will witness it, I dare say, without reading it: and I will give the old lady back her note of hand, and say, which you will confirm, that she and you are quits. I see there is Frosch come back with the cab for my trunks; I shall go to an hotel. You may come in now, policeman; Mr. Morgan and I have arranged our little dispute. If Mrs. Brixham will sign this paper, and you, policeman, will do so, I shall be very much obliged to you both. Mrs. Brixham, you and your worthy landlord, Mr. Morgan, are quits. I wish you joy of him. Let Frosch come and pack the rest of the things."

Frosch, aided by the Slavey, under the calm superintendence of Mr. Morgan, carried Major Pendennis's boxes to the cabs in waiting; and Mrs. Brixham, when her persecutor was not by, came and asked a Heaven's blessing upon the major, her preserver, and the best and quietest and kindest of lodgers. And having given her a finger to shake, which the humble lady received with a courtesy, and over which she was ready to make a speech full of tears, the major cut short that valedictory oration, and walked out of the house to the hotel in Jermyn street, which was not many steps from Morgan's door.

That individual, looking forth from the parlor-window, discharged any thing but blessings at his parting guest; but the stout old boy could afford not to be frightened at Mr. Morgan, and flung him a look of great contempt and humor as he strutted away with his cane.

Major Pendennis had not quitted his house of Bury street many hours, and Mr. Morgan was enjoying his otium, in a dignified manner, surveying the evening fog, and smoking a cigar, on the doorsteps, when Arthur Pendennis, Esq., the hero of this history, made his appearance at the well-known door.

"My uncle out, I suppose, Morgan?" he said to the functionary; knowing full well that to smoke was treason, in the presence of the major.

"Major Pendennis is hout, sir," said Morgan, with gravity, bowing, but not touching the elegant cap which he wore. "Major Pendennis have left this ouse to-day, sir, and I have no longer the honor of being in his service, sir."

"Indeed, and where is he?"

"I believe he ave taken tempory lodgings at Cox's otel, in Jummin street," said Mr. Morgan; and added, after a pause, "Are you in town for some time, pray, sir? Are you in Chambers? I should like to have the honor of waiting on you there: and would be thankful if you would favor me with a quarter of an hour."

"Do you want my uncle to take you back?" asked Arthur, insolent and good-natured.

"I want no such thing; I'd see him—" the man glared at him for a minute, but he stopped. "No, sir, thank you," he said in a softer voice; "it's only with you that I wish to speak, on some business which concerns you; and perhaps you would favor me by walking into my house."

"If it is but for a minute or two, I will listen to you, Morgan," said Arthur; and thought to himself, "I suppose the fellow wants me to patronize him;" and he entered the house. A card was already in the front windows, proclaiming that apartments were to be let, and having introduced Mr. Pendennis into the dining-room, and offered him a chair, Mr. Morgan took one himself, and proceeded to convey some information to him, with which the reader has already had cognizance.

CHAPTER XXXI

IN WHICH PENDENNIS COUNTS HIS EGGS

Our friend had arrived in London on that day only, though but for a brief visit, and having left some fellow-travelers at an hotel to which he had conveyed them from the West, he hastened to the Chambers in Lamb-court, which were basking in as much sun as chose to visit that dreary but not altogether comfortless building. Freedom stands in lieu of sunshine in Chambers; and Templars grumble, but take their ease in their Inn. Pen's domestic announced to him that Warrington was in Chambers too, and, of course, Arthur ran up to his friend's room straightway, and found it, as of old, perfumed with the pipe, and George once more at work at his newspapers and reviews. The pair greeted each other with the rough cordiality which young Englishmen use one to another: and which carries a great deal of warmth and kindness under its rude exterior. Warrington smiled and took his pipe out of his mouth, and said, "Well, young one!" Pen advanced and held out his hand, and said, "How are you, old boy?" And so this greeting passed between two friends who had not seen each other for months. Alphonse and Frederic would have rushed into each other's arms and shrieked Ce bon coeur! ce cher Alphonse! over each other's shoulders. Max and Wilhelm would have bestowed half a dozen kisses, scented with Havanna, upon each other's mustaches. "Well, young one!" "How are you, old boy?" is what two Britons say: after saving each other's lives, possibly, the day before. To-morrow they will leave off shaking hands, and only wag their heads at one another as they come to breakfast. Each has for the other the very warmest confidence and regard: each would share his purse with the other; and hearing him attacked would break out in the loudest and most enthusiastic praise of his friend; but they part with a mere Good-by, they meet with a mere How-d'you-do: and they don't write to each other in the interval. Curious modesty, strange stoical decorum of English friendship! "Yes, we are not demonstrative like those confounded foreigners," says Hardman; who not only shows no friendship, but never felt any all his life long.

"Been in Switzerland?" says Pen. "Yes," says Warrington. "Couldn't find a bit of tobacco fit to smoke till we came to Strasburg, where I got some caporal." The man's mind is full, very likely, of the great sights which he has seen, of the great emotions with which the vast works of nature have inspired it. But his enthusiasm is too coy to show itself, even to his closest friend, and he veils it with a cloud of tobacco. He will speak more fully of confidential evenings, however, and write ardently and frankly about that which he is shy of saying. The thoughts and experience of his travel will come forth in his writings; as the learning, which he never displays in talk, enriches his style with pregnant allusion and brilliant illustration, colors his generous eloquence, and points his wit.

The elder gives a rapid account of the places which he has visited in his tour. He has seen Switzerland, North Italy, and the Tyrol—he has come home by Vienna, and Dresden, and the Rhine. He speaks about these places in a shy, sulky voice, as if he had rather not mention them at all, and as if the sight of them had rendered him very unhappy. The outline of the elder man's tour thus gloomily sketched out, the young one begins to speak. He has been in the country—very much bored—canvassing—uncommonly slow—he is here for a day or two, and going on to—to the neighborhood of Tunbridge Wells, to some friends—that will be uncommonly slow, too. How hard it is to make an Englishman acknowledge that he is happy!

"And the seat in Parliament, Pen? Have you made it all right?" asks Warrington.

"All right—as soon as Parliament meets and a new writ can be issued, Clavering retires, and I step into his shoes," says Pen.

"And under which king does Bezonian speak or die?" asked Warrington. "Do we come out as Liberal Conservative, or as Government man, or on our own hook?"

"Hem! There are no politics now; every man's politics, at least, are pretty much the same. I have not got acres enough to make me a Protectionist; nor could I be one, I think, if I had all the land in the county. I shall go pretty much with Government, and in advance of them upon some social questions which I have been getting up during the vacation; don't grin, you old Cynic, I have been getting up the Blue Books, and intend to come out rather strong on the Sanitary and Colonization questions."

"We reserve to ourselves the liberty of voting against Government, though, we are generally friendly. We are, however, friends of the people avant tout. We give lectures at the Clavering Institute, and shake hands with the intelligent mechanics. We think the franchise ought to be very considerably enlarged; at the same time we are free to accept office some day, when the House has listened to a few crack speeches from us, and the Administration perceives our merit."

"I am not Moses," said Pen, with, as usual, somewhat of melancholy in his voice. "I have no laws from Heaven to bring down to the people from the mountain. I don't belong to the mountain at all, or set up to be a leader and reformer of mankind. My faith is not strong enough for that; nor my vanity, nor my hypocrisy, great enough. I will tell no lies, George, that I promise you: and do no more than coincide in those which are necessary and pass current, and can't be got in without recalling the whole circulation. Give a man at least the advantage of his skeptical turn. If I find a good thing to say in the House, I will say it; a good measure, I will support it; a fair place, I will take it, and be glad of my luck. But I would no more flatter a great man than a mob; and now you know as much about my politics as I do. What call have I to be a Whig? Whiggism is not a divine institution. Why not vote with the Liberal Conservatives? They have done for the nation what the Whigs would never have done without them. Who converted both?—the Radicals and the country outside. I think the Morning Post is often right, and Punch is often wrong. I don't profess a call, but take advantage of a chance. Parlons d'autre chose."

"The next thing at your heart, after ambition, is love, I suppose?" Warrington said. "How have our young loves prospered? Are we going to change our condition, and give up our chambers? Are you going to divorce me, Arthur, and take unto yourself a wife?"

"I suppose so. She is very good-natured and lively. She sings, and she don't mind smoking. She'll have a fair fortune—I don't know how much—but my uncle augurs every thing from the Begum's generosity, and says that she will come down very handsomely. And I think Blanche is devilish fond of me," said Arthur, with a sigh.

"That means that we accept her caresses and her money."

"Haven't we said before that life was a transaction?" Pendennis said. "I don't pretend to break my heart about her. I have told her pretty fairly what my feelings are—and—and have engaged myself to her. And since I saw her last, and for the last two months especially, while I have been in the country, I think she has been growing fonder and fonder of me; and her letters to me, and especially to Laura, seem to show it. Mine have been simple enough—no raptures nor vows, you understand—but looking upon the thing as an affaire faite; and not desirous to hasten or defer the completion."

"And Laura? how is she?" Warrington asked frankly.

"Laura, George," said Pen, looking his friend hard in the face; "by Heaven, Laura is the best, and noblest, and dearest girl the sun ever shone upon." His own voice fell as he spoke: it seemed as if he could hardly utter the words: he stretched out his hand to his comrade, who took it and nodded his head.

"Have you only found out that now, young un?" Warrington said after a pause.

"Who has not learned things too late, George?" cried Arthur, in his impetuous way, gathering words and emotion as he went on. "Whose life is not a disappointment? Who carries his heart entire to the grave without a mutilation? I never knew any body who was happy quite: or who has not had to ransom himself out of the hands of Fate with the payment of some dearest treasure or other. Lucky if we are left alone afterward, when we have paid our fine, and if the tyrant visits us no more. Suppose I have found out that I have lost the greatest prize in the world, now that it can't be mine—that for years I had an angel under my tent, and let her go?—am I the only one—ah, dear old boy, am I the only one? And do you think my lot is easier to bear because I own that I deserve if? She's gone from us. God's blessing be with her! She might have staid, and I lost her; it's like Undine: isn't it, George?"

"She was in this room once," said George.

He saw her there—he heard the sweet low voice—he saw the sweet smile and eyes shining so kindly—the face remembered so fondly—thought of in what night-watches—blest and loved always—gone now! A glass that had held a nosegay—a Bible with Helen's hand-writing—were all that were left him of that brief flower of his life. Say it is a dream: say it passes: better the recollection of a dream than an aimless waking from a blank stupor.

The two friends sate in silence awhile, each occupied with his own thoughts and aware of the other's. Pen broke it presently, by saying that he must go and seek for his uncle, and report progress to the old gentleman. The major had written in a very bad humor; the major was getting old. "I should like to see you in Parliament, and snugly settled with a comfortable house and an heir to the name before I make my bow. Show me these," the major wrote, "and then, let old Arthur Pendennis make room for the younger fellows: he has walked the Pall Mall pavé long enough."

"There is a kindness about the old heathen," said Warrington. "He cares for somebody besides himself, at least for some other part of himself besides that which is buttoned into his own coat;—for you and your race. He would like to see the progeny of the Pendennises multiplying and increasing, and hopes that they may inherit the land. The old patriarch blesses you from the Club window of Bays's, and is carried off and buried under the flags of St. James's Church, in sight of Piccadilly, and the cab-stand, and the carriages going to the levee. It is an edifying ending."

"The new blood I bring into the family," mused Pen, "is rather tainted. If I had chosen, I think my father-in-law, Amory, would not have been the progenitor I should have desired for my race; nor my grandfather-in-law Snell; nor our Oriental ancestors. By the way, who was Amory? Amory was lieutenant of an Indiaman. Blanche wrote some verses about him, about the storm, the mountain wave, the seaman's grave, the gallant father, and that sort of thing. Amory was drowned commanding a country ship between Calcutta and Sydney; Amory and the Begum weren't happy together. She has been unlucky in her selection of husbands, the good old lady, for, between ourselves, a more despicable creature than Sir Francis Clavering, of Clavering Park, Baronet, never—" "Never legislated for his country," broke in Warrington; at which Pen blushed rather.

"By the way, at Baden," said Warrington, "I found our friend the Chevalier Strong in great state, and wearing his orders. He told me that he had quarreled with Clavering, of whom he seemed to have almost as bad an opinion as you have, and in fact, I think, though I will not be certain, confided to me his opinion, that Clavering was an utter scoundrel. That fellow Bloundell, who taught you card-playing at Oxbridge, was with Strong; and time, I think, has brought out his valuable qualities, and rendered him a more accomplished rascal than he was during your undergraduateship. But the king of the place was the famous Colonel Altamont, who was carrying all before him, giving fetes to the whole society, and breaking the bank, it was said."

"My uncle knows something about that fellow—Clavering knows something about him. There's something louche regarding him. But come! I must go to Bury-street, like a dutiful nephew." And, taking his hat, Pen prepared to go.

"I will walk, too," said Warrington. And they descended the stairs, stopping, however, at Pen's chambers, which, as the reader has been informed, were now on the lower story.

Here Pen began sprinkling himself with Eau-de-Cologne, and carefully scenting his hair and whiskers with that odoriferous water.

"What is the matter? You've not been smoking. Is it my pipe that has poisoned you?" growled Warrington.

"I am going to call upon some women," said Pen. "I'm—I'm going to dine with 'em. They are passing through town, and are at an hotel in Jermyn-street."

Warrington looked with good-natured interest at the young fellow dandifying himself up to a pitch of completeness; and appearing at length in a gorgeous shirt-front and neckcloth, fresh gloves, and glistening boots. George had a pair of thick high-lows, and his old shirt was torn about the breast, and ragged at the collar, where his blue beard had worn it.

"Well, young un," said he, simply, "I like you to be a buck, somehow. When I walk about with you, it is as if I had a rose in my button-hole. And you are still affable. I don't think there is any young fellow in the Temple turns out like you; and I don't believe you were ever ashamed of walking with me yet."

"Don't laugh at me, George," said Pen.

"I say, Pen," continued the other, sadly, "if you write—if you write to Laura, I wish you would say 'God bless her' for me." Pen blushed; and then looked at Warrington; and then—and then burst into an uncontrollable fit of laughing.

"I'm going to dine with her," he said. "I brought her and Lady Rockminster up from the country to-day—made two days of it—slept last night at Bath—I say, George, come and dine, too. I may ask any one I please, and the old lady is constantly talking about you."

George refused. George had an article to write. George hesitated; and oh, strange to say! at last he agreed to go. It was agreed that they should go and call upon the ladies; and they marched away in high spirits to the hotel in Jermyn-street. Once more the dear face shone upon him; once more the sweet voice spoke to him, and the tender hand pressed a welcome.

There still wanted half-an-hour to dinner, "You will go and see your uncle now, Mr. Pendennis," old Lady Rockminster said. "You will not bring him to dinner—no—his old stories are intolerable; and I want to talk to Mr. Warrington; I daresay he will amuse us. I think we have heard all your stories. We have been together for two whole days, and I think we are getting tired of each other."

So obeying her ladyship's orders, Arthur went down stairs and walked to his uncle's lodgings.

CHAPTER XXXII

FIAT JUSTITIA

The dinner was served when Arthur returned, and Lady Rockminster began to scold him for arriving late. But Laura, looking at her cousin, saw that his face was so pale and scared, that she interrupted her imperious patroness; and asked, with tender alarm, what had happened? Was Arthur ill?

Arthur drank a large bumper of sherry. "I have heard the most extraordinary news; I will tell you afterward," he said, looking at the servants. He was very nervous and agitated during the dinner. "Don't tramp and beat so with your feet under the table," Lady Rockminster said. "You have trodden on Fido, and upset his saucer. You see Mr. Warrington keeps his boots quiet."

At the dessert—it seemed as if the unlucky dinner would never be over—Lady Rockminster said, "This dinner has been exceedingly stupid. I suppose something has happened, and that you want to speak to Laura. I will go and have my nap. I am not sure that I shall have any tea—no. Good night, Mr.

Warrington. You must come again, and when there is no business to talk about." And the old lady, tossing up her head, walked away from the room with great dignity.

George and the others had risen with her, and Warrington was about to go away, and was saying "Goodnight" to Laura, who, of course was looking much alarmed about her cousin, when Arthur said, "Pray, stay, George. You should hear my news too, and give me your counsel in this case. I hardly know how to act in it."

"It's something about Blanche, Arthur," said Laura, her heart beating, and her cheek blushing, as she thought it had never blushed in her life.

"Yes—and the most extraordinary story," said Pen. "When I left you to go to my uncle's lodgings, I found his servant, Morgan, who has been with him so long, at the door, and he said that he and his master had parted that morning; that my uncle had quitted the house, and had gone to an hotel—this hotel. I asked for him when I came in; but he was gone out to dinner. Morgan then said that he had something of a most important nature to communicate to me, and begged me to step into the house; his house it is now. It appears the scoundrel has saved a great deal of money while in my uncle's service, and is now a capitalist and a millionaire, for what I know. Well, I went into the house, and what do you think he told me? This must be a secret between us all—at least if we can keep it, now that it is in possession of that villain. Blanche's father is not dead. He has come to life again. The marriage between Clavering and the Begum is no marriage."

"And Blanche, I suppose, is her grandfather's heir," said Warrington.

"Perhaps: but the child of what a father! Amory is an escaped convict—Clavering knows it; my uncle knows it—and it was with this piece of information held over Clavering in terrorem that the wretched old man got him to give up his borough to me."

"Blanche doesn't know it," said Laura, "nor poor Lady Clavering."

"No," said Pen; "Blanche does not even know the history of her father. She knew that he and her mother had separated, and had heard, as a child, from Bonner, her nurse, that Mr. Amory was drowned in New South Wales. He was there as a convict, not as a ship's captain, as the poor girl thought. Lady Clavering has told me that they were not happy, and that her husband was a bad character. She would tell me all, she said, some day: and I remember her saying to me, with tears in her eyes, that it was hard for a woman to be forced to own that she was glad to hear her husband was dead: and that twice in her life she should have chosen so badly. What is to be done now? The man can't show and claim his wife: death is probably over him if he discovers himself: return to transportation certainly. But the rascal has held the threat of discovery over Clavering for some time past, and has extorted money from him time after time."

"It is our friend, Colonel Altamont, of course," said Warrington: "I see all now."

"If the rascal comes back," continued Arthur, "Morgan, who knows his secret, will use it over him—and having it in his possession, proposes to extort money from us all. The d—d rascal supposed I was cognizant of it," said Pen, white with anger; "asked me if I would give him an annuity to keep it quiet; threatened me, me, as if I was trafficking with this wretched old Begum's misfortune; and would extort a seat in Parliament out of that miserable Clavering. Good heavens! was my uncle mad, to tamper in such a conspiracy? Fancy our mother's son, Laura, trading on such a treason!"

"I can't fancy it, dear Arthur," said Laura; seizing Arthur's hand, and kissing it.

"No!" broke out Warrington's deep voice, with a tremor; he surveyed the two generous and loving young people with a pang of indescribable love and pain. "No. Our boy can't meddle with such a wretched intrigue as that. Arthur Pendennis can't marry a convict's daughter; and sit in Parliament as member for the hulks. You must wash your hands of the whole affair, Pen. You must break off. You must give no explanations of why and wherefore, but state that family reasons render a match impossible. It is better that those poor women should fancy you false to your word than that they should know the truth. Besides, you can get from that dog Clavering—I can fetch that for you easily enough—an acknowledgement that the reasons which you have given to him as the head of the family are amply sufficient for breaking off the union. Don't you think with me, Laura?" He scarcely dared to look her in the face as he spoke. Any lingering hope that he might have—any feeble hold that he might feel upon the last spar of his wrecked fortune, he knew he was casting away; and he let the wave of his calamity close over him. Pen had started up while he was speaking, looking eagerly at him. He turned his head away. He saw Laura rise up also and go to Pen, and once more take his hand and kiss it. "She thinks so too—God bless her!" said George.

"Her father's shame is not Blanche's fault, dear Arthur, is it?" Laura said, very pale, and speaking very quickly. "Suppose you had been married, would you desert her because she had done no wrong? Are you not pledged to her? Would you leave her because she is in misfortune? And if she is unhappy, wouldn't you console her? Our mother would, had she been here." And, as she spoke, the kind girl folded her arms round him, and buried her face upon his heart.

"Our mother is an angel with God," Pen sobbed out. "And you are the dearest and best of women—the dearest, the dearest and the best. Teach me my duty. Pray for me that I may do it—pure heart. God bless you—God bless you, my sister."

"Amen," groaned out Warrington, with his head in his hands. "She is right," he murmured to himself. "She can't do any wrong, I think —that girl." Indeed, she looked and smiled like an angel. Many a day after he saw that smile—saw her radiant face as she looked up at Pen—saw her putting back her curls, blushing and smiling, and still looking fondly toward him.

She leaned for a moment her little fair hand on the table, playing on it. "And now, and now," she said, looking at the two gentlemen—

"And what now?" asked George.

"And now we will have some tea," said Miss Laura, with her smile.

But before this unromantic conclusion to a rather sentimental scene could be suffered to take place, a servant brought word that Major Pendennis had returned to the hotel, and was waiting to see his nephew. Upon this announcement, Laura, not without some alarm, and an appealing look to Pen, which said "Behave yourself well—hold to the right, and do your duty—be gentle, but firm with your uncle"— Laura, we say, with these warnings written in her face, took leave of the two gentlemen, and retreated to her dormitory. Warrington, who was not generally fond of tea, yet grudged that expected cup very much. Why could not old Pendennis have come in an hour later? Well, an hour sooner or later, what matter? The hour strikes at last? The inevitable moment comes to say Farewell. The hand is shaken, the door closed, and the friend gone; and, the brief joy over, you are alone. "In which of those many windows of the hotel does her light beam?" perhaps he asks himself as he passes down the street. He strides away to the smoking-room of a neighboring club, and there applies himself to his usual solace of a cigar. Men are brawling and talking loud about politics, opera-girls, horse-racing, the atrocious tyranny of the committee; bearing this sacred secret about him, he enters into this brawl. Talk away, each louder than the other. Rattle and crack jokes. Laugh and tell your wild stories. It is strange to take one's place and part in the midst of the smoke and din, and think every man here has his secret ego, most likely, which is sitting lonely and apart, away in the private chamber, from the loud game in which the rest of us is joining!

Arthur, as he traversed the passages of the hotel, felt his anger rousing up within him. He was indignant to think that yonder old gentleman whom he was about to meet, should have made him such a tool and puppet, and so compromised his honor and good name. The old fellow's hand was very cold and shaky when Arthur took it. He was coughing; he was grumbling over the fire; Frosch could not bring his dressing-gown or arrange his papers as that d—d, confounded, impudent scoundrel of a Morgan. The old gentleman bemoaned himself, and cursed Morgan's ingratitude with peevish pathos.

"The confounded impudent scoundrel! He was drunk last night, and challenged me to fight him, Pen; and, bedad, at one time I was so excited that I thought I should have driven a knife into him; and the infernal rascal has made ten thousand pound, I believe—and deserves to be hanged, and will be; but, curse him, I wish he could have lasted out my time. He knew all my ways, and, dammy, when I rang the bell, the confounded thief brought the thing I wanted—not like that stupid German lout. And what sort of time have you had in the country? Been a good deal with Lady Rockminster? You can't do better. She is one of the old school—vieille école, bonne école, hey? Dammy, they don't make gentlemen and ladies now; and in fifty years you'll hardly know one man from another. But they'll last my time. I ain't long for this business: I am getting very old, Pen, my boy; and, gad, I was thinking to-day, as I was packing up my little library, there's a Bible among the books that belonged to my poor mother; I would like you to keep that, Pen. I was thinking, sir, that you would most likely open the box when it was your property, and the old fellow was laid under the sod, sir," and the major coughed and wagged his old head over the fire.

His age—his kindness, disarmed Pen's anger somewhat, and made Arthur feel no little compunction for the deed which he was about to do. He knew that the announcement which he was about to make would destroy the darling hope of the old gentleman's life, and create in his breast a woeful anger and commotion.

"Hey—hey—I'm off, sir," nodded the Elder; "but I'd like to read a speech of yours in the Times before I go—'Mr. Pendennis said, Unaccustomed as I am to public speaking'—hey, sir? hey, Arthur? Begad, you look dev'lish well and healthy, sir. I always said my brother Jack would bring the family right. You must go down into the west, and buy the old estate, sir. Nec tenui pennâ, hey? We'll rise again, sir—rise again on the wing—and, begad, I shouldn't be surprised that you will be a baronet before you die."

His words smote Pen. "And it is I," he thought, "that am going to fling down the poor old fellow's air-castle. Well, it must be. Here goes. I—I went into your lodgings at Bury-street, though I did not find you," Pen slowly began—"and I talked with Morgan, uncle."

"Indeed!" The old gentleman's cheek began to flush involuntarily, and he muttered, "The cat's out of the bag now, begad!"

"He told me a story, sir, which gave me the deepest surprise and pain," said Pen.

The major tried to look unconcerned. "What—that story about— about—What-do-you-call-'em, hey?"

"About Miss Amory's father—about Lady Clavering's first husband, and who he is, and what."

"Hem—a devilish awkward affair!" said the old man, rubbing his nose. "I—I've been aware of that—eh—confounded circumstance, for some time."

"I wish I had known it sooner, or not at all," said Arthur, gloomily.

"He is all safe," thought the senior, greatly relieved. "Gad! I should have liked to keep it from you altogether—and from those two poor women, who are as innocent as unborn babes in the transaction."

"You are right. There is no reason why the two women should hear it; and I shall never tell them—though that villain, Morgan, perhaps may," Arthur said, gloomily. "He seems disposed to trade upon his secret, and has already proposed terms of ransom to me. I wish I had known of the matter earlier, sir. It is not a very pleasant thought to me that I am engaged to a convict's daughter."

"The very reason why I kept it from you—my dear boy. But Miss Amory is not a convict's daughter, don't you see? Miss Amory is the daughter of Lady Clavering, with fifty or sixty thousand pounds for a fortune; and her father-in-law, a baronet and country gentleman, of high reputation, approves of the match, and gives up his seat in Parliament to his son-in-law. What can be more simple?"

"Is it true, sir?"

"Begad, yes, it is true, of course it's true. Amory's dead. I tell you he is dead. The first sign of life he shows, he is dead. He can't appear. We have him at a dead-lock like the fellow in the play—the Critic, hey?—devilish amusing play, that Critic. Monstrous witty man Sheridan; and so was his son. By gad, sir, when I was at the Cape, I remember—" The old gentleman's garrulity, and wish, to conduct Arthur to the Cape, perhaps arose from a desire to avoid the subject which was near est his nephew's heart; but Arthur broke out, interrupting him, "If you had told me this tale sooner, I believe you would have spared me and yourself a great deal of pain and disappointment; and I should not have found myself tied to an engagement from which I can't, in honor, recede."

"No, begad, we've fixed you—and a man who's fixed to a seat in Parliament, and a pretty girl, with a couple of thousand a year, is fixed to no bad thing, let me tell you," said the old man.

"Great Heavens, sir!" said Arthur; "are you blind? Can't you see?"

"See what, young gentleman?" asked the other.

"See, that rather than trade upon this secret of Amory's," Arthur cried out, "I would go and join my father-in-law at the hulks! See, that rather than take a seat in Parliament as a bribe from Clavering for silence, I would take the spoons off the table! See, that you have given me a felon's daughter for a wife;

doomed me to poverty and shame; cursed my career when it might have been—when it might have been so different but for you! Don't you see that we have been playing a guilty game, and have been over-reached; that in offering to marry this poor girl, for the sake of her money, and the advancement she would bring, I was degrading myself, and prostituting my honor?"

"What in Heaven's name do you mean, sir?" cried the old man.

"I mean to say that there is a measure of baseness which I can't pass," Arthur said. "I have no other words for it, and am sorry if they hurt you. I have felt, for months past, that my conduct in this affair has been wicked, sordid, and worldly. I am rightly punished by the event, and having sold myself for money and a seat in Parliament, by losing both."

"How do you mean that you lose either?" shrieked the old gentleman. "Who the devil's to take your fortune or your seat away from you. By G—, Clavering shall give 'em to you. You shall have every shilling of eighty thousand pounds."

"I'll keep my promise to Miss Amory, sir," said Arthur.

"And, begad, her parents shall keep theirs to you."

"Not so, please God," Arthur answered. "I have sinned, but, Heaven help me, I will sin no more. I will let Clavering off from that bargain which was made without my knowledge. I will take no money with Blanche but that which was originally settled upon her; and I will try to make her happy. You have done it. You have brought this on me, sir. But you knew no better: and I forgive—"

"Arthur—in God's name—in your father's, who, by Heavens, was the proudest man alive, and had the honor of the family always at heart—in mine—for the sake of a poor broken down old fellow, who has always been dev'lish fond of you—don't fling this chance away—I pray you, I beg you, I implore you, my dear, dear boy, don't fling this chance away. It's the making of you. You're sure to get on. You'll be a baronet; it's three thousand a year: dammy, on my knees, there, I beg of you, don't do this."

And the old man actually sank down on his knees, and seizing one of Arthur's hands, looked up piteously at him. It was cruel to remark the shaking hands, the wrinkled and quivering face, the old eyes weeping and winking, the broken voice. "Ah, sir," said Arthur, with a groan. "You have brought pain enough on me, spare me this. You have wished me to marry Blanche. I marry her. For God's sake, sir, rise, I can't bear it."

"You—you mean to say that you will take her as a beggar, and be one yourself?" said the old gentleman, rising up and coughing violently.

"I look at her as a person to whom a great calamity has befallen, and to whom I am promised. She can not help the misfortune; and as she had my word when she was prosperous, I shall not withdraw it now she is poor. I will not take Clavering's seat, unless afterward it should be given of his free will. I will not have a shilling more than her original fortune."

"Have the kindness to ring the bell," said the old gentleman. "I have done my best, and said my say; and I'm a dev'lish old fellow. And—and—it don't matter. And—and Shakspeare was right—and Cardinal

Wolsey—begad—'and had I but served my God as I've served you'—yes, on my knees, by Jove, to my own nephew—I mightn't have been—Good-night, sir, you needn't trouble yourself to call again."

Arthur took his hand, which the old man left to him; it was quite passive and clammy. He looked very much oldened; and it seemed as if the contest and defeat had quite broken him.

On the next day he kept his bed, and refused to see his nephew.

CHAPTER XXXIII

IN WHICH THE DECK BEGINS TO CLEAR

When, arrayed in his dressing-gown, Pen walked up, according to custom, to Warrington's chambers next morning, to inform his friend of the issue of the last night's interview with his uncle, and to ask, as usual, for George's advice and opinion, Mrs. Flanagan, the laundress, was the only person whom Arthur found in the dear old chambers. George had taken a carpet-bag, and was gone. His address was to his brother's house, in Suffolk. Packages addressed to the newspaper and review for which he wrote lay on the table, awaiting delivery.

"I found him at the table, when I came, the dear gentleman!" Mrs. Flanagan said, "writing at his papers, and one of the candles was burned out; and hard as his bed is, he wasn't in it all night, sir."

Indeed, having sat at the Club until the brawl there became intolerable to him, George had walked home, and had passed the night finishing some work on which he was employed, and to the completion of which he bent himself with all his might. The labor was done, and the night was worn away somehow, and the tardy November dawn came and looked in on the young man as he sate over his desk. In the next day's paper, or quarter's review, many of us very likely admired the work of his genius, the variety of his illustration, the fierce vigor of his satire, the depth of his reason. There was no hint in his writing of the other thoughts which occupied him, and always accompanied him in his work—a tone more melancholy than was customary, a satire more bitter and impatient than that which he afterward showed, may have marked the writings of this period of his life to the very few persons who knew his style or his name. We have said before, could we know the man's feelings as well as the author's thoughts—how interesting most books would be! more interesting than merry. I suppose harlequin's face behind his mask is always grave, if not melancholy—certainly each man who lives by the pen, and happens to read this, must remember, if he will, his own experiences, and recall many solemn hours of solitude and labor. What a constant care sate at the side of the desk and accompanied him! Fever or sickness were lying possibly in the next room: a sick child might be there, with a wife watching over it terrified and in prayer: or grief might be bearing him down, and the cruel mist before the eyes rendering the paper scarce visible as he wrote on it, and the inexorable necessity drove on the pen. What man among us has not had nights and hours like these? But to the manly heart—severe as these pangs are, they are endurable: long as the night seems, the dawn comes at last, and the wounds heal, and the fever abates, and rest comes, and you can afford to look back on the past misery with feelings that are any thing but bitter.

Two or three books for reference, fragments of torn up manuscript, drawers open, pens and inkstand, lines half visible on the blotting paper, a bit of sealing wax twisted and bitten and broken into sundry pieces—such relics as these were about the table, and Pen flung himself down in George's empty chair—noting things according to his wont, or in spite of himself. There was a gap in the book-case (next to the old College Plato, with the Boniface Arms), where Helen's Bible used to be. He has taken that with him, thought Pen. He knew why his friend was gone. Dear, dear old George!

Pen rubbed his hand over his eyes. O, how much wiser, how much better, how much nobler he is than I, he thought. Where was such a friend, or such a brave heart? Where shall I ever hear such a frank voice, and kind laughter? Where shall I ever see such a true gentleman? No wonder she loved him. God bless him. What was I compared to him? What could she do else but love him? To the end of our days we will be her brothers, as fate wills that we can be no more. We'll be her knights, and wait on her: and when we're old, we'll say how we loved her. Dear, dear old George!

When Pen descended to his own chambers, his eye fell on the letter-box of his outer door, which he had previously overlooked, and there was a little note to A. P., Esq., in George's well-known handwriting, George had put into Pen's box probably as he was going away.

"Dr. Pen—I shall be half way home when you breakfast, and intend to stay over Christmas, in Norfolk, or elsewhere.

"I have my own opinion of the issue of matters about which we talked in J——street yesterday; and think my presence de trop." Vale. G.W.

"Give my very best regards and adieux to your cousin." And so George was gone, and Mrs. Flanagan, the laundress, ruled over his empty chambers.

Pen of course had to go and see his uncle on the day after their colloquy, and not being admitted, he naturally went to Lady Rockminister's apartments, where the old lady instantly asked for Bluebeard, and insisted that he should come to dinner.

"Bluebeard is gone," Pen said, and he took out poor George's scrap of paper, and handed it to Laura, who looked at it—did not look at Pen in return, but passed the paper back to him, and walked away. Pen rushed into an eloquent eulogium upon his dear old George to Lady Rockminister, who was astonished at his enthusiasm. She had never heard him so warm in praise of any body; and told him with her usual frankness, that she didn't think it had been in his nature to care so much about any other person.

As Mr. Pendennis was passing in Waterloo-place, in one of his many walks to the hotel where Laura lived, and whither duty to his uncle carried Arthur every day, Arthur saw issuing from Messrs. Gimcrack's celebrated shop an old friend, who was followed to his Brougham by an obsequious shopman bearing parcels. The gentleman was in the deepest mourning: the Brougham, the driver, and the horse, were in mourning. Grief in easy circumstances, and supported by the comfortablest springs and cushions, was typified in the equipage and the little gentleman, its proprietor.

"What, Foker! Hail, Foker!" cried out Pen—the reader, no doubt, has likewise recognized Arthur's old schoolfellow—and he held out his hand to the heir of the late lamented John Henry Foker, Esq., the master of Logwood and other houses, the principal partner in the great brewery of Foker & Co.: the greater portion of Foker's Entire.

A little hand, covered with a glove of the deepest ebony, and set off by three inches of a snowy wristband, was put forth to meet Arthur's salutation. The other little hand held a little morocco case, containing, no doubt, something precious, of which Mr. Foker had just become proprietor in Messrs. Gimcrack's shop. Pen's keen eyes and satiric turn showed him at once upon what errand Mr. Foker had been employed; and he thought of the heir in Horace pouring forth the gathered wine of his father's vats; and that human nature is pretty much the same in Regent-street as in the Via Sacra.

"Le roi est mort. Vive le roi!" said Arthur.

"Ah!" said the other. "Yes. Thank you—very much obliged. How do you do, Pen? very busy—good-by!" and he jumped into the black Brougham, and sate like a little black Care behind the black coachman. He had blushed on seeing Pen, and showed other signs of guilt and perturbation, which Pen attributed to the novelty of his situation; and on which he began to speculate in his usual sardonic manner.

"Yes: so wags the world," thought Pen. "The stone closes over Harry the Fourth, and Harry the Fifth reigns in his stead. The old ministers at the brewery come and kneel before him with their books; the draymen, his subjects, fling up their red caps, and shout for him. What a grave deference and sympathy the bankers and the lawyers show! There was too great a stake at issue between those two that they should ever love each other very cordially. As long as one man keeps another out of twenty thousand a year, the younger must be always hankering after the crown, and the wish must be the father to the thought of possession. Thank Heaven, there was no thought of money between me and our dear mother, Laura."

"There never could have been. You would have spurned it!" cried Laura. "Why make yourself more selfish than you are, Pen; and allow your mind to own for an instant that it would have entertained such—such dreadful meanness? You make me blush for you, Arthur; you make me—" her eyes finished this sentence, and she passed her handkerchief across them.

"There are some truths which women will never acknowledge," Pen said, "and from which your modesty always turns away. I do not say that I ever knew the feeling, only that I am glad I had not the temptation. Is there any harm in that confession of weakness?"

"We are all taught to ask to be delivered from evil, Arthur," said Laura, in a low voice. "I am glad if you were spared from that great crime; and only sorry to think that you could by any possibility have been led into it. But you never could; and you don't think you could. Your acts are generous and kind: you disdain mean actions. You take Blanche without money, and without a bribe. Yes, thanks be to Heaven, dear brother. You could not have sold yourself away; I knew you could not when it came to the day, and you did not. Praise be—be where praise is due. Why does this horrid skepticism pursue you, my Arthur? Why doubt and sneer at your own heart—at every one's? Oh, if you knew the pain you give me—how I lie awake and think of those hard sentences, dear brother, and wish them unspoken, unthought!"

"Do I cause you many thoughts and many tears, Laura?" asked Arthur. The fullness of innocent love beamed from her in reply. A smile heavenly pure, a glance of unutterable tenderness, sympathy, pity, shone in her face—all which indications of love and purity Arthur beheld and worshiped in her, as you would watch them in a child, as one fancies one might regard them in an angel.

"I—I don't know what I have done," he said, simply, "to have merited such regard from two such women. It is like undeserved praise, Laura—or too much good fortune, which frightens one—or a great post, when a man feels that he is not fit for it. Ah, sister, how weak and wicked we are; how spotless, and full of love and truth, Heaven made you! I think for some of you there has been no fall," he said, looking at the charming girl with an almost paternal glance of admiration. "You can't help having sweet thoughts, and doing good actions. Dear creature! they are the flowers which you bear."

"And what else, sir?" asked Laura. "I see a sneer coming over your face. What is it? Why does it come to drive all the good thoughts away?"

"A sneer, is there? I was thinking, my dear, that nature in making you so good and loving did very well: but—"

"But what? What is that wicked but? and why are you always calling it up?"

"But will come in spite of us. But is reflection. But is the skeptic's familiar, with whom he has made a compact; and if he forgets it, and indulges in happy day-dreams, or building of air castles, or listens to sweet music, let us say, or to the bells ringing to church, But taps at the door, and says, 'Master, I am here. You are my master; but I am yours. Go where you will you can't travel without me. I will whisper to you when you are on your knees at church. I will be at your marriage pillow. I will sit down at your table with your children. I will be behind your death-bed curtain.' That is what But is," Pen said.

"Pen, you frighten me," cried Laura.

"Do you know what But came and said to me just now, when I was looking at you? But said, 'If that girl had reason as well as love, she would love you no more. If she knew you as you are—the sullied, selfish being which you know—she must part from you, and could give you no love and no sympathy.' Didn't I say," he added fondly, "that some of you seem exempt from the fall? Love you know; but the knowledge of evil is kept from you."

"What is this you young folks are talking about?" asked Lady Rockminster, who at this moment made her appearance in the room, having performed in the mystic retirement of her own apartments, and under the hands of her attendant, those elaborate toilet-rites without which the worthy old lady never presented herself to public view "Mr. Pendennis, you are always coming here."

"It is very pleasant to be here," Arthur said; "and we were talking when you came in, about my friend Foker, whom I met just now; and who, as your ladyship knows, has succeeded to his father's kingdom."

"He has a very fine property, he has fifteen thousand a year. He is my cousin. He is a very worthy young man. He must come and see me," said Lady Rockminster, with a look at Laura.

"He has been engaged for many years past to his cousin, Lady—"

"Lady Ann is a foolish little chit," Lady Rockminster said, with much dignity; "and I have no patience with her. She has outraged every feeling of society. She has broken her father's heart, and thrown away fifteen thousand a year."

"Thrown away? What has happened?" asked Pen.

"It will be the talk of the town in a day or two; and there is no need why I should keep the secret any longer," said Lady Rockminster, who had written and received a dozen letters on the subject. "I had a letter yesterday from my daughter, who was staying at Drummington until all the world was obliged to go away on account of the frightful catastrophe which happened there. When Mr. Foker came home from Nice, and after the funeral, Lady Ann went down on her knees to her father, said that she never could marry her cousin, that she had contracted another attachment, and that she must die rather than fulfill her contract. Poor Lord Rosherville, who is dreadfully embarrassed, showed his daughter what the state of his affairs was, and that it was necessary that the arrangements should take place; and in fine, we all supposed that she had listened to reason, and intended to comply with the desires of her family. But what has happened—last Thursday she went out after breakfast with her maid, and was married in the very church in Drummington Park to Mr. Hobson, her father's own chaplain and her brother's tutor; a red-haired widower with two children. Poor dear Rosherville is in a dreadful way: he wishes Henry Foker should marry Alice or Barbara; but Alice is marked with the small-pox, and Barbara is ten years older than he is. And, of course, now the young man is his own master, he will think of choosing for himself. The blow on Lady Agnes is very cruel. She is inconsolable. She has the house in Grosvenor-street for her life, and her settlement, which was very handsome. Have you not met her? Yes, she dined one day at Lady Clavering's—the first day I saw you, and a very disagreeable young man I thought you were. But I have formed you. We have formed him, haven't we, Laura? Where is Bluebeard? let him come. That horrid Grindley, the dentist, will keep me in town another week." To the latter part of her ladyship's speech Arthur gave no ear. He was thinking for whom could Foker be purchasing those trinkets which he was carrying away from the jeweler's. Why did Harry seem anxious to avoid him? Could he be still faithful to the attachment which had agitated him so much, and sent him abroad eighteen months back? Psha! The bracelets and presents were for some of Harry's old friends of the Opera or the French theatre. Rumors from Naples and Paris, rumors, such as are borne to club smoking-rooms, had announced that the young man had found distractions; or, precluded from his virtuous attachment, the poor fellow had flung himself back upon his old companions and amusements—not the only man or woman whom society forces into evil, or debars from good; not the only victim of the world's selfish and wicked laws.

As a good thing when it is to be done can not be done too quickly, Laura was anxious that Pen's marriage intentions should be put into execution as speedily as possible, and pressed on his arrangements with rather a feverish anxiety. Why could she not wait? Pen could afford to do so with perfect equanimity, but Laura would hear of no delay. She wrote to Pen: she implored Pen: she used every means to urge expedition. It seemed as if she could have no rest until Arthur's happiness was complete.

She offered herself to dearest Blanche to come and stay at Tunbridge with her, when Lady Rockminster should go on her intended visit to the reigning house of Rockminster; and although the old dowager scolded, and ordered, and commanded, Laura was deaf and disobedient: she must go to Tunbridge, she would go to Tunbridge: she who ordinarily had no will of her own, and complied, smilingly, with any body's whim and caprices, showed the most selfish and obstinate determination in this instance. The dowager lady must nurse herself in her rheumatism, she must read herself to sleep; if she would not hear her maid, whose voice croaked, and who made sad work of the sentimental passages in the novels—Laura must go, and be with her new sister. In another week, she proposed, with many loves and regards to dear Lady Clavering, to pass some time with dearest Blanche.

Dearest Blanche wrote instantly in reply to dearest Laura's No. 1, to say with what extreme delight she should welcome her sister: how charming it would be to practice their old duets together, to wander o'er the grassy sward, and amidst the yellowing woods of Penshurst and Southborough! Blanche counted the hours till she should embrace her dearest friend.

Laura, No. 2, expressed her delight at dearest Blanche's affectionate reply. She hoped that their friendship would never diminish; that the confidence between them would grow in after years; that they should have no secrets from each other; that the aim of the life of each would be to make one person happy.

Blanche, No. 2 followed in two days. "How provoking! Their house was very small, the two spare bedrooms were occupied by that horrid Mrs. Planter and her daughter, who had thought proper to fall ill (she always fell ill in country houses), and she could not, or would not be moved for some days."

Laura, No. 3. "It was indeed very provoking. L. had hoped to hear one of dearest B.'s dear songs on Friday; but she was the more consoled to wait, because Lady R. was not very well, and liked to be nursed by her. Poor Major Pendennis was very unwell, too, in the same hotel—too unwell even to see Arthur, who was constant in his calls on his uncle. Arthur's heart was full of tenderness and affection. She had known Arthur all her life. She would answer—yes, even in italics she would answer—for his kindness, his goodness, and his gentleness."

Blanche, No. 3. "What is this most surprising, most extraordinary letter from A.P.? What does dearest Laura know about it? What has happened? What, what mystery is enveloped under his frightful reserve?"

Blanche, No. 3, requires an explanation; and it can not be better given than in the surprising and mysterious letter of Arthur Pendennis.

CHAPTER XXXIV

MR. AND MRS. SAM HUXTER

"Dear Blanche," Arthur wrote, "you are always reading and dreaming pretty dramas, and exciting romances in real life, are you now prepared to enact a part of one? And not the pleasantest part, dear Blanche—that in which the heroine takes possession of her father's palace and wealth, and, introducing her husband to the loyal retainers and faithful vassals, greets her happy bridegroom with 'All of this is mine and thine;' but the other character—that of the luckless lady, who suddenly discovers that she is not the prince's wife, but Claude Melnotte's the beggar's; that of Alnaschar's wife, who comes in just as her husband has kicked over the tray of porcelain which was to be the making of his fortune. But stay; Alnaschar, who kicked down the china, was not a married man; he had cast his eye on the vizier's daughter, and his hopes of her went to the ground with the shattered bowls and tea-cups.

"Will you be the vizier's daughter, and refuse and laugh to scorn Alnaschar, or will you be the Lady of Lyons, and love the penniless Claude Melnotte? I will act that part, if you like. I will love you my best in return. I will do my all to make your humble life happy: for humble it will be: at least the odds are against any other conclusion; we shall live and die in a poor, prosy, humdrum way. There will be no stars and epaulets for the hero of our story. I shall write one or two more stories, which will presently be forgotten. I shall be called to the bar, and try to get on in my profession: perhaps some day, if I am very lucky, and work very hard (which is absurd), I may get a colonial appointment, and you may be an Indian judge's lady. Meanwhile I shall buy back the Pall Mall Gazette: the publishers are tired of it since the death of poor Shandon, and will sell it for a small sum. Warrington will be my right hand, and write it up to a respectable sale. I will introduce you to Mr. Finucane, the sub-editor, and I know who, in the end, will be Mrs. Finucane—a very nice, gentle creature, who has lived sweetly through a sad life—and we will jog on, I say, and look out for better times, and earn our living decently. You shall have the opera-boxes, and superintend the fashionable intelligence, and break your little heart in the poet's corner. Shall we live over the offices?—there are four very good rooms, a kitchen, and a garret for Laura, in Catherine-street, in the Strand; or would you like a house in the Waterloo-road?—it would be very pleasant, only there is that halfpenny toll at the bridge. The boys may go to King's College, mayn't they? Does all this read to you like a joke?

"Ah, dear Blanche, it is no joke, and I am sober and telling the truth. Our fine day-dreams are gone. Our carriage has whirled out of sight like Cinderella's: our house in Belgravia has been whisked away into the air by a malevolent Genius, and I am no more a member of Parliament than I am a Bishop on his bench in the House of Lords, or a Duke with a garter at his knee. You know pretty well what my property is, and your own little fortune: we may have enough with those two to live in decent comfort; to take a cab sometimes when we go out to see our friends, and not to deny ourselves an omnibus when we are tired. But that is all: is that enough for you, my little dainty lady? I doubt sometimes whether you can bear the life which I offer you—at least, it is fair that you should know what it will be. If you say, 'Yes, Arthur, I will follow your fate whatever it may be, and be a loyal and loving wife to aid and cheer you'—come to me, dear Blanche, and may God help me so that I may do my duty to you. If not, and you look to a higher station, I must not bar Blanche's fortune—I will stand in the crowd, and see your ladyship go to Court where you are presented, and you shall give me a smile from your chariot window. I saw Lady Mirable going to the drawing-room last season: the happy husband at her side glittered with stars and cordons. All the flowers in the garden bloomed in the coachman's bosom. Will you have these and the chariot, or walk on foot and mend your husband's stockings?

"I can not tell you now—afterward I might, should the day come when we may have no secrets from one another—what has happened within the last few hours which has changed all my prospects in life; but so it is, that I have learned something which forces me to give up the plans which I had formed, and many vain and ambitious hopes in which I had been indulging. I have written and dispatched a letter to Sir Francis Clavering, saying that I can not accept his seat in Parliament until after my marriage; in like manner I can not and will not accept any larger fortune with you than that which has always belonged to you since your grandfather's death, and the birth of your half-brother. Your good mother is not in the least aware—I hope she never may be—of the reasons which force me to this very strange decision. They arise from a painful circumstance, which is attributable to none of our faults; but, having once befallen, they are as fatal and irreparable as that shock which overset honest Alnaschar's porcelain, and shattered all his hopes beyond the power of mending. I write gayly enough, for there is no use in bewailing such a hopeless mischance. We have not drawn the great prize in the lottery, dear Blanche: But I shall be contented enough without it, if you can be so; and I repeat, with all my heart, that I will do my best to make you happy.

"And now, what news shall I give you? My uncle is very unwell, and takes my refusal of the seat in Parliament in sad dudgeon: the scheme was his, poor old gentleman, and he naturally bemoans its failure. But Warrington, Laura, and I had a council of war: they know this awful secret, and back me in my decision. You must love George as you love what is generous and upright and noble; and as for Laura—she must be our sister, Blanche, our saint, our good angel. With two such friends at home, what need we care for the world with-out, or who is member for Clavering, or who is asked or not asked to the great balls of the season?"

To this frank communication came back the letter from Blanche to Laura, and one to Pen himself, which perhaps his own letter justified. "You are spoiled by the world," Blanche wrote; "you do not love your poor Blanche as she would be loved, or you would not offer thus lightly to take her or leave her. No, Arthur, you love me not—a man of the world, you have given me your plighted troth, and are ready to redeem it; but that entire affection, that love whole and abiding, where—where is that vision of my youth? I am but a pastime of your life, and I would be its all;—but a fleeting thought, and I would be your whole soul. I would have our two hearts one; but ah, my Arthur, how lonely yours is! how little you give me of it! You speak of our parting, with a smile on your lip; of our meeting, and you care not to hasten it! Is life but a disillusion, then, and are the flowers of our garden faded away? I have wept—I have prayed—I have passed sleepless hours—I have shed bitter, bitter tears over your letter! To you I bring the gushing poesy of my being—the yearnings of the soul that longs to be loved—that pines for love, love, love, beyond all!—that flings itself at your feet, and cries, Love me, Arthur! Your heart beats no quicker at the kneeling appeal of my love!—your proud eye is dimmed by no tear of sympathy!—you accept my soul's treasure as though 'twere dross! not the pearls from the unfathomable deeps of affection! not the diamonds from the caverns of the heart. You treat me like a slave, and bid me bow to my master! Is this the guerdon of a free maiden—is this the price of a life's passion? Ah me! when was it otherwise? when did love meet with aught but disappointment? Could I hope (fond fool!) to be the exception to the lot of my race; and lay my fevered brow on a heart that comprehended my own? Foolish girl that I was! One by one, all the flowers of my young life have faded away; and this, the last, the sweetest, the dearest, the fondly, the madly loved, the wildly cherished—where is it? But no more of this. Heed not my bleeding heart.—Bless you, bless you always, Arthur!

"I will write more when I am more collected. My racking brain renders thought almost impossible. I long to see Laura! She will come to us directly we return from the country, will she not? And you, cold one!" B.

The words of this letter were perfectly clear, and written in Blanche's neatest hand, upon her scented paper; and yet the meaning of the composition not a little puzzled Pen. Did Blanche mean to accept or to refuse his polite offer? Her phrases either meant that Pen did not love her, and she declined him, or that she took him, and sacrificed herself to him, cold as he was. He laughed sardonically over the letter, and over the transaction which occasioned it. He laughed to think how Fortune had jilted him, and how he deserved his slippery fortune. He turned over and over the musky, gilt-edged riddle. It amused his humor: he enjoyed it as if it had been a funny story.

He was thus seated, twiddling the queer manuscript in his hand, joking grimly to himself, when his servant came in with a card from a gentleman, who wished to speak to him very particularly. And if Pen had gone out into the passage, he would have seen sucking his stick, rolling his eyes, and showing great marks of anxiety, his old acquaintance, Mr. Samuel Huxter.

"Mr. Huxter on particular business! Pray, beg Mr. Huxter to come in," said Pen, amused rather; and not the less so when poor Sam appeared before him.

"Pray take a chair, Mr. Huxter," said Pen, in his most superb manner. "In what way can I be of service to you?"

"I had rather not speak before the flunk—before the man, Mr. Pendennis;" on which Mr. Arthur's attendant quitted the room.

"I'm in a fix," said Mr. Huxter, gloomily.

"Indeed."

"She sent me to you," continued the young surgeon.

"What, Fanny? Is she well? I was coming to see her, but I have had a great deal of business since my return to London."

"I heard of you through my governor and Jack Hobnell," broke in Huxter. "I wish you joy, Mr. Pendennis, both of the borough and the lady, sir. Fanny wishes you joy, too," he added, with something of a blush.

"There's many a slip between the cup and the lip! Who knows what may happen, Mr. Huxter, or who will sit in Parliament for Clavering next session?"

"You can do any thing with my governor," continued Mr. Huxter. "You got him Clavering Park. The old boy was very much pleased, sir, at your calling him in. Hobnell wrote me so. Do you think you could speak to the governor for me, Mr. Pendennis?"

"And tell him what?" "I've gone and done it, sir," said Huxter, with a particular look.

"You—you don't mean to say you have—you have done any wrong to that dear little creature, sir," said Pen, starting up in a great fury.

"I hope not," said Huxter, with a hang-dog look: "but I've married her. And I know there will be an awful shindy at home. It was agreed that I should be taken into partnership when I had passed the College, and it was to have been Huxter and Son. But I would have it, confound it. It's all over now, and the old boy's wrote to me that he's coming up to town for drugs: he will be here to-morrow, and then it must all come out."

"And when did this event happen?" asked Pen, not over well pleased, most likely, that a person who had once attracted some portion of his royal good graces should have transferred her allegiance, and consoled herself for his loss.

"Last Thursday was five weeks—it was two days after Miss Amory came to Shepherd's Inn," Huxter answered.

Pen remembered that Blanche had written and mentioned her visit. "I was called in," Huxter said. "I was in the inn looking after old Cos's leg; and about something else too, very likely: and I met Strong, who told me there was a woman taken ill in Chambers, and went up to give her my professional services. It was the old lady who attends Miss Amory—her housekeeper, or some such thing. She was taken with strong hysterics: I found her kicking and screaming like a good one—in Strong's chamber, along with him and Colonel Altamont, and Miss Amory crying and as pale as a sheet; and Altamont fuming about—a regular kick up. They were two hours in the chambers; and the old woman went whooping off in a cab. She was much worse than the young one. I called in Grosvenor-place next day to see if I could be of any service, but they were gone without so much as thanking me: and the day after I had business of my own to attend to—a bad business too," said Mr. Huxter, gloomily. "But it's done, and can't be undone; and we must make the best of it."

She has known the story for a month, thought Pen, with a sharp pang of grief, and a gloomy sympathy—this accounts for her letter of to-day. She will not implicate her father, or divulge his secret; she wishes to let me off from the marriage—and finds a pretext—the generous girl!

"Do you know who Altamont is, sir?" asked Huxter, after the pause during which Pen had been thinking of his own affairs. "Fanny and I have talked him over, and we can't help fancying that it's Mrs. Lightfoot's first husband come to life again, and she who has just married a second. Perhaps Lightfoot won't be very sorry for it," sighed Huxter, looking savagely at Arthur, for the demon of jealousy was still in possession of his soul; and now, and more than ever since his marriage, the poor fellow fancied that Fanny's heart belonged to his rival.

"Let us talk about your affairs," said Pen. "Show me how I can be of any service to you, Huxter. Let me congratulate you on your marriage, I am thankful that Fanny, who is so good, so fascinating, so kind a creature, has found an honest man, and a gentleman who will make her happy. Show me what I can do to help you."

"She thinks you can, sir," said Huxter, accepting Pen's proffered hand, "and I'm very much obliged to you, I'm sure; and that you might talk over my father, and break the business to him, and my mother, who always has her back up about being a clergyman's daughter. Fanny ain't of a good family, I know, and not up to us in breeding and that—but she's a Huxter now."

"The wife takes the husband's rank, of course," said Pen.

"And with a little practice in society," continued Huxter, imbibing his stick, "she'll be as good as any girl in Clavering. You should hear her sing and play on the piano. Did you ever? Old Bows taught her. And she'll do on the stage, if the governor was to throw me over; but I'd rather not have her there. She can't help being a coquette, Mr. Pendennis, she can't help it. Dammy, sir! I'll be bound to say, that two or three of the Bartholomew chaps, that I've brought into my place, are sitting with her now: even Jack Linton, that I took down as my best man, is as bad as the rest, and she will go on singing and making eyes at him. It's what Bows says, if there were twenty men in a room, and one not taking notice of her, she wouldn't be satisfied until the twentieth was at her elbow."

"You should have her mother with her," said Pen, laughing.

"She must keep the lodge. She can't see so much of her family as she used. I can't, you know, sir, go on with that lot. Consider my rank in life," said Huxter, putting a very dirty hand up to his chin.

"Au fait" said Mr. Pen, who was infinitely amused, and concerning whom mutato nomine (and of course concerning nobody else in the world) the fable might have been narrated.

As the two gentlemen were in the midst of this colloquy, another knock came to Pen's door, and his servant presently announced Mr. Bows. The old man followed slowly, his pale face blushing, and his hand trembling somewhat as he took Pen's. He coughed, and wiped his face in his checked cotton pocket-handkerchief, and sat down, with his hands on his knees, the sun shining on his bald head. Pen looked at the homely figure with no small sympathy and kindness. This man, too, has had his griefs, and his wounds, Arthur thought. This man, too, has brought his genius and his heart, and laid them at a woman's feet; where she spurned them. The chance of life has gone against him, and the prize is with that creature yonder. Fanny's bridegroom, thus mutely apostrophized, had winked meanwhile with one eye at old Bows, and was driving holes in the floor with the cane which he loved.

"So we have lost, Mr. Bows, and here is the lucky winner," Pen said, looking hard at the old man.

"Here is the lucky winner, sir, as you say."

"I suppose you have come from my place?" asked Huxter, who, having winked at Bows with one eye, now favored Pen with a wink of the other—a wink which seemed to say, "Infatuated old boy—you understand—over head and ears in love with her—poor old fool."

"Yes, I have been there ever since you went away. It was Mrs. Sam who sent me after you: who said that she thought you might be doing something stupid—something like yourself, Huxter."

"There's as big fools as I am," growled the young surgeon.

"A few, p'raps," said the old man; "not many, let us trust. Yes, she sent me after you, for fear you should offend Mr. Pendennis; and I daresay because she thought you wouldn't give her message to him, and beg him to go and see her; and she knew I would take her errand. Did he tell you that, sir?"

Huxter blushed scarlet, and covered his confusion with an imprecation. Pen laughed; the scene suited his bitter humor more and more.

"I have no doubt Mr. Huxter was going to tell me," Arthur said, "and very much flattered I am sure I shall be to pay my respects to his wife."

"It's in Charterhouse-lane, over the baker's, on the right hand side as you go from St. John's-street," continued Bows, without any pity. "You know Smithfield, Mr. Pendennis? St. John's-street leads into Smithfield. Dr. Johnson has been down the street many a time with ragged shoes, and a bundle of penny-a-lining for the 'Gent's Magazine.' You literary gents are better off now—eh? You ride in your cabs, and wear yellow kid gloves now."

"I have known so many brave and good men fail, and so many quacks and impostors succeed, that you mistake me if you think I am puffed up by my own personal good luck, old friend," Arthur said, sadly. "Do you think the prizes of life are carried by the most deserving? and set up that mean test of prosperity for merit? You must feel that you are as good as I. I have never questioned it. It is you that are peevish against the freaks of fortune, and grudge the good luck that befalls others. It's not the first time you have unjustly accused me, Bows."

"Perhaps you are not far wrong, sir," said the old fellow, wiping his bald forehead. "I am thinking about myself and grumbling; most men do when they get on that subject. Here's the fellow that's got the prize in the lottery; here's the fortunate youth."

"I don't know what you are driving at," Huxter said, who had been much puzzled as the above remarks passed between his two companions.

"Perhaps not," said Bows, drily. "Mrs. H. sent me here to look after you, and to see that you brought that little message to Mr. Pendennis, which you didn't, you see, and so she was right. Women always are; they have always a reason for every thing. Why, sir," he said, turning round to Pen with a sneer, "she had a reason even for giving me that message. I was sitting with her after you left us, very quiet and comfortable; I was talking away, and she was mending your shirts, when your two young friends, Jack Linton and Bob Blades, looked in from Bartholomew's; and then it was she found out that she had this message to send. You needn't hurry yourself, she don't want you back again; they'll stay these two hours, I daresay."

Huxter rose with great perturbation at this news, and plunged his stick into the pocket of his paletot, and seized his hat.

"You'll come and see us, sir, won't you?" he said to Pen. "You'll talk over the governor, won't you, sir, if I can get out of this place and down to Clavering?"

"You will promise to attend me gratis if ever I fall ill at Fairoaks, will you, Huxter?" Pen said, good-naturedly. "I will do any thing I can for you. I will come and see Mrs. Huxter immediately, and we will conspire together about what is to be done."

"I thought that would send him out, sir," Bows said, dropping into his chair again as soon as the young surgeon had quitted the room. "And it's all true, sir—every word of it. She wants you back again, and sends her husband after you. She cajoles every body, the little devil. She tries it on you, on me, on poor Costigan, on the young chaps from Bartholomew's. She's got a little court of 'em already. And if there's nobody there, she practices on the old German baker in the shop, or coaxes the black sweeper at the crossing."

"Is she fond of that fellow?" asked Pen.

"There is no accounting for likes and dislikes," Bows answered. "Yes, she is fond of him; and having taken the thing into her head, she would not rest until she married him. They had their bans published at St. Clement's, and nobody heard it or knew any just cause or impediment. And one day she slips out of the porter's lodge, and has the business done, and goes off to Gravesend with Lothario; and leaves a note for me to go and explain all things to her ma. Bless you! the old woman knew it as well as I did, though she pretended ignorance. And so she goes, and I'm alone again. I miss her, sir, tripping along that court, and coming for her singing lesson; and I've no heart to look into the porter's lodge now, which looks very empty without her, the little flirting thing. And I go and sit and dangle about her lodgings, like an old fool. She makes 'em very trim and nice, though; gets up all Huxter's shirts and clothes: cooks his little dinner, and sings at her business like a little lark. What's the use of being angry? I lent 'em three pound to go on with: for they haven't got a shilling till the reconciliation, and pa comes down."

When Bows had taken his leave, Pen carried his letter from Blanche, and the news which he had just received, to his usual adviser, Laura. It was wonderful upon how many points Mr. Arthur, who generally followed his own opinion, now wanted another person's counsel. He could hardly so much as choose a waistcoat without referring to Miss Bell: if he wanted to buy a horse he must have Miss Bell's opinion; all which marks of deference tended greatly to the amusement of the shrewd old lady with whom Miss Bell lived, and whose plans regarding her protégée we have indicated.

Arthur produced Blanche's letter then to Laura, and asked her to interpret it. Laura was very much agitated, and puzzled by the contents of the note.

"It seems to me," she said, "as if Blanche is acting very artfully."

"And wishes so to place matters that she may take me or leave me? Is it not so?"

"It is, I am afraid, a kind of duplicity which does not augur well for your future happiness; and is a bad reply to your own candor and honesty, Arthur. Do you know I think, I think—I scarcely like to say what I think," said Laura, with a deep blush; but of course the blushing young lady yielded to her cousin's persuasion, and expressed what her thoughts were. "It looks to me, Arthur, as if there might be—there might be somebody else," said Laura, with a repetition of the blush.

"And if there is," broke in Arthur, "and if I am free once again, will the best and dearest of all women—"

"You are not free, dear brother," Laura said, calmly. "You belong to another; of whom I own it grieves me to think ill. But I can't do otherwise. It is very odd that in this letter she does not urge you to tell her the reason why you have broken arrangements which would have been so advantageous to you; and avoids speaking on the subject. She somehow seems to write as if she knows her father's secret."

Pen said, "Yes, she must know it;" and told the story, which he had just heard from Huxter, of the interview at Shepherd's Inn. "It was not so that she described the meeting," said Laura; and, going to her desk, produced from it that letter of Blanche's which mentioned her visit to Shepherd's Inn. "Another disappointment—only the Chevalier Strong and a friend of his in the room." This was all that Blanche had said. "But she was bound to keep her father's secret, Pen," Laura added. "And yet, and yet—it is very puzzling."

The puzzle was this, that for three weeks after this eventful discovery Blanche had been, only too eager about her dearest Arthur; was urging, as strongly as so much modesty could urge, the completion of the happy arrangements which were to make her Arthur's forever; and now it seemed as if something had interfered to mar these happy arrangements—as if Arthur poor was not quite so agreeable to Blanche as Arthur rich and a member of Parliament—as if there was some mystery. At last she said—

"Tunbridge Wells is not very far off, is it, Arthur? Hadn't you better go and see her?"

They had been in town a week and neither had thought of that simple plan before!

CHAPTER XXXV

SHOWS HOW ARTHUR HAD BETTER HAVE TAKEN A RETURN-TICKET

The train carried Arthur only too quickly to Tunbridge, though he had time to review all the circumstances of his life as he made the brief journey, and to acknowledge to what sad conclusions his selfishness and waywardness had led him. "Here is the end of hopes and aspirations," thought he, "of romance and ambitions! Where I yield or where I am obstinate, I am alike unfortunate; my mother implores me, and I refuse an angel! Say I had taken her: forced on me as she was, Laura would never have been an angel to me. I could not have given her my heart at another's instigation; I never could have known her as she is, had I been obliged to ask another to interpret her qualities and point out her virtues. I yield to my uncle's solicitations, and accept, on his guarantee, Blanche, and a seat in Parliament, and wealth, and ambition, and a career; and see!—fortune comes and leaves me the wife without the dowry, which I had taken in compensation of a heart. Why was I not more honest, or am I not less so? It would have cost my poor old uncle no pangs to accept Blanche's fortune, whencesoever it came; he can't even understand, he is bitterly indignant—heart-stricken, almost—at the scruples which actuate me in refusing it. I dissatisfy every body. A maimed, weak, imperfect wretch, it seems as if I am unequal to any fortune. I neither make myself nor any one connected with me happy. What prospect is there for this poor little frivolous girl, who is to take my obscure name, and share my fortune? I have not even ambition to excite me, or self-esteem enough to console myself, much more her, for my failure. If I were to write a book that should go through twenty editions, why, I should be the very first to sneer at my reputation. Say I could succeed at the bar, and achieve a fortune by bullying witnesses and twisting evidence; is that a fame which would satisfy my longings, or a calling in which my life would be well spent? How I wish I could be that priest opposite, who never has lifted his eyes from his breviary, except when we were in Reigate tunnel, when he could not see; or that old gentleman next him, who scowls at him with eyes of hatred over his newspaper. The priest shuts his eyes to the world, but has his thoughts on the book, which is his directory to the world to come. His neighbor hates him as a monster, tyrant, persecutor; and fancies burning martyrs, and that pale countenance looking on, and lighted up by the flame. These have no doubts; these march on trustfully, bearing their load of logic."

"Would you like to look at the paper, sir?" here interposed the stout gentleman (it had a flaming article against the order of the blackcoated gentleman who was traveling with them in the carriage) and Pen thanked him and took it, and pursued his reverie, without reading two sentences of the journal.

"And yet, would you take either of those men's creeds, with its consequences?" he thought. "Ah me! you must bear your own burden, fashion your own faith, think your own thoughts, and pray your own prayer. To what mortal ear could I tell all, if I had a mind? or who could understand all? Who can tell another's short-comings, lost opportunities, weigh the passions which overpower, the defects which incapacitate reason?—what extent of truth and right his neighbor's mind is organized to perceive and to do?—what invisible and forgotten accident, terror of youth, chance or mischance of fortune, may have altered the whole current of life? A grain of sand may alter it, as the flinging of a pebble may end it. Who can weigh circumstances, passions, temptations, that go to our good and evil account, save One, before whose awful wisdom we kneel, and at whose mercy we ask absolution? Here it ends," thought Pen; "this day or to-morrow will wind up the account of my youth; a weary retrospect, alas! a sad history, with many a page I would fain not look back on! But who has not been tired or fallen, and who has escaped without scars from that struggle?" And his head fell on his breast, and the young man's heart prostrated itself humbly and sadly before that Throne where sits wisdom, and love, and pity for all, and made its confession. "What matters about fame or poverty!" he thought. "If I marry this woman I have chosen, may I have strength and will to be true to her, and to make her happy. If I have children, pray God teach me to speak and to do the truth among them, and to leave them an honest name. There are no splendors for my marriage. Does my life deserve any? I begin a new phase of it; a better than the last may it be, I pray Heaven!".

The train stopped at Tunbridge as Pen was making these reflections; and he handed over the newspaper to his neighbor, of whom he took leave, while the foreign clergyman in the opposite corner still sate with his eyes on his book. Pen jumped out of the carriage then, his carpetbag in hand, and briskly determined to face his fortune.

A fly carried him rapidly to Lady Clavering's house from the station; and, as he was transported thither, Arthur composed a little speech, which he intended to address to Blanche, and which was really as virtuous, honest, and well-minded an oration as any man of his turn of mind, and under his circumstances, could have uttered. The purport of it was—"Blanche, I cannot understand from your last letter what your meaning is, or whether my fair and frank proposal to you is acceptable or no. I think you know the reason which induces me to forego the worldly advantages which a union with you offered, and which I could not accept without, as I fancy, being dishonored. If you doubt of my affection, here I am ready to prove it. Let Smirke be called in, and let us be married out of hand; and with all my heart I purpose to keep my vow, and to cherish you through life, and to be a true and a loving husband to you."

From the fly Arthur sprang out then to the hall-door, where he was met by a domestic whom he did not know. The man seemed to be surprised at the approach of the gentleman with the carpet-bag, which he made no attempt to take from Arthur's hands. "Her ladyship's not at home, sir," the man remarked.

"I am Mr. Pendennis," Arthur said. "Where is Lightfoot?" "Lightfoot is gone," answered the man. "My lady is out, and my orders was—"

"I hear Miss Amory's voice in the drawing-room," said Arthur. "Take the bag to a dressing-room, if you please;" and, passing by the porter, he walked straight toward that apartment, from which, as the door opened, a warble of melodious notes issued.

Our little siren was at her piano singing with all her might and fascinations. Master Clavering was asleep on the sofa, indifferent to the music; but near Blanche sat a gentleman who was perfectly enraptured with her strain, which was of a passionate and melancholy nature.

As the door opened, the gentleman started up with a hullo! the music stopped, with a little shriek from the singer; Frank Clavering woke up from the sofa, and Arthur came forward and said, "What, Foker! how do you do, Foker?" He looked at the piano, and there, by Miss Amory's side, was just such another purple-leather box as he had seen in Harry's hand three days before, when the heir of Logwood was coming out of a jeweler's shop in Waterloo-place. It was opened, and curled round the white-satin cushion within was, oh, such a magnificent serpentine bracelet, with such a blazing ruby head and diamond tail!

"How-de-do, Pendennis?" said Foker. Blanche made many motions of the shoulders, and gave signs of interest and agitation. And she put her handkerchief over the bracelet, and then she advanced, with a hand which trembled very much, to greet Pen. "How is dearest Laura?" she said. The face of Foker looking up from his profound mourning—that face, so piteous and puzzled, was one which the reader's imagination must depict for himself; also that of Master Frank Clavering, who, looking at the three interesting individuals with an expression of the utmost knowingness, had only time to ejaculate the words, "Here's a jolly go!" and to disappear sniggering.

Pen, too, had restrained himself up to that minute; but looking still at Foker, whose ears and cheeks tingled with blushes, Arthur burst out into a fit of laughter, so wild and loud, that it frightened Blanche much more than any the most serious exhibition.

"And this was the secret, was it? Don't blush and turn away, Foker, my boy. Why, man, you are a pattern of fidelity. Could I stand between Blanche and such constancy—could I stand between Miss Amory and fifteen thousand a year?"

"It is not that, Mr. Pendennis," Blanche said, with great dignity. "It is not money, it is not rank, it is not gold that moves me; but it is constancy, it is fidelity, it is a whole, trustful, loving heart offered to me that I treasure—yes, that I treasure!" And she made for her handkerchief, but, reflecting what was underneath it, she paused. "I do not disown, I do not disguise—my life is above disguise—to him on whom it is bestowed, my heart must be forever bare—that I once thought I loved you,—yes, thought I was beloved by you! I own. How I clung to that faith! How I strove, I prayed, I longed to believe it! But your conduct always—your own words so cold, so heartless, so unkind, have undeceived me. You trifled with the heart of the poor maiden! You flung me back with scorn the troth which I had plighted! I have explained all—all to Mr. Foker."

"That you have," said Foker, with devotion, and conviction in his looks.

"What, all?" said Pen, with a meaning look at Blanche. "It is I am in fault is it? Well, well, Blanche, be it so. I won't appeal against your sentence, and bear it in silence. I came down here looking to very different things, Heaven knows, and with a heart most truly and kindly disposed toward you. I hope you may be happy with another, as, on my word, it was my wish to make you so; and I hope my honest old friend here will have a wife worthy of his loyalty, his constancy, and affection. Indeed they deserve the regard of any woman—even Miss Blanche Amory. Shake hands, Harry; don't look askance at me. Has any body told you that I was a false and heartless character?"

"I think you're a—" Foker was beginning, in his wrath, when Blanche interposed.

"Henry, not a word!—I pray you let there be forgiveness!"

"You're an angel, by Jove, you're an angel!" said Foker, at which Blanche looked seraphically up to the chandelier.

"In spite of what has passed, for the sake of what has passed, I must always regard Arthur as a brother," the seraph continued; "we have known each other years, we have trodden the same fields, and plucked the same flowers together. Arthur! Henry! I beseech you to take hands and to be friends! Forgive you!—I forgive you, Arthur, with my heart I do. Should I not do so for making me so happy?"

"There is only one person of us three whom I pity, Blanche," Arthur said, gravely, "and I say to you again, that I hope you will make this good fellow, this honest and loyal creature, happy."

"Happy! O Heavens!" said Harry. He could not speak. His happiness gushed out at his eyes. "She don't know—she can't know how fond I am of her, and—and who am I? a poor little beggar, and she takes me up and says she'll try and I-I-love me. I ain't worthy of so much happiness. Give us your hand, old boy, since she forgives you after your heartless conduct, and says she loves you. I'll make you welcome. I tell you I'll love every body who loves her. By—if she tells me to kiss the ground I'll kiss it. Tell me to kiss the ground! I say, tell me. I love you so. You see I love you so."

Blanche looked up seraphically again. Her gentle bosom heaved. She held out one hand as if to bless Harry, and then royally permitted him to kiss it. She took up the pocket handkerchief and hid her own eyes, as the other fair hand was abandoned to poor Harry's tearful embrace.

"I swear that is a villain who deceives such a loving creature as that," said Pen.

Blanche laid down the handkerchief, and put hand No. 2 softly on Foker's head, which was bent down kissing and weeping over hand No. 1. "Foolish boy!" she said, "it shall be loved as it deserves: who could help loving such a silly creature?"

And at this moment Frank Clavering broke in upon the sentimental trio.

"I say, Pendennis!" he said.

"Well, Frank!"

"The man wants to be paid, and go back. He's had some beer."

"I'll go back with him," cried Pen. "Good-by, Blanche. God bless you, Foker, old friend. You know, neither of you want me here." He longed to be off that instant.

"Stay—I must say one word to you. One word in private, if you please," Blanche said. "You can trust us together, can't you—Henry?" The tone in which the word Henry was spoken, and the appeal, ravished Foker with delight. "Trust you!" said he; "Oh, who wouldn't trust you! Come along, Franky, my boy."

"Let's have a cigar," said Frank, as they went into the hall.

"She don't like it," said Foker, gently.

"Law bless you—she don't mind. Pendennis used to smoke regular," said the candid youth.

"It was but a short word I had to say," said Blanche to Pen, with great calm, when they were alone. "You never loved me, Mr. Pendennis."

"I told you how much," said Arthur. "I never deceived you."

"I suppose you will go back and marry Laura," continued Blanche.

"Was that what you had to say?" said Pen.

"You are going to her this very night, I am sure of it. There is no denying it. You never cared for me."

"Et vous?"

"Et moi c'est différent. I have been spoilt early. I can not live out of the world, out of excitement. I could have done so, but it is too late. If I can not have emotions, I must have the world. You would offer me neither one nor the other. You are blasé in every thing, even in ambition. You had a career before you, and you would not take it. You give it up!—for what?—for a bêtise, for an absurd scruple. Why would you not have that seat, and be such a puritain? Why should you refuse what is mine by right, entendez-vous?"

"You know all then?" said Pen.

"Only within a month. But I have suspected ever since Baymouth —n'importe since when. It is not too late. He is as if he had never been; and there is a position in the world before you yet. Why not sit in Parliament, exert your talent, and give a place in the world to yourself, to your wife? I take celui-là. Il est bon. 1l est riche. Il est—vous le connaissez autant que moi enfin. Think you that I would not prefer un homme, qui fera parler de moi? If the secret appears I am rich à millions. How does it affect me? It is not my fault. It will never appear."

"You will tell Harry every thing, won't you?"

"Je comprends. Vous refusez" said Blanche, savagely. "I will tell Harry at my own time, when we are married. You will not betray me, will you? You, having a defenseless girl's secret, will not turn upon her and use it? S'il me plait de le cacher, mon secret; pourquoi le donnerai-je? Je l'aime, mon pauvre père, voyez-vous? I would rather live with that man than with you fades intriguers of the world. I must have emotions—il m'en donne. Il m'écrit. Il écrit tres-bien, voyez-vous—comme un pirate—comme un Bohémien—comme un homme. But for this I would have said to my mother—Ma mère! quittons ce lâche mari, cette lâche société—retournons à mon père.

"The pirate would have wearied you like the rest," said Pen.

"Eh! Il me faut des émotions" said Blanche. Pen had never seen her or known so much about her in all the years of their intimacy as he saw and knew now: though he saw more than existed in reality. For this young lady was not able to carry out any emotion to the full; but had a sham enthusiasm, a sham hatred, a sham love, a sham taste, a sham grief, each of which flared and shone very vehemently for an instant, but subsided and gave place to the next sham emotion.

CHAPTER XXXVI

A CHAPTER OF MATCH-MAKING

Upon the platform at Tunbridge, Pen fumed and fretted until the arrival of the evening train to London, a full half-hour—six hours it seemed to him: but even this immense interval was passed, the train arrived, the train sped on, the London lights came in view—a gentleman who forgot his carpet-bag in the train rushed at a cab, and said to the man, "Drive as hard as you can go to Jermyn-street." The cabman, although a Hansom cabman, said thank you for the gratuity which was put into his hand, and Pen ran up the stairs of the hotel to Lady Rockminster's apartments. Laura was alone in the drawing-room, reading, with a pale face, by the lamp. The pale face looked up when Pen opened the door. May we follow him? The great moments of life are but moments like the others. Your doom is spoken in a word or two. A single look from the eyes: a mere pressure of the hand may decide it; or of the lips, though they can not speak.

When Lady Rockminster, who has had her after-dinner nap, gets up and goes into her sitting-room, we may enter with her ladyship.

"Upon my word, young people!" are the first words she says, and her attendant makes wondering eyes over her shoulder. And well may she say so; and well may the attendant cast wondering eyes; for the young people are in an attitude; and Pen in such a position as every young lady who reads this has heard tell of, or has seen, or hopes, or at any rate deserves to see.

In a word, directly he entered the room, Pen went up to Laura of the pale face, who had not time even to say, What, back so soon? and seizing her outstretched and trembling hand just as she was rising from her chair, fell down on his knees before her, and said quickly, "I have seen her. She has engaged herself to Harry Foker—and—and NOW, Laura?"

The hand gives a pressure—the eyes beam a reply—the quivering lips answer, though speechless. Pen's head sinks down in the girl's lap, as he sobs out, "Come and bless us, dear mother," and arms as tender as Helen's once more enfold him.

In this juncture it is that Lady Rockminster comes in and says, "Upon my word, young people! Beck! leave the room. What do you want poking your nose in here?"

Pen starts up with looks of triumph, still holding Laura's hand. "She is consoling me for my misfortune, ma'am," he says.

"What do you mean by kissing her hand? I don't know what you will be next doing."

Pen kissed her ladyship's. "I have been, to Tunbridge," he says, "and seen Miss Amory; and find on my arrival that—that a villain has supplanted me in her affections," he says with a tragedy air.

"Is that all? Is that what you were whimpering on your knees about?" says the old lady, growing angry. "You might have kept the news till to-morrow."

"Yes—another has superseded me," goes on Pen; "but why call him villain? He is brave, he is constant, he is young, he is wealthy, he is beautiful."

"What stuff are you talking, sir?" cried the old lady. "What has happened?"

"Miss Amory has jilted me, and accepted Henry Foker, Esq. I found her warbling ditties to him as he lay at her feet; presents had been accepted, vows exchanged, these ten days. Harry was old Mrs. Planter's rheumatism, which kept dearest Laura out of the house. He is the most constant and generous of men. He has promised the living of Logwood to Lady Ann's husband, and given her a splendid present on her marriage; and he rushed to fling himself at Blanche's feet the instant he found he was free."

"And so, as you can't get Blanche, you put up with Laura, is that it, sir?" asked the old lady.

"He acted nobly," Laura said.

"I acted as she bade me," said Pen. "Never mind how, Lady Rockminster; but to the best of my knowledge and power. And if you mean that I am not worthy of Laura, I know it, and pray Heaven to better me; and if the love and company of the best and purest creature in the world can do so, at least I shall have these to help me."

"Hm, hm," replied the old lady to this, looking with rather an appeased air at the young people. "It is all very well; but I should have preferred Bluebeard."

And now Pen, to divert the conversation from a theme which was growing painful to some parties present, bethought him of his interview with Huxter in the morning, and of Fanny Bolton's affairs, which he had forgotten under the immediate pressure and excitement of his own. And he told the ladies how Huxter had elevated Fanny to the rank of wife, and what terrors he was in respecting the arrival of his father. He described the scene with considerable humor, taking care to dwell especially upon that part of it which concerned Fanny's coquetry and irrepressible desire of captivating mankind; his meaning being "You see, Laura, I was not so guilty in that little affair; it was the girl who made love to me, and I who resisted. As I am no longer present, the little siren practices her arts and fascinations upon others. Let that transaction be forgotten in your mind, if you please; or visit me with a very gentle punishment for my error."

Laura understood his meaning under the eagerness of his explanations. "If you did any wrong, you repented, dear Pen," she said, "and you know," she added, with meaning eyes and blushes, "that I have no right to reproach you."

"Hm!" grumbled the old lady; "I should have preferred Bluebeard."

"The past is broken away. The morrow is before us. I will do my best to make your morrow happy, dear Laura," Pen said. His heart was humbled by the prospect of his happiness: it stood awe-stricken in the contemplation of her sweet goodness and purity. He liked his wife better that she had owned to that passing feeling for Warrington, and laid bare her generous heart to him. And she—very likely she was thinking "How strange it is that I ever should have cared for another; I am vexed almost to think I care for him so little, am so little sorry that he is gone away. Oh, in these past two months how I have learned to love Arthur. I care about nothing but Arthur; my waking and sleeping thoughts are about him; he is never absent from me. And to think that he is to be mine, mine! and that I am to marry him, and not to be his servant as I expected to be only this morning; for I would have gone down on my knees to Blanche to beg her to let me live with him. And now—Oh, it is too much. Oh, mother! mother, that you were here!" Indeed, she felt as if Helen were there—by her actually, though invisibly. A halo of happiness beamed from her. She moved with a different step, and bloomed with a new beauty. Arthur saw the change; and the old Lady Rockminster remarked it with her shrewd eyes.

"What a sly, demure little wretch you have been," she whispered to Laura—while Pen, in great spirits, was laughing, and telling his story about Huxter—"and how you have kept your secret!"

"How are we to help the young couple?" said Laura. Of course Miss Laura felt an interest in all young couples, as generous lovers always love other lovers.

"We must go and see them," said Pen. "Of course we must go and see them," said Laura. "I intend to be very fond of Fanny. Let us go this instant. Lady Rockminster, may I have the carriage?"

"Go now!—why, you stupid creature, it is eleven o'clock at night. Mr. and Mrs. Huxter have got their night-caps on, I daresay. And it is time for you to go now. Good-night, Mr. Pendennis."

Arthur and Laura begged for ten minutes more.

"We will go to-morrow morning, then. I will come and fetch you with Martha."

"An earl's coronet," said Pen, who, no doubt, was pleased himself, "will have a great effect in Lamb-court and Smithfield. Stay—Lady Rockminster, will you join us in a little conspiracy?"

"How do you mean conspiracy, young man?"

"Will you please to be a little ill to-morrow; and when old Mr. Huxter arrives, will you let me call him in? If he is put into a good humor at the notion of attending a baronet in the country, what influence won't a countess have on him? When he is softened—when he is quite ripe, we will break the secret upon him; bring in the young people, extort the paternal benediction, and finish the comedy."

"A parcel of stuff," said the old lady. "Take your hat, sir. Come away, Miss. There—my head is turned another way. Good-night, young people." And who knows but the old lady thought of her own early days as she went away on Laura's arm, nodding her head and humming to herself?

With the early morning came Laura and Martha, according to appointment; and the desired sensation was, let us hope, effected in Lamb-court, whence the three proceeded to wait upon Mr. and Mrs. Samuel Huxter, at their residence in Charterhouse-lane.

The two ladies looked at each other with great interest, and not a little emotion on Fanny's part. She had not seen her "guardian," as she was pleased to call Pen in consequence of his bequest, since the event had occurred which had united her to Mr. Huxter.

"Samuel told me how kind you had been," she said. "You were always very kind, Mr. Pendennis. And—and I hope your friend is better, who was took ill in Shepherd's Inn, ma'am."

"My name is Laura," said the other, with a blush. "I am—that is, I was—that is, I am Arthur's sister; and we shall always love you for being so good to him when he was ill. And when we live in the country, I hope we shall see each other. And I shall be always happy to hear of your happiness, Fanny."

"We are going to do what you and Huxter have done, Fanny.—Where is Huxter? What nice, snug lodgings you've got! What a pretty cat!"

While Fanny is answering these questions in reply to Pen, Laura says to herself—"Well, now really! is this the creature about whom we were all so frightened? What could he see in her? She's a homely little thing, but such manners! Well, she was very kind to him—bless her for that." Mr. Samuel had gone out to meet his pa. Mrs. Huxter said that the old gentleman was to arrive that day at the Somerset coffee-house, in the Strand; and Fanny confessed that she was in a sad tremor about the meeting. "If his parents cast him off, what are we to do?" she said. "I shall never pardon myself for bringing ruing on my 'usband's 'ead. You must intercede for us, Mr. Arthur. If mortal man can, you can bend and influence Mr. Huxter senior." Fanny still regarded Pen in the light of a superior being, that was evident. No doubt Arthur thought of the past, as he marked the solemn little tragedy-airs and looks, the little ways, the little trepidations, vanities, of the little bride. As soon as the interview was over, entered Messrs. Linton and Blades, who came, of course, to visit Huxter, and brought with them a fine fragrance of tobacco. They had watched the carriage at the baker's door, and remarked the coronet with awe. They asked of Fanny who was that uncommonly heavy swell who had just driven off? and pronounced the countess was of the right sort. And when they heard that it was Mr. Pendennis and his sister, they remarked that Pen's father was only a sawbones; and that he gave himself confounded airs: they had been in Huxter's company on the night of his little altercation with Pen in the Back Kitchen.

Returning homeward through Fleet-street, and as Laura was just stating to Pen's infinite amusement that Fanny was very well, but that really there was no beauty in her—there might be, but she could not see it—as they were locked near Temple-bar, they saw young Huxter returning to his bride. "The governor had arrived; was at the Somerset coffee-house—was in tolerable good humor—something about the railway: but he had been afraid to speak about—about that business. Would Mr. Pendennis try it on?"

Pen said he would go and call at that moment upon Mr. Huxter, and see what might be done. Huxter junior would lurk outside while that awful interview took place. The coronet on the carriage inspired his soul also with wonder; and old Mr. Huxter himself beheld it with delight, as he looked from the coffee-house window on that Strand, which it was always a treat to him to survey.

"And I can afford to give myself a lark, sir," said Mr. Huxter, shaking hands with Pen. "Of course you know the news? We have got our bill, sir. We shall have our branch line—our shares are up, sir—and we buy your three fields along the Brawl, and put a pretty penny into your pocket, Mr. Pendennis."

"Indeed! that was good news." Pen remembered that there was a letter from Mr. Tatham, at Chambers, these three days; but he had not opened the communication, being interested with other affairs.

"I hope you don't intend to grow rich, and give up practice," said Pen. "We can't lose you at Clavering, Mr. Huxter; though I hear very good accounts of your son. My friend, Dr. Goodenough, speaks most highly of his talents. It is hard that a man of your eminence, though, should be kept in a country town."

"The metropolis would have been my sphere of action, sir," said Mr. Huxter, surveying the Strand. "But a man takes his business where he finds it; and I succeeded to that of my father."

"It was my father's, too," said Pen. "I sometimes wish I had followed it."

"You, sir, have taken a more lofty career," said the old gentleman. "You aspire to the senate: and to literary honors. You wield the poet's pen, sir, and move in the circles of fashion. We keep an eye upon you at Clavering. We read your name in the lists of the select parties of the nobility. Why, it was only the other day that my wife was remarking how odd it was that at a party at the Earl of Kidderminster's your name was not mentioned. To what member of the aristocracy may I ask does that equipage belong from which I saw you descend? The Countess Dowager of Rockminster? How is her ladyship?"

"Her ladyship is not very well; and when I heard that you were coming to town, I strongly urged her to see you, Mr. Huxter," Pen said. Old Huxter felt, if he had a hundred votes for Clavering, he would give them all to Pen.

"There is an old friend of yours in the carriage—a Clavering lady, too—will you come out and speak to her?" asked Pen. The old surgeon was delighted to speak to a coroneted carriage in the midst of the full Strand: he ran out bowing and smiling. Huxter junior, dodging about the district, beheld the meeting between his father and Laura, saw the latter put out her hand, and presently, after a little colloquy with Pen, beheld his father actually jump into the carriage, and drive away with Miss Bell.

There was no room for Arthur, who came back, laughing, to the young surgeon, and told him whither his parent was bound. During the whole of the journey, that artful Laura coaxed and wheedled, and cajoled him so adroitly, that the old gentleman would have granted her any thing; and Lady Rockminster achieved the victory over him by complimenting him on his skill, and professing her anxiety to consult him. What were her ladyship's symptoms? Should he meet her ladyship's usual medical attendant? Mr. Jones was called out of town? He should be delighted to devote his very best energies and experience to her ladyship's service.

He was so charmed with his patient, that he wrote home about her to his wife and family; he talked of nothing but Lady Rockminster to Samuel, when that youth came to partake of beef-steak and oyster-sauce and accompany his parent to the play. There was a simple grandeur, a polite urbanity, a high-bred grace about her ladyship, which he had never witnessed in any woman. Her symptoms did not seem alarming; he had prescribed—Spir:Ammon:Aromat: with a little Spir:Menth:Pip: and orange-flower, which would be all that was necessary.

"Miss Bell seemed to be on the most confidential and affectionate footing with her ladyship. She was about to form a matrimonial connection. All young people ought to marry. Such were her ladyship's words: and the countess condescended to ask respecting my own family, and I mentioned you by name to her ladyship, Sam, my boy. I shall look in to-morrow, when, if the remedies which I have prescribed for her ladyship have had the effect which I anticipate, I shall probably follow them up by a little Spir: Lavend: Comp:—and so set my noble patient up. What is the theater which is most frequented by the—by the higher classes in town, hey, Sam? and to what amusement will you take an old country doctor to-night, hey, sir?"

On the next day, when Mr. Huxter called in Jermyn-street at twelve o'clock, Lady Rockminster had not yet left her room, but Miss Bell and Mr. Pendennis were in waiting to receive him. Lady Rockminster had had a most comfortable night, and was getting on as well as possible. How had Mr. Huxter amused himself? at the theater? with his son? What a capital piece it was, and how charming Mrs. O'Leary looked and sang it! and what a good fellow young Huxter was! liked by every body, an honor to his profession. He has not his father's manners, I grant you, or that old-world tone which is passing away from us, but a more excellent, sterling fellow never lived. "He ought to practice in the country whatever you do, sir," said Arthur, "he ought to marry—other people are going to do so—and settle."

"The very words that her ladyship used yesterday, Mr. Pendennis He ought to marry. Sam should marry, sir."

"The town is full of temptations, sir," continued Pen. The old gentleman thought of that houri, Mrs. O'Leary.

"There is no better safeguard for a young man than an early marriage with an honest affectionate creature."

"No better, sir, no better."

"And love is better than money, isn't it?"

"Indeed it is," said Miss Bell.

"I agree with so fair an authority," said the old gentleman with a bow.

"And—and suppose, sir," Pen said, "that I had a piece of news to communicate to you."

"God bless my soul, Mr. Pendennis! what do you mean?" asked the old gentleman.

"Suppose I had to tell you that a young man carried away by an irresistible passion for an admirable and most virtuous young creature—whom every body falls in love with—had consulted the dictates of reason and his heart, and had married. Suppose I were to tell you that that man is my friend; that our excellent, our truly noble friend the Countess Dowager of Rockminster is truly interested about him (and you may fancy what a young man can do in life when THAT family is interested for him); suppose I were to tell you that you know him—that he is here—that he is—"

"Sam, married! God bless my soul, sir, you don't mean that!"

"And to such a nice creature, dear Mr. Huxter."

"His lordship is charmed with her," said Pen, telling almost the first fib which he has told in the course of this story.

"Married! the rascal, is he?" thought the old gentleman. "They will do it, sir," said Pen; and went and opened the door. Mr. and Mrs. Samuel Huxter issued thence, and both came and knelt down before the old gentleman. The kneeling little Fanny found favor in his sight. There must have been something attractive about her, in spite of Laura's opinion.

"Will never do so any more, sir," said Sam.

"Get up, sir," said Mr. Huxter. And they got up, and Fanny came a little nearer and a little nearer still, and looked so pretty and pitiful, that somehow Mr. Huxter found himself kissing the little crying-laughing thing, and feeling as if he liked it.

"What's your name, my dear?" he said, after a minute of this sport.

"Fanny, papa," said Mrs. Samuel.

CHAPTER XXXVII

EXEUNT OMNES

Our characters are all a month older than they were when the last-described adventures and conversations occurred, and a great number of the personages of our story have chanced to re-assemble at the little country town where we were first introduced to them. Frederic Lightfoot, formerly maître d'hôtel in the service of Sir Francis Clavering, of Clavering Park, Bart., has begged leave to inform the nobility and gentry of——shire that he has taken that well-known and comfortable hotel, the Clavering Arms, in Clavering, where he hopes for the continued patronage of the gentlemen and families of the county. "This ancient and well-established house," Mr. Lightfoot's manifesto states, "has been repaired and decorated in a style of the greatest comfort. Gentlemen hunting with the Dumplingbeare hounds will find excellent stabling and loose boxes for horses at the Clavering Arms. A commodious billiard-room has been attached to the hotel, and the cellars have been furnished with the choicest wines and spirits, selected, without regard to expense, by C.L. Commercial gentlemen will find the Clavering Arms a most comfortable place of resort: and the scale of charges has been regulated for all, so as to meet the economical spirit of the present times."

Indeed, there is a considerable air of liveliness about the old inn. The Clavering Arms have been splendidly repainted over the gate-way. The coffee-room windows are bright and fresh, and decorated with Christmas holly; the magistrates have met in petty sessions in the card-room of the old Assembly. The farmers' ordinary is held as of old, and frequented by increased numbers, who are pleased with Mrs. Lightfoot's cuisine. Her Indian curries and Mulligatawny soup are especially popular: Major Stokes, the respected tenant of Fairoaks Cottage, Captain Glanders, H. P., and other resident gentry, have pronounced in their favor, and have partaken of them more than once, both in private and at the dinner of the Clavering Institute, attendant on the incorporation of the reading-room, and when the chief inhabitants of that flourishing little town met together and did justice to the hostess's excellent cheer. The chair was taken by Sir Francis Clavering, Bart., supported by the esteemed rector, Dr. Portman; the vice-chair being ably filled by——Barker, Esq. (supported by the Rev. J. Simcoe and the Rev. S. Jowls), the enterprising head of the ribbon factory in Clavering, and chief director of the Clavering and Chatteris Branch of the Great Western Railway, which will be opened in another year, and upon the works of which the engineers and workmen are now busily engaged.

"An interesting event, which is likely to take place in the life of our talented townsman, Arthur Pendennis, Esq., has, we understand, caused him to relinquish the intentions which he had of offering himself as a candidate for our borough; and rumor whispers (says the Chatteris Champion, Clavering Agriculturist, and Baymouth Fisherman—that independent county paper, so distinguished for its unswerving principles and loyalty to the British oak, and so eligible a medium for advertisements)—rumor states, says the C. C. C. A. and B.F., that should Sir Francis Clavering's failing health oblige him to relinquish his seat in Parliament, he will vacate it in favor of a young gentleman of colossal fortune and related to the highest aristocracy of the empire, who is about to contract a matrimonial alliance with an accomplished and LOVELY lady, connected by the nearest ties with the respected family at Clavering Park. Lady Clavering and Miss Amory have arrived at the Park for the Christmas holidays; and we understand that a large number of the aristocracy are expected, and that festivities of a peculiarly interesting nature will take place there at the commencement of the new year."

The ingenious reader will be enabled, by the help of the above announcement to understand what has taken place during the little break which has occurred in our narrative. Although Lady Rockminster grumbled a little at Laura's preference for Pendennis over Bluebeard, those who are aware of the latter's secret will understand that the young girl could make no other choice, and the kind old lady who had constituted herself Miss Bell's guardian was not ill-pleased that she was to fulfill the great purpose in life of young ladies and marry. She informed her maid of the interesting event that very night, and of course, Mrs. Beck, who was perfectly aware of every single circumstance, and kept by Martha, of Fairoaks, in the fullest knowledge of what was passing, was immensely surprised and delighted. "Mr. Pendennis's income is so much; the railroad will give him so much more, he states; Miss Bell has so much, and may probably have a little more one day. For persons in their degree, they will be able to manage very well. And I shall speak to my nephew Pynsent, who I suspect was once rather attached to her—but of course that was out of the question" ("Oh! of course, my lady; I should think so indeed!")—"not that you know any thing whatever about it, or have any business to think at all on the subject—I shall speak to George Pynsent, who is now chief secretary of the Tape and Sealing Wax Office, and have Mr. Pendennis made something. And, Beck, in the morning you will carry down my compliments to Major Pendennis, and say that I shall pay him a visit at one o'clock.—Yes," muttered the old lady, "the major must be reconciled, and he must leave his fortune to Laura's children."

Accordingly, at one o'clock, the Dowager Lady Rockminster appeared at Major Pendennis's, who was delighted, as may be imagined, to receive so noble a visitor. The major had been prepared, if not for the news which her ladyship was about to give him, at least with the intelligence that Pen's marriage with Miss Amory was broken off. The young gentleman bethinking him of his uncle, for the first time that day, it must be owned, and meeting his new servant in the hall of the hotel, asked after the major's health from Mr. Frosch; and then went into the coffee-room of the hotel, where he wrote a half-dozen lines to acquaint his guardian with what had occurred. "Dear uncle," he said, "if there has been any question between us, it is over now. I went to Tunbridge Wells yesterday, and found that somebody else had carried off the prize about which we were hesitating. Miss A., without any compunction for me, has bestowed herself upon Harry Foker, with his fifteen thousand a year. I came in suddenly upon their loves, and found and left him in possession.

"And you'll be glad to hear, Tatham writes me, that he has sold three of my fields at Fairoaks to the Railroad Company, at a great figure. I will tell you this, and more when we met; and am always your affectionate—A.P."

"I think I am aware of what you were about to tell me," the major said, with a most courtly smile and bow to Pen's embassadress, "It was a very great kindness of your ladyship to think of bringing me the news. How well you look! How very good you are! How very kind you have always been to that young man!"

"It was for the sake of his uncle," said Lady Rockminster, most politely.

"He has informed me of the state of affairs, and written me a nice note—yes, a nice note," continued the old gentleman; "and I find he has had an increase to his fortune—yes; and all things considered, I don't much regret that this affair with Miss Amory is manquée, though I wished for it once—in fact, all things considered, I am very glad of it."

"We must console him, Major Pendennis," continued the lady; "we must get him a wife." The truth then came across the major's mind, and he saw for what purpose Lady Rockminster had chosen to assume the office of embassadress.

It is not necessary to enter into the conversation which ensued, or to tell at any length how her ladyship concluded a negotiation, which, in truth, was tolerably easy. There could be no reason why Pen should not marry according to his own and his mother's wish; and as for Lady Rockminster, she supported the marriage by intimations which had very great weight with the major, but of which we shall say nothing, as her ladyship (now, of course, much advanced in years) is still alive, and the family might be angry; and, in fine, the old gentleman was quite overcome by the determined graciousness of the lady, and her fondness for Laura. Nothing, indeed, could be more bland and kind than Lady Rockminster's whole demeanor, except for one moment when the major talked about his boy throwing himself away, at which her ladyship broke out into a little speech, in which she made the major understand, what poor Pen and his friends acknowledged very humbly, that Laura was a thousand times too good for him. Laura was fit to be the wife of a king—Laura was a paragon of virtue and excellence. And it must be said, that when Major Pendennis found that a lady of the rank of the Countess of Rockminster seriously admired Miss Bell, he instantly began to admire her himself.

So that when Herr Frosch was requested to walk up-stairs to Lady Rockminster's apartments, and inform Miss Bell and Mr. Arthur Pendennis that the major would receive them, and Laura appeared blushing and happy as she hung on Pen's arm, the major gave a shaky hand to one and the other, with no unaffected emotion and cordiality, and then went through another salutation to Laura, which caused her to blush still more. Happy blushes! bright eyes beaming with the light of love! The story-teller turns from this group to his young audience, and hopes that one day their eyes may all shine so.

Pen having retreated in the most friendly manner, and the lovely Blanche having bestowed her young affections upon a blushing bridegroom, with fifteen thousand a year, there was such an outbreak of happiness in Lady Clavering's heart and family as the good Begum had not known for many a year, and she and Blanche were on the most delightful terms of cordiality and affection. The ardent Foker pressed onward the happy day, and was as anxious as might be expected to abridge the period of mourning which had put him in possession of so many charms and amiable qualities, of which he had been only, as it were, the heir apparent, not the actual owner, until then. The gentle Blanche, every thing that her affianced lord could desire, was not averse to gratify the wishes of her fond Henry. Lady Clavering came up from Tunbridge. Milliners and jewelers were set to work and engaged to prepare the delightful paraphernalia of Hymen. Lady Clavering was in such a good humor, that Sir Francis even benefited by it, and such a reconciliation was effected between this pair, that Sir Francis came to London, sate at the head of his own table once more, and appeared tolerably flush of money at his billiard-rooms and gambling-houses again. One day, when Major Pendennis and Arthur went to dine in Grosvenor place, they found an old acquaintance established in the quality of major-domo, and the gentleman in black, who, with perfect politeness and gravity, offered them their choice of sweet or dry champagne, was no other than Mr. James Morgan. The Chevalier Strong was one of the party; he was in high spirits and condition, and entertained the company with accounts of his amusements abroad.

"It was my lady who invited me," said Strong to Arthur, under his voice—"that fellow Morgan looked as black as thunder when I came in. He is about no good here. I will go away first, and wait for you and Major Pendennis at Hyde Park Gate."

Mr. Morgan helped Major Pendennis to his great coat when he was quitting the house; and muttered something about having accepted a temporary engagement with the Clavering family.

"I have got a paper of yours, Mr. Morgan," said the old gentleman.

"Which you can show, if you please, to Sir Francis, sir, and perfectly welcome," said Mr. Morgan, with downcast eyes. "I'm very much obliged to you, Major Pendennis, and if I can pay you for all your kindness I will."

Arthur overheard the sentence, and saw the look of hatred which accompanied it, suddenly cried out that he had forgotten his handkerchief, and ran up-stairs to the drawing-room again. Foker was still there; still lingering about his siren. Pen gave the siren a look full of meaning, and we suppose that the siren understood meaning looks, for when, after finding the veracious handkerchief of which he came in quest, he once more went out, the siren, with a laughing voice, said, "O, Arthur—Mr. Pendennis—I want you to tell dear Laura something?" and she came out to the door.

"What is it?" he asked, shutting the door.

"Have you told Harry? Do you know that villain Morgan knows all."

"I know it," she said.

"Have you told Harry?"

"No, no," she said. "You won't betray me?"

"Morgan will," said Pen.

"No, he wont," said Blanche. "I have promised him—n'importe. Wait until after our marriage—O, until after our marriage—O, how wretched I am," said the girl, who had been all smiles, and grace, and gayety during the evening.

Arthur said, "I beg and implore you to tell Harry. Tell him now. It is no fault of yours. He will pardon you any thing. Tell him tonight."

"And give her this—Il est là—with my love, please; and I beg your pardon for calling you back; and if she will be at Madame Crinoline's at half-past three, and if Lady Rockminster can spare her, I should so like to drive with her in the park;" and she went in, singing and kissing her little hand, as Morgan the velvet-footed came up the carpeted stair.

Pen heard Blanche's piano breaking out into brilliant music as he went down to join his uncle; and they walked away together. Arthur briefly told him what he had done. "What was to be done?" he asked.

"What is to be done, begad?" said the old gentleman. "What is to be done but to leave it alone? Begad, let us be thankful," said the old fellow, with a shudder, "that we are out of the business, and leave it to those it concerns."

"I hope to Heaven she'll tell him," said Pen.

"Begad, she'll take her own course," said the old man. "Miss Amory is a dev'lish wide-awake girl, sir, and must play her own cards; and I'm doosid glad you are out of it—doosid glad, begad. Who's this smoking? O, it's Mr. Strong again. He wants to put in his oar, I suppose. I tell you, don't meddle in the business, Arthur."

Strong began once or twice, as if to converse upon the subject, but the major would not hear a word. He remarked on the moonlight on Apsley House, the weather, the cab-stands—any thing but that subject. He bowed stiffly to Strong, and clung to his nephew's arm, as he turned down St. James's-street, and again cautioned Pen to leave the affair alone. "It had like to have cost you so much, sir, that you may take my advice," he said.

When Arthur came out of the hotel, Strong's cloak and cigar were visible a few doors off. The jolly chevalier laughed as they met. "I'm an old soldier too," he said. "I wanted to talk to you, Pendennis. I have heard of all that has happened, and all the chops and changes that have taken place during my absence. I congratulate you on your marriage, and I congratulate you on your escape, too—you understand me. It was not my business to speak, but I know this, that a certain party is as arrant a little—well—well, never mind what. You acted like a man, and a trump, and are well out of it."

"I have no reason to complain," said Pen. "I went back to beg and entreat poor Blanche to tell Foker all: I hope, for her sake, she will; but I fear not. There is but one policy, Strong, there is but one."

"And lucky he that can stick to it," said the chevalier. "That rascal Morgan means mischief. He has been lurking about our chambers for the last two months: he has found out that poor mad devil Amory's secret. He has been trying to discover where he was: he has been pumping Mr. Bolton, and making old Costigan drunk several times. He bribed the Inn porter to tell him when we came back: and he has got into Clavering's service on the strength of his information. He will get very good pay for it, mark my words, the villain." "Where is Amory?" asked Pen.

"At Boulogne, I believe. I left him there, and warned him not to come back. I have broken with him, after a desperate quarrel, such as one might have expected with such a madman. And I'm glad to think that he is in my debt now, and that I have been the means of keeping him out of more harms than one."

"He has lost all his winnings, I suppose," said Pen.

"No: he is rather better than when he went away, or was a fortnight ago. He had extraordinary luck at Baden: broke the bank several nights, and was the fable of the place. He lied himself there, with a fellow by the name of Bloundell, who gathered about him a society of all sorts of sharpers, male and female, Russians, Germans, French, English. Amory got so insolent, that I was obliged to thrash him one day within an inch of his life. I couldn't help myself; the fellow has plenty of pluck, and I had nothing for it but to hit out."

"And did he call you out?" said Pen.

"You think if I had shot him I should have done nobody any harm? No, sir; I waited for his challenge, but it never came: and the next time I met him he begged my pardon, and said, 'Strong, I beg your pardon; you whopped me and you served me right.' I shook hands: but I couldn't live with him after that. I paid him what I owed him the night before," said Strong with a blush. "I pawned every thing to pay him, and then I went with my last ten florins, and had a shy at the roulette. If I had lost, I should have let him shoot me in the morning. I was weary of my life. By Jove, sir, isn't it a shame that a man like me, who may have had a few bills out, but who never deserted a friend, or did an unfair action, shouldn't be able to turn his hand to any thing to get bread? I made a good night, sir, at roulette, and I've done with that. I'm going into the wine business. My wife's relations live at Cadiz. I intend to bring over Spanish wine and hams; there's a fortune to be made by it, sir—a fortune—here's my card. If you want any sherry or hams, recollect Ned Strong is your man." And the chevalier pulled out a handsome card, stating that Strong and Company, Shepherd's Inn, were sole agents of the celebrated Diamond Manzanilla of the Duke of Garbanzos, Grandee of Spain of the First Class; and of the famous Toboso hams, fed on acorns only in the country of Don Quixote. "Come and taste 'em, sir—come and try 'em at my chambers. You see, I've an eye to business, and by Jove, this time I'll succeed."

Pen laughed as he took the card. "I don't know whether I shall be allowed to go to bachelors' parties," he said. "You know I'm going to—"

"But you must have sherry, sir. You must have sherry."

"I will have it from you, depend on it," said the other. "And I think you are very well out of your other partnership. That worthy, Altamont and his daughter correspond, I hear," Pen added after a pause "Yes; she wrote him the longest rigmarole letters that I used to read: the sly little devil; and he answered under cover to Mrs. Bonner. He was for carrying her off the first day or two, and nothing would content him but having back his child. But she didn't want to come, as you may fancy; and he was not very eager about it." Here the chevalier burst out in a laugh. "Why, sir, do you know what was the cause of our quarrel and boxing match? There was a certain widow at Baden, a Madame la Baronne de la Cruche-cassée, who was not much better than himself, and whom the scoundrel wanted to marry; and would, but that I told her he was married already. I don't think that she was much better than he was. I saw her on the pier at Boulogne the day I came to England."

And now we have brought up our narrative to the point, whither the announcement in the Chatteris Champion had already conducted us.

It wanted but very, very few days before that blissful one when Foker should call Blanche his own; the Clavering folks had all pressed to see the most splendid new carriage in the whole world, which was standing in the coach-house at the Clavering Arms; and shown, in grateful return for drink, commonly, by Mr. Foker's head coachman. Madame Fribsby was occupied in making some lovely dresses for the tenants' daughters, who were to figure as a sort of bridemaids' chorus at the breakfast and marriage ceremony. And immense festivities were to take place at the Park upon this delightful occasion.

"Yes, Mr. Huxter, yes; a happy tenantry, its country's pride, will assemble in the baronial hall, where the beards will wag all. The ox shall be slain, and the cup they'll drain; and the bells shall peal quite genteel; and my father-in-law, with the tear of sensibility bedewing his eye, shall bless us at his baronial porch. That shall be the order of proceedings, I think, Mr. Huxter; and I hope we shall see you and your lovely bride by her husband's side; and what will you please to drink, sir? Mrs. Lightfoot, madam, you will give to my excellent friend and body surgeon, Mr. Huxter, Mr. Samuel Huxter, M.R.C.S., every refreshment that your hostel affords, and place the festive amount to my account; and Mr. Lightfoot, sir, what will you take? though you've had enough already, I think; yes, ha."

So spoke Harry Foker in the bar of the Clavering Arms. He had apartments at that hotel, and had gathered a circle of friends round him there. He treated all to drink who came. He was hail-fellow with every man. He was so happy! He danced round Madam Fribsby, Mrs. Lightfoot's great ally, as she sate pensive in the bar. He consoled Mrs. Lightfoot, who had already begun to have causes of matrimonial disquiet; for the truth must be told, that young Lightfoot, having now the full command of the cellar, had none over his own unbridled desires, and was tippling and tipsy from morning till night. And a piteous sight it was for his fond wife to behold the big youth reeling about the yard and coffee-room, or drinking with the farmers and tradesmen his own neat wines and carefully-selected stock of spirits.

When he could find time, Mr. Morgan the butler came from the Park, and took a glass at the expense of the landlord of the Clavering Arms. He watched poor Lightfoot's tipsy vagaries with savage sneers. Mrs. Lightfoot felt always doubly uncomfortable when her unhappy spouse was under his comrade's eye. But a few months married, and to think he had got to this. Madame Fribsby could feel for her. Madame Fribsby could tell her stories of men every bit as bad. She had had her own woes too, and her sad experience of men. So it is that nobody seems happy altogether; and that there's bitters, as Mr. Foker remarked, in the cup of every man's life. And yet there did not seem to be any in his, the honest young fellow! It was brimming over with happiness and good-humor.

Mr. Morgan was constant in his attentions to Foker. "And yet I don't like him somehow," said the candid young man to Mrs. Lightfoot. "He always seems as if he was measuring me for my coffin somehow. Pa-in-law's afraid of him; pa-in-law's, a-hem! never mind, but ma-in-law's a trump, Mrs. Lightfoot."

"Indeed my lady was;" and Mrs. Lightfoot owned, with a sigh, that perhaps it had been better for her had she never left her mistress.

"No, I do not like thee, Dr. Fell: the reason why I can not tell," continued Mr. Foker; "and he wants to be taken as my head man. Blanche wants me to take him. Why does Miss Amory like him so?"

"Did Miss Blanche like him so?" The notion seemed to disturb Mrs. Lightfoot very much; and there came to this worthy landlady another cause for disturbance. A letter bearing the Boulogne postmark, was brought to her one morning, and she and her husband were quarreling over it as Foker passed down the stairs by the bar, on his way to the Park. His custom was to breakfast there, and bask awhile in the presence of Armida; then, as the company of Clavering tired him exceedingly, and he did not care for sporting, he would return for an hour or two to billiards and the society of the Clavering Arms; then it would be time to ride with Miss Amory, and, after dining with her, he left her and returned modestly to his inn.

Lightfoot and his wife were quarreling over the letter. What was that letter from abroad? Why was she always having letters from abroad? Who wrote 'em?—he would know. He didn't believe it was her brother. It was no business of his? It was a business of his; and, with a curse, he seized hold of his wife, and dashed at her pocket for the letter.

The poor woman gave a scream; and said, "Well, take it." Just as her husband seized on the letter, and Mr. Foker entered at the door, she gave another scream at seeing him, and once more tried to seize the paper. Lightfoot opened it, shaking her away, and an inclosure dropped down on the breakfast table.

"Hands off, man alive!" cried little Harry, springing in. "Don't lay hands on a woman, sir. The man that lays his hand upon a woman, save in the way of kindness, is a—hallo! it's a letter for Miss Amory. What's this, Mrs. Lightfoot?"

Mrs. Lightfoot began, in piteous tones of reproach to her husband— "You unmanly! to treat a woman so who took you off the street. O you coward, to lay your hand upon your wife! Why did I marry you? Why did I leave my lady for you? Why did I spend eight hundred pound in fitting up this house that you might drink and guzzle?"

"She gets letters, and she won't tell me who writes letters," said Mr. Lightfoot, with a muzzy voice, "it's a family affair, sir. Will you take any thing, sir?"

"I will take this letter to Miss Amory, as I am going to the Park," said Foker, turning very pale; and taking it up from the table, which was arranged for the poor landlady's breakfast, he went away.

"He's comin'—dammy, who's a-comin'? Who's J.A., Mrs. Lightfoot —curse me, who's J.A.," cried the husband.

Mrs. Lightfoot cried out, "Be quiet, you tipsy brute, do,"—and running to her bonnet and shawl, threw them on, saw Mr. Foker walking down the street, took the by-lane which skirts it, and ran as quickly as she could to the lodge-gate, Clavering Park. Foker saw a running figure before him, but it was lost when he got to the lodge-gate. He stopped and asked, "Who was that who had just come in? Mrs. Bonner, was it?" He reeled almost in his walk: the trees swam before him. He rested once or twice against the trunks of the naked limes.

Lady Clavering was in the breakfast-room with her son, and her husband yawning over his paper. "Good-morning, Harry," said the Begum. "Here's letters, lots of letters; Lady Rockminster will be here on Tuesday instead of Monday, and Arthur and the major come to-day; and Laura is to go Dr. Portman's, and come to church from there: and—what's the matter, my dear? What makes you so pale Harry?"

"Where is Blanche?" asked Harry, in a sickening voice "not down yet?"

"Blanche is always the last," said the boy, eating muffins; "she's a regular dawdle, she is. When you're not here, she lays in bed till lunch time."

"Be quiet, Frank," said the mother.

Blanche came down presently, looking pale, and with rather an eager look toward Foker; then she advanced and kissed her mother, and had a face beaming with her very best smiles on when she greeted Harry.

"How do you do, sir?" she said, and put out both her hands.

"I'm ill," answered Harry. "I—I've brought a letter for you, Blanche."

"A letter, and from whom is it pray? Voyons" she said.

"I don't know—I should like to know," said Foker.

"How can I tell until I see it?" asked Blanche. "Has Mrs. Bonner not told you?" he said, with a shaking voice; "there's some secret. You give her the letter, Lady Clavering."

Lady Clavering, wondering, took the letter from poor Foker's shaking hand, and looked at the superscription. As she looked at it, she too began to shake in every limb, and with a scared face she dropped the letter, and running up to Frank, clutched the boy to her, and burst out with a sob, "Take that away—it's impossible, it's impossible."

"What is the matter?" cried Blanche, with rather a ghastly smile, "the letter is only from—from a poor pensioner and relative of ours."

"It's not true, it's not true," screamed Lady Clavering. "No, my Frank—is it Clavering?"

Blanche had taken up the letter, and was moving with it toward the fire, but Foker ran to her and clutched her arm, "I must see that letter," he said; "give it to me. You shan't burn it."

"You—you shall not treat Miss Amory so in my house," cried the baronet; "give back the letter, by Jove!"

"Read it—and look at her," Blanche cried, pointing to her mother; "it—it was for her I kept the secret! Read it, cruel man!"

And Foker opened and read the letter:

"I have not wrote, my darling Bessy, this three weeks; but this is to give her a father's blessing, and I shall come down pretty soon as quick as my note, and intend to see the ceremony, and my son-in-law. I shall put up at Bonner's. I have had a pleasant autumn, and am staying here at an hotel where there is good company, and which is kep' in good style. I don't know whether I quite approve of your throwing over Mr. P. for Mr. F., and don't think Foker's such a pretty name, and from your account of him he seems a muff, and not a beauty. But he has got the rowdy, which is the thing. So no more, my dear little Betsy, till we meet, from your affectionate father,"

"J. AMORY ALTAMONT."

"Read it, Lady Clavering; it is too late to keep it from you now," said poor Foker; and the distracted woman, having cast her eyes over it, again broke out into hysterical screams, and convulsively grasped her son.

"They have made an outcast of you, my boy," she said. "They've dishonored your old mother; but I'm innocent, Frank; before God, I'm innocent. I didn't know this, Mr. Foker; indeed, indeed, I didn't."

"I'm sure you didn't," said Foker, going up and kissing her hand.

"Generous, generous Harry," cried out Blanche in an ecstasy. But he withdrew his hand, which was upon her side, and turned from her with a quivering lip. "That's different," he says.

"It was for her sake—for her sake, Harry." Again Miss Amory is in an attitude.

"There was something to be done for mine" said Foker. "I would have taken you, whatever you were. Every thing's talked about in London. I knew that your father had come to—to grief. You don't think it was—it was for your connection I married you? D—it all! I've loved you with all my heart and soul for two years, and you've been playing with me, and cheating me," broke out the young man, with a cry. "Oh, Blanche, Blanche, it's a hard thing, a hard thing!" and he covered his face with his hands, and sobbed behind them.

Blanche thought, "Why didn't I tell him that night when Arthur warned me?"

"Don't refuse her, Harry," cried Lady Clavering. "Take her, take every thing I have. It's all hers, you know, at my death. This boy's disinherited."—(Master Frank, who had been looking as scared at the strange scene, here burst into a loud cry.)—"Take every shilling. Give me just enough to live, and to go and hide my head with this child, and to fly from both. Oh, they've both been bad, bad men. Perhaps he's here now. Don't let me see him. Clavering, you coward, defend me from him."

Clavering started up at this proposal. "You ain't serious, Jemima? You don't mean that?" he said. "You won't throw me and Frank over? I didn't know it, so help me—. Foker I'd no more idea of it than the dead—until the fellow came and found me out, the d—d escaped convict scoundrel."

"The what?" said Foker. Blanche gave a scream.

"Yes," screamed out the baronet in his turn, "yes, a d—d runaway convict—a fellow that forged his father-in-law's name—a d—d attorney, and killed a fellow in Botany Bay, hang him—and ran into the Bush, curse him; I wish he'd died there. And he came to me, a good six years ago and robbed me; and I've been ruining myself to keep him, the infernal scoundrel! And Pendennis knows it, and Strong knows it, and that d—d Morgan knows it, and she knows it, ever so long; and I never would tell it, never: and I kept it from my wife."

"And you saw him, and you didn't kill him, Clavering, you coward?" said the wife of Amory. "Come away, Frank; your father's a coward. I am dishonored, but I'm your old mother, and you'll—you'll love me, won't you?"

Blanche eploree, went up to her mother; but Lady Clavering shrank from her with a sort of terror. "Don't touch me," she said; "you've no heart; you never had. I see all now. I see why that coward was going to give up his place in Parliament to Arthur; yes, that coward! and why you threatened that you would make me give you half Frank's fortune. And when Arthur offered to marry you without a shilling, because he wouldn't rob my boy, you left him, and you took poor Harry. Have nothing to do with her, Harry. You're good, you are. Don't marry that—that convict's daughter. Come away, Frank, my darling; come to your poor old mother. We'll hide ourselves; but we're honest, yes, we are honest."

All this while a strange feeling of exultation had taken possession of Blanche's mind. That month with poor Harry had been a weary month to her. All his fortune and splendor scarcely sufficed to make the idea of himself supportable. She was weaned of his simple ways, and sick of coaxing and cajoling him.

"Stay, mamma; stay, madam!" she cried out with a gesture, which was always appropriate, though rather theatrical; "I have no heart? have I? I keep the secret of my mother's shame. I give up my rights to my half-brother and my bastard brother—yes, my rights and my fortune. I don't betray my father, and for this I have no heart. I'll have my rights now, and the laws of my country shall give them to me. I appeal to my country's laws—yes, my country's laws! The persecuted one returns this day. I desire to go to my father." And the little lady swept round her hand, and thought that she was a heroine.

"You will, will you?" cried out Clavering, with one of his usual oaths. "I'm a magistrate, and dammy, I'll commit him. Here's a chaise coming; perhaps it's him. Let him come."

A chaise was indeed coming up the avenue; and the two women shrieked each their loudest, expecting at that moment to see Altamont arrive.

The door opened, and Mr. Morgan announced Major Pendennis and Mr. Pendennis, who entered, and found all parties engaged in this fierce quarrel. A large screen fenced the breakfast-room from the hall; and it is probable that, according to his custom, Mr. Morgan had taken advantage of the screen to make himself acquainted with all that occurred.

It had been arranged on the previous day that the young people should ride; and at the appointed hour in the afternoon, Mr. Foker's horses arrived from the Clavering Arms. But Miss Blanche did not accompany him on this occasion. Pen came out and shook hands with him on the door-steps; and Harry Foker rode away, followed by his groom, in mourning. The whole transactions which have occupied the most active part of our history were debated by the parties concerned during those two or three hours. Many counsels had been given, stories told, and compromises suggested; and at the end, Harry Foker rode away, with a sad "God bless you!" from Pen. There was a dreary dinner at Clavering Park, at which the lately installed butler did not attend; and the ladies were both absent. After dinner, Pen said, "I will walk down to Clavering and see if he is come." And he walked through the dark avenue, across the bridge and road by his own cottage—the once quiet and familiar fields of which were flaming with the kilns and forges of the artificers employed on the new railroad works; and so he entered the town, and made for the Clavering Arms.

It was past midnight when he returned to Clavering Park. He was exceedingly pale and agitated. "Is Lady Clavering up yet?" he asked. Yes, she was in her own sitting-room. He went up to her, and there found the poor lady in a piteous state of tears and agitation. "It is I—Arthur," he said, looking in; and entering, he took her hand very affectionately and kissed it. "You were always the kindest of friends to me, dear Lady Clavering," he said. "I love you very much. I have got some news for you."

"Don't call me by that name," she said, pressing his hand. "You were always a good boy, Arthur; and it's kind of you to come now—very kind. You sometimes look very like your ma, my dear."

"Dear, good Lady Clavering," Arthur repeated, with particular emphasis, "something very strange has happened."

"Has any thing happened to him?" gasped Lady Clavering. "O, it's horrid to think I should be glad of it—horrid!"

"He is well. He has been and is gone, my dear lady. Don't alarm yourself—he is gone, and you are Lady Clavering still."

"Is it true? what he sometimes said to me," she screamed out—"that he—"

"He was married before he married you," said Pen. "He has confessed it to-night. He will never come back." There came another shriek from Lady Clavering, as she flung her arms round Pen, and kissed him, and burst into tears on his shoulder.

What Pen had to tell, through a multiplicity of sobs and interruptions, must be compressed briefly, for behold our prescribed limit is reached, and our tale is coming to its end. With the Branch Coach from the railroad, which had succeeded the old Alacrity and Perseverance, Amory arrived, and was set down at the Clavering Arms. He ordered his dinner at the place under his assumed name of Altamont, and, being of a jovial turn, he welcomed the landlord, who was nothing loth, to a share of his wine. Having extracted from Mr. Lightfoot all the news regarding the family at the Park, and found, from examining his host, that Mrs. Lightfoot, as she said, had kept his counsel, he called for more wine of Mr. Lightfoot, and at the end of this symposium, both being greatly excited, went into Mrs. Lightfoot's bar.

She was there taking tea with her friend, Madame Fribsby; and Lightfoot was by this time in such a happy state as not to be surprised at any thing which might occur, so that, when Altamont shook hands with Mrs. Lightfoot as an old acquaintance, the recognition did not appear to him to be in the least strange, but only a reasonable cause for further drinking. The gentlemen partook then of brandy-and-water, which they offered to the ladies, not heeding the terrified looks of one or the other.

While they were so engaged, at about six o'clock in the evening, Mr. Morgan, Sir Francis Clavering's new man, came in, and was requested to drink. He selected his favorite beverage, and the parties engaged in general conversation.

After awhile Mr. Lightfoot began to doze. Mr. Morgan had repeatedly given hints to Mrs. Fribsby to quit the premises; but that lady, strangely fascinated, and terrified, it would seem, or persuaded by Mrs. Lightfoot not to go, kept her place. Her persistence occasioned much annoyance to Mr. Morgan, who vented his displeasure in such language as gave pain to Mrs. Lightfoot, and caused Mr. Altamont to say, that he was a rum customer, and not polite to the sex.

The altercation between the two gentlemen became very painful to the women, especially to Mrs. Lightfoot, who did every thing to soothe Mr. Morgan; and, under pretense of giving a pipe-light to the stranger, she handed him a paper on which she had privily written the words, "He knows you. Go." There may have been something suspicious in her manner of handing, or in her guest's of reading the paper; for when he got up a short time afterward, and said he would go to bed, Morgan rose too, with a laugh, and said it was too early to go to bed.

The stranger then said, he would go to his bedroom. Morgan said he would show him the way.

At this the guest said, "Come up. I've got a brace of pistols up there to blow out the brains of any traitor or skulking spy," and glared so fiercely upon Morgan, that the latter, seizing hold of Lightfoot by the collar, and waking him, said, "John Amory, I arrest you in the Queen's name. Stand by me, Lightfoot. This capture is worth a thousand pounds."

He put forward his hand as if to seize his prisoner, but the other, doubling his fist, gave Morgan with his left hand so fierce a blow on the chest, that it knocked him back behind Mr. Lightfoot. That gentleman, who was athletic and courageous, said he would knock his guest's head off, and prepared to do so, as the stranger, tearing off his coat, and cursing both of his opponents, roared to them to come on.

But with a piercing scream Mrs. Lightfoot flung herself before her husband, while with another and louder shriek Madame Fribsby ran to the stranger, and calling out "Armstrong, Johnny Armstrong!" seized hold of his naked arm, on which a blue tattooing of a heart and M.F. were visible.

The ejaculation of Madame Fribsby seemed to astound and sober the stranger. He looked down upon her, and cried out, "It's Polly, by Jove."

Mrs. Fribsby continued to exclaim, "This is not Amory. This is Johnny Armstrong, my wicked—wicked husband, married to me in St. Martin's Church, mate on board an Indiaman, and he left me two months after, the wicked wretch. This is John Armstrong—here's the mark on his arm which he made for me."

The stranger said, "I am John Armstrong, sure enough, Polly. I'm John Armstrong, Amory, Altamont—and let 'em all come on, and try what they can do against a British sailor. Hurray, who's for it!"

Morgan still called, "Arrest him!" But Mrs. Lightfoot said, "Arrest him! arrest you, you mean spy! What! stop the marriage and ruin my lady, and take away the Clavering Arms from us?"

"Did he say he'd take away the Clavering Arms from us?" asked Mr. Lightfoot, turning round, "Hang him, I'll throttle him." "Keep him, darling, till the coach passes to the up train. It'll he here now directly."

"D—him, I'll choke him if he stirs," said Lightfoot. And so they kept Morgan until the coach came, and Mr. Amory or Armstrong went away hack to London.

Morgan had followed him: but of this event Arthur Pendennis did not inform Lady Clavering, and left her invoking blessings upon him at her son's door, going to kiss him as he was asleep. It had been a busy day.

We have to chronicle the events of but one day more, and that was a day when Mr. Arthur, attired in a new hat, a new blue frock-coat, and blue handkerchief, in a new fancy waistcoat, new boots, and new shirt-studs (presented by the Right Honorable the Countess Dowager of Rockminster), made his appearance at a solitary breakfast-table, in Clavering Park, where he could scarce eat a single morsel of food. Two letters were laid by his worship's plate; and he chose to open the first, which was in a round clerk-like hand, in preference to the second more familiar superscription.

Note 1 ran as follows:

"GARBANZOS WINE COMPANY, SHEPHERD'S INN.—Monday.

"MY DEAR PENDENNIS—In congratulating you heartily upon the event which is to make you happy for life, I send my very kindest remembrances to Mrs. Pendennis, whom I hope to know even longer than I have already known her. And when I call her attention to the fact, that one of the most necessary articles to her husband's comfort is pure sherry, I know I shall have her for a customer for your worship's sake.

"But I have to speak to you of other than my own concerns. Yesterday afternoon, a certain J.A. arrived at my chambers from Clavering, which he had left under circumstances of which you are doubtless now aware. In spite of our difference, I could not but give him food and shelter (and he partook freely both of the Garbanzos Amontillado and the Toboso ham), and he told me what had happened to him, and many other surprising adventures. The rascal married at sixteen, and has repeatedly since performed that ceremony—in Sidney, in New Zealand, in South America, in Newcastle, he says first, before he knew our poor friend the milliner. He is a perfect Don Juan.

"And it seemed as if the commendatore had at last overtaken him, for, as we were at our meal, there came three heavy knocks at my outer door, which made our friend start. I have sustained a siege or two here, and went to my usual place to reconnoiter. Thank my stars I have not a bill out in the world, and besides, those gentry do not come in that way. I found that it was your uncle's late valet, Morgan, and a policeman (I think a sham policeman), and they said they had a warrant to take the person of John Armstrong, alias Amory, alias Altamont, a runaway convict, and threatened to break in the oak. Now, sir, in my own days of captivity I had discovered a little passage along the gutter into Bows and Costigan's window, and I sent Jack Alias along this covered way, not without terror of his life, for it had grown very cranky; and then, after a parley, let in Mons. Morgan and friend.

"The rascal had been instructed about that covered way, for he made for the room instantly, telling the policeman to go down stairs and keep the gate; and he charged up my little staircase as if he had known, the premises. As he was going out of the window we heard a voice that you know, from Bow's garret, saying, 'Who are ye, and hwhat the divvle are ye at? You'd bette leave the gutther; bedad there's a man killed himself already.'

"And as Morgan, crossing over and looking into the darkness, was trying to see whether this awful news was true, he took a broom-stick, and with a vigorous dash broke down the pipe of communication—and told me this morning, with great glee, that he was reminded of that 'aisy sthratagem by remembering his dorling Emilie, when she acted the pawrt of Cora in the Plee—and by the bridge in Pezawro, bedad: I wish that scoundrel Morgan had been on the bridge when the general tried his 'sthratagem.'

"If I hear more of Jack Alias I will tell you. He has got plenty of money still, and I wanted him to send some to our poor friend the milliner; but the scoundrel laughed and said, he had no more than he wanted, but offered to give any body a lock of his hair. Farewell—be happy! and believe me always truly yours.

"E. STRONG."

"And now for the other letter," said Pen. "Dear old fellow!" and he kissed the seal before he broke it.

"WARRINGTON, Tuesday.

"I must not let the day pass over without saying a God bless you, to both of you. May heaven make you happy, dear Arthur, and dear Laura. I think, Pen, that you have the best wife in the world; and pray that, as such, you will cherish her and tend her. The chambers will be lonely without you, dear Pen; but if I am tired, I shall have a new home to go to in the house of my brother and sister. I am practicing in the nursery here, in order to prepare for the part of Uncle George. Farewell! make your wedding tour, and come back to your affectionate

"G. W."

Pendennis and his wife read this letter together after Doctor Portman's breakfast was over, and the guests were gone; and when the carriage was waiting amidst the crowd at the doctor's outer gate. But the wicket led into the church-yard of St Mary's where the bells were pealing with all their might, and it was here, over Helen's green grass, that Arthur showed his wife George's letter. For which of those two—for grief was it or for happiness, that Laura's tears abundantly fell on the paper? And once more, in the presence of the sacred dust, she kissed and blessed her Arthur.

There was only one marriage on that day at Clavering Church; for in spite of Blanche's sacrifices for her dearest mother, honest Harry Foker could not pardon the woman who had deceived her husband, and justly argued that she would deceive him again. He went to the Pyramids and Syria, and there left his malady behind him, and returned with a fine beard, and a supply of tarbooshes and nargillies, with which he regales all his friends. He lives splendidly, and through Pen's mediation, gets his wine from the celebrated vintages of the Duke of Garbanzos.

As for poor Cos, his fate has been mentioned in an early part of this story. No very glorious end could be expected to such a career. Morgan is one of the most respectable men in the parish of St. James's, and in the present political movement has pronounced himself like a man and a Briton. And Bows—on the demise of Mr. Piper, who played the organ at Clavering, little Mrs. Sam Huxter, who has the entire command of Doctor Portman, brought Bows down from London to contest the organ chair loft, and her candidate carried the chair. When Sir Francis Clavering quitted this worthless life, the same little indefatigable canvasser took the borough by storm, and it is now represented by Arthur Pendennis, Esq.. Blanche Amory, it is well known, married at Paris, and the saloons of Madame la Comtesse de Montmorenci de Valentinois were among the most suivis of that capital. The duel between the count and the young and fiery Representative of the Mountain, Alcide de Mirobo, arose solely from the latter questioning at the Club the titles borne by the former nobleman. Madame de Montmorenci de Valentinois traveled after the adventure: and Bungay bought her poems, and published them, with the countess's coronet emblazoned on the countess's work.

Major Pendennis became very serious in his last days, and was never so happy as when Laura was reading to him with her sweet voice, or listening to his stories. For this sweet lady is the friend of the young and the old: and her life is always passed in making other lives happy.

"And what sort of a husband would this Pendennis be?" many a reader will ask, doubting the happiness of such a marriage, and the fortune of Laura. The querists, if they meet her, are referred to that lady herself, who, seeing his faults and wayward moods—seeing and owning that there are men better than he—loves him always with the most constant affection. His children or their mother have never heard a harsh word from him; and when his fits of moodiness and solitude are over, welcome him back with a never-failing regard and confidence. His friend is his friend still—entirely heart-whole. That malady is never fatal to a sound organ. And George goes through his part of godpapa perfectly, and lives alone. If Mr. Pen's works have procured him more reputation than has been acquired by his abler friend, whom no one knows, George lives contented without the fame. If the best men do not draw the great prizes in life, we know it has been so settled by the Ordainer of the lottery. We own, and see daily, how the false and worthless live and prosper, while the good are called away, and the dear and young perish untimely—we perceive in every man's life the maimed happiness, the frequent falling, the bootless endeavor, the struggle of Right and Wrong, in which the strong often succumb and the swift fail: we see flowers of good blooming in foul places, as, in the most lofty and splendid fortunes, flaws of vice and meanness, and stains of evil; and, knowing how mean the best of us is, let us give a hand of charity to Arthur Pendennis, with all his faults and shortcomings, who does not claim to be a hero but only a man and a brother.

William Makepeace Thackeray – A Short Biography

William Makepeace Thackeray, was born on July 18th, 1811 in Calcutta, then British India, where his father, Richmond Thackeray was the secretary to the Board of Revenue in the British East India Company. His mother, Anne Becher also worked for the British East India Company.

His father died in 1815, and his mother sent Thackeray to England the following year while she remained in India and would, sometime later, marry her childhood sweetheart. En-route to England the ship stopped for provisions on St. Helena. The Imprisoned Napoleon was pointed out to him by a servant with the words that he "eats three sheep every day, and all the little children he can lay hands on!"

Finally, back in England the young Thackeray was sent to school, initially in Southampton and Chiswick, before being moved to Charterhouse School. Charterhouse and Thackeray did not take to each other but the time became a valuable source for his later work "Slaughterhouse". Despite his less than respectful recalling of his time with them Charterhouse placed a monument in the chapel after his death.

In his final year at Charterhouse a troubling illness delayed his departure to attend Cambridge University. Over the course of his life Thackeray would suffer from ill health, much of it brought about for his fondness for "gluttling and gorging". Excess was something he could enjoy and for a man who stood some 6' 3" it would appear to the eye that, initially at least, his large frame could absorb much of that excess.

However, Thackeray's lazy attitude to completely mastering anything he set his mind too, especially where ambition for academia was involved, meant he departed Cambridge little more than a year after joining. He had however published two short works in University periodicals. As an author, he would have quite some impact on English literature in the years to come, so it seems difficult to reconcile that he felt no urgency to pursue writing at that time.

He now spent some time travelling across Europe stopping at both Paris, to study art, and to winter in Weimar. Back in London a final attempt was made on a professional career. This time studying law at Middle Temple. It lasted no more than a few months.

Now, having reached 21, he received his father's inheritance. It was a very substantial estate of 17,000 pounds, an enormous sum of money at the time. However, although Thackeray had youth he lacked a little in energy and certainly much financial experience. He funded not one but two newspapers, and neither was to prove successful. Gambling seemed enjoyable and certainly he had money to lose, which he did on a regular basis. Further investments in two soon-to-fail Indian banks quickly ensured little of his good fortune remained.

He now had to consider taking up yet another profession. Thackeray turned to art hoping that his studies in Paris would prove of benefit. Unfortunately, they did not. His ambivalent attitude continued until on August 20th, 1836 he married the 20-year-old, Isabella Gethin Shawe. It seemed to prove a turning point in many ways.

The marriage would produce three daughters; Anne Isabella in 1837, Jane, in 1838, who tragically died in infancy and Harriet Marian in 1840.

Now, as a husband and father, Thackeray seemed at last to understand his responsibilities to nurture and provide.

His early efforts at "writing for his life" were to establish his career as a foremost author. His main employment was with Fraser's Magazine, a sharp-witted and sharp-tongued conservative publication for which he produced art criticism, short fictional sketches, and who would also serialise two of his novels.

He also found time, between 1837 and 1840 to review books for The Times and to make regular contributions to The Morning Chronicle and The Foreign Quarterly Review.

In his earliest works, which he wrote under various pseudonyms including; Charles James Yellowplush, Michael Angelo Titmarsh and George Savage Fitz-Boodle, he tended towards savagery in his attacks on high society, military prowess, the institution of marriage and hypocrisy.

Between May 1839 and February 1840 Fraser's published Catherine. Originally intended as a satire of the Newgate school of crime fiction, it ended up being more of a picaresque tale. Thackeray also began work on what would eventually become A Shabby Genteel Story.

However, Thackeray, having successfully found a career that he cared about and had the talent for, found that his personal life was about to descend into chaos. After the birth of her third child in 1840, Isabella, sank into depression. At first Thackeray, didn't think too much of it. He needed to work to earn an income to support his family and finding that Isabella was distracting both herself and him he realised he could get no work done at home and so spent more and more time away until finally, in September 1840, it dawned upon him how serious his wife's condition had become. Struck by guilt, he set out with his wife to Ireland. During the boat crossing she threw herself into the sea, but was thankfully pulled from the waters. Her mother who had little understanding of her daughter's illness was of little help and perhaps a hinderance. After four-weeks they returned to England. From November 1840 to February 1842 Isabella was in and out of professional care, as her condition waxed and waned.

Isabella eventually deteriorated into a permanent state of detachment. Thackeray desperately sought cures for her, but nothing worked, and she ended up in two different asylums in or near Paris until 1845, after which Thackeray took her back to England, where he installed her with a Mrs Bakewell at Camberwell. Despite her condition Isabella would outlive her husband by 3 decades.

After his wife's illness Thackeray became a de facto widower, never able to establish another permanent relationship.

In 1843, through his connection to the illustrator John Leech, whom he had met at Charterhouse, he began writing for the newly created magazine Punch, in which he published The Snob Papers, later collected as The Book of Snobs. Thackeray was a regular contributor to Punch until 1854.

Thackeray had earlier received some success with two travel books, The Paris Sketch Book and The Irish Sketch Book, the latter marked by hostility to Irish Catholics. The book appealed to British prejudices, and on that basis Thackeray now became Punch's Irish expert, often under the pseudonym Hibernis Hibernior. It was Thackeray's writings that were the basis for Punch's notoriously harsh, hostile and condescending depictions of the Irish during the devastating Irish Famine (1845–51).

As well as his regular columns and contributions Thackeray worked on his novels. In The Luck of Barry Lyndon, which was serialised in Fraser's in 1844, he explored the situation of an outsider trying to achieve status in high society, a theme he developed more successfully a few years later with Vanity Fair.

Thackeray achieved more recognition with his Snob Papers (serialised 1846/7, and published as a book in 1848), but the work that really established his fame was the novel Vanity Fair, which first appeared in serialised instalments beginning in January 1847.

Published as a book the novel had a slow start but eventually sales rose to 7,000 copies a month. Just as importantly, it was the book that everybody was talking about. Thackeray finally had a name that gained notice and was reviewed in journals such as the famed, and much sought after, Edinburgh Review.

The accolades and success also gave him a respite from writing everything in a manner that would help ensure income rather than literary respect. Even before Vanity Fair completed its serial run Thackeray had become a celebrity, sought after by the very lords and ladies whom he satirised. with the character of Becky Sharp, the artist's daughter who rises high by manipulating all around her.

Pendennis followed in 1849-50, but it was interrupted halfway through writing for 3 months by a severe illness. Some accounts say it was cholera. Pendennis is a semi-autobiographical bildungsroman that draws on, among other things, Thackeray's disappointments in college, his ambivalent relationship with his mother, and his insider's knowledge of the London publishing world.

This novel ran at the same time as Charles Dicken's David Copperfield, and their dual appearance brought about the first of many comparisons with Dickens. Thackeray, for his part, felt that he and Dickens were battling for supremacy, though he would never equal Dickens's popularity, except with the critics.

Interestingly the two were involved in a spat which became known as the "Garrick Club affair". Thackeray and Dickens had skirmished over the "Dignity of Literature" and had other slight disagreements but this literary quarrel caused a rift in their friendship that lasted almost until the end of Thackeray's life. The relationship was healed only in Thackeray's last months, through a surprise meeting and handshake on the steps of a London club. Thackeray had taken offense at some personal remarks in a column by Edmund Yates and demanded an apology, eventually taking the affair to the Garrick Club committee. Already upset with Thackeray for an indiscreet remark about his affair with Ellen Ternan, Dickens championed Yates, helping him to write letters both to Thackeray and, in his defense, to the club's committee. Despite the intervention of Dickens, Yates eventually lost the vote of the Club's members, but the quarrel was laid out for the public in journal articles and pamphlets. "What pains me most," Thackeray said at the time, "is that Dickens should have been his adviser, and next that I should have had to lay a heavy hand on a young man who, I take it, has been cruelly punished by the issue of the affair, and I believe is hardly aware of the nature of his own offence, and doesn't even now understand that a gentleman should resent the monstrous insult which he volunteered".

Aside from these quarrelsome, distracting literary disagreements and Isabella's on-going illness life was good for Thackeray. He was to remain as he put it "at the top of the tree," for the rest of his life. The works for which he is so well remembered; Vanity Fair and Barry Lyndon had established that but he continued to write and produce novels, stories, sketches and works profusely.

To remain at such a high level in both quality and quantity is somewhat surprising given the continuation and escalation of various illnesses which continued to haunt him.

With Isabella still unwell Thackeray did seek out other women, in particular Mrs Jane Brookfield. Despite his hopes, it always felt that he was pursuing her as she battled the problems of her own marriage and turned to Thackeray for comfort and support. A source for these relationships often came on the lecture tours of Great Britain and the United States which he now entertained. These tours gave the public a chance to see and hear their hero's and provided another valuable source of income for those invited to tour. Whilst in in New York he met the Baxter family. Sally, the eldest daughter, enchanted the novelist—as a number of vibrant, intelligent, beautiful young women had done before her—and she became the model for Ethel Newcome. He visited her on his second tour of the States when she was married to a South Carolina gentleman. His choosing of married women in the shape of both Jane and Sally was ill-advised and both relationships led nowhere but did take quite some time to disassemble and for reason to set in.

In 1852, The History of Henry Esmond was published as a 3-volume novel without first being serialised and in a special type meant to imitate the appearance of an eighteenth-century book. This was the most carefully planned of Thackeray's novels. The book was celebrated for its brilliance, and Thackeray recognized it as "the very best I can do". At the time, it caused a sensation thanks to its controversial ending, wherein the hero marries a woman who early in the novel seemed more like a "mother" to him.

The eighteenth-century held a great attraction for Thackeray and he had previously set both Barry Lyndon and Catherine there as well as the sequel to Esmond, The Virginians, which takes place in North America and includes George Washington as a character.

Thackeray had twice visited the United States on lecture tours during this period as well as given lectures in London on the English humorists of the eighteenth century, and on the first four Hanoverian monarchs. The latter were published in a book as The Four Georges.

Interestingly Thackeray also decided that Politics was something he could more than dabble in. In Oxford he stood as an independent for Parliament. He was narrowly beaten by Cardwell, a politician who was substituted for the man Thackeray thought he was going to run against, although Thackeray's advocacy of entertainment on the Sabbath would have done little to help his campaign. Even so the margin of his defeat was only 1,070 votes, to Thackeray's 1,005.

In 1860 Thackeray became editor of the newly established Cornhill Magazine, a role he never felt truly comfortable in, preferring to contribute as a columnist on the Roundabout Papers. However, the financial compensation was by all accounts quite extraordinary. The Cornhill began its history with a record circulation and a number of distinguished contributors swayed onboard by Thackeray's reputation. It was in the Cornhill that he serialised his last complete novel, The Adventures of Philip in 1861-62. (After his death, the incomplete Denis Duval would also appear there in 1864).

After two years as editor he stepped down, primarily to concentrate on writing novels again. A piece he wrote for the Cornhill at this time "Thorns in the Cushion," one of The Roundabout Papers, fondly assembles the pains he felt in rejecting manuscripts on the one hand and receiving criticism of the magazine on the other. It seemed a good time to move on.

Thackeray's health had worsened during the 1850s and he was plagued by a recurring stricture of the urethra that laid him up for days at a time. He also felt that he had lost much of his creative impetus. He worsened matters by excessively eating and drinking, and avoiding exercise, though he enjoyed horseback-riding. He has been described as "the greatest literary glutton who ever lived". Indeed, his main activity apart from writing was eating and drinking and many of his stories include elaborate scenes and themes on his fondness for them.

On December 23rd, 1863, William Makepeace Thackeray, after returning from dining out and before dressing for bed, suffered a massive stroke. He was found dead on his bed the following morning. He was only fifty-two.

His death was entirely unexpected, and shocked family, friends and indeed the entire Nation.

It is said that at his funeral service thousands of mourners turned out to witness his passing. He was buried on December 29th at Kensal Green Cemetery, London.

William Makepeace Thackeray – A Concise Bibliography

The Yellowplush Papers (1837)
Catherine (1839–40)
A Shabby Genteel Story (1840)
Second Funeral of Napoleon (1841)
The Irish Sketchbook (1843)
The Luck of Barry Lyndon (1844)
Notes of a Journey from Cornhill to Grand Cairo (1846)
Mrs. Perkins's Ball (1846), under the name M. A. Titmarsh
Stray Papers: Being Stories, Reviews, Verses, and Sketches (1821-1847)
The Book of Snobs (1848)
Vanity Fair (1848)
Pendennis (1848–1850)
Rebecca and Rowena (1850)
The Paris Sketchbook (1840)
Men's Wives (1852)
The History of Henry Esmond (1852)
The English Humorists of the Eighteenth Century (1853)
The Newcomes (1855)
The Rose and the Ring (1855)
The Virginians (1857–1859)
Lovel the Widower (1860)
Four Georges (1860-1861)
The Adventures of Philip (1862)
Roundabout Papers (1863)
Denis Duval (1864)
The English Humorists of the eighteenth century: A Series of Six Lectures (1867)
Ballads (1869)
Burlesques (1869)
The Orphan of Pimlico (1876)

Thackeray wrote a numerous number of articles for magazines and the like as well as contributing many picture sketches to articles and his own books. Many were then collected and published together. We have listed his major works only for this bibliography.

Printed in Great Britain
by Amazon

62215733R00154